*Show
Me
a
Hero*

OTHER PERSEA ANTHOLOGIES

———

FIRST SIGHTINGS: Contemporary Stories of American Youth
Edited by John Loughery

INTO THE WIDENING WORLD: International Coming-of-Age Stories
Edited by John Loughery

AMERICA STREET: A Multicultural Anthology of Stories
Edited by Anne Mazer

GOING WHERE I'M COMING FROM: Memoirs of American Youth
Edited by Anne Mazer

IMAGINING AMERICA: Stories from the Promised Land
Edited by Wesley Brown and Amy Ling

VISIONS OF AMERICA: Personal Narratives from the Promised Land
Edited by Wesley Brown and Amy Ling

PAPER DANCE: 55 Latino Poets
Edited by Victor Hernández Cruz, Leroy V. Quintana, and Virgil Suarez

POETS FOR LIFE: Seventy-Six Poets Respond to AIDS
Edited by Michael Klein

IN THE COMPANY OF MY SOLITUDE: American Writing from
the AIDS Pandemic
Edited by Marie Howe and Michael Klein

SHOW
ME
A
HERO

*Great
Contemporary
Stories About
Sports*

Edited by Jeanne Schinto

PERSEA BOOKS  NEW YORK

ACKNOWLEDGMENTS

Thanks to Karen Braziller; to all the writers, publishers, and agents who have
granted me permission to use these stories; and to the Interlibrary Loan
Department of Memorial Hall Library, Andover, Massachusetts.

*Since this page cannot legibly accommodate all copyright notices,
pages 263–265 constitute an extension of the copyright page.*

Library of Congress Cataloging-in-Publication Data
*Show me a hero : great contemporary stories about sports | edited by
Jeanne Schinto.*
p. cm.
*Summary: A collection of twenty-one sports stories which explore
aspects of everyday life experiences.*
ISBN 0-89255-209-3 (pbk.)
*1. Sports stories, American. 2. American fiction—20th century.
[1. Sports—Fiction. 2. Short stories.] I. Schinto, Jeanne, 1951–.*
PS648.S78S56 1995
813'.0108355—dc20 94-47955
CIP
AC

Designed by REM Studio, Inc.
Set in Italian Old Style by ComCom, Allentown, Pennsylvania
Printed and bound by Haddon Craftsmen, Scranton, Pennsylvania
Cover printed by Lynn Art, New York, New York

First Edition

For my parents,
Josephine
and
Henry Schinto

CONTENTS

———

INTRODUCTION

It's odd to think that I, of all people, have edited an anthology of stories about sports. In high school, a season of synchronized swimming was my sole athletic activity. As a kid, instead of shooting baskets, I wrote to pen pals. I seemed to lack any of the skills that athletic feats require: speed, strength, agility, and above all, aggression. In gym class, when forced to play sports, if I did happen to start winning, I would end up feeling sorry for the opponent and back down.

Yet later in life, sports liberated me. At age thirty-five, when I started to play serious year-round tennis, I also learned how to take risks; how to make quick decisions; and, for the first time, how to enjoy competition. On the tennis court I also honed the skills of perseverance and concentration (necessary for writers, too, I had discovered years ago, when I taught myself to write). Eventually, as part of a league that competed all over Greater Boston, where I live, I learned to win.

Through tennis I've also met people from all classes and cultures—acquaintances I never would have made if I hadn't taken up the sport. This includes fellow competitors from ages six to eighty-six, and from five continents (Africa and Antarctica are the exceptions, but give me time). More importantly, tennis brought me closer to my family, especially my mother.

In fact, Mom and I forged an enviable friendship because I came to share with her a passion for hitting a fuzzy yellow ball back and forth across a net. As a child I had sat on the sidelines and watched her play; she had frequently encouraged me to join in, but hadn't pushed. And I had always refused. Now I'm glad I wasn't coerced; surely I would have rebelled and never learned to love the game.

Still, the delay also makes me sad. My late start is the reason my mother and I competed against each other for only a few years, doing what ideal opponents always do: force each other to play his or her best. Just as I was working up to her level, she was growing older, more inclined to play golf with Dad, although in phone conversations, she still gives me pointers, and I still listen.

Do not assume, however, that just because my experience with sports turned out so well this volume is an unbridled paean. It has been said that one of the emblems of the trivialization of American life is our obsession with sports, and I find myself agreeing with that statement when I encounter people who say they love sports but who fail to see any of the resonances between it and "real" human conflicts and resolutions. More radical critics than I believe that sports is not only trivial but wastes time and energy that might be channeled into more "useful" activities. The most radical critics of all argue that sports teaches militarism, authoritarianism, racism, and sexism, especially to the young.

This last view, while extreme, isn't unfounded. Much of the sports world remains entrenched in patriarchal attitudes and values as well as narrow concepts of masculinity and femininity even as other segments of society move beyond those oppressive constraints. Ideally, athletics equals physical emancipation, but when the positive effects of strict discipline and rigorous training are combined with some of the inimical forces in our culture, the union can be quite literally lethal. Witness the abuse of steroids and other performance-enhancing drugs by young men and the prevalence of eating disorders among young women engaged in gymnastics, figure skating, and other competitive sports that prize a "feminine" appearance.

It's also no secret that there is trouble in the realm of professional athletics. And although our amateur competitions resemble the

pros' only in passing, the media's obsession with the "lifestyle" problems of certain millionaire megastars—their latest failed drug test,
drunken-driving arrest, paternity suit—can have a negative impact on
immature minds.

One place from which some semblance of the truth about the
pressures of playing for profit might logically emerge is sports figures'
autobiographies; certainly there is no shortage of these largely ghost-
written books. Unfortunately, this "literature" is often superficial, eva-
sive, full of fluffy gossip; "inspirational," oozing suspect praise for
various sponsors and associates; even occasionally rancorous, when cat-
tiness is substituted for candor.

Indeed, these books that pander to the public's taste for titilla-
tion, simplism, and escape frequently tell us more about the state of
commercial publishing than they do about commercial sports.

Luckily, many of our finest serious fiction writers (and some ace
rookies, too) have written stories using contemporary sports as their
theme. In fact, the twenty-one stories collected here—all of them first
and foremost great fiction, no matter what their subject matter—are
only a sampling of the dozens and dozens of excellent pieces I have read
and reread while making my final selections for this book.

Be forewarned, however: I have made no attempt to include a
story about every sport—an impossible task in any event. My intention
is not to explore sports per se, but rather the themes and issues that
sports evoke, including the reasons why athletic competitions can so en-
thrall us and why they seem to be able to embody our deepest desires
and fears.

To that end, the stories are grouped into thematic categories.
"Out of Bounds" leads off the volume. Each of its stories is about what
happens to people who refuse to conform to the human categories to
which society would have them belong. I wanted readers to know at the
outset that this book shouldn't be mistaken for an ordinary compen-
dium of sports fiction. How could it be when the first piece is Jim Shepard's "Ida," which portrays a pro-football-playing mother and son;
the next is Ann Packer's "HORSE," about a failed high-school cheer-
leader; and another is John Edgar Wideman's "Doc's Story," Doc being
a blind basketball player, star of the playground pick-up games in his
ghetto neighborhood, who causes Wideman's narrator to dream: *"If a
blind man could play basketball, surely we . . ."*?

Feel free, of course, to rethink the clusters. You might, for instance, want to compare and contrast all the parent-child conflict stories

(Ethan Canin's "The Year of Getting to Know Us," Jonathan Baumbach's "The Return of Service," and Jay Woodruff's "The Secret to
Not Getting Stuck" are three). Or all the ones in which the protagonists
are winners (try pairing Mark Helprin's "Palais de Justice" with David
Michael Kaplan's "Doe Season"). Or those whose protagonists decide
to walk away from their sport (Chris Fisher's "Playing the Garden,"
Garrison Keillor's "What Did We Do Wrong?" and Don Lee's "Yellow" make an interesting trio). My hope is that individual works will
accumulate even more meaning when read in conjunction with other
titles.

Beyond thematic considerations, I also tried to assemble a range
of writing styles and traditions. There's high humor, black humor; real-
ism, surrealism; and everything in between. In a section called "Dream
Teams," for example, you'll find T. Coraghessan's now classic "The
Hector Quesadilla Story," which is about rebirth as much as it is about a
fantastical game of baseball; and you'll also find John Sayles's insis-
tently realistic "The 7–10 Split," a story ostensibly about bowling that
is actually about nothing less than the possibility of human perfection.

Boyle's portrayal of a Latino pitcher trying to make a comeback
and Sayles's tale of a working-class woman who surprises her ten-pin
league reminds me that an unusual number of writers of stories about
sports take on personae at odds with their own. Maybe it's because
sports—particularly the spectator variety—encourages the pleasures of
vicarious experience as much as reading does.

I speak of pleasure, but in fact, during my search for stories for
this volume, I found many more "dark" pieces than "happy" ones from
which to choose. "Show me a hero," F. Scott Fitzgerald wrote, "and I'll
write you a tragedy."

The adage seems to be especially true of the stories about sports
and women, who often face cultural obstacles to athletic success that
men do not. Elizabeth Spencer's "The Girl Who Loved Horses," which
depicts the South of the 1950s (though the piece wasn't published until
1979), shows what was then popularly thought to happen to women who
tried stepping outside a certain narrow circle of prescribed behavior. Indeed, the story could have gone into the "Out of Bounds" section as
easily as it went into the one I have called "Dark Victories."

Yet after reading Monica Wood's "Disappearing," which is
about a young woman of the 1980s who carries too far her resolve to lose
weight by swimming, I had to conclude that the situation really hasn't
changed all that much. Thanks to the Federal law known as Title IX,

two million girls and young women participate in interscholastic sports today (compared to 300,000 before the landmark legislation was passed by Congress in 1972); but the hopeful figures obviously don't tell the whole story. As an iconoclastic girls' soccer coach laments in "Offsides" by Marisa Labozzetta: "Something happened to [female athletes after age fourteen]. Just when they were beginning to believe they could do it, they turned self-conscious on him. Then, one by one, they dropped out, feeling more comfortable on the sidelines of some boys' competition."

All I can say is I'm awfully glad Ellen Gilchrist and Toni Cade Bambara have given us such plucky preadolescent females as those featured in "Revenge" and "Raymond's Run." Both depict states of mind and body worthy of anybody's aspiration.

It particularly pleases me that one of those dauntless girls is white and one is black. I began this project determined that the volume would reflect the reality of our country's racial composition. At the same time, however, I wanted to avoid creating the impression that sports matters more to people of color than it matters to anybody else.

That stereotype exists because athletics is viewed as one of the few arenas where merit truly counts, where the playing field is supposedly level, and where non-whites seem to get a fair shake. Yet while racial barriers to professional athletic careers are gone, we know that prejudice in our society is still a virulent force when sports heroes are the *only* heroes for some youngsters who don't see many other people like themselves being celebrated or revered.

It's shameful too that the minuscule number of young men and women good enough for big-league sports are often exploited for their talents. A scholarship is a gift, after all, only if the recipient really does get an education. (Susan Straight's story, "Off-Season," tells what happens to a college basketball star who never even learns to read or write competently.)

Anyway, consider this: only five percent of the college sports scholarships awarded in this country go to people of color. Surprised? If you think about who is underrepresented in higher education in general, it makes sad sense.

Speaking of schooling reminds me that, as a teacher, I'm always on the lookout for fiction that I hope will appeal to young adults. I'm eager to use these stories in my classroom to teach not only contemporary literature but also what sports teaches so easily and so often: lessons about life itself.

One unexpected lesson I have learned from tennis is the importance of imagination—knowledge that might more properly belong in the domain of fiction reading and writing, it's true; yet I have discovered that I'll play more effectively if, *before* I get to the court, I visualize myself stroking the ball correctly, winning the point, winning the match. Many other kinds of athletes use the same precompetition technique to picture what they want their bodies to do and, by extension, what they want themselves to be.

A similar instruction about the power of that kind of seeing is voiced by a sightless runner in Thomas Fox Averill's story, "Running Blind."

"Want to improve?" he asks his slower, sighted companion. "Running's inside you. Don't watch what's around you, pay attention to what's inside."

So don't be fooled. Though this very much resembles a volume of superlative stories about football, baseball, basketball, and more, it is actually a book about the world beyond winning and losing that lies deep within us all.

—*Jeanne Schinto*

I

---

*Out
of
Bounds*

IDA

Jim Shepard

Millions roar. The Three Rivers Stadium scoreboard lights up, the thick letters turning the rectangle from black to yellow: DEE—FENSE. DEE—FENSE. Over the line, the Pittsburgh Steelers hunch taut, ready to explode. I straighten up. Time-out! I call, Time-out! and trot to the sidelines. My father waits, his arms folded. He didn't want the time-out; against Pittsburgh we'll need them later.

Greenwood and Banaszak are way wide, I explain. He doesn't say anything. The corners are in tight, I add almost desperately, I think it's a dog. My mother trots over, stands beside me for support, lets her mouthpiece slip from her mouth. He waits agonizing seconds more before answering.

Okay, he says. Go with Ida here on the blast.

It's the wrong call, the worst call, but I don't argue; we turn and trot back onto the field. The crowd seems to swell physically in the stands; the Steelers sidle back to their positions. It's not at all strange to me that we join a dark, brilliant-purple Minnesota Viking huddle even though we are in a championship game and the Steelers, the home team, are already in black. It seems, the rich purple against the black, the way it should be. We earned this spot, I know. I have no memory of who we beat, but I know we earned this spot.

In the huddle, my mother bends at the waist, slips her mouthpiece back in, doesn't look up as I call her number. On the way out of the huddle she straightens her face mask angrily, uselessly.

On the snap Greenwood roars in, Cole fills the gap beside him on the blitz and, hurtling the line, meets my mother head on in the opening we both knew would be, cruelly, not an opening at all but an avenue for the oncoming blitz. She is savaged backward, driven into and across the cold artificial surface, and again I think that's it, she's finished. I wave to the sidelines, motioning toward my mother, but my father remains oblivious; no replacement starts out onto the field.

Damn you, I think. Why're you doing this to her? I call another time-out, for her sake. On the way to the sidelines I see him throw his hands up in the air and turn his back to me.

Once there I unsnap my chin strap and lick my first three fingers, peering at the scoreboard while I talk with my father's brother. We're in the fourth quarter and it's 0–0; we haven't been able to move because my mother has gotten every call and the Steelers are ready for her and us each time. My uncle tells me she has fifty-six carries for seventeen yards. We have seventeen yards total offense. The Steelers have not scored because their offense is not allowed on the field; when we are stopped and must punt, we receive the ball we've punted. The Steelers know they've been cheated and they're frustrated, gambling. They're blitzing often and hitting late and grabbing for the ball, but my mother's fumbled only once, only once in fifty-six carries, and I fell on it. Thank you, Son, she'd said, with great dignity, rising from her knees after we'd all unpiled.

The crowd, too, senses the injustice; they are always loud, bitter, and they unceasingly roar with delight as my mother receives each assault. The sound itself seemed to slow our reflexes when they saw the ball squirt straight up, a comic, precious seed, the one time my mother fumbled.

Hey, my uncle is saying. Let's go. I turn, sheepish, and head back across the field to my teammates. It's second and eleven. They watch me, their eyes pleading this one time for a pass. My uncle's signals from the sidelines are clear: Ida on the 23 Pitch. I anger when they sag and snap at them irritably: maybe if we'd work a little harder we could spring her.

My mother bends, exhausted, to her three-point stance.

Over the line I can see Lambert inching to the right. He knows. Banaszak, too, inches over. They're all waiting, peering up at me from lowered helmets. I won't let it happen again, I think, but at the snap the ball is out of my hands, flipping end over end, before I've realized it, my pitch hitting my mother perfectly in the hands seconds before Lambert and Banaszak and Donnie Shell bury her.

Sprawled across the artificial surface, our team despairs. My mother lies on her back, eyes closed to the gray Pittsburgh sky, wheezing painfully. Kneeling over her, I call another time-out, and my father explodes on the far sidelines, flinging his clipboard past the ducking heads of caped Vikings.

On the sidelines with him I try it again. They're wide open for Sammy or Ahmad deep. We both glance out to the teams, my mother kneeling, her head down, her hands on her thighs.

Go with the pitch again, he says.

This time, no. I almost say it aloud to Lambert, across the line. His missing front teeth make his eyeteeth fangs. I look back at my mother already in her stance; she'd accepted the call without any visible reaction. This will be fifty-eight carries.

She takes the pitch and veers unexpectedly away from our blocking and has almost five yards on the sheer boldness of her cut before lowering her head and taking on Donnie Shell helmet to helmet. In the impact, she spins off helpless, absurdly frail, into a slash of Pittsburgh tacklers, the ball punched free and jerking past me, rolling innocent toward our goal line, and a host of Steelers are after it, Greenwood, Greene, Cole, and, running alongside, I can't even reach the one— Greenwood—who finally gets control of it and carries it aloft into the end zone, the sound from the Pittsburgh fans coming down at us like thunder.

I crouch over my mother, on the bench. Blood is flecked in tiny red dots across the white of her face mask. I'm sorry, she says. I had it, but it must've popped out when they hit me. This is finished, I think. He's got to listen.

But he doesn't move on the sidelines, watching the kickoff team swarmed over, listening to the headset. No, he answers suddenly. We don't have to throw. We're only six down. Run her on some misdirection. He stares into me. She's a professional, he says. She gets paid to do this.

Pittsburgh's waiting for the misdirection, too, and Greenwood drives her onto her back so that the people on the sidelines can hear the impact.

Mom, I say over her, and I start to cry. She swims in my vision, her head lolling from side to side. I wave, stand and wave, enraged in mime, but no replacement comes. My mother gets back on her feet. I lean into the huddle. I want to call a pass, but I can't: there are no routes for my receivers, and I have no faith in my arm.

So I call the 23 Pitch to my mother and move down the line at the snap only to plant and cut rather than pitching, Lambert's astonished face flashing by, my teammates shouting, whooping, pounding along behind in useless support before Donnie Shell slants in on me inexorably and slams me down as a betrayer, a cheat, riding up and over me in his anger as we tumble along the sidelines.

The crowd, stunned, erupts anyway. It is the first first-down of the game. My father is frantically trying to signal for a time-out, but he can't, we've used them all, I've used them all.

That's like you, Dad, I think, bringing the team back to the huddle. But we're not listening now. On the next play I'm swarmed under, astounded at the viciousness of the tackles, hobbled. I hold my knee. Lambert stands over me, nodding. No more diagonal cuts.

I limp up, my father sends a replacement out for me, I wave him back. Suddenly all the anger and frustration hits and I'm near tears again, the crossbars in the Steeler end zone mocking us over their helmets. We'll never get this in, I think bitterly. My mother, leaning forward in the huddle, hands on thighs, says, It's okay.

I look into her eyes in fear and wonder, her tone settling me as I do, and I want to tell her I love her, want desperately to show her in my eyes how much support she has from me, if not physical, now, then mental, emotional; want desperately for my support to help.

Call the play, she says. Everyone's waiting.

Twenty-three Pitch, I say.

She takes it and is driven out of bounds, into spectators, yard markers, the bench. Equipment flies. She returns to the huddle breathing noisily from her mouth. Call it again, she says. She lowers her head, drives forward, collides with Shell, staggers, and keeps going. The referee signals first down, and I rush over and hug her to her feet. She still has not let go of the ball. In the huddle she sways slightly. Run it again, she whispers.

And she drives forward again and again, exchanging yards for the punishment her body absorbs until the goalposts loom high above us.

There're two minutes left, she says. Her teeth, in the huddle, are red. Time-out is given to both benches for the two-minute warning, and my father is halfway out onto the field, trying to get us over to the sideline.

I look at her closely. We don't have to go, I remind her. He's still the coach, she says. And I want to get these taped up. She stares critically at her hand, the smaller two fingers dangling uselessly, flapping a bit as she walks.

They wrap my mother's hand while my uncle yells tendencies, patterns, picked up from up in the booth, in my ear. My father, so desperate to get us to the sidelines, seems unable to speak. He grabs my arm, then my mother's, gesticulates. He seems terrified, overwhelmed. I feel content, all at once; surprised and pleased and superior. My mother raises her hand to signal enough and they snip the tape. Now listen to what Coach said, my uncle says finally. We trot back out onto the pale green expanse, our teammates, the Steelers, millions waiting.

The scoreboard flashes STOP, then IDA. STOP—IDA. The crowd responds, picking up the chant.

I hug her again, my teammates embarrassed, bewildered, our helmets clacking together earhole to earhole, and whisper, They can't. I know that now. When I let her go, she looks at me as though I still have more to learn. The lights are on now, reflecting in yellow circles off the high-gloss purple of her helmet, refracting in the scars in the plastic. The sky is blue black and a wind picks up. Across the line, hands on hips, Greenwood shivers.

I call the play. Halfway down to her stance, my mother says behind me, Either we do it here or we don't do it at all.

The scoreboard announces, belatedly, that my mother's sixty-six carries are a National Football League record. The crowd boos.

I pitch it and my mother gains three yards, leaping and being spun in midair, bouncing on her shoulder.

I pitch it and she gains three more, cutting back inside, her head snapping around as her face mask is grabbed and her body flies out from under her. Face mask! I yell, searching wildly for an official, but there are none.

And again, and again. Once more, she says in the huddle, coughing, and over center I realize the Steelers are crouching in their own end zone and there are eight men up on the line, thighs quivering, ready to shoot every gap. The scoreboard shows five seconds and I wonder where the time went.

I pitch it a final time, both hands supplicating, supporting, as they follow the flight of the ball, and the Steelers have her completely shut off to the sideline, and as she plants her foot to cut, Lambert's helmet catches her flush in the face and Greenwood's in the chest, and she's knocked five yards backward in a splinter of face-mask pieces, catching herself with her free hand, somehow keeping her balance, reversing herself, heading instinctively, blindly, for the opposite sideline, gaining speed as she runs back past me, face bloody, eyes closed; jagged pieces of face mask jutting out from the helmet. I spin and head for the end zone, her only blocker, both teams caught and tangled at the other side of the field. There's only Cole and as he throws himself at my mother I throw myself at him, and we pile up, brutally, my mother underneath with the ball over the goal line.

My teammates mob her, and I'm caught in the crush, still tangled with Cole, and the coaching staff mobs her, bald-headed, paunchy men leaping and shrieking among the purple of the uniforms, and the Steelers, too, and suddenly I'm scared for her, trying to fight my way over to her, up on somebody's shoulders, and I can't, and I shout, Mom! Mom! and she turns and sees me. Across the field my father stands alone, alone in the horizontal expanse of the empty sideline, and above me the scoreboard announces 15:00, the start of a fifth quarter. Mom! I yell above the tumult. We've still got overtime! and she yells something back and I can't hear her and try to fight closer and she says, I said it never really will stop. But we can get a handle on it anyway, and as the mob carries her back toward our sideline my throwing arm and knee both recover and surge with energy, as if looking forward to their supporting role.

HORSE

Ann Packer

When I entered the ninth grade I had just turned fourteen and I wanted more than anything to be a pompon girl. My desire had formed over the course of the summer: my friends and I customarily ate lunch on the benches near the English office, but during the long idle months I had taken to imagining myself moved as if by magic to the picnic table in front of the snack machines, which was handed down, with all the arrogance and inevitability attached to the turning over of a monarchy, from one pompon squad to the next. Our school colors were red and yellow— crimson and gold, we called them—and by the end of the first day of school the idea of owning one of those short, flip-skirted red and yellow dresses had taken over my mind. The football season pompon girls had shown up in their new outfits, and I was enamored even of the spotless white Keds they wore. Tryouts for the basketball pompon squad weren't until the beginning of October, but within days I had cleared out our garage and claimed it as my practice area. I set up my record player on the shelf where my mother kept the tools, and I listened to all of my albums, over and over again, in an effort to find a song that would inspire me to make up a winning routine. The routine, according to the printed rules I got from the girls' P.E. office, would be composed of a series of "steps"—dance steps, I decided—of my devising. The only fundamental thing about pompon was pompon step itself, a kind of miniature running in place that would form the basis of everyone's routine. The rest was up to me.

One Saturday morning, as I passed through the kitchen on my way to the garage, my mother cleared her throat and said she wanted to talk to me. She was sitting at the table, stacks of envelopes and her big, ledger-style checkbook lined up in front of her. She was paying the bills.

She pulled her reading glasses down onto the tip of her nose and looked up at me. "Found a song yet?" she asked evenly.

"Not yet," I said.

She nodded, and I wondered whether she was finally going to condemn my pompon dreams. So far, she hadn't come out against them—she hadn't, for instance, told me that she thought the whole concept was sexist or exploitative or elitist or even just plain silly—and because of her very neutrality I'd been assuming the worst. It wasn't like her not to comment.

"I got a call last night from Jim Baranski," she said, naming our down-the-street neighbor, who coached basketball at the local college. "One of his players needs a place to live and Jim thought we might let him have the guest room."

"Why would we do that?" I said.

"That's what I asked Jim. I'm not looking to be anybody's frat mother."

"So that was that?"

"The poor guy was supposed to have a full scholarship, but it fell through. If he can't find a place to live for free he's going to have to leave school. Jim says he's willing to do yardwork in exchange for a room."

"If we need yardwork done," I said, "maybe we should just get a gardener."

"We're not exactly rich at this point," my mother said, her voice tight and controlled. She cleared her throat and went on in a friendlier tone. "Jim said it might be nice for Danny to have a guy around. You know, an older guy—someone he could do things with. Play basketball and stuff."

Now I understood; and I understood that she wasn't asking my

opinion so much as pleading with me not to say no. My father had died a
year earlier, a heart attack at forty-five, and my ten-year-old brother
Danny had become a big source of worry to her. He spent all his time in
his room, reading Planet of the Apes books and drawing highly detailed
maps of outer space. The maps were really good: all the lines were
meticulously drawn; the planets were colored in to look like real spheres;
and everything was carefully labeled in his tiny, scientist's script.

"When's he moving in?" I said.

"Elizabeth."

"Well?"

She began flipping through the bills. "I told Jim we'd try it for a
month. And if any of us doesn't like it that'll be that." She looked up at
me, a small, desperate smile on her lips. "His name's Bobby. He's going
to bring his things over tomorrow."

"OK."

"Really?"

I forced a smile. "Sure," I said. "It'll be good for Danny." But I
thought, a basketball player? It seemed like an insult to my father's
memory: he had taught philosophy at the college, and his favorite and
only sport had been speed-reading paperback mysteries.

The guest room was right next to my room, and I got up early the next
morning to take a last look at it. My room had been decorated—very
decorated—according to my specifications six or seven years earlier; it
was all pink and white, and whenever I felt the girlishness of it too
keenly I would go into the guest room and lie on the bed in there. It was
a big, square, airy room, full of plain oak furniture. The only adornment
was an elaborate cut glass water pitcher on the dresser; anywhere else it
might have looked gaudy, but it was the perfect touch in that austere
room.

I stood in the doorway and tried to imagine a college basketball
player living next door to me. The room was empty except for when my
grandmother came to visit, and although I could never really hear her, I
always felt aware of her when she was there—of her breathing, of her
sighing, of her rolling over in bed in the middle of the night.

I went down to the garage and, as I had every day for the past
two weeks, I worked on my pompon step. It wasn't, I had quickly
learned, as easy as it looked. You had to jump from foot to foot, pointing
first your left toes, then your right toes, then your left toes, then your
right toes, and all the while you had to keep your hands at your waist,

but not around your waist: they had to be bent at the knuckles so your fingers and thumbs wouldn't show. It was a little boring, but I didn't mind spending so much time on it because the next thing I had to do was settle on a song and start working on my routine. I knew it would have to involve some kicking, some little flips of the shoulder, and, most important, the splits, and although I'd been stretching every day I could only get down to about eight inches off the ground.

Early in the afternoon, a car came up the driveway and stopped just on the other side of the garage. I turned off my music. A couple of doors slammed; then I heard a deep voice.

"Nice deal, Bobby. Maybe they'll go away a lot and you can have some parties."

"Quiet." His voice was clear and rather high for a man's. "They might be able to hear us."

I lowered the arm of the record player back onto the album I was playing, turned the volume up, and sat down on the garage floor, my bare legs touching the cold concrete. I listened to the muffled sounds of people going back and forth, from car to house, for the next five or ten minutes. After a while the commotion stopped, and I knew my mother and Danny were talking to Bobby and his friend. She had probably offered them iced tea, maybe even sandwiches. The only thing I had with me to read was the pompon tryouts instruction sheet, and I read it through several times, trying to concentrate on all the details—what kind of gloves you were supposed to wear, how long your routine should be, when the winners' names would be posted. There was one paragraph that I kept going back to. It said, "The pompon girls represent everyone at Murphy Junior High. They are our ambassadors to schools all over the county. Even when they're not in uniform they feel like pompon girls, and it's important that they look that way, too. This means extra special attention to personal hygiene and grooming. Any girl who doesn't know what this means should speak to Mrs. Donovan in the P.E. office as soon as possible."

I didn't know what it meant—I assumed it had something to do either with shaving under your arms or getting your period—but I wasn't about to ask Mrs. Donovan. With my mother I had only recently managed to shut down communication about such things; as far as I was concerned, we had covered what needed to be covered. The occasional appearance on my desk of pamphlets entitled "Your Changing Body" or "A Single Egg" suggested that she disagreed.

Finally, I heard the car starting up again, and I turned the music off in time to hear the low-voiced guy say, "Later, bro."

"See you at practice," Bobby said.

They said a few more things, but in voices pitched so low I couldn't hear them. I imagined they were talking about me: saying how strange it was my mother hadn't made me say hello, that I must be one of those shy girls who couldn't look anybody in the eye. Either that, or they were wondering what I looked like, what color hair I had. What my body was like.

At six Danny came out to tell me dinner was ready.

"What are we having?" I asked.

"Steak," he said. "Baked potatoes with sour cream. Corn on the cob with butter. Chocolate cream pie."

He was joking. All we ever had now was fish. Sometimes she put a sauce called Mock Hollandaise on our vegetables, but usually it was just lemon juice and pepper. There was no salt in the house anymore, no butter.

I laughed. "What'd you read today?"

"I didn't really read."

I turned from him and began stacking my records together.

"She invited him to eat with us," he said.

I didn't reply.

"That guy. Bobby."

I wheeled around. "I know who you mean. What do you think I am, stupid?"

His face turned a delicate shade of pink, the color he used to get when he had a fever. He was wearing a nerdy little plaid shirt with a too-big collar, and his head looked unbearably small to me.

"I'm sorry, Dan," I said. I took hold of his shoulders and pulled him to me. "You're almost as tall as I am, sonny-boy."

"Won't be long now, moony-girl." He pulled away from me and I followed him into the house.

Bobby Johansen was very tall: six foot four, I later learned. His hair was pale blond, almost colorless. He was leaning against the kitchen counter, wearing shorts, and I thought his legs would probably come up to my chest if we stood close.

My mother was washing lettuce. *"Here* she is," she said, as if my whereabouts had been a mystery. "Elizabeth, this is Bobby Johansen."

"Hi," I said. The table was set for four, and my mother had even used cloth placemats; lately even the usual woven straw ones had gone missing more often than not.

"Hey, Elizabeth," he said. "How's it goin'?"

I looked up at him and shrugged. "OK."

He didn't seem to know what to do with his hands. First they were on the counter behind him, then they were clasped in front of his fly, then crossed tightly over his chest. "What do you go by?" he said. "Liz? I've got a cousin Liz, just about your age."

"Elizabeth," I said.

"We used to call her Bit, though," my mother said. "Didn't we, honey?"

"We?" I said.

She pursed her lips. "Danny did. He couldn't say Elizabeth, he said *Elizabit*. Then it was just Bit. Right, Dan?"

"A few hundred years ago," Danny said.

"Well, anyway," my mother said to me. "We were thinking maybe after dinner the four of us could play a game. Monopoly or something."

"Can't," I said. "Math test tomorrow."

My mother yanked a square of paper towel from the roll and began arranging the wet lettuce leaves on it.

"I used to be pretty good at math," Bobby said. "If you need any help."

"That's OK," I said. It was in my mind to say, I'm pretty good at math, too; but I managed to stifle it. "Thanks, though."

There was a silence. I was still holding my records, so I went upstairs to put them in my room. The guest room door was ajar and I pushed it open. A couple of worn-looking green duffel bags were lying on the bed, with T-shirts and sweat clothes and towels spilling out as if they were someone's cast-offs at a garage sale. I tiptoed across the room and opened the closet door. It was empty except for three pairs of high-topped white leather sneakers arranged in a row on the floor. I bent over and picked up a shoe. It was longer than my forearm and it smelled: of dirty laundry and of sweat, but of something else, too—a sharp, leathery scent. It was, I decided, the smell of arrogance.

·   ·   ·

The following Friday, at the lunch-time rally that was the official end of the school day—during football season we got out early for away-games—I stood by myself and studied the football pompon girls' new routine. They would do it again at half-time later that afternoon, but I wasn't going to the game; none of my friends ever went, and I was too shy to go to an away-game alone. If I'd been asked why I wanted to go, I would only have been able to say that it had something to do with my father dying: that it wasn't the game so much as the way everyone looked after the game as they poured onto the field from the bleachers, uniform expressions of joy or despair on their faces.

I rode my bicycle home through the college, thinking that I would have the house to myself for the afternoon. Students were lying on the grass in little groups, and I looked at them more carefully than usual, wondering if Bobby was among them. I hadn't seen him since the day he moved in. He had a meal plan at one of the dorms and he studied at the library, so all I knew of him so far was the sound of his footsteps on the stairs as I was falling asleep. He didn't even leave his toothbrush in the bathroom.

The guest room door was closed. I went into my room, put my books on my desk, and lay down on my bed. I closed my eyes and waited to see what would materialize—the glittering ballroom, the dark restaurant, the umbrella-shaded outdoor cafe: at that time the arena of my fantasy life was limited to places where I would not be alone with the object of my idylls. After a moment, the restaurant hovered into view. The walls were lined with smoky mirrors, the tables covered with pale pink linen and set with gold-rimmed china. I was tall and sleek in a clingy silver gown sewn all over with shimmering little beads. A handsome, square-jawed man—with whom I never, in all the adolescent hours I spent in his company, exchanged a word—met me at the door and guided me to our secluded table, his hand in the small of my back. (I had just learned about the small of your back; it was where you were supposed to aim your tampon, and although that was nearly as unpleasant to think of as it was to do, the idea of that spot had a kind of power over me. It suggested romance—not the candlelight and flowers kind, but something easier, more intimate.)

I heard a noise from Bobby's room. It wasn't much of a noise: low and repetitive and only vaguely vocal. But before I was really even aware of the sound, I'd convinced myself that sex was taking place on the other side of the wall.

I turned my radio on, loud, and sat at my desk looking at my Latin book, my heart pounding. A moment later I got up and clomped past the guest room and down the stairs. I paused in the kitchen, but the idea of the two of them—Bobby in pajama bottoms, a tousle-haired girl in the matching pajama top—coming down in search of something to drink sent me out to the garage.

Leaning against the wall was a brand-new basketball hoop attached to a backboard. I looked it over for a minute or two: the backboard was white with jaunty red trim; the basket itself was a metal circle from which hung a flimsy-looking white net. I bent my knees and tried to lift it, but it was surprisingly heavy.

"Careful with that, it's heavier than it looks."

I turned around and Bobby was standing in the doorway, his long arms dangling by his sides.

"I was going to put that up for Danny this afternoon," he said. He was wearing gym shorts and a gray T-shirt, and there were big dark stains where he'd been sweating. I must have been staring, because he said, "I was doing sit-ups."

"Danny's not much of an athlete," I said.

"Everyone likes to shoot baskets."

"Does my mother know?"

He gave me a funny look. "She bought it."

I turned from him and examined the hoop again. "These strings don't seem too sturdy," I said.

He laughed and came over to where I was standing. "They're not meant to hold any weight. They hug the ball when it goes through so it'll drop down gently instead of flying all over the court. Stick around while I put it up and I'll show you."

"I have homework," I said.

He nodded. "More math?"

"Latin."

"Can't help you there. The only Latin I know is pig."

I edged toward the door. "Well," I said. "See you later."

"O-say ong-lay," he said with a smile.

A few nights later my mother came into my room on her way to bed. I was rearranging my closet, and she sat at my desk and watched me.

"I guess we should get you a new parka this year," she said.

"This one's OK." I hung it on a hook inside the closet door.

"Maybe a down one," she said. "I was thinking we should go up to Tahoe in February. Try again." When I was eight or nine the four of us had spent a miserable weekend trying to learn to ski; we'd never gone back. My father had liked to say that we were the only family in California who *didn't* love the fact that the mountains were only five hours from the beach.

"Down jackets aren't good for skiing," I said. "Too bulky."

"Elizabeth," she said. "Why do you have to be so difficult?"

I looked at her; her lips were pressed into a narrow line. "I'm not being difficult. I just don't happen to want a down jacket."

"That's not the point," she said. "I mention skiing and you don't react at all. Can't you at least say, 'Yes, Mother dear, a ski trip would be lovely,' or 'No, Mother dear, the idea of trying to ski again makes my legs turn to jelly'?"

I turned back to the closet. Very quietly, I said, "I'll go if you want me to."

"I want you to have an *opinion.*"

I shrugged, but suddenly there were tears running down my face. I stared at my clothes.

"Eliz?"

"I can't."

She came over and touched my shoulder and I turned around. "What is it?" she said. She pulled me close and held me, and my shoulders started to shake. "What is it?"

I shook my head.

She ran her hand up and down my back. "Tell me," she said. "Poor baby, to have such a brute of a mother. Tell me."

I pulled away from her, got a Kleenex from my desk, and blew my nose. "Why do you have to get so mad at me?"

"I'm sorry." She sat down on my bed and shook her head. She looked very small, sitting there; small and tired. There were wrinkles around her eyes and mouth, and her hair looked thin and lifeless.

I heard the sound of someone—Bobby—opening and closing the front door and coming up the stairs. A moment later, the guest room door closed.

"I'm sorry," my mother said again. "I'll try to be better."

I held my forefinger up to my lips, then pointed at the wall dividing my room from Bobby's. *He can hear us,* I mouthed.

She smiled at me. "He doesn't care," she whispered.

"Well," I whispered back, "I do."

.   .   .

With the coming of the basketball hoop Bobby was around more, and I had to find a new place to work on my pompon routine. I moved down to the basement, and against the muffled yet insistent sounds of the basketball bouncing on the asphalt and—thud—hitting the backboard, I settled on the Beach Boys' "I Get Around," and began to choreograph my moves.

Late one afternoon, when my routine was going badly and the Beach Boys' falsettos were all but drowned out by the hammer of the basketball, I decided that I'd had enough. I marched up the stairs and out to the driveway, icily polite equivalents to WILL YOU PLEASE SHUT UP running through my mind. But when I saw Danny standing there looking at the ball, which seemed bigger around than he was, I couldn't say anything. I watched.

"OK," Bobby said, glancing at me, "dribble a couple of times and then when you shoot try for some backspin." He held his hand up, palm to the sky, and flicked his wrist a couple of times. "Roll the ball up your fingers."

Danny bounced the ball, then threw it at the basket; it hit the rim with a metallic clang and careened past me. I turned and ran after it, then carried it back and handed it to Bobby.

"Want to try?" he said.

I shook my head.

He gave the ball back to Danny. "That was better," he said. "Try again."

On the fifth shot, the ball hit the backboard, rolled around the rim, and went through the net. "Great," Bobby said, giving Danny's shoulder a little shake. "That's the stuff."

He took the ball and without looking at me backed up so that he was standing just a few feet from me. Without seeming to aim, he tossed the ball and it sailed through the air and went cleanly through the basket without touching the backboard or the rim. "Swish," he said.

Danny caught the ball and came running over. "Can we play HORSE?" he said.

Bobby looked at me and smiled. "Only if your sister will try a shot first."

"Blackmailer," I said.

Danny handed me the ball and I moved closer to the basket. I held the ball in front of my face, closed my eyes, and threw.

"Two points," Bobby yelled. "Whoo!"

Danny clapped and called, "Maybe you should try out to *play* instead."

"Ha ha," I said. I tugged at my shirt, which had ridden up and exposed my stomach when I threw the ball.

"Play HORSE with us," Danny said. "Please?"

"HORSE?" I glanced at Bobby; he stood there with the ball tucked under his arm, looking at me. "I don't think so, Dan."

"You don't even know what it is. Let me at least explain it to you." Danny held out his hands and Bobby threw him the ball. He bounced it and looked up at the basket. "Say I go first. I stand wherever I want and try for a basket. If I make it, the next person has to stand in the same spot and shoot. And if they don't make it they get an H. And you keep moving around and whoever spells out HORSE first loses. Get it? They're a horse. Come on, it's fun."

"Sorry, kid," I said. "Got to practice. I have no time for this 'fun' of which you speak."

"Your graciousness," he said, and bowed to me.

"Your majesty," I said, bowing back.

I turned and headed for the house. "Bye, Elizabeth," Bobby called to me as I reached the kitchen door. "Nice to see you again."

I needed some white gloves. My mother had said not to worry; she had several pairs I could choose from. The Saturday before tryouts I asked her to let me see them.

She led me up to her bedroom and pulled a shoebox from the back of her closet. "I know you can't believe it," she said, "but your mother used to be the picture of elegance."

We both laughed; she was wearing blue jeans and an old checked shirt, her usual weekend attire. Even when she went to work I thought she looked a little mannish—she dressed in somber colors, never wore jewelry.

She slipped the top off the box and pulled away some tissue paper. "God," she said.

I looked into the box, and it was a strange sight: over a dozen gloves, some white, some beige, even a single navy blue one, all lying in a tangle. "How orderly," I said.

"Don't give me any lip, kid," she said, smiling. She set the box on the bed and we began sorting through it, putting the gloves in pairs.

"Where's the other blue one?" I said.

"Long gone." A dreamy look came over her face and for a moment I thought she was going to tell me a story. But all she said was "Lost to another era."

There were four pairs of white gloves in all, but none of them seemed right to me.

"What's wrong with these, Elizabeth?"

"The rules didn't say anything about buttons."

"Well, what about these?"

"There's a huge stain on the left one."

"It's on the palm, no one'll see it."

"Mom."

"These?"

"Too long."

Finally she sat on the bed and looked at me, her mouth in a half-frown.

"I'll ride over to the shopping center and buy some," I said. I began piling the gloves back into the box.

She grabbed my wrist. "Elizabeth, for God's sake, you're only going to wear them for ten minutes."

I shook her hand off. "I want to look nice."

She stood up and cut me a disgusted look, then stalked out of the room. I hurried after her and caught up with her on the stairs.

"Why shouldn't I get new gloves?" I said. "What do you care? I'll pay for them."

"I don't care," she snapped.

"Mom," I said.

We reached the bottom of the stairs and she turned to face me. "It's just so silly, Elizabeth," she said quietly. "It's beneath you."

I opened my mouth, but nothing came out.

"Your father would—"

"Well, lucky for me he's not here to see it!" I jerked open the front door and hurried out of the house. My bicycle was locked, and I had to twist the dial several times before I got the lock to open.

Twenty minutes later I was at the shopping center—without a cent. I decided to look around anyway; when I found the gloves I wanted I would ask the saleslady to hold them for me, then go back home for my wallet.

I went into Penney's and found the glove department. There was no one behind the counter, so I circled the glass case, looking. There were leather gloves and wool gloves and gloves made of bright red satin, but I couldn't find a single pair of white gloves.

"Can I help you?"

A woman stood behind the counter, blue hair piled on top of her head. I told her what I wanted and she said, "Oh, we haven't carried white gloves in ten years, dear. Is it for Halloween?"

"Um, no."

"Prom?" she asked, cocking her head gaily.

"No, I just need them for school."

She raised her eyebrows. "School play?"

"No, I—thanks anyway." I turned and hurried away.

"You might try Peaches and Cream, dear," she called after me.

I got outside the store and leaned against the wall. My face felt hot. At the other end of the shopping center was Bullock's, where my mother took me twice a year for school clothes. I decided to go there first, even though Peaches and Cream was on the way; Peaches and Cream was a shop full of breakable knickknacks and precious little silk flower arrangements, and although I'd never been in it I had always held it in a kind of contempt: it seemed to have nothing to do with real life.

But Bullock's didn't have white gloves, either. I wandered around the ground floor of the store, and, as if I were languishing in a boat on a hot day and needed the feel of the water, my hand trailed behind me, touching whatever I passed: wool, leather, chrome. In the makeup department I slowed even more, studying the nail polish and lipstick at first one counter, then another. A young woman in a salmon-colored lab coat caught my eye.

"Free makeovers today," she said. "Would you like one?"

"I don't have any money," I said.

"They're *free.*"

"But I won't be able to buy anything after."

She patted the seat of a chair set against one of the counters. "You'll feel better."

I glanced around the area; it was nearly empty. I climbed onto the chair.

"I'm Kristen," she said. "Tell me a little about what you usually wear. Makeup-wise, I mean."

"Oh, just a little eyeshadow and lip gloss," I said, although in truth I never wore a stroke of either.

"What's your name, honey?"

"Elizabeth."

"Well, Elizabeth, I'm going to start with a little foundation." She unscrewed the top of a small white bottle, tipped some liquid onto her fingers, and began dabbing the stuff onto my face.

Another salmon-coated woman appeared. "Oh, *fun*," she said. "Wild Sage on her lids, don't you think?"

"I was thinking Midnight Velvet," Kristen said.

They joined forces. They mixed colors. They tried a little of this and a little of that. Half an hour later Kristen offered me a hand mirror. "You're going to love this, Elizabeth," she said.

I searched the image for signs of myself, but I looked like a stranger—not just someone I didn't recognize, but someone who wasn't quite human. My cheeks had unnatural-looking hollows, and across each cheekbone was a slash of pink. They had used so much mascara it looked as if I were wearing false eyelashes.

"Well?" Kristen said.

"She has to get used to it," the other woman said. "It's a change."

I handed Kristen the mirror. "It's a whole new me."

She gave me a wide smile. "I knew you'd like it."

I thanked them and left the store. There were some benches arranged around a fountain and I slumped onto one. I closed my eyes and felt the sun on my hair and skin. My face felt odd, as if I'd washed it and let it dry without rinsing the soap off. I thought about the pompon tryouts instruction sheet, the part about hygiene and grooming. I wondered whether everyone else would be wearing a lot of makeup for the tryouts: I knew that the other girls who were trying out were the kind who *did* wear eyeshadow and lip gloss to school every day. I imagined myself in the girls' gym on the day of the tryouts, standing there in my forest green polyester one-piece gymsuit and my white gloves, waiting for my turn; my stomach did a queasy dance. Then I thought about what my mother had said, and I stood up, ready to try Peaches and Cream.

And there was Bobby.

He was coming toward me, but he hadn't seen me yet. I thought of running, but I knew that would attract more attention than anything. Hoping I would somehow be invisible to him, I sat down on the bench again and stared at the ground.

"Elizabeth?"

I looked up. "Hi."

He did a quick double-take, so subtle that if I hadn't been looking for his reaction I might not have noticed it. "What are you doing?" He put his foot up on the bench next to me.

"Shopping."

"What have you bought? I need socks."

"Nothing," I said. "I forgot my wallet."

He laughed. "Window shopping, more like, huh?" He turned and sat on the bench, a few feet away from me.

"I guess so."

We sat there staring straight ahead, not talking. I was certain that he thought I was the most pathetic person on earth, that he felt too sorry for me to make a getaway.

"So," he said.

"So," I said.

"Can I ask you a question?"

I turned to look at him.

"What happened to your face?"

I felt, surprisingly, that I had a choice: I could die of embarrassment or not, it was up to me. I smiled, and a moment later we were both laughing. "I had a makeover," I said.

"In there?"

I nodded. "There were two of them, Kristen and someone else. It took half an hour. It was free."

"What a bargain," he said, and we both laughed. "I don't know, I think Kristen and her friend are in the wrong line of work."

"What? You don't think they're artists?" I stood up and struck a pose.

"More like morticians."

"So that's why I couldn't recognize myself in the mirror. I look dead."

We both started to laugh again, but a shadow of unhappiness fell over me and although I kept laughing, I was thinking about my father; we'd had an open casket, against my wishes, and when I saw him lying there, a false rosiness on his waxy cheeks, I felt a tiny pinprick of shock, as if I had to learn all over again of his death.

I looked at Bobby and he was biting his lip. He smiled quickly and stood up.

"Maybe I could help you buy your socks," I said. "I mean, I'm sure you don't need help, but maybe I could go with you."

"Actually," he said. "I do need help. I can never decide on colors. Red and yellow or blue and green."

"You wear red socks?"

"No, no," he said, laughing, "the bands on top. I need tube socks. For practice." He dribbled an imaginary basketball, then shot it into the sky.

"Would you like to go to a movie tonight?" my mother said at dinner that evening. I'd been back and forth to the shopping center until the middle of the afternoon—I'd finally found some gloves at Peaches and Cream—and since I'd gotten home she and I had been distant and polite when we'd seen each other, as if we were strangers whose paths kept crossing in some foreign city.

"No, thank you," I said. "I've got to spend some time on things that are beneath me."

She colored, and Danny looked down at his plate. "I'm sorry, honey," she said. "I didn't mean it, it was a dumb thing to say. I just don't want you to be disappointed."

"When I don't make it?" I asked, standing up to clear the table.

Danny all but leapt from his chair and hurried from the room.

"Oh," my mother said quietly, and covered her mouth with her hand. She shook her head, and I could see she was fighting tears. After a moment she turned and faced the door, following Danny's path with her eyes. "Should I—"

I went over to her and held her head to my chest. "He's OK," I said. "I think we should just leave him alone."

"The old laissez-faire attitude was never my strong suit," she said. The vibrations her jaw made against my stomach as she spoke felt strange. She sighed and put her hands on my hips and I moved away. She looked up at me. "Show us your dance, honey," she said. "I think it would mean a lot to Danny."

I nodded. *Dance,* I thought.

"And to me, too, of course."

"Tomorrow," I said.

But the next day, a Sunday, Danny had been invited by a friend's family to go to San Francisco, and it wasn't until Monday night, just two days before tryouts, that I allowed my mother and Danny into the basement to watch me run through my routine.

"OK," I said when we got downstairs, "I'm going to pretend you guys are the judges."

Danny had perched on the washing machine. My mother leaned against the dryer. "How many are there?" she said uneasily.

"Six," I said. There would be Mrs. Donovan; Coach Simpson; Sally Chin, the head pompon girl for the football season; two guys from the basketball team; and Miss Rosenthal, a Home Ec teacher—*my* Home Ec teacher, as it happened, and it was she who worried me most. We had somehow, already, not hit it off; the other girls in the class were already on their A-line skirts, but I just couldn't finish my pot holder. I was afraid she would take it out on me in the judging.

"Six?" my mother said.

"The competition is going to be tough," Danny said. "We've got some very critical judges, ladies and gentlemen, and only five of these fifty beautiful young ladies will be selected. Sam, tell us a little about how the competition works."

"Fifty!" my mother said.

"He's joking, Mom. It's twenty-two."

"Oh, that's not so bad," my mother said. "Five out of twenty-two." But she looked unhappy.

"And now, from our own Manzanita Drive, it's Elizabeth Earle," Danny shouted.

"Quiet," my mother said, elbowing him.

I winked at Danny and turned to start the music. I stood with my back to them, my hands at my waist, my right knee bent. Then, on cue, I whipped around and started the routine.

It was the first time I had done it in front of anyone, and the thing I was most conscious of was the fact that I could not keep a smile on my face: Smile, I would tell myself, and my lips would slide open, and I would think about the kick I was doing (was my knee straight? were my toes pointed?) and I would realize my mouth was twisted into a tight knot again.

I finished with the splits, my arms upstretched in a V for Victory.

"Yes," Danny cried, leaping off the washing machine. He high-fived me and ran up the stairs to the kitchen.

My mother smiled at me. "Very nice," she said.

I sighed and turned around.

"Really, honey," she said. "It's good—you got all the way down on your splits. I'll bet most of the other girls can't do that."

Danny came running back down the stairs, waving a piece of

paper on which he'd written "9.9" with a thick pen. "An amazing routine from Elizabeth Earle," he cried.

"Thanks, Dan." I looked at my mother. "Well, it'll all be over in two days."

"Who knows?" she said. "Maybe it'll just be beginning."

They went upstairs while I took the record off the turntable and put it back in its paper sleeve. I wiped my sweaty palms off on my shorts—I'd decided not to wear the gloves for practicing, to keep them clean—then I turned the basement light off and climbed the stairs.

My mother and Bobby were sitting at the kitchen table. When my mother saw me she said, "Elizabeth's got her tryouts day after tomorrow."

Bobby looked at me. "Nervous?"

I nodded.

"Twenty-two girls are trying out for five spots," my mother said.

"OK, Mom." I looked at Bobby's feet. "Are you wearing your new socks?"

He pulled up one leg of his jeans to display the bright red and yellow bands around the top of his sock. "Listen," he said, "try not to be too nervous. It'll show, and that'll be the thing that gets you. Know what I mean?" He turned to my mother. "They totally watch for whether the girl has the right look. You know, smiley, bouncy. Believe me, I was once a judge for one of these things."

"Maybe you should do your routine for Bobby," my mother said.

"Absolutely not." His words had sent my heartbeat out of control. Eyeshadow and lip gloss, I thought, like it or not.

"Please?" he said.

I shook my head.

"Well, just remember," he said. "You've got to smile."

I felt my face fill with color.

My mother coughed and said, "You know, honey, you did look a little fierce down there."

I gave them a frozen grin. "Like this?" I said through clenched teeth.

"That's the one," Bobby said. "Glue it on."

"Goodnight," I said. Without looking at either of them, I got myself a glass of water and climbed the stairs.

"Elizabeth?" Danny called from his room.

I stopped in his doorway. He was lying on his bed, our giant world atlas open in front of him. "Planning a trip?" I asked. I sat down next to him and glanced at the atlas; it was open to a page showing the whole of Africa. "They say Morocco is nice this time of year."

"It was good," he said. "I'm sure you'll make it."

I shrugged. "Not according to Mr. Basketball down there."

"What did he say?"

"Nothing. I can just tell. He thinks I'm not pretty enough."

"God," Danny said. "He does not. You are so puerile sometimes."

"Puerile?" I laughed and reached over to tickle his neck. "Little Mr. Vocabulary."

"Don't call me little." He scrambled off the bed and assumed a body-builder's stance. Then he put his hands on his hips and began mimicking my pompon kicks. "Do they have pompon girls in Morocco?"

"Danny!"

He started wiggling around, his arms snaking out from his sides. "I'm a Moroccan pompon girl," he said. "Elizabethahad Earlakim."

"Danny," I said. "Stop, tell me the truth. Did I look fierce?"

Of course I didn't make it. Ten or twelve years later, at parties, I would offer up the comic spectacle of myself standing in the girls' gym, my back to the judges, my eyelids powder blue, my white-gloved hands clenched into fists, my right knee bent: my hopeful, embarrassed self waiting for the music to start. I would say that as I slid down into the splits at the end, my arms in their V, I caught Miss Rosenthal's eye and mistook her horsey grin for congratulations on a job well done, when in fact she was trying to get me to smile. I would perhaps also say—although this wasn't true, I was far too nervous for such fancies—that as I stood in the locker room changing out of my gymsuit, I had a triumphant vision of myself on the floor of the basketball court at half-time, facing the crowded bleachers in my crimson and gold dress, and that I felt a thrill of fear at the idea of doing something so marvelously alien. I would say, in closing, that I was lucky: no one could admit to actually having been a pompon girl. The cachet was in having wanted to, and failed.

Here's what I never said: After the list was posted I telephoned my mother to come pick me up; it was nearly six o'clock and the afternoon light was fading. I was sitting on the curb in the parking lot hoping

that Bobby wouldn't be around when I got home, when the memory of
my mother's voice came to me. "Your father would—" it said. Your
father would, your father would . . . And I was filled with sickness because I realized that she might have been wrong. Wouldn't he, after all,
have been on my side? What would he have thought? *Well, lucky for me
he isn't here to see it.*

A little while later my mother arrived; neither of us spoke on the way
home.

As we turned into our street, I saw that Danny and Bobby were
outside the house, shooting baskets. "No," I said, turning to her. "Oh,
please."

"What?" She put her foot on the brake.

"I can't face him right now. Can't we go to the store or
something?"

"You look fine, honey."

"Mom," I said. "It's not how I look. He'll think I'm such a loser.
He'll try to get me to play basketball. Please."

She steered the car to the curb and cut the engine. She turned to
face me. "You don't get it, do you?" she said. "He doesn't think you're a
loser. He's scared of you."

"Bobby?"

"Terrified. You're what's standing between him and a place to
live. Next week his month is up, and if we say he can't stay he's in big
trouble. He's scared you want him out."

My mouth fell open. "He told you this?"

"Elizabeth," she said. "Believe me. No, he didn't tell me, but I
know. You can be—formidable."

I looked out the window at our house. Dusk was coming on
quickly now, but still they played. I watched Danny make three baskets
in a row. Then Bobby took the ball, backed up to the foot of the driveway, and drove in for a lay-up. "That was a good shot," I said. I turned
back to my mother.

She had picked up my gloves, which I'd thrown onto the seat
between us, and was pulling them on. She held her hands up in front of
her face and looked at them. Then she reached out and ran her finger
down my cheek, a soft, velvety touch. "I'm sorry you didn't win," she
said.

I sat without speaking for a while. Then I took her hand and
pulled at the fingertip of the glove. "What am I going to do with these?"

"I know of this shoebox," she said. She smiled at me; then she started the car and drove the last hundred yards to our house.

When they saw us, Danny and Bobby stopped playing. I got out of the car, and for a moment neither of them said anything. Then Bobby said, "I'm sorry, Elizabeth—it's too bad." He brushed the hair off his forehead and I could see he was trying to think of something to add.

"Thanks," I said.

Danny bounced the basketball a couple of times. Without quite looking at me he said, "We could play one game of HORSE before dinner."

"I'm kind of tired, Dan."

He bounced the ball again.

"We could just play GOAT," Bobby said. "That would be quicker."

"Or DOG," Danny said, smiling.

I set my books on the trunk of the car. "Jeez, guys—I'm not in a hurry. Let's play RHINOCEROS."

"All right," Danny said, jumping up and down. "You'll play."

I looked at Bobby and we exchanged an amused smile.

"I know," Danny went on. "I have a great idea. Let's play AN-TIDISESTABLISHMENTARIANISM."

"What?" Bobby said.

"*Antidisestablishmentarianism,*" Danny said. "It's the longest word in the English language."

That was something he'd gotten from our father. As a game at dinner we used to have these sort of spelling bees, and Danny always insisted that the longer a word was, the harder it would be to spell; our father gave him "antidisestablishmentarianism" once to show that he was wrong.

"Danny," I said, "spell *puerile.*"

"Hold on, you two," said Bobby. "I think it has to be an animal."

DOC'S STORY

John Edgar Wideman

He thinks of her small, white hands, blue veined, gaunt, awkwardly knuckled. He'd teased her about the smallness of her hands, hers lost in the shadow of his when they pressed them together palm to palm to measure. The heavy drops of color on her nails barely reached the middle joints of his fingers. He'd teased her about her dwarf's hands but he'd also said to her one night when the wind was rattling the windows of the apartment on Cedar and they lay listening and shivering though it was summer on the brass bed she'd found in a junk store on Haverford Avenue, near the Woolworth's five-and-dime they'd picketed for two years, that God made little things closer to perfect than he ever made big things. Small, compact women like her could be perfectly formed, proportioned, and he'd smiled out loud running his hand up and down the just-right fine lines of her body, celebrating how good she felt to him.

She'd left him in May, when the shadows and green of the park had started to deepen. Hanging out, becoming a regular at the basketball court across the street in Regent Park was how he'd coped. No questions asked. Just the circle of stories. If you didn't want to miss anything good you came early and stayed late. He learned to wait, be patient. Long hours waiting were not time lost but time doing nothing because there was nothing better to do. Basking in sunshine on a stone bench, too beat to play any longer, nowhere to go but an empty apartment, he'd watch the afternoon traffic in Regent Park: dog strollers, baby carriages, winos, kids, gays, students with blankets they'd spread out on the grassy banks of the hollow and books they'd pretend to read, the black men from the neighborhood who'd search the park for braless young mothers and white girls on blankets who didn't care or didn't know any better than to sit with their crotches exposed. When he'd sit for hours like that, cooking like that, he'd feel himself empty out, see himself seep away and hover in the air, a fine mist, a little, flattened-out gray cloud of something wavering in the heat, a presence as visible as the steam on the window as he stares for hours at winter.

He's waiting for summer. For the guys to begin gathering on the court again. They'll sit in the shade with their backs against the Cyclone fencing or lean on cars parked at the roller-coaster curb or lounge in the sun on low, stone benches catty-corner from the basketball court. Some older ones still drink wine, but most everybody cools out on reefer, when there's reefer passed along, while they bullshit and wait for winners. He collects the stories they tell. He needs a story now. The right one now to get him through this long winter because she's gone and won't leave him alone.

In summer fine grit hangs in the air. Five minutes on the court and you're coughing. City dirt and park dust blowing off bald patches from which green is long gone, and deadly ash blowing over from New Jersey. You can taste it some days, bitter in your spit. Chunks pepper your skin, burn your eyes. Early fall while it's still warm enough to run outdoors the worst time of all. Leaves pile up against the fence, higher and higher, piles that explode and jitterbug across the court in the middle of a game, then sweep up again, slamming back where they blew from. After a while the leaves are ground into coarse, choking powder. You eat leaf trying to get in a little hoop before the weather turns, before those days when nobody's home from work yet but it's dark already and too cold to run again till spring. Fall's the only time sweet syrupy wine beats reefer. Ripple, Manischewitz, Taylor's Tawny Port coat your throat. He takes a hit when the jug comes round. He licks the sweetness from his lips, listens for his favorite stories one more time before everybody gives it up till next season.

His favorite stories made him giggle and laugh and hug the others, like they hugged him when a story got so good nobody's legs could hold them up. Some stories got under his skin in peculiar ways. Some he liked to hear because they made the one performing them do crazy stuff with his voice and body. He learned to be patient, learned his favorites would be repeated, get a turn just like he got a turn on the joints and wine bottles circulating the edges of the court.

Of all the stories, the one about Doc had bothered him most. Its orbit was unpredictable. Twice in one week, then only once more last summer. He'd only heard Doc's story three times, but that was enough to establish Doc behind and between the words of all the other stories. In a strange way Doc presided over the court. You didn't need to mention him. He was just there. Regent Park stories began with Doc and ended with Doc and everything in between was preparation, proof the circle was unbroken.

They say Doc lived on Regent Square, one of the streets like Cedar, dead-ending at the park. On the hottest afternoons the guys from the court would head for Doc's stoop. Jars of ice water, the good feeling and good talk they'd share in the shade of Doc's little front yard was what drew them. Sometimes they'd spray Doc's hose on one another. Get drenched like when they were kids and the city used to turn on fire hydrants in the summer. Some of Doc's neighbors would give them dirty looks. Didn't like a whole bunch of loud, sweaty, half-naked niggers backed up in their nice street where Doc was the only colored on the block. They say Doc didn't care. He was just out there like everybody else having a good time.

Doc had played at the University. Same one where Doc taught for a while. They say Doc used to laugh when white people asked him if he was in the Athletic Department. No reason for niggers to be at the University if they weren't playing ball or coaching ball. At least that's what white people thought, and since they thought that way, that's the way it was. Never more than a sprinkle of black faces in the white sea of the University. Doc used to laugh till the joke got old. People freedom-marching and freedom-dying, Doc said, but some dumb stuff never changed.

He first heard Doc's story late one day, after the yellow streetlights had popped on. Pooner was finishing the one about gang warring in North Philly: Yeah. They sure nuff lynched this dude they caught on their turf. Hung him up on the goddamn poles behind the backboard. Little kids found the sucker in the morning with his tongue all black and shit down his legs, and the cops had to come cut him down. Worst part is them little kids finding a dead body swinging up there. Kids don't be needing to find nothing like that. But those North Philly gangs don't play. They don't even let the dead rest in peace. Run in a funeral parlor and fuck up the funeral. Dumping over the casket and tearing up the flowers. Scaring people and turning the joint out. It's some mean shit. But them gangs don't play. They kill you they ain't finished yet. Mess with your people, your house, your sorry-ass dead body to get even. Pooner finished telling it and he looked round at the fellows and people were shaking their heads and then there was a chorus of You got that right, man. It's a bitch out there, man. Them niggers crazy, boy, and Pooner holds out his hand and somebody passes the joint. Pooner pinches it in two fingers and takes a deep drag. Everybody knows he's finished, it's somebody else's turn.

One of the fellows says, I wonder what happened to old Doc. I always be thinking about Doc, wondering where the cat is, what he be doing now . . .

Don't nobody know why Doc's eyes start to going bad. It just happen. Doc never even wore glasses. Eyes good as anybody's far as anybody knew till one day he come round he got goggles on. Like Kareem. And people kinda joking, you know. Doc got him some goggles. Watch out, youall. Doc be skyhooking youall to death today. Funning, you know. Cause Doc like to joke and play. Doc one the fellas like I said, so when he come round in goggles he subject to some teasing and one another thing like that cause nobody thought nothing serious wrong. Doc's eyes just as good as yours or mine, far as anybody knew.

Doc been playing all his life. That's why you could stand him on the foul line and point him at the hoop and more times than not, Doc could sink it. See he be remembering. His muscles know just what to do. You get his feet aimed right, line him up so he's on target, and Doc would swish one for you. Was a game kinda. Sometimes you get a sucker and Doc win you some money. Swish. Then the cat lost the dough start crying. He ain't blind. Can't no blind man shoot no pill. Is you really blind, brother? You niggers trying to steal my money, trying to play me for a fool. When a dude start crying the blues like that Doc wouldn't like it. He'd walk away. Wouldn't answer.

Leave the man lone. You lost fair and square. Doc made the basket so shut up and pay up, chump.

Doc practiced. Remember how you'd hear him out here at night when people sleeping. It's dark but what dark mean to Doc? Blacker than the rentman's heart but don't make no nevermind to Doc, he be steady shooting fouls. Always be somebody out there to chase the ball and throw it back. But shit, man. When Doc into his rhythm, didn't need nobody chase the ball. Ball be swishing with that good backspin, that good arch bring it back blip, blip, blip, three bounces and it's coming right back to Doc's hands like he got a string on the pill. Spooky if you didn't know Doc or know about foul shooting and understand when you got your shit together don't matter if you blindfolded. You put the motherfucker up and you know it's spozed to come running back just like a dog with a stick in his mouth.

Doc always be hanging at the court. Blind as wood but you couldn't fool Doc. Eyes in his ears. Know you by your walk. He could tell if you wearing new sneaks, tell you if your old ones is laced or not. Know you by your breath. The holes you make in the air when you jump. Doc was hip to who fucking who and who was getting fucked. Who could play ball and who was jiving. Doc use to be out here every weekend, steady rapping with the fellows and doing his foul-shot thing between games. Every once in a while somebody tease him, Hey, Doc. You want to run winners next go? Doc laugh and say, No, Dupree . . . I'm tired today, Dupree. Besides which you ain't been on a winning team in a week have you, Du? And everybody laugh. You know, just funning cause Doc one the fellas.

But one Sunday the shit got stone serious. Sunday I'm telling youall about, the action was real nice. If you wasn't ready, get back cause the brothers was cooking. Sixteen points, rise and fly. Next. Who got next? . . . Come on out here and take your ass kicking. One them good days when it's hot and everybody's juices is high and you feel you could play till next week. One them kind of days and a run's just over. Doc gets up and he goes with Billy Moon to the foul line. Fellas hanging under the basket for the rebound. Ain't hardly gon be a rebound Doc get hisself lined up right. But see, when the ball drop through the net you want to be the one grab it and throw it back to Billy. You want to be out there part of Doc shooting fouls just like you want to run when the running's good.

Doc bounce the ball, one, two, three times like he does. Then he raise it. Sift it in his fingers. You know he's a ballplayer, a shooter already way the ball spin in them long fingers way he raises it and cocks his wrist. You know Doc can't see a damn thing through his sunglasses but swear to God you'd think he was looking at the hoop way he study and measure. Then he shoots and ain't a sound in whole Johnson. Seems like everybody's heart stops. Everybody's breath behind that ball pushing it and steadying it so it drops through clean as new money.

But that Sunday something went wrong. Couldna been wind cause wasn't no wind. I was there. I know. Maybe Doc had playing on his mind. Couldn't help have playing on his mind cause it was one those days wasn't nothing better to do in the world than play. Whatever it was, soon as the ball left his hands, you could see Doc was missing, missing real bad. Way short and way off to the left. Might hit the backboard if everybody blew on it real hard.

A young boy, one them skinny, jumping-jack young boys got pogo sticks for legs, one them kids go up and don't come back down till they ready, he was standing on the left side the lane and leap up all the sudden catch the pill out the air and jams it through. Blam. A monster dunk and everybody break out in Goddamn. Do it, Sky, and Did you see that nigger get up? People slapping five and all that mess. Then Sky, the young boy they call Sky, grinning like a Chessy cat and strutting out with the ball squeezed in one hand to give it to Doc. In his glory. Grinning and strutting.

Gave you a little help, Doc.

Didn't ask for no help, Sky. Why'd you fuck with my shot, Sky?

Well, up jumped the Devil. The joint gets real quiet again real quick. Doc ain't cracked smile the first. He ain't playing.

Sorry, Doc. Didn't mean no harm, Doc.

You must think I'm some kind of chump fucking with my shot that way.

People start to feeling bad. Doc is steady getting on Sky's case. Sky just a young, light-in-the-ass kid. Jump to the moon but he's just a silly kid. Don't mean no harm. He just out there like everybody else trying to do his thing. No harm in Sky but Doc ain't playing and nobody else says shit. It's quiet like when Doc's shooting. Quiet as death and Sky don't know what to do. Can't wipe that lame look off his face and can't back off and can't hand the pill to Doc neither. He just stands there with his arm stretched out and his rusty fingers wrapped round the ball. Can't hold it much longer, can't let it go.

Seems like I coulda strolled over to Doc's stoop for a drinka water and strolled back and those two still be standing there. Doc and Sky. Billy Moon off to one side so it's just Doc and Sky.

Everybody holding they breath. Everybody want it over with and finally Doc says, Forget it, Sky. Just don't play with my shots anymore. And then Doc say, Who has next winners?

If Doc was joking nobody took it for no joke. His voice still hard. Doc ain't kidding around.

Who's next? I want to run.

Now Doc knows who's next. Leroy got next winners and Doc knows Leroy always saves a spot so he can pick up a big man from the losers. Leroy tell you to your face, I got my five, man, but everybody know Leroy saving a place so he can build him a winner and stay on the court. Leroy's a cold dude that way, been that way since he first started coming round and ain't never gon change and Doc knows that, everybody knows that but even Leroy ain't cold enough to say no to Doc.

I got it, Doc.

You got your five yet?

You know you got a spot with me, Doc. Always did.

Then I'ma run.

Say to myself, Shit . . . Good God Almighty. Great Googa-Mooga. What is happening here? Doc can't see shit. Doc blind as this bench I'm sitting on. What Doc gon do out there?

Well, it ain't my game. If it was, I'd a lied and said I had five. Or maybe not. Don't know what I'da done, to tell the truth. But Leroy didn't have no choice. Doc caught him good. Course Doc knew all that before he asked.

Did Doc play? What kinda question is that? What you think I been talking about all this time, man? Course he played. Why the fuck he be asking for winners less he was gon play? Helluva run as I remember. Overtime and shit. Don't remember who won. Somebody did, sure nuff. Leroy had him a strong unit. You know how he is. And Doc? Doc ain't been out on the court for a while but Doc is Doc, you know. Held his own . . .

If he had tried to tell her about Doc, would it have made a difference? Would the idea of a blind man playing basketball get her attention or would she have listened the way she listened when he told her stories he'd read about slavery days when Africans could fly, change themselves to cats and hummingbirds, when black hoodoo priests and conjure queens were feared by powerful whites even though ordinary black lives weren't worth a penny. To her it was folklore, superstition. Interesting because it revealed the psychology, the pathology of the oppressed. She listened intently, not because she thought she'd hear truth. For her, belief in magic was like belief in God. Nice work if you could get it. Her skepticism, her hardheaded practicality, like the smallness of her hands, appealed to him. Opposites attracting. But more and more as the years went by, he'd wanted her with him, wanted them to be together . . .

They were walking in Regent Park. It was clear to both of them that things weren't going to work out. He'd never seen her so beautiful, perfect.

There should have been stars. Stars at least, and perhaps a sickle moon. Instead the edge of the world was on fire. They were walking in Regent Park and dusk had turned the tree trunks black. Beyond them in the distance, below the fading blue of sky, the colors of sunset were pinched into a narrow, radiant band. Perhaps he had listened too long. Perhaps he had listened too intently for his own voice to fill the emptiness. When he turned back to her, his eyes were glazed, stinging. Grit, chemicals, whatever it was coloring, poisoning the sky, blurred his vision. Before he could blink her into focus, before he could speak, she was gone.

If he'd known Doc's story he would have said: *There's still a chance. There's always a chance. I mean this guy, Doc. Christ. He was stone blind. But he got out on the court and played. Over there. Right over there. On that very court across the hollow from us. It happened. I've talked to people about it many times. If Doc could do that, then anything's possible. We're possible . . .*

If a blind man could play basketball, surely we . . . If he had known Doc's story, would it have saved them? He hears himself saying the words. The ball arches from Doc's fingertips, the miracle of it sinking. Would she have believed any of it?

WHAT DID WE DO WRONG?

Garrison Keillor

The first woman to reach the big leagues said she wanted to be treated like any other rookie, but she didn't have to worry about that. The Sparrows nicknamed her Chesty and then Big Numbers the first week of spring training, and loaded her bed at the Ramada with butterscotch pudding. Only the writers made a big thing about her being the First Woman. The Sparrows treated her like dirt.

Annie Szemanski arrived in camp fresh from the Federales League of Bolivia, the fourth second baseman on the Sparrows roster, and when Drayton stepped in a hole and broke his ankle Hemmie put her in the lineup, hoping she would break hers. "This was the front office's bright idea," he told the writers. "Off the record, I think it stinks." But when she got in she looked so good that by the third week of March she was a foregone conclusion. Even Hemmie had to admit it. A .346 average tells no lies. He disliked her purely because she was a woman—there was nothing personal about it. Because she was a woman, she was given the manager's dressing room, and Hemmie had to dress with the team. He was sixty-one, a heavyweight, and he had a possum tattooed on his belly alongside the name "Georgene," so he was shy about taking his shirt off in front of people. He hated her for making it necessary. Other than that, he thought she was a tremendous addition to the team.

Asked how she felt being the first woman to make a major-league team, she said, "Like a pig in mud," or words to that effect, and then turned and released a squirt of tobacco juice from the wad of rum-soaked plug in her right cheek. She chewed a rare brand of plug called Stuff It, which she learned to chew when she was playing Nicaraguan summer ball. She told the writers, "They were so mean to me down there you couldn't write it in your newspaper. I took a gun everywhere I went, even to bed. *Especially* to bed. Guys were after me like you can't believe. That's when I discovered that life is essentially without meaning. That's when I started chewing tobacco—because, no matter how bad anybody treats you, it's not as bad as this. This is the worst chew in the world. After this, everything else is peaches and cream." The writers elected Gentleman Jim, the Sparrows' PR guy, to bite off a chunk and tell them how it tasted, and as he sat and chewed it tears ran down his old sunburned cheeks and he couldn't talk for a while. Then he whispered, "You've been chewing this for two years? I had no idea it was so hard to be a woman."

When thirty-two thousand fans came to Cold Spring Stadium on April 4 for Opening Day and saw the scrappy little freckle-faced woman with tousled black hair who they'd been reading about for almost two months, they were dizzy with devotion. They chanted her name and waved Annie flags and Annie caps ($8.95 and $4.95) and held up hand-painted bedsheets ("EVERY DAY IS LADIES' DAY," "A WOMAN'S PLACE—AT SECOND BASE," "ERA & RBI," "THE GAME AIN'T OVER TILL THE BIG LADY BATS"), but when they saw No. 18 trot out to second with a load of chew as big as if she had mumps it was a surprise. Then, bottom of the second, when she leaned over in the on-deck circle and dropped a stream of brown juice in the sod, the stadium experienced a moment of thoughtful silence.

One man in Section 31 said, "Hey, what's the beef? She can chew if she wants to. This is 1987. Grow up."

"I guess you're right," his next-seat neighbor said. "My first reaction was nausea, but I think you're right."

"Absolutely. She's a woman, but, more than that, she's a *person.*"

Other folks said, "I'm with you on that. A woman can carry a quarter-pound of chew in her cheek and spit in public, same as any man—why should there be any difference?"

And yet. Nobody wanted to say this, but the plain truth was that No. 18 was not handling her chew well at all. Juice ran down her chin and dripped onto her shirt. She's bit off more than she can chew, some people thought to themselves, but they didn't want to say that.

Arnie (The Old Gardener) Brixius mentioned it ever so gently in his "Hot Box" column the next day:

> It's only this scribe's opinion, but isn't it about time baseball cleaned up its act and left the tobacco in the locker? Surely big leaguers can go two hours without nicotine. Many a fan has turned away in disgust at the sight of grown men (and now a member of the fair sex) with a faceful, spitting gobs of the stuff in full view of paying customers. Would Frank Sinatra do this onstage? Or Anne Murray? Nuff said.

End of April, Annie was batting .278, with twelve RBIs, which for the miserable Sparrows was stupendous, and at second base she was surprising a number of people, including base runners who thought she'd be a pushover on the double play. A runner heading for second quickly found out that Annie had knees like ball-peen hammers and if he tried to eliminate her from the play she might eliminate him from the rest of the week. One night, up at bat against the Orioles, she took a step toward the mound after an inside pitch and yelled some things, and when the dugouts emptied she was in the thick of it with men who had never been walloped by a woman before. The home-plate ump hauled her off a guy she was pounding the cookies out of, and a moment later he threw her out of the game for saying things to him, he said, that he had never heard in his nineteen years of umping. ("Like what, for example?" writers asked. "Just tell us one thing." But he couldn't; he was too upset.)

The next week, the United Baseball Office Workers local passed a resolution in support of Annie, as did the League of Women Voters and the Women's Softball Caucus, which stated, "Szemanski is a model for all women who are made to suffer guilt for their aggressiveness, and we declare our solidarity with her heads-up approach to the game.

While we feel she is holding the bat too high and should bring her hips into her swing more, we're behind her one hundred percent."

Then, May 4, at home against Oakland—seventh inning, two outs, bases loaded—she dropped an easy pop-up and three runs came across home plate. The fans sent a few light boos her way to let her know they were paying attention, nothing serious or overtly political, just some folks grumbling, but she took a few steps toward the box seats and yelled something at them that sounded like—well, like something she shouldn't have said—and after the game she said some more things to the writers that Gentleman Jim pleaded with them not to print. One of them was Monica Lamarr, of the *Press,* who just laughed. She said, "Look. I spent two years in the Lifestyles section writing about mother-hood vs. career and the biological clock. Sports is my way out of the gynecology ghetto, so don't ask me to eat this story. It's a hanging curve and I'm going for it. I'm never going to write about day care again." And she wrote it:

SZEMANSKI RAPS FANS AS "SMALL PEOPLE" AFTER DUMB ERROR GIVES GAME TO A'S

FIRST WOMAN ATTRIBUTES BOOS TO SEXUAL INADEQUACY IN STANDS

Jim made some phone calls and the story was yanked and only one truckload of papers went out with it, but word got around, and the next night, though Annie went three for four, the crowd was depressed, and even when she did great the rest of the home stand and became the first woman to hit a major-league triple, the atmosphere at the ballpark was one of moodiness and hurt. Jim went to the men's room one night and found guys standing in line there, looking thoughtful and sad. One of them said, "She's a helluva ballplayer," and other guys murmured that yes, she was, and they wouldn't take anything away from her, she was great and it was wonderful that she had opened up baseball to women, and then they changed the subject to gardening, books, music, aesthet-ics, anything but baseball. They looked like men who had been stood up.

Gentleman Jim knocked on her door that night. She wore a blue chenille bathrobe flecked with brown tobacco-juice stains, and her black hair hung down in wet strands over her face. She spat into a Dixie cup she was carrying. "Hey! How the Fritos are you? I haven't seen your Big

Mac for a while," she said, sort of. He told her she was a great person and a great ballplayer and that he loved her and wanted only the best for her, and he begged her to apologize to the fans.

"Make a gesture—*anything*. They *want* to like you. Give them a chance to like you."

She blew her nose into a towel. She said that she wasn't there to be liked, she was there to play ball.

It was a good road trip. The Sparrows won five out of ten, lifting their heads off the canvas, and Annie raised her average to .291 and hit the first major-league home run ever by a woman, up into the left-field screen at Fenway. Sox fans stood and cheered for fifteen minutes. They whistled, they stamped, they pleaded, the Sparrows pleaded, umpires pleaded, but she refused to come out and tip her hat until the public-address announcer said, "No. 18, please come out of the dugout and take a bow. No. 18, the applause is for you and is not intended as patronizing in any way," and then she stuck her head out for 1.5 seconds and did not tip but only touched the brim. Later, she told the writers that just because people had expectations didn't mean she had to fulfill them—she used other words to explain this, but her general drift was that she didn't care very much about living up to anyone else's image of her, and if anyone thought she should, they could go watch wrist wrestling.

The forty thousand who packed Cold Spring Stadium June 6 to see the Sparrows play the Yankees didn't come for a look at Ron Guidry. Banners hung from the second deck: "WHAT DID WE DO WRONG?" and "ANNIE COME HOME" and "WE LOVE YOU, WHY DO YOU TREAT US THIS WAY" and "IF YOU WOULD LIKE TO DISCUSS THIS IN A NONCONFRONTATIONAL, MUTUALLY RESPECTFUL WAY, MEET US AFTER THE GAME AT GATE C." It was Snapshot Day, and all the Sparrows appeared on the field for photos with the fans except you know who. Hemmie begged her to go. "You owe it to them," he said.

"Owe?" she said. *"Owe?"*

"Sorry, wrong word," he said. "What if I put it this way: it's a sort of tradition."

"Tradition?" she said. "I'm supposed to worry about *tradition?"*

That day, she became the first woman to hit .300. A double in the fifth inning. The scoreboard flashed the message, and the crowd gave her a nice hand. A few people stood and cheered, but the fans around them told them to sit down. "She's not that kind of person," they said. "Cool it. Back off." The fans were trying to give her plenty of space. After the game, Guidry said, "I really have to respect her. She's got that small strike zone and she protects it well, so she makes you pitch to her." She said, "Guidry? Was that his name? I didn't know. Anyway, he didn't show me much. He throws funny, don't you think? He reminded me a little bit of a southpaw I saw down in Nicaragua, except she threw inside more."

All the writers were there, kneeling around her. One of them asked if Guidry had thrown her a lot of sliders.

She gave him a long, baleful look. "Jeez, you guys are out of shape," she said. "You're wheezing and panting and sucking air, and you just took the elevator *down* from the press box. You guys want to write about sports, you ought to go into training. And then you ought to learn how to recognize a slider. Jeez, if you were writing about agriculture, would you have to ask someone if those were Holsteins?"

Tears came to the writer's eyes. "I'm trying to help," he said. "Can't you see that? We're all on your side. Don't you know how much we care about you? Sometimes I think you put up this tough exterior to hide your own insecurity."

She laughed and brushed the wet hair back from her forehead. "It's no exterior," she said as she unbuttoned her jersey. "It's who I am." She peeled off her socks and stepped out of her cubicle a moment later, sweaty and stark naked. The towel hung from her hand. She walked slowly around them. "You guys learned all you know about women thirty years ago. That wasn't me back then, that was my mother." The writers bent over their notepads, writing down every word she said and punctuating carefully. Gentleman Jim took off his glasses. "My mother was a nice lady, but she couldn't hit a curveball to save her Creamettes," she went on. "And now, gentlemen, if you'll excuse me, I'm going to take my insecurity and put it under a hot shower." They pored over their notes until she was gone, and then they piled out into the hallway and hurried back to the press elevator.

Arnie stopped at the Shortstop for a load of Martinis before he went to the office to write the "Hot Box," which turned out to be about love:

Baseball is a game but it's more than a game, baseball is people, damn it, and if you are around people you can't help but get involved in their lives and care about them and then you don't know how to talk to them or tell them how much you care and how come

we know so much about pitching and we don't know squat about
how to communicate? I guess that is the question.

The next afternoon, Arnie leaned against the batting cage before the
game, hung over, and watched her hit line drives, fifteen straight, and
each one made his head hurt. As she left the cage, he called over to her.
"Later," she said. She also declined a pregame interview with Joe
Garagiola, who had just told his NBC "Game of the Week" television
audience, "This is a city in love with a little girl named Annie Szemanski," when he saw her in the dugout doing deep knee bends. "Annie!
Annie!" he yelled over the air. "Let's see if we can't get her up here," he
told the home audience. "Annie! Joe Garagiola!" She turned her back to
him and went down into the dugout.

That afternoon, she became the first woman to steal two bases in
one inning. She reached first on a base on balls, stole second, went to
third on a sacrifice fly, and headed for home on the next pitch. The
catcher came out to make the tag, she caught him with her elbow under
the chin, and when the dust cleared she was grinning at the ump, the
catcher was sprawled in the grass trying to inhale, and the ball was halfway to the backstop.

The TV camera zoomed in on her, head down, trotting toward
the dugout steps, when suddenly she looked up. Some out-of-town fan
had yelled at her from the box seats. ("A profanity which also refers to a
female dog," the *News* said.) She smiled and, just before she stepped out
of view beneath the dugout roof, millions observed her right hand
uplifted in a familiar gesture. In bars around the country, men looked at
each other and said, "Did she do what I think I saw her do? She didn't
do that, did she?" In the booth, Joe Garagiola was observing that it was
a clean play, that the runner has a right to the base path, but when her
hand appeared on the screen he stopped. At home, it sounded as if he
had been hit in the chest by a rock. The screen went blank, then went to
a lite sausage commercial. When the show resumed, it was the middle of
the next inning.

On Monday, for "actions detrimental to the best interests of
baseball," Annie was fined a thousand dollars by the Commissioner and
suspended for two games. He deeply regretted the decision, etc. "I
count myself among her most ardent fans. She is good for baseball, good
for the cause of equal rights, good for America." He said he would be
happy to suspend the suspension if she would make a public apology,
which would make him the happiest man in America.

Gentleman Jim went to the bank Monday afternoon and got the money, a thousand dollars, in a cashier's check. All afternoon, he called Annie's number over and over, waiting thirty or forty rings, then trying again. He called from a pay phone at the Stop 'N' Shop, next door to the Cityview Apartments, where she lived, and between calls he sat in his car and watched the entrance, waiting for her to come out. Other men were parked there, too, in front, and some in back—men with Sparrows bumper stickers. After midnight, about eleven of them were left. "Care to share some onion chips and clam dip?" one guy said to another guy. Pretty soon all of them were standing around the trunk of the clam-dip guy's car, where he also had a case of beer.

"Here, let me pay you something for this beer," said a guy who had brought a giant box of pretzels.

"Hey, no. Really. It's just good to have other guys to talk to tonight," said the clam-dip owner.

"She changed a lot of very basic things about the whole way that I look at myself as a man," the pretzel guy said quietly.

"I'm in public relations," said Jim. "But even I don't understand all that she has meant to people."

"How can she do this to us?" said a potato-chip man. "All the love of the fans, how can she throw it away? Why can't she just play ball?"

Annie didn't look at it that way. "Pall Mall! I'm not going to crawl just because some Tootsie Roll says crawl, and if they don't like it, then bull shit, they can go butter their Hostess Twinkies," she told the writers as she cleaned out her locker on Tuesday morning. They had never seen the inside of her locker before. It was stuffed with dirty socks, half-unwrapped gifts from admiring fans, a set of ankle weights, and a small silver-plated pistol. "No way I'm going to pay a thousand dollars, and if they expect an apology—well, they better send out for lunch, because it's going to be a long wait. Gentlemen, goodbye and hang on to your valuable coupons." And she smiled her most winning smile and sprinted up the stairs to collect her paycheck. They waited for her outside the Sparrows office, twenty-six men, and then followed her down the ramp and out of Gate C. She broke into a run and disappeared into the lunchtime crowd on West Providence Avenue, and that was the last they saw of her—the woman of their dreams, the love of their lives, carrying a red gym bag, running easily away from them.

II

Dream
Teams

RAYMOND'S RUN

Toni Cade Bambara

I don't have much work to do around the house like some girls. My mother does that. And I don't have to earn my pocket money by hustling; George runs errands for the big boys and sells Christmas cards. And anything else that's got to get done, my father does. All I have to do in life is mind my brother Raymond, which is enough.

Sometimes I slip and say my little brother Raymond. But as any fool can see he's much bigger and he's older too. But a lot of people call him my little brother cause he needs looking after cause he's not quite right. And a lot of smart mouths got lots to say about that too, especially when George was minding him. But now, if anybody has anything to say to Raymond, anything to say about his big head, they have to come by me. And I don't play the dozens or believe in standing around with somebody in my face doing a lot of talking. I much rather just knock you down and take my chances even if I am a little girl with skinny arms and a squeaky voice, which is how I got the name Squeaky. And if things get too rough, I run. And as anybody can tell you, I'm the fastest thing on two feet.

There is no track meet that I don't win the first place medal. I use to win the twenty-yard dash when I was a little kid in kindergarten. Nowadays it's the fifty-yard dash. And tomorrow I'm subject to run the quarter-meter relay all by myself and come in first, second, and third. The big kids call me Mercury cause I'm the swiftest thing in the neighborhood. Everybody knows that—except two people who know better, my father and me.

He can beat me to Amsterdam Avenue with me having a two fire-hydrant headstart and him running with his hands in his pockets and whistling. But that's private information. Cause can you imagine some thirty-five-year-old man stuffing himself into PAL shorts to race little kids? So as far as everyone's concerned, I'm the fastest and that goes for Gretchen, too, who has put out the tale that she is going to win the first place medal this year. Ridiculous. In the second place, she's got short legs. In the third place, she's got freckles. In the first place, no one can beat me and that's all there is to it.

I'm standing on the corner admiring the weather and about to take a stroll down Broadway so I can practice my breathing exercises, and I've got Raymond walking on the inside close to the buildings cause he's subject to fits of fantasy and starts thinking he's a circus performer and that the curb is a tightrope strung high in the air. And sometimes after a rain, he likes to step down off his tightrope right into the gutter and slosh around getting his shoes and cuffs wet. Then I get hit when I get home. Or sometimes if you don't watch him, he'll dash across traffic to the island in the middle of Broadway and give the pigeons a fit. Then I have to go behind him apologizing to all the old people sitting around trying to get some sun and getting all upset with the pigeons fluttering around them, scattering their newspapers and upsetting the wax-paper lunches in their laps. So I keep Raymond on the inside of me, and he plays like he's driving a stage coach which is O.K. by me so long as he doesn't run me over or interrupt my breathing exercises, which I have to do on account of I'm serious about my running and don't care who knows it.

Now some people like to act like things come easy to them, won't let on that they practice. Not me. I'll high prance down 34th Street like a rodeo pony to keep my knees strong even if it does get my mother uptight so that she walks ahead like she's not with me, don't know me, is all by herself on a shopping trip, and I am somebody else's crazy child.

Now you take Cynthia Procter for instance. She's just the opposite. If there's a test tomorrow, she'll say something like, "Oh I guess I'll play handball this afternoon and watch television tonight," just to let you know she ain't thinking about the test. Or like last week when she won the spelling bee for the millionth time, "A good thing you got 'receive,' Squeaky, cause I would have got it wrong. I completely forgot about the spelling bee." And she'll clutch the lace on her blouse like it was a narrow escape. Oh, brother.

But of course when I pass her house on my early morning trots around the block, she is practicing the scales on the piano over and over and over and over. Then in music class, she always lets herself get bumped around so she falls accidently on purpose onto the piano stool and is so surprised to find herself sitting there, and so decides just for fun to try out the ole keys and what do you know—Chopin's waltzes just spring out of her fingertips and she's the most surprised thing in the world. A regular prodigy. I could kill people like that.

I stay up all night studying the words for the spelling bee. And you can see me anytime of day practicing running. I never walk if I can trot and shame on Raymond if he can't keep up. But of course he does, cause if he hangs back someone's liable to walk up to him and get smart, or take his allowance from him, or ask him where he got that great big pumpkin head. People are so stupid sometimes.

So I'm strolling down Broadway breathing out and breathing in on counts of seven, which is my lucky number, and here comes Gretchen and her sidekicks—Mary Louise who used to be a friend of mine when she first moved to Harlem from Baltimore and got beat up by everybody till I took up for her on account of her mother and my mother used to sing in the same choir when they were young girls, but people ain't grateful, so now she hangs out with the new girl Gretchen and talks about me like a dog; and Rosie who is as fat as I am skinny and has a big mouth where Raymond is concerned and is too stupid to know that there is not a big deal of difference between herself and Raymond and that she can't afford to throw stones. So they are steady coming up Broadway and I see right away that it's going to be one of those Dodge City scenes cause the street ain't that big and they're close to the buildings just as we are. First I think I'll step into the candy store and look over the new comics and let them pass. But that's chicken and I've got a reputation to consider. So then I think I'll just walk straight on through them or over them if necessary. But as they get to me, they slow down. I'm ready to fight, cause like I said I don't feature a whole lot of

chitchat, I much prefer to just knock you down right from the jump and
save everybody a lotta precious time.

"You signing up for the May Day races?" smiles Mary Louise,
only it's not a smile at all.

A dumb question like that doesn't deserve an answer. Besides,
there's just me and Gretchen standing there really, so no use wasting my
breath talking to shadows.

"I don't think you're going to win this time," says Rosie, trying
to signify with her hands on her hips all salty, completely forgetting that
I have whupped her behind many times for less salt than that.

"I always win cause I'm the best," I say straight at Gretchen
who is, as far as I'm concerned, the only one talking in this ventrilo-
quist-dummy routine.

Gretchen smiles but it's not a smile and I'm thinking that girls
never really smile at each other because they don't know how and don't
want to know how and there's probably no one to teach us how cause
grown-up girls don't know either. Then they all look at Raymond who
has just brought his mule team to a standstill. And they're about to see
what trouble they can get into through him.

"What grade you in now, Raymond?"

"You got anything to say to my brother, you say it to me, Mary
Louise Williams of Raggedy Town, Baltimore."

"What are you, his mother?" sasses Rosie.

"That's right, Fatso. And the next word out of anybody and I'll
be their mother too." So they just stand there and Gretchen shifts from
one leg to the other and so do they. Then Gretchen puts her hands on
her hips and is about to say something with her freckle-face self but
doesn't. Then she walks around me looking me up and down but keeps
walking up Broadway, and her sidekicks follow her. So me and Raymond smile at each other and he says "Gidyap" to his team and I continue with my breathing exercises, strolling down Broadway toward the
icey man on 145th with not a care in the world cause I am Miss Quicksil-
ver herself.

I take my time getting to the park on May Day because the track
meet is the last thing on the program. The biggest thing on the program
is the May Pole dancing which I can do without, thank you, even if my
mother thinks it's a shame I don't take part and act like a girl for a
change. You'd think my mother'd be grateful not to have to make me a
white organdy dress with a big satin sash and buy me new white baby-
doll shoes that can't be taken out of the box till the big day. You'd think

she'd be glad her daughter ain't out there prancing around a May Pole getting the new clothes all dirty and sweaty and trying to act like a fairy or a flower or whatever you're supposed to be when you should be trying to be yourself, whatever that is, which is, as far as I am concerned, a poor Black girl who really can't afford to buy shoes and a new dress you only wear once a lifetime cause it won't fit next year.

I was once a strawberry in a Hansel and Gretel pageant when I was in nursery school and didn't have no better sense than to dance on tiptoe with my arms in a circle over my head doing umbrella steps and being a perfect fool just so my mother and father could come dressed up and clap. You'd think they'd know better than to encourage that kind of nonsense. I am not a strawberry. I do not dance on my toes. I run. That is what I am all about. So I always come late to the May Day program, just in time to get my number pinned on and lay in the grass till they announce the fifty-yard dash.

I put Raymond in the little swings, which is a tight squeeze this year and will be impossible next year. Then I look around for Mr. Pearson who pins the numbers on. I'm really looking for Gretchen if you want to know the truth, but she's not around. The park is jam-packed. Parents in hats and corsages and breast-pocket handkerchiefs peeking up. Kids in white dresses and light blue suits. The parkees unfolding chairs and chasing the rowdy kids from Lenox as if they had no right to be there. The big guys with their caps on backwards, leaning against the fence swirling the basketballs on the tips of their fingers waiting for all these crazy people to clear out the park so they can play. Most of the kids in my class are carrying bass drums and glockenspiels and flutes. You'd think they'd put in a few bongos or something for real like that.

Then here comes Mr. Pearson with his clipboard and his cards and pencils and whistles and safety pins and fifty million other things he's always dropping all over the place with his clumsy self. He sticks out in a crowd cause he's on stilts. We used to call him Jack and the Beanstalk to get him mad. But I'm the only one that can outrun him and get away, and I'm too grown for that silliness now.

"Well, Squeaky," he says checking my name off the list and handing me number seven and two pins. And I'm thinking he's got no right to call me Squeaky, if I can't call him Beanstalk.

"Hazel Elizabeth Deborah Parker," I correct him and tell him to write it down on his board.

"Well, Hazel Elizabeth Deborah Parker, going to give someone else a break this year?" I squint at him real hard to see if he is seriously thinking I should lose the race on purpose just to give someone else a break.

"Only six girls running this time," he continues, shaking his head sadly like it's my fault all of New York didn't turn out in sneakers. "That new girl should give you a run for your money." He looks around the park for Gretchen like a periscope in a submarine movie. "Wouldn't it be a nice gesture if you were . . . to ahhh . . ."

I give him such a look he couldn't finish putting that idea into words. Grownups got a lot of nerve sometimes. I pin number seven to myself and stomp away—I'm so burnt. And I go straight for the track and stretch out on the grass while the band winds up with "Oh the Monkey Wrapped His Tail Around the Flag Pole," which my teacher calls by some other name. The man on the loudspeaker is calling everyone over to the track and I'm on my back looking at the sky trying to pretend I'm in the country, but I can't, because even grass in the city feels hard as sidewalk and there's just no pretending you are anywhere but in a "concrete jungle" as my grandfather says.

The twenty-yard dash takes all of the two minutes cause most of the little kids don't know no better than to run off the track or run the wrong way or run smack into the fence and fall down and cry. One little kid though has got the good sense to run straight for the white ribbon up ahead so he wins. Then the second graders line up for the thirty-yard dash and I don't even bother to turn my head to watch cause Raphael Perez always wins. He wins before he even begins by psyching the runners, telling them they're going to trip on their shoelaces and fall on their faces or lose their shorts or something, which he doesn't really have to do since he is very fast, almost as fast as I am. After that is the forty-yard dash which I use to run when I was in first grade. Raymond is hollering from the swings cause he knows I'm about to do my thing cause the man on the loudspeaker has just announced the fifty-yard dash, although he might just as well be giving a recipe for Angel Food cake cause you can hardly make out what he's saying for the static. I get up and slip off my sweat pants and then I see Gretchen standing at the starting line kicking her legs out like a pro. Then as I get into place I see that ole Raymond is in line on the other side of the fence, bending down with his fingers on the ground just like he knew what he was doing. I was going to yell at him but then I didn't. It burns up your energy to holler.

Every time, just before I take off in a race, I always feel like I'm in a dream, the kind of dream you have when you're sick with fever and feel all hot and weightless. I dream I'm flying over a sandy beach in the early morning sun, kissing the leaves of the trees as I fly by. And there's always the smell of apples, just like in the country when I was little and use to think I was a choo-choo train, running through the fields of corn and chugging up the hill to the orchard. And all the time I'm dreaming this, I get lighter and lighter until I'm flying over the beach again, getting blown through the sky like a feather that weighs nothing at all. But once I spread my fingers in the dirt and crouch over for the Get on Your Mark, the dream goes and I am solid again and am telling myself, Squeaky you must win, you must win, you are the fastest thing in the world, you can even beat your father up Amsterdam if you really try. And then I feel my weight coming back just behind my knees then down to my feet then into the earth and the pistol shot explodes in my blood and I am off and weightless again, flying past the other runners, my arms pumping up and down and the whole world is quiet except for the crunch as I zoom over the gravel in the track. I glance to my left and there is no one. To the right a blurred Gretchen who's got her chin jutting out as if it would win the race all by itself. And on the other side of the fence is Raymond with his arms down to his side and the palms tucked up behind him, running, in his very own style and the first time I ever saw that and I almost stop to watch my brother Raymond on his first run. But the white ribbon is bouncing toward me and I tear past it racing into the distance till my feet with a mind of their own start digging up footfuls of dirt and brake me short. Then all the kids standing on the side pile on me, banging me on the back and slapping my head with their May Day programs, for I have won again and everybody on 151st Street can walk tall for another year.

"In first place . . ." the man on the loudspeaker is clear as a bell now. But then he pauses and the loudspeaker starts to whine. Then static. And I lean down to catch my breath and here comes Gretchen walking back for she's overshot the finish line too, huffing and puffing with her hands on her hips taking it slow, breathing in steady time like a real pro and I sort of like her a little for the first time. "In first place . . ." and then three or four voices get all mixed up on the loudspeaker and I dig my sneaker into the grass and stare at Gretchen who's staring back, we both wondering just who did win. I can hear old Beanstalk arguing with the man on the loudspeaker and then a few others running their mouths about what the stop watches say.

Then I hear Raymond yanking at the fence to call me and I wave to shush him, but he keeps rattling the fence like a gorilla in a cage like in them gorilla movies, but then like a dancer or something he starts climbing up nice and easy but very fast. And it occurs to me, watching how smoothly he climbs hand over hand and remembering how he looked running with his arms down to his side and with the wind pulling his mouth back and his teeth showing and all, it occurred to me that Raymond would make a very fine runner. Doesn't he always keep up with me on my trots? And he surely knows how to breathe in counts of seven cause he's always doing it at the dinner table, which drives my brother George up the wall. And I'm smiling to beat the band cause if I've lost this race, or if me and Gretchen tied, or even if I've won, I can always retire as a runner and begin a whole new career as a coach with Raymond as my champion. After all, with a little more study I can beat Cynthia and her phony self at the spelling bee. And if I bugged my mother, I could get piano lessons and become a star. And I have a big rep as the baddest thing around. And I've got a roomful of ribbons and medals and awards. But what has Raymond got to call his own?

So I stand there with my new plan, laughing out loud by this time as Raymond jumps down from the fence and runs over with his teeth showing and his arms down to the side which no one before him has quite mastered as a running style. And by the time he comes over I'm jumping up and down so glad to see him—my brother Raymond, a great runner in the family tradition. But of course everyone thinks I'm jumping up and down because the men on the loudspeaker have finally gotten themselves together and compared notes and are announcing "In first place—Miss Hazel Elizabeth Deborah Parker." (Dig that.) "In second place—Miss Gretchen P. Lewis." And I look over at Gretchen wondering what the P stands for. And I smile. Cause she's good, no doubt about it. Maybe she'd like to help me coach Raymond; she obviously is serious about running, as any fool can see. And she nods to congratulate me and then she smiles. And I smile. We stand there with this big smile of respect between us. It's about as real a smile as girls can do for each other, considering we don't practice real smiling every day you know, cause maybe we too busy being flowers or fairies or strawberries instead of something honest and worthy of respect . . . you know . . . like being people.

THE HECTOR QUESADILLA STORY

T. Coraghessan Boyle

He was no Joltin' Joe, no Sultan of Swat, no Iron Man. For one thing, his feet hurt. And God knows no legendary immortal ever suffered so prosaic a complaint. He had shin splints too, and corns and ingrown toenails and hemorrhoids. Demons drove burning spikes into his tailbone each time he bent to loosen his shoelaces, his limbs were skewed so awkwardly that his elbows and knees might have been transposed and the once-proud knot of his *frijole*-fed belly had fallen like an avalanche. Worse: he was old. Old, old, old, the graybeard hobbling down the rough-hewn steps of the senate building, the ancient mariner chewing on his whiskers and stumbling in his socks. Though they listed his birthdate as 1942 in the program, there were those who knew better: it was way back in '54, during his rookie year for San Buitre, that he had taken Asunción to the altar, and even in those distant days, even in Mexico, twelve-year-olds didn't marry.

When he was younger—really young, nineteen, twenty, tearing

up the Mexican League like a saint of the stick—his ears were so sensitive he could hear the soft rasping friction of the pitcher's fingers as he massaged the ball and dug in for a slider, fastball, or change-up. Now he could barely hear the umpire bawling the count in his ear. And his legs. How they ached, how they groaned and creaked and chattered, how they'd gone to fat! He ate too much, that was the problem. Ate prodigiously, ate mightily, ate as if there were a hidden thing inside him, a creature of all jaws with an infinite trailing ribbon of gut. *Huevos con chorizo* with beans, *tortillas, camarones* in red sauce, and a twelve-ounce steak for breakfast, the chicken in *mole* to steady him before afternoon games, a sea of beer to wash away the tension of the game and prepare his digestive machinery for the flaming *machaca*-and-pepper salad Asunción prepared for him in the blessed evenings of the home stand.

Five foot seven, one hundred eighty-nine and three-quarters pounds. Hector Hernán Jesús y María Quesadilla. Little Cheese, they called him. Cheese, Cheese, Cheesus, went up the cry as he stepped in to pinch-hit in some late-inning crisis, Cheese, Cheese, Cheesus, building to a roar until Chavez Ravine resounded as if with the holy name of the Saviour Himself when he stroked one of the clean line-drive singles that were his signature or laid down a bunt that stuck like a finger in jelly. When he fanned, when the bat went loose in the fat brown hands and he went down on one knee for support, they hissed and called him *Viejo.*

One more season, he tells himself, though he hasn't played regularly for nearly ten years and can barely trot to first after drawing a walk. One more. He tells Asunción too—One more, one more—as they sit in the gleaming kitchen of their house in Boyle Heights, he with his Carta Blanca, she with her mortar and pestle for grinding the golden, petrified kernels of maize into flour for the tortillas he eats like peanuts. *Una más,* she mocks. What do you want, the Hall of Fame? Hang up your spikes, Hector.

He stares off into space, his mother's Indian features flattening his own as if the legend were true, as if she really had taken a spatula to him in the cradle, and then, dropping his thick lids as he takes a long slow swallow from the neck of the bottle, he says: Just the other day, driving home from the park, I saw a car on the freeway, a Mercedes with only two seats, a girl in it, her hair out back like a cloud, and you know what the license plate said? His eyes are open now, black as pitted olives. Do you? She doesn't. Cheese, he says. It said Cheese.

Then she reminds him that Hector Jr. will be twenty-nine next month and that Reina has four children of her own and another on the way. You're a grandfather, Hector—almost a great-grandfather, if your son ever settled down. A moment slides by, filled with the light of the sad, waning sun and the harsh Yucatano dialect of the radio announcer. *Hombres* on first and third, one down. *Abuelo,* she hisses, grinding stone against stone until it makes his teeth ache. Hang up your spikes, *abuelo.*

But he doesn't. He can't. He won't. He's no grandpa with hair the color of cigarette stains and a blanket over his knees, he's no toothless old gasser sunning himself in the park—he's a big-leaguer, proud wearer of the Dodger blue, wielder of stick and glove. How can he get old? The grass is always green, the lights always shining, no clocks or periods or halves or quarters, no punch-in and punch-out: this is the game that never ends. When the heavy hitters have fanned and the pitchers' arms gone sore, when there's no joy in Mudville, taxes are killing everybody, and the Russians are raising hell in Guatemala, when the manager paces the dugout like an attack dog, mind racing, searching high and low for the canny veteran to go in and do single combat, there he'll be—always, always, eternal as a monument—Hector Quesadilla, utility infielder, with the .296 lifetime batting average and service with the Reds, Phils, Cubs, Royals, and L.A. Dodgers.

So he waits. Hangs on. Trots his aching legs round the outfield grass before the game, touches his toes ten agonizing times each morning, takes extra batting practice with the rookies and slumping millionaires. Sits. Watches. Massages his feet. Waits through the scourging road trips in the Midwest and along the East Coast, down to muggy Atlanta, across to stormy Wrigley, and up to frigid Candlestick, his gut clenched round an indigestible cud of meatloaf and instant potatoes and wax beans, through the terrible night games with the alien lights in his eyes, waits at the end of the bench for a word from the manager, for a pat on the ass, a roar, a hiss, a chorus of cheers and catcalls, the marimba pulse of bat striking ball, and the sweet looping arc of the clean base hit.

And then comes a day, late in the season, the homeboys battling for the pennant with the big-stick Braves and the sneaking Jints, when he wakes from honeyed dreams in his own bed that's like an old friend with the sheets that smell of starch and soap and flowers, and feels the pain stripped from his body as if at the touch of a healer's fingertips. Usually he dreams nothing, the night a blank, an erasure, and opens his eyes on the agonies of the martyr strapped to a bed of nails. Then he limps to the toilet, makes a poor discolored water, rinses the dead taste from his mouth, and staggers to the kitchen table, where food, only food, can revive in him the interest in drawing another breath. He butters tortillas and folds them into his mouth, spoons up egg and melted jack cheese and *frijoles refritos* with the green *salsa,* lashes into his steak as if it were cut from the thigh of Kerensky, the Atlanta relief ace who'd twice that season caught him looking at a full-count fastball with men in scoring position. But not today. Today is different, a sainted day, a day on which sunshine sits in the windows like a gift of the Magi and the chatter of the starlings in the crapped-over palms across the street is a thing that approaches the divine music of the spheres. What can it be?

In the kitchen it hits him: *pozole* in a pot on the stove, *carnitas* in the saucepan, the table spread with sweetcakes, *buñuelos,* and the little marzipan *dulces* he could kill for. *Feliz cumpleaños,* Asunción pipes as he steps through the doorway. Her face is lit with the smile of her mother, her mother's mother, the line of gift givers descendant to the happy conquistadors and joyous Aztecs. A kiss, a *dulce,* and then a knock at the door and Reina, fat with life, throwing her arms around him while her children gobble up the table, the room, their grandfather, with eyes that swallow their faces. Happy birthday, Daddy, Reina says, and Franklin, her youngest, is handing him the gift.

And Hector Jr.?

But he doesn't have to fret about Hector Jr., his firstborn, the boy with these same great sad eyes who'd sat in the dugout in his Reds uniform when they lived in Cincy and worshiped the pudgy icon of his father until the parish priest had to straighten him out on his hagiography; Hector Jr., who studies English at USC and day and night writes his thesis on a poet his father has never heard of, because here he is, walking in the front door with his mother's smile and a store-wrapped gift—a book, of course. Then Reina's children line up to kiss the *abuelo*—they'll be sitting in the box seats this afternoon—and suddenly he knows so much: he will play today, he will hit, oh yes, can there be a doubt? He sees it already. Kerensky, the son of a whore. Extra innings. Koerner or Manfredonia or Brooksie on third. The ball like an orange, a mango, a muskmelon, the clean swipe of the bat, the delirium of the crowd, and the gimpy *abuelo,* a big-leaguer still, doffing his cap and taking a tour of the bases in a stately trot, Sultan for a day.

Could things ever be so simple?

In the bottom of the ninth, with the score tied at 5 and Reina's kids full of Coke, hotdogs, peanuts, and ice cream and getting restless, with Asunción clutching her rosary as if she were drowning and Hector

Jr.'s nose stuck in some book, Dupuy taps him to hit for the pitcher with two down and Fast Freddie Phelan on second. The eighth man in the lineup, Spider Martinez from Muchas Vacas, D.R., has just whiffed on three straight pitches, and Corcoran, the Braves' left-handed relief man, is all of a sudden pouring it on. Throughout the stadium a hush has fallen over the crowd, the torpor of suppertime, the game poised at apogee. Shadows are lengthening in the outfield, swallows flitting across the face of the scoreboard, here a fan drops into his beer, there a big mama gathers up her purse, her knitting, her shopping bags and parasol, and thinks of dinner. Hector sees it all. This is the moment of catharsis, the moment to take it out.

As Martinez slumps toward the dugout, Dupuy, a laconic, embittered man who keeps his suffering inside and drinks Gelusil like water, takes hold of Hector's arm. His eyes are red-rimmed and paunchy, doleful as a basset hound's. Bring the runner in, champ, he rasps. First pitch fake a bunt, then hit away. Watch Booger at third. Uh-huh, Hector mumbles, snapping his gum. Then he slides his bat from the rack—white ash, tape-wrapped grip, personally blessed by the archbishop of Guadalajara and his twenty-seven acolytes—and starts for the dugout steps, knowing the course of the next three minutes as surely as his blood knows the course of his veins. The familiar cry will go up—Cheese, Cheese, Cheesus—and he'll amble up to the batter's box, knocking imaginary dirt from his spikes, adjusting the straps of his golf gloves, tugging at his underwear, and fiddling with his batting helmet. His face will be impenetrable. Corcoran will work the ball in his glove, maybe tip back his cap for a little hair grease, and then give him a look of psychopathic hatred. Hector has seen it before. Me against you. My record, my career, my house, my family, my life, my mutual funds and beer distributorship against yours. He's been hit in the elbow, the knee, the groin, the head. Nothing fazes him. Nothing. Murmuring a prayer to Santa Griselda, patroness of the sun-blasted Sonoran village where he was born like a heat blister on his mother's womb, Hector Hernán Jesús y María Quesadilla will step into the batter's box, ready for anything.

But it's a game of infinite surprises.

Before Hector can set foot on the playing field, Corcoran suddenly doubles up in pain, Phelan goes slack at second, and the catcher and shortstop are hustling out to the mound, tailed an instant later by trainer and pitching coach. First thing Hector thinks is groin pull, then appendicitis, and finally, as Corcoran goes down on one knee, poison.

He'd once seen a man shot in the gut at Obregón City, but the report had been loud as a thunderclap, and he hears nothing now but the enveloping hum of the crowd. Corcoran is rising shakily, the trainer and pitching coach supporting him while the catcher kicks meditatively in the dirt, and now Mueller, the Atlanta *cabeza,* is striding big-bellied out of the dugout, head down as if to be sure his feet are following orders. Halfway to the mound, Mueller flicks his right hand across his ear quick as a horse flicking its tail, and it's all she wrote for Corcoran.

Poised on the dugout steps like a bird dog, Hector waits, his eyes riveted on the bullpen. Please, he whispers, praying for the intercession of the Niño and pledging a hundred votary candles—at least, at least. Can it be?—yes, milk of my mother, yes—Kerensky himself strutting out onto the field like a fighting cock. Kerensky!

Come to the birthday boy, Kerensky, he murmurs, so certain he's going to put it in the stands he could point like the immeasurable Bambino. His tired old legs shuffle with impatience as Kerensky stalks across the field, and then he's turning to pick Asunción out of the crowd. She's on her feet now, Reina too, the kids come alive beside her. And Hector Jr., the book forgotten, his face transfigured with the look of rapture he used to get when he was a boy sitting on the steps of the dugout. Hector can't help himself: he grins and gives them the thumbs-up sign.

Then, as Kerensky fires his warm-up smoke, the loudspeaker crackles and Hector emerges from the shadow of the dugout into the tapering golden shafts of the late-afternoon sun. That pitch, I want that one, he mutters, carrying his bat like a javelin and shooting a glare at Kerensky, but something's wrong here, the announcer's got it screwed up: BATTING FOR RARITAN, NUMBER 39, DAVE TOOL. What the—? And now somebody's tugging at his sleeve and he's turning to gape with incomprehension at the freckle-faced batboy, Dave Tool striding out of the dugout with his big forty-two-ounce stick, Dupuy's face locked up like a vault, and the crowd, on its feet, chanting Tool, Tool, Tool! For a moment he just stands there, frozen with disbelief. Then Tool is brushing by him and the idiot of a batboy is leading him toward the dugout as if he were an old blind fisherman poised on the edge of the dock.

He feels as if his legs have been cut out from under him. Tool! Dupuy is yanking him for Tool? For what? So he can play the lefty-righty percentages like some chess head or something? Tool, of all people. Tool, with his thirty-five home runs a season and lifetime BA of .234; Tool, who's worn so many uniforms they had to expand the league to make room for him—what's he going to do? Raging, Hector flings down his bat and comes at Dupuy like a cat tossed in a bag. You crazy, you jerk, he sputters. I woulda hit him, I woulda won the game. I dreamed it. And then, his voice breaking: It's my birthday, for Christ's sake!

But Dupuy can't answer him, because on the first pitch Tool slams a real worm burner to short and the game is going into extra innings.

By seven o'clock, half the fans have given up and gone home. In the top of the fourteenth, when the visitors came up with a pair of runs on a two-out pinch-hit home run, there was a real exodus, but then the Dodgers struck back for two to knot it up again. Then it was three up and three down, regular as clockwork. Now, at the end of the nineteenth, with the score deadlocked at 7 all and the players dragging themselves around the field like gut-shot horses, Hector is beginning to think he may get a second chance after all. Especially the way Dupuy's been using up players like some crazy general on the Western Front, yanking pitchers, juggling his defense, throwing in pinch runners and pinch hitters until he's just about gone through the entire roster. Asunción is still there among the faithful, the foolish, and the self-deluded, fumbling with her rosary and mouthing prayers for Jesus Christ Our Lord, the Madonna, Hector, the home team, and her departed mother, in that order. Reina too, looking like the survivor of some disaster, Franklin and Alfredo asleep in their seats, the niñitas gone off somewhere—for Coke and dogs, maybe. And Hector Jr. looks like he's going to stick it out too, though he should be back in his closet writing about the mystical so-and-so and the way he illustrates his poems with gods and men and serpents. Watching him, Hector can feel his heart turn over.

In the bottom of the twentieth, with one down and Gilley on first—he's a starting pitcher but Dupuy sent him in to run for Manfredonia after Manfredonia jammed his ankle like a turkey and had to be helped off the field—Hector pushes himself up from the bench and ambles down to where Dupuy sits in the corner, contemplatively spitting a gout of tobacco juice and saliva into the drain at his feet. Let me hit, Bernard, come on, Hector says, easing down beside him.

Can't, comes the reply, and Dupuy never even raises his head. Can't risk it, champ. Look around you—and here the manager's voice quavers with uncertainty, with fear and despair and the dull edge of hopelessness—I got nobody left. I hit you, I got to play you.

No, no, you don't understand—I'm going to win it, I swear.

And then the two of them, like old bankrupts on a bench in Miami Beach, look up to watch Phelan hit into a double play.

A buzz runs through the crowd when the Dodgers take the field for the top of the twenty-second. Though Phelan is limping, Thorkelsson's asleep on his feet, and Dorfman, fresh on the mound, is the only pitcher left on the roster, the moment is electric. One more inning and they tie the record set by the Mets and Giants back in '64, and then they're making history. Drunk, sober, and then drunk again, saturated with fats and nitrates and sugar, the crowd begins to come to life. Go, Dodgers! Eat shit! Yo Mama! Phelan's a bum!

Hector can feel it too. The rage and frustration that had consumed him back in the ninth are gone, replaced by a dawning sense of wonder—he could have won it then, yes, and against his nemesis Kerensky too—but the Niño and Santa Griselda have been saving him for something greater. He sees it now, knows it in his bones: he's going to be the hero of the longest game in history.

As if to bear him out, Dorfman, the kid from Albuquerque, puts in a good inning, cutting the bushed Braves down in order. In the dugout, Doc Pusser, the team physician, is handing out the little green pills that keep your eyes open and Dupuy is blowing into a cup of coffee and staring morosely out at the playing field. Hector watches as Tool, who'd stayed in the game at first base, fans on three straight pitches, then he shoves in beside Dorfman and tells the kid he's looking good out there. With his big cornhusker's ears and nose like a tweezer, Dorfman could be a caricature of the green rookie. He says nothing. Hey, don't let it get to you, kid—I'm going to win this one for you. Next inning or maybe the inning after. Then he tells him how he saw it in a vision and how it's his birthday and the kid's going to get the victory, one of the biggest of all time. Twenty-four, twenty-five innings maybe.

Hector had heard of a game once in the Mexican League that took three days to play and went seventy-three innings, did Dorfman know that? It was down in Culiacán. Chito Marití, the converted bullfighter, had finally ended it by dropping down dead of exhaustion in center field, allowing Sexto Silvestro, who'd broken his leg rounding third, to crawl home with the winning run. But Hector doesn't think this game will go that long. Dorfman sighs and extracts a bit of wax from his ear as Pantaleo, the third-string catcher, hits back to the pitcher to end the inning. I hope not, he says, uncoiling himself from the bench; my arm'd fall off.

Ten o'clock comes and goes. Dorfman's still in there, throwing breaking stuff and a little smoke at the Braves, who look as if they just stepped out of *The Night of the Living Dead*. The home team isn't doing much better. Dupuy's run through the whole team but for Hector, and three or four of the guys have been in there since two in the afternoon; the rest are a bunch of ginks and gimps who can barely stand up. Out in the stands, the fans look grim. The vendors ran out of beer an hour back, and they haven't had dogs or kraut or Coke or anything since eight-thirty.

In the bottom of the twenty-seventh Phelan goes berserk in the dugout and Dupuy has to pin him to the floor while Doc Pusser shoves something up his nose to calm him. Next inning the balls-and-strikes ump passes out cold, and Dorfman, who's beginning to look a little fagged, walks the first two batters but manages to weasel his way out of the inning without giving up the go-ahead run. Meanwhile, Thorkelsson has been dropping ice cubes down his trousers to keep awake, Martinez is smoking something suspicious in the can, and Ferenc Fortnoi, the third baseman, has begun talking to himself in a tortured Slovene dialect. For his part, Hector feels stronger and more alert as the game goes on. Though he hasn't had a bite since breakfast he feels impervious to the pangs of hunger, as if he were preparing himself, mortifying his flesh like a saint in the desert.

And then, in the top of the thirty-first, with half the fans asleep and the other half staring into nothingness like the inmates of the asylum of Our Lady of Guadalupe, where Hector had once visited his halfwit uncle when he was a boy, Pluto Morales cracks one down the first-base line and Tool flubs it. Right away it looks like trouble, because Chester Bubo is running around right field looking up at the sky like a birdwatcher while the ball snakes through the grass, caroms off his left foot, and coasts like silk to the edge of the warning track. Morales meanwhile is rounding second and coming on for third, running in slow motion, flat-footed and hump-backed, his face drained of color, arms flapping like the undersized wings of some big flightless bird. It's not even close. By the time Bubo can locate the ball, Morales is ten feet from the plate, pitching into a face-first slide that's at least three parts collapse, and that's it, the Braves are up by one. It looks black for the hometeam. But Dorfman, though his arm has begun to swell like a sausage, shows some grit, bears down, and retires the side to end the historic top of the unprecedented thirty-first inning.

Now, at long last, the hour has come. It'll be Bubo, Dorfman, and Tool for the Dodgers in their half of the inning, which means that Hector will hit for Dorfman. *I been saving you, champ,* Dupuy rasps, the empty Gelusil bottle clenched in his fist like a hand grenade. *Go on in there,* he murmurs, and his voice fades away to nothing as Bubo pops the first pitch up in back of the plate. *Go on in there and do your stuff.*

Sucking in his gut, Hector strides out onto the brightly lit field like a nineteen-year-old, the familiar cry in his ears, the haggard fans on their feet, a sickle moon sketched in overhead as if in some cartoon strip featuring drunken husbands and the milkman. Asunción looks as if she's been nailed to the cross, Reina wakes with a start and shakes the little ones into consciousness, and Hector Jr. staggers to his feet like a battered middleweight coming out for the fifteenth round. They're all watching him. The fans whose lives are like empty sacks, the wife who wants him home in front of the TV, his divorced daughter with the four kids and another on the way, his son, pride of his life, who reads for the doctor of philosophy while his crazy *padrecito* puts on a pair of long stockings and chases around after a little white ball like a case of arrested development. He'll show them. He'll show them some *cojones,* some true grit and desire: the game's not over yet.

On the mound for the Braves is Bo Brannerman, a big mustachioed machine of a man, normally a starter but pressed into desperate relief service tonight. A fine pitcher—Hector would be the first to admit it—but he just pitched two nights ago and he's worn thin as wire. Hector steps up to the plate, feeling legendary. He glances over at Tool in the on-deck circle, and then down at Booger, the third-base coach. All systems go. He cuts at the air twice and then watches Brannerman rear back and release the ball: strike one. Hector smiles. Why rush things? Give them a thrill. He watches a low outside slider that just about bounces to even the count, and then stands like a statue as Brannerman slices the corner of the plate for strike two. From the stands, a chant of *Viejo, Viejo,* and Asunción's piercing soprano, *Hit him, Hector!*

Hector has no worries, the moment eternal, replayed through games uncountable, with pitchers who were over the hill when he was a rookie with San Buitre, with pups like Brannerman, with big-leaguers and Hall of Famers. Here it comes, Hector, 92 MPH, the big *gringo* trying to throw it by you, the matchless wrists, the flawless swing, one terrific moment of suspended animation—and all of a sudden you're starring in your own movie.

How does it go? The ball cutting through the night sky like a comet, arching high over the center fielder's hapless scrambling form to slam off the wall while your legs churn up the base paths, you round first in a gallop, taking second, and heading for third . . . but wait, you spill hot coffee on your hand and you can't feel it, the demons apply the live wire to your tailbone, the legs give out and they cut you down at third while the stadium erupts in howls of execration and abuse and the *niñitos* break down, faces flooded with tears of humiliation, Hector Jr. turning his back in disgust and Asunción raging like a harpie, *Abuelo! Abuelo! Abuelo!*

Stunned, shrunken, humiliated, you stagger back to the dugout in a maelstrom of abuse, paper cups, flying spittle, your life a waste, the game a cheat, and then, crowning irony, that bum Tool, worthless all the way back to his washerwoman grandmother and the drunken muttering whey-faced tribe that gave him suck, stands tall like a giant and sends the first pitch out of the park to tie it. Oh, the pain. Flat feet, fire in your legs, your poor tired old heart skipping a beat in mortification. And now Dupuy, red in the face, shouting: The game could be over but for you, you crazy gimpy old beaner washout! You want to hide in your locker, bury yourself under the shower-room floor, but you have to watch as the next two men reach base and you pray with fervor that they'll score and put an end to your debasement. But no, Thorkelsson whiffs and the new inning dawns as inevitably as the new minute, the new hour, the new day, endless, implacable, world without end.

But wait, wait: who's going to pitch? Dorfman's out, there's nobody left, the astonishing thirty-second inning is marching across the scoreboard like an invading army, and suddenly Dupuy is standing over you—no, no, he's down on one knee, begging. Hector, he's saying, didn't you use to pitch down in Mexico when you were a kid, didn't I hear that someplace? Yes, you're saying, yes, but that was—

And then you're out on the mound, in command once again, elevated like some half-mad old king in a play, and throwing smoke. The first two batters go down on strikes and the fans are rabid with excitement, Asunción will raise a shrine, Hector Jr. worships you more than all the poets that ever lived, but can it be? You walk the next three and then give up the grand slam to little Tommy Oshimisi! Mother of God, will it never cease? But wait, wait, wait: here comes the bottom of the thirty-second and Brannerman's wild. He walks a couple, gets a couple out, somebody reaches on an infield single and the bases are loaded for you, Hector Quesadilla, stepping up to the plate now like the Iron Man himself. The wind-up, the delivery, the ball hanging there like a *piñata,* like a birthday gift, and then the stick flashes in your hands like an archangel's sword, and the game goes on forever.

THE 7–10 SPLIT

John Sayles

If you don't have your own shoes they rent you a pair for fifty cents. None of us are any big athletes, we meet at the lanes once a week, Thursday night. But some of us have our own shoes. Bobbi for instance, she got a pair cause the rented shoes have their size on the heel in a red leather number and Bobbi doesn't want everybody seeing how big her feet are. She's real conscious of things like that, real conscious of her appearance, like you'd expect a hairdresser to be.

We play two teams, four girls each, and take up a pair of lanes. It's Bobbi and Janey and Blanche and me against Rose Teta, Pat and Vi, and Evelyn Chambers. We've worked it out over the years so the sides are pretty even. A lot of the time the result comes down to whether I been on days at the Home or if Blanche is having problems with her corns. She's on her feet all day at the State Office Building cafeteria and sometimes the corns act up. I figure that I roll around 175 if I'm on graveyard but drop down to 140 if I already done my shift in the morning. Janey works with me at the Home and doesn't seem to mind either which way, but she's the youngest of us.

"Mae," she always says to me, "it's all in your head. If you let yourself *think* you're tired, you'll *be* tired. All in your head."

That might be so for her, but you get my age and a lot of what used to be in your head goes directly to your legs.

And Janey is just one of those people was born with a lot of *pep*. Night shift at the Home, in between bed checks when all the aides and nurses are sitting around the station moaning about how little sleep they got during the day, Janey is always working like crazy on her macrame plant-hangers. She sells them to some hippie store downtown for the extra income. She's a regular little Christmas elf, Janey, her hands never stop moving. It's a wonder to me how she keeps her looks, what with the lack of rest and the load she's been saddled with, the hand she's been dealt in life. She's both mother and father to her little retarded boy, Scooter, and still she keeps her sweet disposition. We always send her up to the desk when the pinspotter jams, cause Al, who runs the lanes and is real slow to fix things, is sweet on her. You can tell because he takes his earplugs out when she talks to him. Al won't do that for just anybody. Of course, he's married and kind of greasy-looking, but you take your compliments where you can.

It's a real good bunch though, and we have a lot of fun. Rose Teta and Vi work together at the Woolworth's and are like sisters, always borrowing each other's clothes and kidding around. They ought to be on TV, those two. The other night, the last time we played, they started in on Bobbi before we even got on the boards. Bobbi owns a real heavy ball, a sixteen-pounder. It's this milky-blue marbled thing, real feminine-looking like everything Bobbi has. Only last week it's at the shop having the finger holes redrilled, so she has to find one off the rack at the lanes. At Al's the lighter ones, for women and children, are red, and the heavier ones the men use are black. Bobbie is over checking on the black ones when Rose and Vi start up about there she goes handling the men's balls again, and when she blushes and pretends she doesn't hear they go on about her having her holes drilled. Bobbi hates anything vulgar, or at least she makes like she does, so she always keeps Pat in between her and the Woolworth's girls when we sit on the bench. Pat is a real serious Catholic, and though she laughs at Rose and Vi she never does it out loud. Pat's gonna pop a seam some day, laughing so hard with her hand clapped over her mouth.

It was just after the men's-balls business with Bobbi that Evelyn walked in and give us the news. We could tell right off something was wrong—she wasn't carrying her ball bag and she looked real tired, didn't have any makeup on. She walks in and says, "I'm sorry I didn't call you, girls, but I just now come to my decision. I won't be playing Thursdays anymore, I'm joining the Seniors' League."

You could of heard a pin drop. Evelyn is the oldest of us, true, and her hair has mostly gone gray, but she's one of the liveliest women I know. She and Janey always used to make fun of the Seniors' League, all the little kids' games they do and how they give out a trophy every time you turn around. Used to say the Seniors' was for people who had given up, that they set the handicaps so high all you had to do to average 200 was to write your name on the scorecard.

Well, we all wanted to know her reasons and tried to talk her out of it. Since she retired from the State last year, bowling was the only time any of us got to see Evelyn and we didn't want to lose her. She's one of those women makes you feel all right about getting older, at least till this Seniors' business come up. We tried every argument we could think of but she'd made up her mind. She nodded down the alley at the AMF machine clacking the pins into place and she says, "I'm the only one here remembers when they used to be a boy behind there, setting them up by hand. You give him a tip at the end of the night, like a golf caddy. I remember when Al had all his teeth, when the hot dogs here had beef in them. I'm the only one here remembers a lot of things and it's time I quit kidding myself and act my age. You girls can get on without me."

Then she said her good-byes to each of us and walked out, tired-looking and smaller than I'd remembered her. Wasn't a dry eye in the house.

But, like they say, life must go on. We evened the sides up by having either me or Blanche sit out every other game and keep score. While we were putting on our shoes we tried to figure out who we could get to replace Evelyn and even up the teams again. June Hundley's name was mentioned, and Edie McIntyre and Lorraine DeFillippo. Of course Bobbi had some objection to each of them, but that's just how she is so we didn't listen. Janey didn't say a word all the while, she seemed real depressed.

Janey and Evelyn were really tight. In one way it's hard to figure since there's so much age difference between them, but then again it makes sense. They've both had a real hard row to hoe, Evelyn's husband dying and Janey's running off. And they both had a child with mental problems. Evelyn had her Buddy, who was Mongoloid and lived till he was twenty-seven. She kept him at home the whole while, even when he got big and hard to manage, and loved him like she would a normal child. Never gave up on him. To his dying day Evelyn was trying to teach Buddy to read, used to sit with him for hours with travel brochures. Buddy liked all the color pictures.

And Janey always puts me in mind of that poor Terry on *General Hospital,* or any of the nice ones on the daytime stories who are always going blind or having their men stolen or losing their memories. Just one thing after another—as if having Scooter wasn't enough trouble in one lifetime. Janey has to bring Scooter on Thursdays cause there isn't a babysitter who could handle him. Al allows it cause like I said, he's sweet on her. There's no keeping Scooter still, he's ten years old, real stocky and wild-eyed, like a little animal out of control. At the Home they'd keep him full of Valium and he'd be in a fog all day, but Janey won't let the school use drugs on him. Says he's at least entitled to his own sensations, and from what I seen from my patients I agree with her. Scooter is all over the lanes, dancing down the gutters, picking the balls up, drawing on score sheets, playing all the pinball and safari-shoot games in the back even when there's no coin in them. Scooter moves faster than those flippers and bumpers ever could, even pinball must seem like a slow game to him. The only thing he does that Al won't stand for is when he goes to the popcorn machine and laps his tongue on the chute where it comes out. He likes the salt and doesn't understand how he might be putting people off their appetite.

Anyhow, you could just look at Janey and tell she was feeling low. She's usually got a lot of color in her cheeks, it glows when she smiles and sets off nice against her hair. Natural blond, not bottled like Bobbi's is. Well, after Evelyn left she was all pale, no color to her at all, and when we started bowling she didn't have the little bounce in her approach like she usually does. One of the things that's fun is watching the different styles the girls bowl. Like I said, Janey usually comes up to the line really bouncy, up on her toes, and lays the ball down so smooth it's almost silent. You're surprised when you hear the pins crash. Rose and Vi both muscle it down the alley, they're as hard on the boards as they are on the pins, and when they miss a spare clean the ball cracks against the back wall so hard it makes you wince. But when they're in the pocket you should see those pins fly, like an explosion. Bobbi uses that heavy ball and can let it go a lot slower—she always freezes in a picture pose on her follow-through, her arm pointing at the headpin, her back leg up in the air, and her head cocked to the side. She looks like a bowling trophy—sometime we'll have her bronzed while she's waiting for her ball to connect. Pat plays by those little arrows on the boards behind the foul line, she doesn't even look at the pins. She's like a machine—same starting spot, same four-and-a-half steps, same little kneeling dip as she lets go, like she's genuflecting. Blanche has this awful hook to her ball, some kind of funny hitch she does with her elbow on her backswing. She has to stand way over to the right to have a shot at the pocket and sometimes when she's tired she'll lay one right in the gutter on her first ball. She gets a lot of action when she connects with that spin, though she leaves the 10–pin over on the right corner a lot and it's hard for her to pick up.

I'm a lefty, so the lanes are grooved in my favor, but I don't know what I look like. The girls say I charge the line too fast and foul sometimes, but I'm not really aware of it.

The other thing with Janey's style is the 7–10 split. It's the hardest to pick up, the two pins standing on opposite sides of the lane, and because Janey throws a real straight ball she sees it a lot. Most people settle for an open frame, hit one or the other of the pins solid and forget about trying to convert, but Janey always tries to pick it up. You have to shade the outside of one of the pins perfectly so it either slides directly over to take out the other or bangs off the back wall and nails it on the rebound. Even the pros don't make it very often and there's always a good chance you'll throw a gutter ball and end up missing both pins. But Janey always goes for it, even if we're in a tight game and that one sure pin could make the difference. That's just how she plays it. It drives Bobbi nuts, whenever Janey leaves a 7–10 Bobbi moans and rolls her eyes.

Of course Bobbi is a little competitive with Janey, they're the closest in age and both still on the market. Bobbi is always saying in that high breathy voice of hers that's so surprising coming from such a—well, such a *big* woman—she's always saying, "I just can't understand why Janey doesn't have a man after her. What with all her nice qualities." Like it's some fault of Janey's—like working split shifts at a nursing home and taking care of a kid who makes motorcycle sounds and bounces off the walls all day leaves you much time to go looking for a husband.

Not that Janey doesn't try. She gets herself out to functions at the PNA and the Sons of Italy Hall and Ladies' Nite at Barney's when they let you in free to dance. The trouble is, she's got standards, Janey.

Nothing unreasonable, but considering what's available in the way of unattached men, having any standards at all seems crazy. Janey won't have any truck with the married ones or the drinkers, which cuts the field in half to start with. And what's left isn't nothing to set your heart going pitter-pat. When I think of what Janey's up against it makes me appreciate my Earl and the boys, though they're no bargain most of the time. Janey's not getting any younger, of course, and any man interested in her has got to buy Scooter in the same package and that's a lot to ask. But Janey hasn't given up. "There's always an outside chance, Mae," she says. "And even if nothing works out, look at Evelyn. All that she's been through, and she hasn't let it beat her. Nope, you got to keep trying, there's always an outside chance." Like with her 7–10 splits, always trying to pick them up.

But she never made a one of them. All the times she's tried, she's never hit it just right, never got the 7–10 spare. Not a one.

Anyhow, last Thursday after Evelyn left we got into our first string and Janey started out awful. Honey, it was just pitiful to see. None of the girls were really up to form, but Janey was the worst, no bounce in her approach, just walked up flat-footed and dropped the ball with a big thud onto the boards. Turned away from the pins almost before she seen what the ball left, with this pinched look on her face that showed up all the wrinkles she's starting to get. Leaving three, four pins in a cluster on her first ball, then missing the spares. The teams were all out of balance without Evelyn, *we* were all out of balance. Blanche's hook was even worse than usual and Pat couldn't seem to find the right arrows on the boards and I couldn't for the life of me keep behind that foul line. Everyone was real quiet, Rose and Vi weren't joking like always, and the noise of the lanes took over.

Usually I like it, the girls all talking and laughing, that strange bright light all around you, the rumbling and crashing. It reminds me of the Rip Van Winkle story they told in school when I was a girl, how the dwarfs bowling on the green were the cause of thunder and lightning. It's exciting, kind of. But that night with Evelyn gone and the girls so quiet it scared me. The pins sounded real hollow when they were hit, the sound of the bowling balls on the wood was hollow too, sounded like we were the only people left in the lanes. It gave me the creeps and I tried to concentrate on keeping score.

Scooter was drawing all over the score sheet like he always does, making his motorcycle revving noise, but we've gotten used to reading through his scribble and I didn't pay it no mind. All of a sudden Janey reaches over and smacks his hand, real hard. It was like a gunshot, Pat near jumped out of her seat. Usually Janey is the most patient person in the world, she'll explain to Scooter for the millionth time why he shouldn't lick the popcorn chute while she steers him away from it real gentle. I remember how upset she got when she first come to the Home and saw how some of the girls would slap a patient who was mean or just difficult. She always offered to take those patients off their hands, and found some calmer way to deal with them.

But here she'd just smacked Scooter like she really meant it and for once his engine stalled, and he just stood and stared at her like the rest of us did. Then Bobbi's ball finally reached the pocket and broke the spell, Scooter zoomed away and we all found something else to look at.

It put me in mind of when Evelyn's husband Boyd had his stroke and come to the Home for his last days. It was right when they'd moved Janey to the men's ward to help me with the heavy lifting cause the orderlies were so useless. Evelyn would come every night after work and sit by Boyd, and in between checks Janey would go in to keep her company. Boyd was awake a lot of the time but wasn't much company, as he'd had the kind where your motor control goes and all he could say was "ob-bob-bob-bob" or something like that. What impressed Janey most was how Evelyn kept planning this trip to Florida they'd set up before the stroke, as if the rehabilitation was going to make a miracle and Boyd would ever get to leave the Home. She'd ask him questions about what they'd bring or where they'd visit and he'd answer by nodding. Kept him alive for a good six months, planning that trip. "How bout this Parrot Jungle, Boyd," I'd hear when I'd walk by the room to answer a bell, "would you like to stop there?" Then she'd wait for a nod. Janey would come out of that room with a light in her eyes, it was something to see. And honey, three weeks after Boyd went out, didn't Evelyn go and take her Buddy down to Florida all by herself, stopped in every place they'd planned together and sent us all postcards.

Anyhow, the night went on. Sometimes it can get to be work, the bowling, and by the fourth string everybody was looking half dead. Dropping the ball instead of rolling it, bumping it against their legs on the backswing, waving their thumb blisters over the little air vent on the return rack—a real bunch of stiffs. Almost no one was talking and Bobbi had taken out her little mirror and was playing with her hair, a sure sign that she's in a nasty mood. We'd had a few lucky strikes but no one had hit for a double or a turkey and there were open frames all over the place. Everybody was down twenty to forty points from their average and we'd only ordered one round of Cokes and beers. Usually we keep Al hopping cause talking and yelling gets us so thirsty. When I felt how heavy my legs were I remembered I still had to pull my eleven-to-seven shift, had to get urine samples from all the diabetics on the ward and help with old Sipperly's tube-feeding, I started feeling very old, like *I* should be joining the Seniors', not Evelyn.

Then in the eighth frame Janey laid one right on the nose of the headpin, first time she hit the pocket square all night, and there it stood. The 7–10 split. Sort of taunting, like a gap-toothed grin staring at her. It was real quiet in the lanes then, the way it goes sometimes, like a break in the storm. Janey stood looking at it with her hands on her hips while her ball came back in slow motion. She picked it up and got her feet set and then held still for the longest time, concentrating. She was going for it, we could tell she was going to try to make it and we all held our breaths.

Janey stepped to the line with a little bounce and rolled the ball smooth and light, rolled it on the very edge of the right-hand gutter with just the slightest bit of reverse English on it and it teetered on the edge all the way down, then faded at the end just barely nipping the 10, sliding it across to tip the 7–pin as it went down, tilting that 7 on its edge and if we'd had the breath we'd of blown it over but then the bastard righted itself, *righted* and began to wobble, wobbled a little Charlie Chaplin walk across the wood and plopped flat on its back into the gutter.

Well, we all set up a whoop and Janey turned to us with this little hopeful smile on her face, cheeks all glowing again like a little girl who just done her First Communion coming back down the aisle looking to her folks for approval and even Bobbi, who was up next, even Bobbi give her a big hug while little Scooter drew *X*'s all over the score sheet.

III

*Double
Plays*

THE YEAR OF GETTING TO KNOW US

Ethan Canin

I told my father not to worry, that love is what matters, and that in the end, when he is loosed from his body, he can look back and say without blinking that he did all right by me, his son, and that I loved him.

And he said, "Don't talk about things you know nothing about."

We were in San Francisco, in a hospital room. I.V. tubes were plugged into my father's arms; little round Band-Aids were on his chest. Next to his bed was a table with a vase of yellow roses and a card that my wife, Anne, had brought him. On the front of the card was a photograph of a golf green. On the wall above my father's head an electric monitor traced his heartbeat. He was watching the news on a TV that stood in the corner next to his girlfriend, Lorraine. Lorraine was reading a magazine.

I was watching his heartbeat. It seemed all right to me: the blips made steady peaks and drops, moved across the screen, went out at one end, and then came back at the other. It seemed that this was all a heart could do. I'm an English teacher, though, and I don't know much about it.

"It looks strong," I'd said to my mother that afternoon over the phone. She was in Pasadena. "It's going right across, pretty steady. Big bumps. Solid."

"Is he eating all right?"

"I think so."

"Is *she* there?"

"Is Lorraine here, you mean?"

She paused. "Yes, Lorraine."

"No," I said. "She's not."

"Your poor father," she whispered.

I'm an only child, and I grew up in a big wood-frame house on Huron Avenue in Pasadena, California. The house had three empty bedrooms and in the back yard a section of grass that had been stripped and leveled, then seeded and mowed like a putting green. Twice a week a Mexican gardener came to trim it, wearing special moccasins my father had bought him. They had soft hide soles that left no imprints.

My father was in love with golf. He played seven times every week and talked about the game as if it were a science that he was about to figure out. "Cut through the outer rim for a high iron," he used to say at dinner, looking out the window into the yard while my mother passed him the carved-wood salad bowl, or "In hot weather hit a high-compression ball." When conversations paused, he made little putting motions with his hands. He was a top amateur and in another situation might have been a pro. When I was sixteen, the year I was arrested, he let me caddie for the first time. Before that all I knew about golf was his clubs—the Spalding made-to-measure woods and irons, Dynamiter sand wedge, St. Andrews putter—which he kept in an Abercrombie & Fitch bag in the trunk of his Lincoln, and the white leather shoes with long tongues and screw-in spikes, which he stored upside down in the hall closet. When he wasn't playing, he covered the club heads with socks that had little yellow dingo balls on the ends.

He never taught me to play. I was a decent athlete—could run, catch, throw a perfect spiral—but he never took me to the golf course. In the summer he played every day. Sometimes my mother asked if he would take me along with him. "Why should I?" he answered. "Neither of us would like it."

Every afternoon after work he played nine holes; he played eighteen on Saturday, and nine again on Sunday morning. On Sunday afternoon, at four o'clock, he went for a drive by himself in his white Lincoln Continental. Nobody was allowed to come with him on the drives. He was usually gone for a couple of hours. "Today I drove in the country," he would say at dinner, as he put out his cigarette, or "This afternoon I looked at the ocean," and we were to take from this that he had driven north on the coastal highway. He almost never said more, and across our blue-and-white tablecloth, when I looked at him, my silent father, I imagined in his eyes a pure gaze with which he read the waves and currents of the sea. He had made a fortune in business and owed it to being able to see the truth in any situation. For this reason, he said, he liked to drive with all the windows down. When he returned from his trips his face was red from the wind and his thinning hair lay fitfully on his head. My mother baked on Sunday afternoons while he was gone, walnut pies or macaroons that she prepared on the kitchen counter, which looked out over his putting green.

I teach English in a high school now, and my wife, Anne, is a journalist. I've played golf a half-dozen times in ten years and don't like it any more than most beginners, though the two or three times I've hit a drive that sails, that takes flight with its own power, I've felt something that I think must be unique to the game. These were the drives my father used to hit. Explosions off the tee, bird flights. But golf isn't my game, and it never has been, and I wouldn't think about it at all if not for my father.

Anne and I were visiting in California, first my mother, in Los Angeles, and then my father and Lorraine, north in Sausalito, and Anne suggested that I ask him to play nine holes one morning. She'd been wanting me to talk to him. It's part of the project we've started, part of her theory of what's wrong—although I don't think that much is. She had told me that twenty-five years changes things, and since we had the time, why not go out to California.

She said, "It's not too late to talk to him."

My best friend in high school was named Nickie Apple. Nickie had a thick chest and a voice that had been damaged somehow, made a little hoarse, and sometimes people thought he was twenty years old. He lived in a four-story house that had a separate floor for the kids. It was the top story, and his father, who was divorced and a lawyer, had agreed never to come up there. That was where we sat around after school. Because of the agreement, no parents were there, only kids. Nine or ten of us, usually. Some of them had slept the night on the big pillows that were scattered against the walls: friends of his older brothers, in Stetson hats and flannel shirts; girls I had never seen before.

Nickie and I went to Shrier Academy, where all the students carried around blue-and-gray notebooks embossed with the school's heraldic seal. SUMUS PRIMI, the seal said. Our gray wool sweaters said it; our green exam books said it; the rear window decal my mother brought home said it. My father wouldn't put the sticker on the Lincoln, so she pressed it onto the window above her kitchen sink instead. ƧUMUƧ IMIЯꟼ I read whenever I washed my hands. At Shrier we learned Latin in the eighth grade and art history in the ninth, and in the tenth I started getting into some trouble. Little things: cigarettes, graffiti. Mr. Goldman, the student counselor, called my mother in for a premonition visit. "I have a premonition about Leonard," he told her in the counseling office one afternoon in the warm October when I was sixteen. The office was full of plants and had five floor-to-ceiling windows that let in sun like a greenhouse. They looked over grassy, bushless knolls. "I just have a feeling about him."

That October he started talking to me about it. He called me in and asked me why I was friends with Nickie Apple, a boy going nowhere. I was looking out the big windows, opening and closing my fists beneath the desk top. He said, "Lenny, you're a bright kid—what are you trying to tell us?" And I said, "Nothing. I'm not trying to tell you anything."

Then we started stealing, Nickie and I. He did it first, and took things I didn't expect: steaks, expensive cuts that we cooked on a grill by the window in the top story of his house; garden machinery; luggage. We didn't sell it and we didn't use it, but every afternoon we went someplace new. In November he distracted a store clerk and I took a necklace that we thought was diamonds. In December we went for a ride in someone else's car, and over Christmas vacation, when only gardeners were on the school grounds, we threw ten rocks, one by one, as if we'd paid for them at a carnival stand, through the five windows in Mr. Goldman's office.

"You look like a train station," I said to my father as he lay in the hospital bed. "All those lines coming and going everywhere."

He looked at me. I put some things down, tried to make a little bustle. I could see Anne standing in the hall just beyond the door.

"Are you comfortable, Dad?"

"What do you mean, 'comfortable'? My heart's full of holes, leaking all over the place. Am I comfortable? No, I'm dying."

"You're not dying," I said, and I sat down next to him. "You'll be swinging the five iron in two weeks."

I touched one of the tubes in his arm. Where it entered the vein, the needle disappeared under a piece of tape. I hated the sight of this. I moved the bedsheets a little bit, tucked them in. Anne had wanted me to be alone with him. She was in the hall, waiting to head off Lorraine.

"What's the matter with her?" he asked, pointing at Anne.

"She thought we might want to talk."

"What's so urgent?"

Anne and I had discussed it the night before. "Tell him what you feel," she said. "Tell him you love him." We were eating dinner in a fish restaurant. "Or if you don't love him, tell him you don't."

"Look, Pop," I said now.

"What?"

I was forty-two years old. We were in a hospital and he had tubes in his arms. All kinds of everything: needles, air, tape. I said it again.

"Look, Pop."

Anne and I have seen a counselor, who told me that I had to learn to accept kindness from people. He saw Anne and me together, then Anne alone, then me. Children's toys were scattered on the floor of his office. "You sound as if you don't want to let people near you," he said. "Right?"

"I'm a reasonably happy man," I answered.

I hadn't wanted to see the counselor. Anne and I have been married seven years, and sometimes I think the history of marriage can be written like this: People Want Too Much. Anne and I have suffered no plague; we sleep late two mornings a week; we laugh at most of the same things; we have a decent house in a suburb of Boston, where, after the commuter traffic has eased, a quiet descends and the world is at peace. She writes for a newspaper, and I teach the children of lawyers and insurance men. At times I'm alone, and need to be alone; at times she does too. But I can always count on a moment, sometimes once in a day, sometimes more, when I see her patting down the sheets on the bed, or watering the front window violets, and I am struck by the good fortune of my life.

Still, Anne says I don't feel things.

It comes up at dinner, outside in the yard, in airports as we wait

for planes. You don't let yourself feel, she tells me; and I tell her that I
think it's a crazy thing, all this talk about feeling. What do the African
Bushmen say? They say, Will we eat tomorrow? Will there be rain?

When I was sixteen, sitting in the back seat of a squad car, the policeman stopped in front of our house on Huron Avenue, turned around
against the headrest, and asked me if I was sure this was where I lived.
　　"Yes, sir," I said.
　　He spoke through a metal grate. "Your daddy owns this house?"
　　"Yes, sir."
　　"But for some reason you don't like windows."
　　He got out and opened my door, and we walked up the porch
steps. The swirling lights on the squad car were making crazy patterns
in the French panes of the living room bays. He knocked. "What's your
daddy do?"
　　I heard lights snapping on, my mother moving through the
house. "He's in business," I said. "But he won't be home now." The
policeman wrote something on his notepad. I saw my mother's eye
through the glass in the door, and then the locks were being unlatched,
one by one, from the top.

When Anne and I came to California to visit, we stayed at my mother's
for three days. On her refrigerator door was a calendar with men's
names marked on it—dinner dates, theater—and I knew this was done
for our benefit. My mother has been alone for fifteen years. She's still
thin, and her eyes still water, and I noticed that books were lying open
all through the house. Thick paperbacks—*Doctor Zhivago, The Thorn
Birds*—in the bathroom and the studio and the bedroom. We never
mentioned my father, but at the end of our stay, when we had packed
the car for our drive north along the coast, after she'd hugged us both
and we'd backed out of the driveway, she came down off the lawn into
the street, her arms crossed over her chest, leaned into the window, and
said, "You might say hello to your father for me."
　　We made the drive north on Highway 1. We passed mission
towns, fields of butter lettuce, long stretches of pumpkin farms south of
San Francisco. It was the first time we were going to see my father with
Lorraine. She was a hairdresser. He'd met her a few years after coming
north, and one of the first things they'd done together was take a trip
around the world. We got postcards from the Nile delta and Bangkok.
When I was young, my father had never taken us out of California.

His house in Sausalito was on a cliff above a finger of San Francisco Bay. A new Lincoln stood in the carport. In his bedroom was a teak-framed king-size waterbed, and on the walls were bits of African artwork—opium pipes, metal figurines. Lorraine looked the same age as Anne. One wall of the living room was glass, and after the first night's dinner, while we sat on the leather sofa watching tankers and yachts move under the Golden Gate Bridge, my father put down his scotch and water, touched his jaw, and said, "Lenny, call Dr. Farmer."

It was his second one. The first had been two years earlier, on the golf course in Monterey, where he'd had to kneel, then sit, then lie down on the fairway.

At dinner the night after I was arrested, my mother introduced her idea. "We're going to try something," she said. She had brought out a chicken casserole, and it was steaming in front of her. "That's what we're going to do. Max, are you listening? This next year, starting tonight, is going to be the year of getting to know us better." She stopped speaking and dished my father some chicken.

"What do you mean?" I asked.

"I mean it will be to a small extent a theme year. Nothing that's going to change every day of our lives, but in this next year I thought we'd all make an attempt to get to know each other better. Especially you, Leonard. Dad and I are going to make a better effort to know you."

"I'm not sure what you mean," said my father.

"All kinds of things, Max. We'll go to movies together, and Lenny can throw a party here at the house. And I personally would like to take a trip, all of us together, to the American Southwest."

"Sounds all right to me," I said.

"And Max," she said, "you can take Lenny with you to play golf. For example." She looked at my father.

"Neither of us would like it," he said.

"Lenny never sees you."

I looked out the window. The trees were turning, dropping their leaves onto the putting green. I didn't care what he said, one way or the other. My mother spooned a chicken thigh onto my plate and covered it with sauce. "All right," my father said. "He can caddie."

"And as preparation for our trip," my mother said, "can you take him on your Sunday rides?"

My father took off his glasses. "The Southwest," he said, wiping the lenses with a napkin, "is exactly like any other part of the country."

.   .   .

Anne had an affair once with a man she met on an assignment. He was young, much younger than either of us—in his late twenties, I would say from the one time I saw him. I saw them because one day on the road home I passed Anne's car in the lot of a Denny's restaurant. I parked around the block and went in to surprise her. I took a table at the back, but from my seat in the corner I didn't realize for several minutes that the youngish-looking woman leaning forward and whispering to the man with a beard was my wife.

I didn't get up and pull the man out with me into the parking lot, or even join them at the table, as I have since thought might have been a good idea. Instead I sat and watched them. I could see that under the table they were holding hands. His back was to me, and I noticed that it was broad, as mine is not. I remember thinking that she probably liked this broadness. Other than that, though, I didn't feel very much. I ordered another cup of coffee just to hear myself talk, but my voice wasn't quavering or fearful. When the waitress left, I took out a napkin and wrote on it, "You are a forty-year-old man with no children and your wife is having an affair." Then I put some money on the table and left the restaurant.

"I think we should see somebody," Anne said to me a few weeks later. It was a Sunday morning, and we were eating breakfast on the porch.

"About what?" I asked.

On a Sunday afternoon when I was sixteen I went out to the garage with a plan my mother had given me. That morning my father had washed the Lincoln. He had detergent-scrubbed the finish and then sun-dried it on Huron Avenue, so that in the workshop light of the garage its highlights shone. The windshield molding, the grille, the chrome side markers had been cloth-dried to erase water spots. The keys hung from their magnetic sling near the door to the kitchen. I took them out and opened the trunk. Then I hung them up again and sat on the rear quarter panel to consider what to do. It was almost four o'clock. The trunk of my father's car was large enough for a half-dozen suitcases and had been upholstered in a gray medium-pile carpet that was cut to hug the wheel wells and the spare-tire berth. In one corner, fastened down by straps, was his toolbox, and along the back lay the golf bag. In the shadows the yellow dingos of the club socks looked like baby chicks. He was going to come out in a few minutes. I reached in, took off four of the club socks, and made a pillow for my head. Then I stepped into the trunk. The shocks bounced once and stopped. I lay down with my head propped on the quarter panel and my feet resting in the taillight berth, and then I reached up, slammed down the trunk, and was in the dark.

This didn't frighten me. When I was very young, I liked to sleep with the shades drawn and the door closed so that no light entered my room. I used to hold my hand in front of my eyes and see if I could imagine its presence. It was too dark to see anything. I was blind then, lying in my bed, listening for every sound. I used to move my hand back and forth, close to my eyes, until I had the sensation that it was there but had in some way been amputated. I had heard of soldiers who had lost limbs but still felt them attached. Now I held my open hand before my eyes. It was dense black inside the trunk, colorless, without light.

When my father started the car, all the sounds were huge, magnified as if they were inside my own skull. The metal scratched, creaked, slammed when he got in; the bolt of the starter shook all the way through to the trunk; the idle rose and leveled; then the gears changed and the car lurched. I heard the garage door glide up. Then it curled into its housing, bumped once, began descending again. The seams of the trunk lid lightened in the sun. We were in the street now, heading downhill. I lay back and felt the road, listened to the gravel pocking in the wheel wells.

I followed our route in my mind. Left off Huron onto Telscher, where the car bottomed in the rain gulley as we turned, then up the hill to Santa Ana. As we waited for the light, the idle made its change, shifting down, so that below my head I heard the individual piston blasts in the exhaust pipe. Left on Santa Ana, counting the flat stretches where I felt my father tap the brakes, numbering the intersections as we headed west toward the ocean. I heard cars pull up next to us, accelerate, slow down, make turns. Bits of gravel echoed inside the quarter panels. I pulled off more club socks and enlarged my pillow. We slowed down, stopped, and then we accelerated, the soft piston explosions becoming a hiss as we turned onto the Pasadena freeway.

"Dad's rides," my mother had said to me the night before, as I lay in bed, "would be a good way for him to get to know you." It was the first week of the year of getting to know us better. She was sitting at my desk.

"But he won't let me go," I said.

"You're right." She moved some things around on a shelf. The room wasn't quite dark, and I could see the outline of her white blouse. "I talked to Mr. Goldman," she said.

"Mr. Goldman doesn't know me."

"He says you're angry." My mother stood up, and I watched her white blouse move to the window. She pulled back the shade until a triangle of light from the streetlamp fell on my sheets. "Are you angry?"

"I don't know," I said. "I don't think so."

"I don't think so either." She replaced the shade, came over and kissed me on the forehead, and then went out into the hall. In the dark I looked for my hand.

A few minutes later the door opened again. She put her head in. "If he won't let you come," she said, "sneak along."

On the freeway the thermal seams whizzed and popped in my ears. The ride had smoothed out now, as the shocks settled into the high speed, hardly dipping on curves, muffling everything as if we were under water. As far as I could tell, we were still driving west, toward the ocean. I sat halfway up and rested my back against the golf bag. I could see shapes now inside the trunk. When we slowed down and the blinker went on, I attempted bearings, but the sun was the same in all directions and the trunk lid was without shadow. We braked hard. I felt the car leave the freeway. We made turns. We went straight. Then more turns, and as we slowed down and I was stretching out, uncurling my body along the diagonal, we made a sharp right onto gravel and pulled over and stopped.

My father opened the door. The car dipped and rocked, shuddered. The engine clicked. Then the passenger door opened. I waited.

If I heard her voice today, twenty-six years later, I would recognize it.

"Angel," she said.

I heard the weight of their bodies sliding across the back seat, first hers, then his. They weren't three feet away. I curled up, crouched into the low space between the golf bag and the back of the passenger compartment. There were two firm points in the cushion where it was displaced. As I lay there, I went over the voice again in my head: it was nobody I knew. I heard a laugh from her, and then something low from him. I felt the shift of the trunk's false rear, and then, as I lay behind them, I heard the contact: the crinkle of clothing, arms wrapping, and the half-delicate, muscular sounds. It was like hearing a television in the next room. His voice once more, and then the rising of their breath, slow; a minute of this, maybe another; then shifting again, the friction of cloth on the leather seat and the car's soft rocking. "Dad," I whispered. Then rocking again; my father's sudden panting, harder and harder, his half-words. The car shook violently. "Dad," I whispered. I shouted, "Dad!"

The door opened.

His steps kicked up gravel. I heard jingling metal, the sound of the key in the trunk lock. He was standing over me in an explosion of light.

He said, "Put back the club socks."

I did and got out of the car to stand next to him. He rubbed his hands down the front of his shirt.

"What the hell," he said.

"I was in the trunk."

"I know," he said. "What the goddamn."

The year I graduated from college, I found a job teaching junior high school in Boston. The school was a cement building with small windows well up from the street, and dark classrooms in which I spent a lot of time maintaining discipline. In the middle of an afternoon that first winter a boy knocked on my door to tell me I had a phone call. I knew who it was going to be.

"Dad's gone," my mother said.

He'd taken his things in the Lincoln, she told me, and driven away that morning before dawn. On the kitchen table he'd left a note and some cash. "A lot of cash," my mother added, lowering her voice. "Twenty thousand dollars."

I imagined the sheaf of bills on our breakfast table, held down by the ceramic butter dish, the bank notes ruffling in the breeze from the louvered windows that opened onto his green. In the note he said he had gone north and would call her when he'd settled. It was December. I told my mother that I would visit in a week, when school was out for Christmas. I told her to go to her sister's and stay there, and then I said that I was working and had to get back to my class. She didn't say anything on the other end of the line, and in the silence I imagined my father crisscrossing the state of California, driving north, stopping in Palm Springs and Carmel, the Lincoln riding low with the weight.

"Leonard," my mother said, "did you know anything like this was happening?"

.   .   .

During the spring of the year of getting to know us better I caddied for him a few times. On Saturdays he played early in the morning, when the course was mostly empty and the grass was still wet from the night. I learned to fetch the higher irons as the sun rose over the back nine and the ball, on drying ground, rolled farther. He hit skybound approach shots with backspin, chips that bit into the green and stopped. He played in a foursome with three other men, and in the locker room, as they changed their shoes, they told jokes and poked one another in the belly. The lockers were shiny green metal, the floor clean white tiles that clicked under the shoe spikes. Beneath the mirrors were jars of combs in green disinfectant. When I combed my hair with them it stayed in place and smelled like limes.

We were on the course at dawn. At the first fairway the other men dug in their spikes, shifted their weight from leg to leg, dummy-swung at an empty tee while my father lit a cigarette and looked out over the hole. "The big gun," he said to me, or, if it was a par three, "The lady." He stepped on his cigarette. I wiped the head with the club sock before I handed it to him. When he took the club, he felt its balance point, rested it on one finger, and then, in slow motion, he gripped the shaft. Left hand first, then right, the fingers wrapping pinkie to index. Then he leaned down over the ball. On a perfect drive the tee flew straight up in the air and landed in front of his feet.

Over the weekend his heart lost its rhythm for a few seconds. It happened Saturday night, when Anne and I were at the house in Sausalito, and we didn't hear about it until Sunday. "Ventricular fibrillation," the intern said. "Circus movements." The condition was always a danger after a heart attack. He had been given a shock and his heartbeat had returned to normal.

"But I'll be honest with you," the intern said. We were in the hall. He looked down, touched his stethoscope. "It isn't a good sign."

The heart gets bigger as it dies, he told me. Soon it spreads across the x-ray. He brought me with him to a room and showed me strips of paper with the electric tracings: certain formations. The muscle was dying in patches, he said. He said things might get better, they might not.

My mother called that afternoon. "Should I come up?"

"He was a bastard to you," I said.

When Lorraine and Anne were eating dinner, I found the intern again. "I want to know," I said. "Tell me the truth." The intern was tall and thin, sick-looking himself. So were the other doctors I had seen around the place. Everything in that hospital was pale—the walls, the coats, the skin.

He said, "What truth?"

I told him that I'd been reading about heart disease. I'd read about EKGs, knew about the medicines—lidocaine, propranolol. I knew that the lungs filled up with water, that heart failure was death by drowning. I said, "The truth about my father."

The afternoon I had hidden in the trunk, we came home while my mother was cooking dinner. I walked up the path from the garage be-hind my father, watching the pearls of sweat on his neck. He was whis-tling a tune. At the door he kissed my mother's cheek. He touched the small of her back. She was cooking vegetables, and the steam had fogged up the kitchen windows and dampened her hair. My father sat down in the chair by the window and opened the newspaper. I thought of the way the trunk rear had shifted when he and the woman had moved into the back of the Lincoln. My mother was smiling.

"Well?" she said.

"What's for dinner?" I asked.

"Well?" she said again.

"It's chicken," I said. "Isn't it?"

"Max, aren't you going to tell me if anything unusual happened today?"

My father didn't look up from the newspaper. "Did anything unusual happen today?" he said. He turned the page, folded it back smartly. "Why don't you ask Lenny?"

She smiled at me.

"I surprised him," I said. Then I turned and looked out the window.

"I have something to tell you," Anne said to me one Sunday morning in the fifth year of our marriage. We were lying in bed. I knew what was coming.

"I already know," I said.

"What do you already know?"

"I know about your lover."

She didn't say anything.

"It's all right," I said.

It was winter. The sky was gray, and although the sun had risen only a few hours earlier, it seemed like late afternoon. I waited for Anne to say something more. We were silent for several minutes. Then she said, "I wanted to hurt you." She got out of bed and began straightening out the bureau. She pulled my sweaters from the drawer and refolded them. She returned all our shoes to the closet. Then she came back to the bed, sat down, and began to cry. Her back was toward me. It shook with her gasps, and I put my hand out and touched her. "It's all right," I said.

"We only saw each other a few times," she answered. "I'd take it back if I could. I'd make it never happen."

"I know you would."

"For some reason I thought I couldn't really hurt you."

She had stopped crying. I looked out the window at the tree branches hung low with snow. It didn't seem I had to say anything.

"I don't know why I thought I couldn't hurt you," she said. "Of course I can hurt you."

"I forgive you."

Her back was still toward me. Outside, a few snowflakes drifted up in the air.

"*Did* I hurt you?"

"Yes, you did. I saw you two in a restaurant."

"Where?"

"At Denny's."

"No," she said. "I mean, where did I hurt you?"

The night he died, Anne stayed awake with me in bed. "Tell me about him," she said.

"What about?"

"Stories. Tell me what it was like growing up, things you did together."

"We didn't do that much," I said. "I caddied for him. He taught me things about golf."

That night I never went to sleep. Lorraine was at a friend's apartment and we were alone in my father's empty house, but we pulled out the sheets anyway, and the two wool blankets, and we lay on the fold-out sofa in the den. I told stories about my father until I couldn't think of any more, and then I talked about my mother until Anne fell asleep.

In the middle of the night I got up and went into the living room. Through the glass I could see lights across the water, the bridges, Belvedere and San Francisco, ships. It was clear outside, and when I walked out to the cement carport the sky was lit with stars. The breeze moved inside my nightclothes. Next to the garage the Lincoln stood half-lit in the porch floodlight. I opened the door and got in. The seats were red leather and smelled of limes and cigarettes. I rolled down the window and took the key from the glove compartment. I thought of writing a note for Anne, but didn't. Instead I coasted down the driveway in neutral and didn't close the door or turn on the lights until the bottom of the hill, or start the engine until I had swung around the corner, so that the house was out of sight and the brine smell of the marina was coming through the open windows of the car. The pistons were almost silent.

I felt urgent, though I had no route in mind. I ran one stop sign, then one red light, and when I reached the ramp onto Highway 101, I squeezed the accelerator and felt the surge of the fuel-injected, computer-sparked V–8. The dash lights glowed. I drove south and crossed over the Golden Gate Bridge at seventy miles an hour, its suspension cables swaying in the wind and the span rocking slowly, ocean to bay. The lanes were narrow. Reflectors zinged when the wheels strayed. If Anne woke, she might come out to the living room and then check for me outside. A light rain began to fall. Drops wet my knees, splattered my cheek. I kept the window open and turned on the radio; the car filled up with wind and music. Brass sounds. Trumpets. Sounds that filled my heart.

The Lincoln drove like a dream. South of San Francisco the road opened up, and in the gulley of a shallow hill I took it up over a hundred. The arrow nosed rightward in the dash. Shapes flattened out. "Dad," I said. The wind sounds changed pitch. I said, "The year of getting to know us." Signposts and power poles were flying by. Only a few cars were on the road, and most moved over before I arrived. In the mirror I could see the faces as I passed. I went through San Mateo, Pacifica, Redwood City, until, underneath a concrete overpass, the radio began pulling in static and I realized that I might die at this speed. I slowed down. At seventy drizzle wandered in the windows again. At fifty-five the scenery stopped moving. In Menlo Park I got off the freeway.

It was dark still, and off the interstate I found myself on a road without streetlights. It entered the center of town and then left again, curving up into shallow hills. The houses were large on either side. They were spaced far apart, three and four stories tall, with white shutters or ornament work that shone in the perimeter of the Lincoln's headlamps. The yards were large, dotted with eucalyptus and laurel. Here and there a light was on. Sometimes I saw faces: someone on an upstairs balcony; a man inside the breakfast room, awake at this hour, peering through the glass to see what car could be passing. I drove slowly, and when I came to a high school with its low buildings and long athletic field I pulled over and stopped.

The drizzle had become mist. I left the headlights on and got out and stood on the grass. I thought, This is the night your father has passed. I looked up at the lightening sky. I said it, "This is the night your father has passed," but I didn't feel what I thought I would. Just the wind on my throat, the chill of the morning. A pickup drove by and flashed its lights at me on the lawn. Then I went to the trunk of the Lincoln, because this was what my father would have done, and I got out the golf bag. It was heavier than I remembered, and the leather was stiff in the cool air. On the damp sod I set up: dimpled white ball, yellow tee. My father would have swung, would have hit drives the length of the football field, high irons that disappeared into the gray sky, but as I stood there I didn't even take the clubs out of the bag. Instead I imagined his stance. I pictured the even weight, the deliberate grip, and after I had stood there for a few moments, I picked up the ball and tee, replaced them in the bag, and drove home to my wife.

The year I was sixteen we never made it to the American Southwest. My mother bought maps anyway, and planned our trip, talking to me about it at night in the dark, taking us in her mind across the Colorado River at the California border, where the water was opal green, into Arizona and along the stretch of desert highway to New Mexico. There, she said, the canyons were a mile deep. The road was lined with sagebrush and a type of cactus, jumping cholla, that launched its spines. Above the desert, where a man could die of dehydration in an afternoon and a morning, the peaks of the Rocky Mountains turned blue with sun and ice.

We didn't ever go. Every weekend my father played golf, and at last, in August, my parents agreed to a compromise. One Sunday morning, before I started the eleventh grade, we drove north in the Lincoln to a state park along the ocean. Above the shore the cliffs were planted with ice plant to resist erosion. Pelicans soared in the thermal currents. My mother had made chicken sandwiches, which we ate on the beach, and after lunch, while I looked at the crabs and swaying fronds in the tide pools, my parents walked to the base of the cliffs. I watched their progress on the shallow dunes. Once when I looked, my father was holding her in his arms and they were kissing.

She bent backward in his hands. I looked into the tide pool where, on the surface, the blue sky, the clouds, the reddish cliffs were shining. Below them rock crabs scurried between submerged stones. The afternoon my father found me in the trunk, he introduced me to the woman in the back seat. Her name was Christine. She smelled of perfume. The gravel drive where we had parked was behind a warehouse, and after we shook hands through the open window of the car, she got out and went inside. It was low and long, and the metal door slammed behind her. On the drive home, wind blowing all around us in the car, my father and I didn't say much. I watched his hands on the steering wheel. They were big and red-knuckled, the hands of a butcher or a carpenter, and I tried to imagine them on the bend of Christine's back.

Later that afternoon on the beach, while my mother walked along the shore, my father and I climbed a steep trail up the cliffs. From above, where we stood in the carpet of ice plant, we could see the hue of the Pacific change to a more translucent blue—the drop-off and the outline of the shoal where the breakers rose. I tried to see what my father was seeing as he gazed out over the water. He picked up a rock and tossed it over the cliff. "You know," he said without looking at me, "you could be all right on the course." We approached the edge of the palisade, where the ice plant thinned into eroded cuts of sand. "Listen," he said. "We're here on this trip so we can get to know each other a little bit." A hundred yards below us waves broke on the rocks. He lowered his voice. "But I'm not sure about that. Anyway, you don't *have* to get to know me. You know why?"

"Why?" I asked.

"You don't have to get to know me," he said, "because one day you're going to grow up and then you're going to *be* me." He looked at me and then out over the water. "So what I'm going to do is teach you how to hit." He picked up a long stick and put it in my hand. Then he showed me the backswing. "You've got to know one thing to drive a golf ball," he told me, "and that's that the club is part of you." He stood behind me and showed me how to keep the left arm still. "The club is your hand," he said. "It's your bone. It's your whole arm and your skeleton and your heart." Below us on the beach I could see my mother walking the waterline. We took cut after cut, and he taught me to visualize the impact, to sense it. He told me to whittle down the point of energy so that the ball would fly. When I swung he held my head in position. "Don't just watch," he said. *"See."* I looked. The ice plant was watery-looking and fat, and at the edge of my vision I could see the tips of my father's shoes. I was sixteen years old and waiting for the next thing he would tell me.

COMING TO

Nance Van Winckel

After Donna passed out on the floor of the church in her wedding gown, and after a groomsman brought a metal folding chair and helped her mother prop her up on it, everyone just went on with the ceremony. They barely missed a beat. They only had the church for an hour.

Donna never knew what hit her. Her head bent sideways, a few of her meticulously pinned curls had come undone and trailed down her cheek. She looked like a bride doll thrown carelessly on a closet shelf. Her mother stood at her side, fanning her with an old church bulletin. Then, while the minister went on with his spiel, Donna's mother supplied her daughter's missing lines. "She does." "She will."

I never took Donna for the type who'd go weak in the knees. A couple of years ago, when we were seniors in high school, we'd been doubles partners on the tennis team, and we were almost unbeatable, though ours was a small team in a small town. And even as kids then, which already seems a long time ago, we'd seen a few things. We weren't strangers to sadness. So I was, frankly, surprised to see her fold under pressure. Of course when I learned later that she had been almost five months pregnant and had cinched herself up in two pairs of control top panty hose, her fainting made more sense.

Each time I came back to town I felt the past more keenly as the *past*—a thing with clear perimeters, more strictly enclosed and defined. Driving by the tennis courts, I'd stopped suddenly, stepped out of the car, and stood looking across the grassy field behind the courts to where Vern's place used to stand. Donna and I had played several victorious matches on those courts, and we'd known the exact location of every crack, every leaf stain.

But getting to the courts—mornings and afternoons—we had to walk by Vern's place. Since there was not an iota of space left for him in his house, he'd taken to sleeping in the trunk of his car. A dingy khaki army blanket around his shoulders, he'd sit up and stare at us as we walked by. "Whatever," Donna'd say. "That car's going nowhere."

We weren't the kind to taunt him, to call him Wild Billy No-Brains or Rat Face, but we watched for him. If he wasn't in the trunk, we looked in every direction around his house, which was stacked to the ceiling with towers of junk. We could see it through the house's windows: the yellowed newspapers and magazines, cans of coffee grounds, pillars of empty cereal boxes.

I was thinking then, but could not say yet, about where people's fear came from—the fear that provoked them to make up the names; and the fear that would eventually prompt Manmouth County Services to step in and cart Vern off to a clean institutional bed. Later they'd raze his house, sending the rats scurrying through the smoke. The fear came from a deep down place, but a locked place, a place no one wanted to have opened, not ever, to the light of day.

I hadn't talked with Donna much at her wedding shower. I wasn't sure what to think about all her quickly made decisions. She was going to marry Mike and live with him in the basement of her parents' place, a huge dairy farm out on Highway Y. I doubt even her closest friends knew then about the baby on the way. The party was at Coleen's house, Coleen who was just married herself, as were so many our age, and like the others, Coleen seemed to need to promote marriage. It was, after all, a main, if not the main, undertaking of their lives so far.

The shower included the sale of lingerie, somewhat on the same principle as Tupperware; only, as Coleen cautioned us, we couldn't try things on. We had to, she said, "simply imagine" ourselves in the skimpy outfits, which came in small pastel-colored boxes with matching tissue paper. Donna, as co-hostess and guest of honor, opened the boxes and held up each tiny costume as if it were the dried husk of an insect. The girls hooted and giggled. I remember it had hit me then that I wasn't even wearing a bra. I was in college, newly liberated, and I scoffed at the lingerie, which had names like Lilac Lust and Pandora's Passion. I turned away. I smoked a cigarette alone in the kitchen.

Then we gave Donna our real presents—cookbooks, casserole dishes, a flannel nightie, a set of towels. Coleen saved the bows and made them into a bouquet, and I kept the list of givers and their gifts. It was all organized. Donna smiled over each item as she lifted it from its box. In the big armchair, with the presents piling up around her, she seemed to shrink further and further into herself and away from us, past all the corny jokes.

We used to take the long way to school, a back way down gravel roads. This gave us time to trade earrings, share a smoke, and gossip about our tennis opponents, though I suppose what we were really doing was taking our time, lingering in the quiet of a long slow wakefulness, not the sudden jolt of streets crowded with teenagers. Not a parking lot full of loud cars and catcalls. By letting the day seep gradually through our bodies, we were warmed by slow degrees.

In the spring the grass was high and damp, and it brushed our ankles as we walked. Occasionally during our practices we'd look out across the tennis courts over an expanse of neat grass and a few trees that were school property and beyond to Vern's place: the weeds and scrub oak, the cracked windows of the small house, and the chaos of trash and litter everywhere in the yard—bottles of all sizes and colors, car parts, filthy bathtubs and sinks, old carpets, miscellaneous shirts and coats nailed to trees like the ghosts of former selves. This was how our lives came to have their brief and slight intersection with Vern's. We'd pass by his place and see weeds and sometimes a flower growing heartily from one of Vern's castoff rubber workboots.

It was odd how after we'd walked a few times down the gravel road past his place, everything about it began to seem ordinary. Even the smell, which on a warm spring day was quite musty—a slight tinge of camphor and a hint of some strong vegetable, beets perhaps? But it was a smell we expected to be always recognizable among the smells of the world, though we would never smell it again, except in dreams.

Donna was slower than I was to come fully awake in the mornings. At first as we walked to school, she watched my face as I talked. After a couple of blocks she'd get around to muttering a few monosyllabic responses to my questions. Then one sentence, then two. Her eyes would brighten. Finally her deep laughter floated up. She had a new boyfriend, Mike, who kept her out late and brought on lectures from her mother. Donna had questions about sex and boys' bodies I couldn't answer, though I tried. Was it really painful, as Mike claimed, for a boy to go on and on unfulfilled? And why? We made up explanations that sounded plausible. The blood pumping too fast, too hard, too long.

When we'd pass Vern's and see him rise from the trunk of his car and throw off his blanket, we knew our laughter had roused him. We'd walk by quietly. Vern would sit up stiffly and blink in the harsh early light like someone resurrected, brought back against his wishes to his litter-strewn life.

The Donna I'd seen that day at her wedding shower wasn't at all like the Donna I'd known in school—back in those days when we'd put our long hair high over our ears in two ponytails that whirled wildly when we swung our rackets. Seeing her there among the presents, so shy among the jokesters, reminded me of another side of her I had known too but had almost forgotten. It was the year before we'd become tennis partners and friends. She'd been sick and home from school for a week, and I'd volunteered to stop by her house with a few books and homework assignments. There were usually chickens in her front yard, and I'd often driven slowly by their place to watch them. The chickens were beautiful—so brightly colored against Donna's old white clapboard house. And how did they know not to run into the road? They roamed the yard, pecking at what seemed like nothing in the sparse grass.

It was a cold, snowy afternoon and already growing dark when I arrived at Donna's. On her front porch was an old floral print couch, soggy and visibly lumpy. Not a chicken in sight. After I'd knocked on the front door and stood waiting a moment, Donna's mother peered at me though the living room curtains. "Go around back," she mouthed to me through the glass. I followed the gravel drive, and as I passed the garage, I heard the chickens clucking and cooing inside.

Donna's mother opened the back door and I stepped into a laundry room, maneuvering along a narrow path between big winter coats and boots piled on the floor. Her mother explained how they kept the living room closed off in the winter. The government, she said, was in cahoots with the gas company to drive up the cost of heat. Then Donna appeared at the kitchen door in her pink robe and slippers. A red bandana around her head.

Not taking off my coat, I started to tell her the assignments right there in the laundry room. I hadn't ever really talked to her much before that day.

"You girls come and sit here at the kitchen table," Donna's mother said. "I've got some cider all heated up."

For a moment Donna didn't move. She just stood in the doorway as if waiting for some sign from me. I took off my coat, laid it on top of a huge stack of coats, and stepped into the warm kitchen.

That's when I saw the baby crib, right there in the kitchen, though I didn't see at first the kind of baby inside. We drank our cider and turned pages in our algebra books. Her mother moved on to another room, humming. Then the baby turned in its crib, and the crib shook violently. I looked over and saw his two feet, way too big to be a baby's, pressed up against the slats at the end.

"That's my brother," Donna said. I was still staring at his feet. "He's got spina bifada. He likes to stay in here where it's nice and toasty." Then she asked me about a certain equation, did I get how it worked, and what in the world it was for. I tried to explain it plainly, the difficult theory I'd just learned about that day.

Not until I stood up to leave did I see, at the other end of the boy's five- or six-year-old body, his tiny infant's head, his eyes staring up blankly, registering nothing. It had been completely dark when I left, and I remember how, when I'd stepped outside, I'd felt my eyes moisten, which may or may not have been from the sudden blast of cold air.

The days we didn't have tennis matches, we practiced for matches. We didn't suspect then that those were our last days of joyful greetings in the hallways, the last times we'd be so happily recognized by our peers, our names spoken in that easy casual way we'd surely never hear again.

It was on one of those days as we fussed over our serves—getting the ball to touch down in a spot we'd chalked on the court and then fly off close to the ground—that we saw the bulldozer appear on the gravel road and slowly grind its way toward Vern's. He was nowhere in sight.

As the dozer went about its business, we went about ours. As the house fell, wall by wall, to ruin, we'd pause to say the score, and as we did, we'd catch sight of the strange contents of Vern's life being scraped into a huge scoop and dumped into a dump truck.

Donna was way out ahead. I looked up to see one of her famous lobs coming at me and saw rats at the same time. I shrieked and lost hold of my racket. The rats were swarming around the maze of towering magazines and egg cartons. The four walls of the house were already down, and the insides laid bare like relics from the tomb of an insane monarch.

We stood at the green metal fence and watched the rats running—wild, lost, as if insane themselves. They were the size of cats. And for a moment we thought we heard them, a high-pitched squealing that somehow reached us even over the low drone of the dozers. "Is that *them?*" Donna asked, giving me a quick look. We could barely tear our eyes from the scene. "I didn't know rats even made noise," she said.

Later we'd laugh off how we'd lost the final match of the division tournament. We'd forgive ourselves and each other, though the latter took a little time. The forgiveness had happened one day as we stood in the hallway talking to a girl who worked afternoons as a nurse's aide. She'd helped with Vern when they'd brought him to the hospital. She told us they'd had to scrape the dirt off him with a metal kitchen spatula. She told us about the unbelievable length of his toenails and fingernails, and she told us the names of the bugs they'd found in his hair. We stood huddled by the girl's locker and listened. Then I'd grabbed Donna's arm, and she'd squeezed my hand. We'd been okay after that.

Of the final game itself, I only remember a few things—how I felt a little slow, just a step too late to reach my mark, and only missing by an inch or two the spot at which I'd aimed my last few serves, as if someone had moved my X. At one point, as Donna and I were running to make a return—at the same time reversing our positions at the net—we collided. I landed hard on the ground on my butt. The ball went soaring over both our heads. Our game just went downhill after that.

Watching Donna come to in the church now, her eyes swimming back to focus on the faces of her new husband and her old father, who, together, carry her out into the warm sunshine, I'm filled with relief. I see Donna's face brighten as the blood comes back. And though I hear her low laugh, I'm still at the place in my memory where I remember how our two bodies had collided that day on the courts. Donna had jumped up quickly, regained her balance, and gone back to her place to resume her serve. But I had sat there, still reeling from the collision, my mind gone dark. I didn't know who or what we were. I didn't know what game it was. I knew no one. I was nowhere.

THE RETURN OF SERVICE

Jonathan Baumbach

I am in a tennis match against my father. He is also the umpire and comes to my side of the court to advise me of the rules. "You have only one serve," he says. "My advice is not to miss." I thank him—we have always been a polite family—and wait for his return to the opposing side. Waiting for him to take his place in the sun, I grow to resent the limitation imposed on my game. (Why should he have two serves, twice as many chances, more margin for error?) I bounce the ball, waiting for him—he takes his sweet time, always has—and plan to strike my first service deep to his forehand. And what if I miss, what if ambition overreaches skill? The ordinary decencies of a second chance have been denied me.

"Play is in," says the umpire.

The irreversibility of error gives me pause. It may be the height of folly to attempt the corner of his service box—my shoulder a bit stiff from the delay—and risk losing the point without a contest. The moral imperative in a challenge match is to keep the ball in play. If I aim the service for the optical center of his box, margin for error will move it right or left, shallow or deep, some small or remarkable distance from its failed intention. Easily enough done. Yet there is a crowd watching and an unimaginative, riskless service will lower their regard for me. My opponent's contempt, as the night the day, would follow.

I can feel the restiveness of the crowd. The umpire holds his pocket watch to his ear. "Play is in," he says again. "Play is in, but alas it is not in."

It is my father, the umpire, a man with a long-standing commitment to paradox.

Paradox will only take a man so far. How can my father be in the judge's chair and on the other side of the net at the same time? One of the men resembling my father is an imposter. Imposture is an old game with him. No matter the role he takes, he has the trick of showing the same face.

I rush my first serve and fault, a victim of disorientation, the ball landing two, perhaps three inches deep. I plan to take a second serve as a form of protest—a near miss rates a second chance in my view—and ready myself for the toss.

The umpire blows his whistle. "Over and done," he says. "Next point."

This one seems much too laconic to be my father, a man who tends to carry his case beyond a listener's capacity to suffer his words. (Sometimes it is hard to recognize people outside the context in which you generally experience them.) I indicate confusion, a failed sense of direction, showing my irony to the few sophisticates in the audience, disguising it from the rest.

My latest intuition is that neither man is my father, but that both, either by circumstance or design, are stand-ins for him, conventional surrogates.

I protest to the umpire the injustice of only being allowed a single service.

"I'm sorry life isn't fair," he says.

I can tell he isn't sorry, or if he is, it is no great burden of sorrow.

The toss is a measure low and somewhat behind me. Concentrated to a fine degree, I slice the ball into the backhand corner of my father's box. The old man, coming out of his characteristic crouch, slides gracefully to his left and though the ball is by him, he somehow manages to get it back. A short lob, which I put away, smashing the overhead at an acute angle, leaving no possibility of accidental return.

A gratifying shot. I replay it in the imagination. The ball in the air, a lovely arc. The player, myself, stepping back to let it bounce, then racket back, waiting for the ball to rise again, uncharacteristically patient, feeling it lift off the ground, swelling, rising, feeling myself rise with the ball. My racket, that extension of myself, meets the ball at its penultimate height as if they had arranged in advance to meet at that moment and place, the racket delivering the message, the ball the message itself. I am the agent of their coming together, the orchestrator of their perfect conjunction.

I didn't want to leave that point to play another, hated to go on to what, at its best, would be something less. I offered to play the point again. There was some conversation about my request, a huddle of heads at the umpire's chair. The crowd, in traditional confusion, applauded.

The decision was to go on. My father advised, and I appreciated his belated concern, against living in the past.

What a strange man! I wondered if he thought the same about me, and if he did—strange men hold strange opinions—was there basis in fact for his view of my strangeness?

We were positioned to play the third point of the first game. It was getting dark and I expected that time would be called after this exchange or after the next. If I won the first of what I had reason to believe would be the last two points, I was assured of at least a draw. Not losing had always been my main objective. Winning was merely a more affirmative statement of the same principle. I took refuge in strategy, thought to tame the old man at his own game. (I kept forgetting that it wasn't really him, only somebody curiously like him.)

I took a practice toss which drew a reprimand from the umpire's chair. I said I was sorry, mumbled my excuses. It's not something, the toss of a ball, you have any hope of undoing when done. "This is for real," I said.

My credibility was not what it had been. I could feel the murmurs of disbelief whistling through the stands, an ill wind.

"Let's get the road on the show," said the umpire.

My service, impelled by anger, came in at him, the ball springing at his heart, requiring a strategic retreat.

I underestimated his capacity for survival. His return, surprising in itself, was forceful and deep, moving me to the backhand corner, against my intention to play there, with disadvantageous haste. "Good shot," I wanted to say to him, though there wasn't time for that.

There's hardly ever time, I thought, to do the graceful thing. I was busy in pursuit of the ball (my failure perhaps was compliment enough), staving off defeat. Even if I managed the ball's return, and I would not have run this far without that intention, the stroke would not have enough arm behind it to matter. It would merely ask my opponent for an unforced error, a giving up of self-interest.

There were good reasons, then, not to make the exceptional effort necessary to put the ball in my father's court, and if I were a less stubborn man (or a more sensible one), I would not have driven myself in hopeless pursuit. My return was effected by a scooplike shot off the backhand, an improvised maneuver under crisis conditions. Wherever the ball would go, I had done the best I could.

My father tapped the ball into the open court for the point. His gentleness and restraint were a lesson to us all.

I was more dangerous—my experience about myself—coming from behind. Large advantages had always seemed to me intolerable burdens.

The strain of being frontrunner was beginning to tell on my father. His hair had turned white between points, was turning whiter by the moment, thinning and whitening. I perceived this erratic acceleration in the aging process as another one of his strategies. He was a past master in evoking guilt in an adversary.

The umpire was clearing his throat, a means of attracting attention to himself. "Defecate or desist from the pot," he said, winking at the crowd.

Such admonishments were intolerable. He had never let me do anything at my own time and pace. As if in speeded-up motion, I smashed the ball past my opponent—he seemed to be looking the wrong way—for the first service ace of the match.

There was no call from the umpire, the man humming to himself some private tune. We looked at each other a moment without verbal communication, a nod of understanding sufficient. I was readying the toss for the next serve when he called me back. "Let's see that again," he said.

Why again?

"Didn't see it. P'raps should. However didn't. 'Pologize." He wiped some dampness from the corner of his eye with a finger. I could see that he was trying to be fair, trying against predilection to control all events in his path, to perceive history as if it were the prophecy of his will.

I said I would play the point over, though under protest and with perceptible displeasure.

"I will not have this match made into a political spectacle," the umpire said. He gestured me back to the deuce court, world weary and disapproving, patient beyond human forbearance.

I would only accept the point, I said, if it were awarded to me in the proper spirit. I had already agreed to play it again and would not retract that agreement.

The umpire, my father, crossed his arms in front of him, an implacable figure. "Are we here to argue or play tennis?" he asked no one in particular.

I started to protest, then said, "Oh forget it," and returned to the court he had gestured me to, embarrassed at getting my way. I was about to toss the ball for the serve when I noticed that my opponent was sitting cross-legged just inside his own service box.

I asked the umpire if time had been called and he said, "Time calls though is almost never called to account," which made little sense in my present mood. My father, I remembered, tended to treat words as if they were playthings.

"Are you ready?" I shouted across the net. "I'm going to serve."

My opponent cocked his head as if trying to make out where the voice was coming from.

"I'm going to count to five," I said, "and then put the ball into play. One . . ."

There was no point in counting—the old man had no intention of rousing himself—though I was of the mind that one ought to complete what one started. I wasn't going to be the one to break a promise.

I finished counting in a businesslike way and served the ball.

"Indeed," said my father as it skittered off his shoe. The point was credited to my account.

My father stood in the center of the court, arms out, eyes toward the heavens, asking God what he had done to deserve ingratitude.

I would not let him shame me this time, not give him that false advantage.

The umpire coughed while my father got himself ready, dusting off the seat of his shorts, combing his hair.

I hit the next serve into the net cord, the ball catapulting back at me. I caught it with a leap, attracting the crowd's applause.

"Deuce," said the umpire with his characteristic ambiguity.

I had lost count, thought I was either ahead or behind, felt nostalgic for an earlier time when issues tended to have decisive resolutions.

I suspected the umpire not of bias, not so much that, no more than anyone's, but of attempting to prolong the match beyond its natural consequence.

The umpire spoke briefly, and not without eloquence, on the need to set our houses in order. "Sometimes wounds have to be healed in the process." He spoke as if the healing of wounds was at best a necessary evil.

My opponent said the present dispute was a family matter and would be decided at home if his prodigal son returned to the fold.

What prodigal son? I was too old, too grown up, to live with my parents. I had in fact a family of my own somewhere which, in the hurly-burly of getting on, I had somehow misplaced. "Why not stop play at this point," I said, "and continue the match at a later date under more convivial circumstances. Or . . ."

"What alternative, sir, are you proposing?" said my father from the umpire's chair, a hint of derision in the query.

I had planned to say that I would accept a draw, though thought it best to let the suggestion emerge elsewhere.

"I will not be the first one to cry *enough,*" said my father. "Don't look to me for concessions. On the other hand . . ."

The umpire interrupted him. "The match will continue until one of the contestants demonstrates a clear superiority." His message was announced over the loud speaker and drew polite applause from the gallery.

My plan was to alternate winning and losing points. There was nothing to be gained, I thought, in beating him decisively and no need to take the burden of a loss on myself.

If I won the deuce point, I could afford to give away the advantage. I could afford to give it away so long as I created the illusion that it was being taken from me.

"Can't win for losing," I quipped after the second deuce.

"Deuces are wild," I said after the fourth tie.

These remarks seemed to anger my adversary. He spat into the wind, sending some of it my way, swore to teach me a lesson in manners.

When he lost the next point after an extended rally he flung his racket and threw himself to the ground, lamenting his limitations and the blind malignity of chance.

I turned my back, embarrassed for him, kicked a few balls to show that I was not without passion myself.

I had served the last ad point into the net and assumed a repetition of that tactic would invite inordinate suspicion among an ordinarily wary and overbred audience. My inclination was to hit the serve wide to the backhand, an expression of overreaching ambition, beyond reproach.

A poor toss—the ball thrown too close—defeated immediate intention. I swung inside out (as they say in baseball when a batter hits an inside pitch to the opposite field), a desperation stroke whose only design was to go through the motions of design. (Perhaps this is rationalization after the fact. The deed of course manifests the intention.) The ball, which had no business clearing the net, found the shallow corner of his box, ticking the line. As if anticipating my accidental shot, he came up quickly. He seemed to have a way of knowing what I was going to do—perhaps it was in the blood—even before I knew myself. He was coming up, his thin knotted legs pushing against the artificial surface as he drove himself forward. There was a small chance that he might reach the ball on its first bounce, the smallest of chances.

His moment arrived and was gone.

My father swung majestically and connected with space, with platonic delusion, the ball moving in its own cycle, disconnected from his intention.

Game and match to the challenger. My father came to the net on the run as is the fashion, hand outstretched. We never did get to shake hands, our arms passing like ships in the night. "I was lucky," I said. "That serve had no business going where it did."

He looked through me, said in the iciest of voices, "I'm grateful for your lesson," and walked off.

Murmurs went through the gallery, an ominous buzzing sound. I asked one of the linesmen, a sleepy old man with thick glasses, what the murmurs signified.

"Well, sir," he wheezed, "this may be out of line, my saying this, but there's some feeling among the old heads that your final service was not in the best traditions of fair play."

I was perfectly willing to concede the point, I said, an unintentional ambiguity. "Why don't we call the match a stalemate."

The old linesman said that it was not within his authority to grant such dispensation. He suggested that I talk directly to my father.

"If I could talk directly to my father, if either of us could talk to the other, we would never have gotten into this match." (That wasn't wholly true. Sometimes you said things because they had a pleasant turn to them.)

"Sir," said the linesman, "a broken heart is not easily repaired."

I walk up and down the now deserted corridors of the stadium, looking for the old man. He is, as always, deceptively difficult to find.

Someone comes up to me in the dark and asks if I'd be interested in a match against an aggressive and skillful opponent.

I say that I am looking for my father, perhaps another time.

"Hold on," he says, holding me by the shoulder. "What's this father of yours look like? An old dude passed here maybe ten minutes ago, tears running down his ancient face."

"The old man was crying?"

"Crying! Jesus, the falls of Niagara were nothing to those tears. I mean, it was not a good scene."

I try to get by, but my companion, a younger man with a viselike grip, holds fast. "Excuse me," I say.

"After we play, we'll talk," says my companion. "I want to show you my new serve."

I am in no mood to look at serves and say so in a kind way, not wanting to hurt his feelings or not wanting to hurt them to excess.

"I may be your last chance, pal," the kid says in his brash way. "To count on chances beyond the second is to live a life of unreproved illusion."

His remark, like most nonsense, has a ring of truth.

I return to the playing area alongside my insinuating companion. We take our places on opposing sides of center court, though I have not at any time, by word or sign, agreed to play him.

My father, or someone like him, is again in the umpire's chair and announces, after a few preliminary hits, that the match is begun.

It is the moment I've been waiting for. "I have not agreed to play this young man a match," I say. "This is not a contest for which I feel the slightest necessity."

My refusal to play either comes too late or goes unheard. My opponent has already tossed the ball for his service, a brilliant toss rising

like a sun to the highest point of his extension. The meeting of racket
and ball resounds through the stadium like the crash of cymbals.

The ball is arriving. Before I can ready myself, before I can coordinate arm and racket, before I can coordinate mind and arm, the ball
will be here and gone, a dream object, receding into the distance like a
ghost of the imagination. The first point is lost. And so the game. And
so the match. Waiting for the ball's arrival—it is on the way, it has not
yet reached me—I concede nothing.

RUNNING BLIND

Thomas Fox Averill

"Why do you do it?" he asks. I talk of feeling trim, breathing deep, of burned calories, heart rate, endorphins, of T-shirts—a lifetime supply after five years of organized runs. I talk of sky, sun, wind, earth, asphalt, concrete. "Will you take me sometime?" he asks. My friend is blind.

Week one, one mile: asphalt high-school track. His legs are longer than mine. We stutter, finding our stride, his hand at my elbow. I describe the curves, teach him to lean. By the back stretch he is winded. I close my eyes. "What's wrong?" he asks, but I say, "Nothing, you're just tired."

Week eight, three miles: asphalt park roads. We run faster now. I describe trees, the elegant rose garden, the zoo, the amphitheatre, the incredible blue of early summer sky, clouds billowing like runner's breath. Eyes on the road, I anticipate gradual rises and falls, corners, patches of loose gravel, dead limbs. "Just another half-mile," I say when his breath shortens and his hand loses my elbow for a second. He grunts:

"Tell me in time. Time means more than distance." I say, "Okay, four minutes or so to go."

Week twelve, five miles: country roads. His hand pushes my elbow, begging for speed. We climb hills as steeply pitched as ladders. I call out the views, lush green, hazy with humidity. Downhills we run so fast I'm afraid for him. "Let go," he says, "just let yourself move. Don't talk, I know where I am now." I breathe hard. We run faster than I ever have before.

Week fifteen, 10k: downtown, intricate concrete course. "How fast?" I ask as we wait for the gun. He stretches his long, sinewy legs, says, "As fast as you can." He is calm, confident. I weave us through the congestion of bodies. We race. With two-tenths left he leans against me, asks, "Straightaway?" and I gasp, "Yes," and he passes me, sprinting. Someone stops him at the finish.

From then on: he runs with faster companions. He tells me: "Want to improve? Running's inside you. Don't watch what's around you, pay attention to what's inside." He's right, but free again, I slow down, enjoy the view.

IV

*One
on
One*

PALAIS DE JUSTICE

Mark Helprin

In a lesser chamber of Suffolk County Courthouse on a day in early August, 1965—the hottest day of the year—a Boston judge slammed down his heavy gavel, and its pistol-like report threw the room into disarray. Within a few minutes, everyone had gone—judge, court reporters, blue-shirted police, and a Portuguese family dressed as if for a wedding to witness the trial of their son. The door was shut. Wood and marble remained at attention in dead silence. For quite a while the room must have been doing whatever rooms do when they are completely empty. Perhaps air currents were stabilizing, coming to a halt, or spiders were beginning to crawl about, up high in the woodwork. The silence was beginning to set when the door opened and the defense attorney re-entered to retrieve some papers. He went to his seat, sat down, and ran his hands over the smooth tabletop—no papers. He glanced at the chairs, and then bent to see under the table—no papers. He touched his nose and looked perplexed. "I know I left them here," he said to the empty courtroom. "I thought I left them here. Memory must be going, oh well."

But his memory was excellent, as it had always been. He enjoyed pretending that in his early sixties he was losing his faculties, and he delighted in the puzzlement of where the papers had gone. The first was an opportunity for graceful abstention and serene neutrality, the second a problem designed to fill a former prosecutor's mind as he made his way out of the courthouse, passing through a great hall arched like a cathedral and mitered by hot white shafts of grainy light.

Years before, when he had had his first trial, one could not see the vault of the roof. It was too high and dark. But then they had put up a string of opaque lighting globes, which clung to the paneled arches like risen balloons and lit the curving ceiling.

One day a clerk had been playing a radio so loudly that it echoed through the building. The Mayor of Boston appeared unexpectedly and stood in the middle of the marble floor, emptiness and air rising hundreds of feet above him. "Turn that radio off!" he screamed, but the clerk could not hear him. Alone on the floor with a silent crowd staring from the perimeter, the Mayor turned angrily and scanned halls and galleries trying to find direction for his rage, but could not tell from where the sound came and so pivoted on the smooth stone and filled the chamber with his voice. "I am your mayor. Turn it off, do you hear me, damn you to hell. I am your mayor!" The radio was silenced and all that could be heard was the echo of the Mayor's voice. The defense attorney had looked up as if to see its last remnants rising through rafters of daylight, and had seen several birds, flushed from hidden nesting places, coursing to and fro near the ceiling, threading through the light rays. No one but the defense attorney saw them or the clerk, a homely, frightened woman who, when the Mayor had long gone, came out and carefully peered over a balcony to see where he had stood. It was then that the defense attorney saw the intricate motif of the roof—past the homely woman, the birds, and the light.

Now he went from chamber to chamber, and hall to hall, progressing through layers of rising temperature until he stood on the street in a daze. It was so hot that people moved as if in a baking desert, their expressions as blank and beaten as a Tuareg's mask and impassive eyes. The stonework radiated heat. A view of Charlestown—mountains and forests of red brick, and gray shark-colored warships drawn up row upon row at the Navy Yard—danced in bright waves of air like a mirage. Across the harbor, planes made languid approaches to whitened runways. They glided so slowly it looked as if they were hesitant to come down. Despite the heat there was little haze, even near the sea. A Plains August had grasped New England, and Boston was quiet.

"Good," thought the defense attorney, "there won't be a single soul on the river. I'll have it all to myself, and it'll be as smooth as glass." He had been a great oarsman. Soon it would be half a century of near-silent speed up and down the Charles in thin light racing shells, always alone. The fewer people on the river, the better. He often saw wonderful sights along the banks, even after the new roads and bridges had been built. Somehow, pieces of the countryside held out and the idea of the place stayed much the same, though in form it was a far cry from the hot meadows, dirt roads, and wooden fences he had gazed upon in his best and fastest years. But just days before, he had seen a mother and her infant son sitting on the weir, looking out at the water and at him as he passed. The child was so beautiful as the woman held up his head and pointed his puzzled stare out over river and fields, that the defense attorney had shaken in his boat—having been filled with love for them. Then there were the ducks, who slept standing with heads tucked under their wings. Over fifty years he had learned to imitate them precisely, and often woke them as he passed, oars dipping quietly and powerfully to speed him by. Invariably, they looked up to search for another duck.

"You shouldn't be going out today, Professor," said Pete, who was in charge of the boathouse. "No one's out. It's too hot."

He was a stocky Dubliner with a dialect strong enough to make plants green. When he carried one end of the narrow craft down the sloping dock to the river he seemed to the defense attorney to resemble the compact engines which push and pull ships in the Panama Canal. Usually the oarsman holding the stern was hardly as graceful or deliberative as Pete, but struggled to avoid getting splinters in his bare feet.

"I haven't seen one boat all of today." Pete looked at him, waiting for him to give up and go home. The defense attorney knew that Pete wanted to call the Department of Athletics and have the boathouse closed at two so he could go to tend his garden. "Really, not one boat. You could get heat stroke, you know. I saw it in North Africa during the War—terrible thing, terrible thing. Like putting salt on a leech."

The defense attorney was about to give in, when someone else walked up to the log book and signed so purposefully that Pete changed his strategy, saying to both of them, "If I were you now, I wouldn't stay out too long, not in this weather."

They went as they did each day to get S–40, the best of the old boats. It was the last boat Pat Shea had built for Harvard before he was killed overseas. Though already a full professor in the Law School and over draft age, the defense attorney had volunteered, and did not see his wife or his children for three solid years. When he returned—and those were glorious days when his children were young and suddenly talking, and his wife more beautiful than she had ever been—he went down to the boathouse and there was S—40, gleaming from disuse. Pat Shea was dead in the Pacific, but his boat was as ready as a thoroughbred in the paddock. For twenty years the defense attorney had rowed loyally in S—40, preferring it to the new boats of unpronounceably named resins—computer designed, from wind tunnels, with riggers lighter than air and self-lubricating ball bearings on the sliding seat, where S—40 had the same brass wheels Pat Shea had used when he had begun building boats in 1919. S—40 had seasoned into a dark blood color, and the defense attorney knew its every whim.

As they carried it from the shadows into blinding light, the defense attorney noticed the other sculler. He could not have been much over twenty, but was so large that he made the two older men feel diminutive. He was lean, muscled, and thick at the neck and shoulders. His face was pitted beneath a dark tan, and his hair long and tied up on his head in an Iroquois topknot. He looked like a Spartan with hair coiled before battle, and was ugly and savage in his stance. Nevertheless, the defense attorney, fond of his students and of his son who had just passed that age, smiled as he passed. He received as recompense a sneer of contempt, and he heard the words "old man" spoken with astonishing hatred.

"Who the hell is that?" asked the defense attorney of Pete as they set S—40 down on the lakelike water.

"I don't know. I never seen him before, and I don't like the looks of him. He brought his own boat, too, one of those new ones. He wants me to help him bring it down. Of course I'll have to. I'll take me time, and you can get a good head start so's you'll be alone up river," said Pete, knowing that informal races were common, and that if two boats pulled up even it nearly always became a contest. He wanted to spare the defense attorney the humiliation of being beaten by the unpleasant young man who had meanwhile disappeared into the darkness of the boathouse.

As S—40 pulled out and made slowly for the Anderson Bridge, the young man, whom the defense attorney had already christened "the barbarian," walked down the ramp, with his boat across his shoulders.

Even from one hundred feet out the defense attorney heard Pete say, "You didn't have to do that. I would have helped you." No matter, thought the defense attorney, by the time he gets it in the water, places his oars, and fine tunes all his alloy locks and stretchers, I'll be at the Eliot Bridge and in open water with a nice distance between us. He had no desire to race, because he knew that although he could not beat a young athlete in a boat half as light as S—40, he would try his best to do so. On such a hot day, racing was out of the question. In fact, he resolved to let the young man pass should he be good enough to catch up. For it was better to be humiliated and alive than dead at the finish line. He cannot possibly humiliate me anyway, he thought. A young man in a new-style boat will obviously do better than a man three times his age in a wood shell. But, he thought, this boat and I know the river. I have a good lead. I can pace myself as I watch him, and what I do not have in strength I may very well possess in concentration and skill.

And so he started at a good pace, sweeping across glass-faced waters in the large swelling of the stream just north of the Anderson Bridge, gauging his speed expertly from the passage of round turbulent spots where the oars had been, and sensing on the periphery of vision the metered transit of tall ranks of sycamores on the Cambridge side. He was the only man on the river, which was glossy and green with a thick tide of beadlike algae. Always driven to the river by great heat, dogs loped along with the gait of trained horses, splashing up a wave as they ran free in the shallows. S—40 had taut blue canvas decking, and oars of lacquered yellow wood with black and white blades. The riggers were silver-colored, an alloy modification, and the only thing modern about the boat. The defense attorney was lean and tanned, with short white hair. His face was kind and quiet, and though small in stature, he was very strong, and looked impressive in his starched white rowing shorts. The blue decking shone against the green water as in a filtered photograph of a sailing regatta.

It seemed to him that the lonely condition upon the river was a true condition. Though he had had a lot of love in his life, he knew from innumerable losses and separations that one stands alone or not at all. And yet, he had sought the love of women and the friendship of men as if he were a dog rasping through the bushes in search of birds or game. Women were for him so lovely and central to all he found important that their absence, as in the war, was the stiffest sentence he could imagine, and he pictured hell as being completely without them—although from experience he knew that they must have filled a wing or two there to the brim. Often, as he rowed, he slackened to think of the grace and beauty of girls and women he had known or loved. He remembered how some-time in the middle Twenties, when he was courting his wife, he had passed a great bed of water lilies in the wide bay before Watertown. He grasped one for her as he glided by, and put it in the front of the boat. But when he reached the dock the flower had wilted and died. The next day he stopped his light craft and pulled deep down on a long supple stem. Then he tied it to the riggers and rowed back with the lily dan-gling in the water so that he was able to preserve it, a justly appreciated rare flower. But people did not "court" anymore.

He resumed his pace, even though, without straining, he was as dripping wet as if he had been in a sauna for five minutes. Rounding the bend before the Eliot Bridge, he saw the young man in his new-style boat, making excellent speed toward him. He had intended to go beyond the Eliot, Arsenal Street, and North Beacon bridges to the bay where the lilies still grew, where it was easy to turn (although he could turn in place) and then to come back. All told, it was a course of six miles. It would not pay to go fast over that distance in such killing heat. If they were to race, the finish would have to be the last bridge out. By the time he passed under the Eliot Bridge, with two more bridges to go, the young man had closed to within a few hundred yards.

His resolutions fell away as if they were light November ice easy to break with oars and prow. Almost automatically, he quickened his pace to that of the young man, who, after a furious initial sprint, had been forced to slow somewhat and retrieve his breath. The defense at-torney knew that once he had it he would again pour on speed in the excessive way youth allowed, and so the defense attorney husbanded his strength, going as fast as his opponent but with the greatest possible economy. This he achieved by relaxing, saying to himself, "Easy. Easy. The fight is yet to come. Easy now, easy."

Though the young athlete was a hundred yards downriver the defense attorney could see dark lines of sweat in his knotted hair, and could hear heavy breathing. "I'm a fool," he said, "for racing in this heat. It's over one hundred degrees. I have nothing to prove. I'll let him pass, and I'll let him sneer. I don't care. My wisdom is far more power-ful than his muscular energy." And yet, his limbs automatically kept up the pace, draining him of water, causing salt to burn his eyes. He simply could not stop.

He remembered Cavafy's *Waiting for the Barbarians,* which he— in a clearly Western way—had orginally assumed to be a lament. Upon reading it he discovered that the poet shared in the confusion, for it was indeed a lament, that the barbarians were not still on their way. But for the defense attorney this was unthinkable, for he dearly loved the West and had never thought that to constitute itself it required the expectation of a golden horde. And he believed that if one man were to remain strong and upholding, if just one man were not to wilt, then the light he saw and loved could never be destroyed, despite the barbarism of the war, of soulless materialism, of the self-righteous students who thought to remake this intricate and marvelously fashioned world with one blink of an untutored eye. If a man can be said to grit his teeth over a span of years, then the defense attorney had done just this, knowing that it would both pass and come again, as had the First War, and the Second, in which he had learned the great lessons of his life, in which he had been broken and battered repeatedly—only to rise up again.

He did not want to concede the minor victory of a river race on a hot day in August, not even that, not even such a small thing as that to yet another wave of ignorance and violence. He started with rage in remembering the sneer. Contempt meant an attack against perceived weakness, and did not weakness merit compassion? If this barbarian had thought him weak, he was up against the gates of a city he did not know, a stone-built city of towers and citadels. The defense attorney increased the rapidity of his stroke to meet his opponent's ominously growing speed.

The young man was gaining, but by very small increments. Were the defense attorney to have kept up his pace he would have reached the North Beacon Street Bridge first, even if only by a few feet. But two things were wrong. First, such a close margin afforded no recourse in a final sprint. Because of the unpredictability of the young man's capacities, the defense attorney was forced to build an early lead, which would as well demoralize his rival. Second, not even halfway to the finish, he was beginning to go under. Already breathing extremely hard, he could feel his heart in his chest as if it were a fist pounding on a door.

He was lucky, because he knew the river so well that he had no need of turning to see where he was headed. So precise had the fifty years rendered his navigational sense that he did not even look when he approached bridges, and shot through the arches at full speed always right in the center. However, the young man had to turn for guidance every minute or so to make sure he was not straying from a straight course—which would have meant defeat. That he had to turn was another advantage for the defense attorney, for the young man not only broke his rhythm and sometimes lost his stroke or made a weak stroke when doing so, but he was also forced to observe his adversary still in the lead. If the defense attorney saw the leather thong in the young man's haircomb begin to dip, and saw the muscles in his back uplift a bit, making a slightly different shadow, he knew he was about to turn. This caused the defense attorney to assume an expression of ease and relaxation, as if he were not even racing, and to make sure that his strokes were deep, perfect, and classically executed. He had been in many contests, both ahead and behind.

Though it was a full-blooded race, he realized that he was going no more than half the sustained speed of which he normally was capable. Like a cargo of stone, the heat dragged all movement into viscous slow motion. Time was caught in its own runners, and its elements repeated. Two dogs at the riverside were fighting over a dead carp lapping in the green water. He saw them clash at the neck. Later, when he looked back, he saw the same scene again. Perhaps because of the blood and the heat and the mist in front of his eyes, the salt-stung world seemed to unpiece in complex dissolution. There was a pattern which the darkness and the immediacy of the race made him unable to decipher. Intensified summer colors drifted one into the other without regard to form, and the laziness was shattered only when a bright white gull, sliding down the air, passed before his sight in a heartening straight line.

Though he felt almost ready to die and thought that he might, the defense attorney decided to implement his final strategy. About a mile was left. They were nearing the Arsenal Street Bridge. Here the river's high walls and banks stopped the wind, and the waters were always smooth. With no breeze whatsoever, it was all the hotter. In this quiet stretch races were won or lost. A completely tranquil surface allowed a burst of energy after the slight rest it provided. Usually a racer determined to begin his build-up just at the bridge. Two boats could not clear the northern arch simultaneously. Thus the rear boat had no hope of passing and usually resolved upon commencement of its grand effort after the natural delineation of the bridge. Knowing it could not be passed, the lead boat rested to get strength before the final stretch. But the defense attorney knew that his position was in great danger. A few hundred yards from the bridge, he was only two or three boatlengths ahead. He could see the young man, glistening and red, breathing as if struggling for life. But his deep breathing had not the patina of weakness the defense attorney sensed in his own. He was certain to maintain his lead to the bridge, though, and beyond it for perhaps a quarter of a mile. But he knew that then the superior strength of the younger man would finally put the lighter boat ahead. If it were to be a contest of endurance, steady and torturesome as it had been, he knew he would not win.

But he had an idea. He would try to demoralize the young man. He would begin his sprint even before the Arsenal Street Bridge, with the benefit of the smooth water and the lead-in of the arch. What he did was to mark out in his mind a closer finish which he made his goal— knowing that there he would have to stop, a good half mile before the last bridge. But with luck the shocking lead so far in advance of all expectations would convince the struggling young man to surrender to his own exhaustion. An experienced man would guess the stratagem. A younger man might, and might not. If he did, he would maintain an even pace and eventually pass the defense attorney dead in the water a good distance before the finish line.

A hundred yards before the Arsenal Street Bridge, the defense attorney began his massive strokes. One after another, they were in clear defiance of the heat and his age. He began to increase his lead. When he passed through the dark shadow of the bridge, he was already five boat-lengths ahead. He heard the echo of his heart from the cool concrete, for it was a hollow chamber. Back in bright light, clubbed by the sun, he went even faster. The young man had to turn every few seconds to guide himself through the arch. When he did so he lost much time in weak strokes, adjustments to course, and breaking rhythm. But far more important was what he saw ahead. The old man had begun a powerful sprint, as if up to that point he had only been warming up.

Three quarters of a mile before the finish the defense attorney was going full blast. From a distance he looked composed and unruffled, because all his strength was perfectly channeled. Because of this the young man's stroke shattered in panic. The defense attorney beat toward his secret finish, breathing as though he were a woman lost deep in love. The breaths were loud and desperate, abandoned and raw, as if of birth or a struggle not to die. He was ten boatlengths ahead, and nearing his finish.

He had not time to think of what he had endured in his life, of the loss which had battered him, and beaten him, and reduced him at times to nothing but a shadow of a man. He did not think of the men he had seen killed in war, whose screams were loud enough to echo in his dreams decades after. He did not think of the strength it had taken to love when not loved, to raise faltering children in the world, to see his parents and his friends die and fall away. He did not think of things he had seen as the century moved on, nor of how he had risen each time to survive in the palace of the world by a good and just fight, by luck, by means he sometimes did not understand. He simply beat the water with his long oars, and propelled himself ahead. One more stroke, he said, and another, and another. He was almost at his end.

He looked back, and a beautiful sight came to his eyes. The young man was bent over and gliding. His oars no longer moved but only brushed the top of the water. Then he began to work his port oar and turn around, for he had given up. He vanished through the bridge.

The defense attorney was alone on the river, in a thickly wooded green stretch full of bent willows. It was so hot that for a moment he forgot exactly who he was or where he was. He rowed slowly to the last bridge. There he rested in the cool shadow of a great and peaceful arch.

OFF-SEASON

Susan Straight

For six years I had been sitting on hard bleachers watching Donnie play basketball, watching him run until his chest and neck gleamed gold brown like smooth palm tree wrapping. All those years my butt bones got tired, and I slid down to rest them on the wooden boards where feet belong, propping up my thighs on the bench in front of me. Donnie always came up during practice or warm-ups and told me to close my legs because I looked like a boy. Now we were married and I was a wife, so I was supposed to sit normal and put my hands on my knees, knit, or read romance novels like the other team's wives opposite me, plump and pale, screaming politely when they thought they should.

I wanted desperately to slump down in comfort and figure out why these white boys from the suburbs were beating Donnie's team by eight, but I slid a little and couldn't arrange my legs over the bleacher seat because of the bruises. Donnie had decorated my thighs when he threw me around the apartment, put serious rainbow stuff there, first rosy, then purple, and now fading to gold and green. Team colors, Notre Dame.

Since the week before when he did it, I'd been sleeping in the front room on the mattress we called a couch. That morning, I woke up thinking I heard the shiver of the windowpane, the pause and roar of a winter Santa Ana wind at home in Rio Seco, on the Westside. The sun, shining warm on my eyelids, had fooled me into thinking that this was California, but then the wind came through the cracks around the window, icy and silent, and I realized that there were no palm fronds hurling themselves against each other, no eucalyptus leaves to whistle and hold the air. I pushed the shade and looked outside to see the glare of light on February snow, and then heard Donnie in the bedroom getting ready for the game. His size fourteens crashed to the floor after he took them from the closet shelf.

Past the metal railing in front of our second-story door, I could see the long, empty lot that led down to the park where people sold weed in the summer, when we first moved in. The snow was thin over the ground in some places, steel gray the color of trash cans. Donnie came into the kitchen and looked at me. I could tell by how quickly he turned away that he was scared to say anything. Good, I thought, maybe if he's chicken he won't do it again. He sat on the folding chair and reached down to jerk his shoelaces tight, the muscles in his arms pulling downward, fluid like silty, dark water. The two tiny marks where I had stabbed him were flat black now, healed over so they could pass for beauty marks. When he'd bent my arm backwards, I poked him with the closest thing I could reach, and two drops of blood like ruby stud earrings stood out on his bicep. He'd been using his hands, his best weapons, and I found mine, the pen I practiced writing sports stories with, the pen with a long, sharp nub.

I pulled on two pairs of sweats, so I could go along, when he came close to the front door. "I thought you wouldn't want to be with me," he said.

"Nobody else to be with," I said. "Only game on TV is Indiana and Northwestern. I ain't hardly staying here and freezing to watch them." I stopped at the door, near him, and smelled the sleep on his skin, the little bit of my perfume that was still in the sheets. He looked away, like he couldn't stand to not touch me, and I smiled. Maybe if he won today, I would feel the same longing I always had, for touching wet curls at his ears, for everyone watching when I did, when I tasted the salt on his skin. The familiar feel of all those eyes on him might make Donnie into himself again.

But these country boys from Middlefield were playing Danny Ainge ball, that scrambly kind full of flying elbows and guys who pretended to fall and then tried to low-bridge somebody. One dude was using his beer belly as a second man to guard James, the skinny forward who had asked Donnie to play in this tournament. We were in a junior-high gym outside Hartford, at the second round of the Middlefield YMCA Tournament.

Donnie's team was all black and Puerto Rican guys from the city, and when they walked in, everybody looked nervous and started whispering. They hadn't been playing together but a week, though, and I could tell by the way the other team warmed up that they went way back. I didn't want to watch a bunch of pink-skinned, raw-kneed guys on TV, but here they were. The point guard was one of those little ones who stomps his feet between the legs of whoever's dribbling, constantly trying to steal the ball, pushing his eyebrows up all cocky and excited. Donnie had gotten three jams in the first-round game, dunks that everybody had heard about, James said, and the Middlefield crowd loved it now when this guard rogued Donnie's ball and got a clean, practice drill lay-up. You could tell their kind: they hated big-city flashiness on the court, which they automatically associated with car theft, annoying rap music, and the loss of their in-dash stereos when they drove into Hartford. Good team ball was the American way, hustle was much better than black and cool, and they'd much rather see one of theirs fall out of bounds for a save than see Donnie do a one-handed slam. "You show that big guy, he's not so tough," somebody yelled from the Middlefield ladies to my right after the steal.

"He ain't about nothin, Donnie," I said loudly. It was habit. "Come on, box out." He wasn't supposed to be the big guy, at center; he was a power forward, and he should have been putting the ball on the floor the way he loved to, hiding in the corner now and then to shoot his old low-trajectory jumper, rebounding better than anyone else. I had watched a hundred times while he positioned himself surely, his hands slanting nervously up and down like fins to guide him in his own part of the water, his long arms fencing out the others behind him. He would sway for a second, his mouth hung in a triangle and eyes rolled upward, waiting for the ball to leap within reach, as it almost always did. It was like he knew instantly from the rotation of the shot where it would fly.

But now he backed up in the key and swung his head around to look at the backboard, all wrong, late. Middlefield's center was old, with a hairy, concave chest and those ancient player smarts from pickup games. He could tell Donnie's familiarity and ease were gone when his back was to the basket, and I saw him smile again and again. He threw Donnie off with a pinch to the side and snatched the ball off the boards, passing it way downcourt to the cherry-picking little guard. They were up by five a few minutes before halftime.

"Don't let him get happy yet," I called out.

"Tell him, baby," Three said, from the row below me. Three was Donnie's oldest brother, Charles Morris King III. "Get back downcourt, man."

"You shouldn't have kept him out so late, Three," I said. "Coming home at two, and he had a nine o'clock game."

"Shit, we was workin, Rosa."

"First time all week. This on-call stuff ain't getting it."

"It's better than bein at home workin on the truck with Pops. That make you old before your time." Three looked back at the court. "He gettin tore up. Donnie ain't about no center. Look at that gray boy doggin him."

I always had to smile when Three called people gray. My mother was white, my father light-skinned, and I came out sort of gray, especially in winter, when I didn't get much sun. Here in the cold, my hands looked see-through and smoky as cheap paper, and my eyes had wells of pencil-colored skin underneath.

When I was fourteen and Donnie had taken me for the first time to see Three, in back of the high school where Three and his cousin Scooter laughingly coerced change from small white students to buy malt liquor for lunch, I could tell by the way Donnie stood still and held his face carefully that he was worried about his favorite brother's estimation.

"So my brother here tell me your mama from some other country," Three had said, stroking his chin with two fingers. "You got some exotic foreign blood in you, huh?"

"She ain't no regular ghostie, cuz?" Snooter said, and the faces around him waited to laugh. I waited for somebody to say "half-breed," but I heard nothing. I wondered what "exotic" meant to Three.

"My mother's Swiss," I said, and Three's face stretched in surprise.

"Don-nay, man, don't you know Sweden is where they be mak-

ing all them porno flicks and thangs? They *free* over there! Oh, ho, ho,"
he laughed.

"Swiss people are from Switzerland," I said. "It's far away from
Sweden."

"Yeah, baby, I was just jokin with you. Check her out, she blu-
shin," Three said.

"You better be careful, man," Donnie said. "She got brains.
And a mouth."

"Long as the brains don't outweigh the better parts, bruh,"
Three said. Each word was separate, like a pronouncement, and when
he looked around, they laughed. Donnie's hand had been wet and cold
in mine.

We watched him walk toward the drinking fountain now.
"Didn't you give him no early morning lovin?" Three said, and I was
angry when he didn't even bother to look at me. "He need some of that
sweetness to keep his game sharp."

"Shit," I said. I was tired of Three being the only reason we'd
moved to Hartford after Donnie quit college ball and ran out of money.
He'd been hauling trash from construction sites with his Uncle Floyd,
listening to Three talk about how the East Coast was live every time he
called. All I'd been able to find was a secretary job, and Donnie the part-
time guard. Winter didn't seem live to me. "He need some sharpness in
his head."

'Y'all can't be fightin, now. You still eligible for the Newlywed
Game and shit," Three said.

I looked at Donnie's back, bent over while he breathed. "It ain't
a game," I said. They were beating up on him under the boards because
he'd gotten so big. Donnie was six-five, and the bulk he'd put on during
college was still there. He was up to 220. Sometimes I couldn't believe I
held him up when he lay on top of me, but in all our time together, it
hadn't mattered how heavy or light he was, only whether I wanted him
or not. When I put my arms around his neck and pulled him down the
way I had all those years, the way I had when we first came to Hartford,
his flat stomach fit over mine and my ribs had room to fall up and down
when I pulled in my breath sharp with love. But now I couldn't breathe
under him, felt only his chest crushing mine and his hipbones against
my thighs.

He sat on the bottom bleacher while James argued with the other
guys about strategy. Sweat dripped from his chin onto the floor, and his
face was glossy and blank. The strategy before had been to get it to Don-

nie, and at center, he wasn't doing what he was supposed to do. I knew
he was going to ignore them and go where he pleased after halftime.

"Man, what up?" Three said. "Why you lettin the old dude
make you look bad and shit?"

"Shoot, he got it figured out so he don't have to run nowhere,
just pick off the back and elbow silly under there," Donnie said. He
waited, watching me. He was wondering if I had kept track.

"Ten points," I said. "Only seven boards." For years, I had
named the number of rebounds I wanted, and I had to pay in kisses.
"You're slow. Why don't you guys try a backdoor?"

"Shit. With who? Williams?" Donnie looked back at the court.
Williams was the other forward. He'd been shooting bricks all morning,
even missing two lay-ups.

The third quarter was all Middlefield boys, playing hustle ball,
harassing James and kicking passes away, clunking up plays. There was
no rhythm, no city ball; they didn't allow jumpers and trade-off that
they couldn't have kept up with. Donnie got some tip-ins, but the team
stayed five or six points down. I saw Donnie coming back up slower and
slower, going outside the key and leaving the basket unprotected, trying
to fade into the corner. His skin flushed red where it stretched over his
collarbone.

At the start of the fourth quarter, Middlefield's center reached in
to try another steal from Donnie as he whirled much too slowly in the
key. He poked Donnie in the face. I knew what would happen, remembered how many times he'd said, "They can hit me anywhere they want,
bow me and shit, but don't be messin with my eyes. I only got two." He
popped the center in the mouth, chased him to the corner, his big shoulders rounded like a bear's with anger and concentration. I had never
seen him fight. People pulled him away, and he shook them off, walked
to the fountain. "Chill out, D, man," Three called, and I felt fear rising
at the back of my scalp. When he walked back toward the stands, the
center laughed and said something I couldn't hear, but I knew what it
was, because Donnie went after him again. I closed my eyes. Donnie
used to break up fights, not pursue them with legs stiff as a boxer. The
Middlefield crowd was shouting, and after Donnie was ejected and sat
on the bench, they stared at his back with disgust and pointed him out to
the people coming in for the next game.

Thin icicles had attached the underside of our car to the street
like web threads when we went outside. "I don't want to hear it," he
said, and I waited while he tried to scrape the ice off the windshield. I

looked at all the trees. Some had delicate bare branches standing straight up like the piece of elegant coral my mother had found somewhere and kept on the table at home. There were other trees like coaches' heads, with square-edged crew cuts, bristled and stiff. Everything was black, white, and gray here. I tried to watch the wind blow, but you couldn't see anything move here. Donnie walked back toward the gym to say something to James, and I saw that the stiff heaps of dirty snow covered anything light, anything that would move. At home, the wind would mean tumbleweeds piled so high outside my mother's door that we couldn't open it, and pink pepper berries, ferny leaves and bits of mesh from the palms, ribbons of eucalyptus bark all collected in banks by the sidewalks, in piles behind the cement barriers in the parking lots. And I was always in those parking lots during winter, during the season, at the city college gyms or the convention centers, watching practice, coming early with the team for the games, telling Donnie to watch out for the pick and roll the other team always ran, packing down his hair a little more where it was uneven near his ears. His hair grew faster there.

When we were back at the apartment, I drank bitter herb tea my mother had sent me, something she said was good for stomachaches. Donnie stomped around, hanging his wet clothes outside on the railing, turning on the TV. "Why you gotta drink that stuff?" he said. "It stinks up the kitchen. Why you can't drink something normal like soda?"

"Soda's bad for you," I said.

"Miss Body, the one always got a stomachache cause she so healthy."

"I got that because of you, fool."

"Now I gotta be a fool."

"You don't gotta be, you *wanna* be." That was what we had said into each other's ears in the dark before. I watched him lie on the bed. "You going to work tonight?"

"They said they don't have nothin for a couple of days."

"They never have anything for you anymore. You and Three got all kind of time on your hands."

"You *been* asked me about fifty times, and I told you it's slow." The light from the TV, in the dark bedroom, jumped back and forth, and the glare made his face shift crazily.

I had found a Xerox copy of one of the incident reports the security guards were required to write for each job site. Donnie's illegible handwriting and secret-code spelling, which only I could unlock, had been circled and someone had written, "This is not acceptable." I knew, but I wanted him to admit it.

"Why don't you go find another job, then? Maybe you could chase some lizards out from somewhere." Donnie sucked his teeth and swung his head around, away from me. "Yeah, remember when you called me and said you found a job. Coach got it for you. 'I bounce the basketball in the gym, in case any lizards and snakes get inside, so I'll scare em away.' Really prepared you for the outside world, huh, baby?"

"Rosa, you getting on my third nerve. I'll look for another slave, okay? Let me get some rest."

"Yeah," I said, and then I stopped. I'd seen him back in Rio Seco when he quit school, carrying a small piece of paper in his wallet; he had copied his address from a bill, because when he filled out applications he couldn't spell Picasso, the street he lived on, or Rio Seco. I couldn't say it to him. In the kitchen, I picked through a bowl of pinto beans, looking for small stones that sometimes got into the bin. It seemed that every night we ate beans and rice, or *raui roesti,* the Swiss-fried potatoes and onions I had eaten daily as a child. From the kitchen window, I could see the back of the Puerto Rican restaurant across the alley. Hartford had been an escape, an adventure at first, the crowded streets, red leaves in piles, the good smell of the Puerto Rican food. But now the long tangle of icicles on the black waterpipes wasn't clear and sparkling; it was milky and old, no longer fascinating. When our car broke down, Donnie had to pay someone to fix it, because he couldn't lie on his back in the snow. We turned up the heat to seventy-nine degrees on my twentieth birthday, in December. We had read the temperature in Los Angeles in the newspaper, and we wore shorts all morning and laughed. It wasn't funny when the bill came. We had no family but Three, no one to call when the pipes in the toilet froze, when somebody slashed our tires. We were suckers of the world.

Donnie switched the TV to his favorite cartoon, "Thunder the Barbarian." I had always been amazed and irritated that he and Three watched Saturday cartoons, staring and still like children.

"So we're going to have some intellectual stimulation now, since we worked out our muscles with early-morning boxing," I said, unable to stay out of the bedroom, to stop talking to him. I pulled clothes off the edge of the closet door that stuck out from under our mattress. We'd bought the bed from a hotel, and it sagged in the middle. We slid one of the closet doors underneath and sat on the shelf it made at the foot of the bed to watch TV, since there was nothing else in the room.

Donnie said, "At least Thundar got a woman who keeps her mouth shut. Maybe I should jump on into cartoon life, cause mine ain't about shit."

"You the one laying around here waiting for something to fly to you. You refuse to go back to school. You can't find another job. And you want to stay here forever because you chicken to go home and be a nobody. That's the only reason we're still here. One time you were a bighead star, everybody wanting to know what you thought about the Skyline game and what about your knee, is it better for tonight? Now you know you're gonna hear, 'Donnie King? He couldn't hang, man.' I can say it for you right here, any time. I'll be your friends *for* you and tell you all about yourself."

But he didn't put his hand over my mouth, which was how most of our fights began. He ignored me for Thundar. I pushed at his shoulder, and the flexible closet door bent a little under his weight. "You got nothing to say?" I prodded.

'You gon whup me with your tongue and then when I get mad I'ma do something you don't like. I just want to say shut up now, okay?"

When we fought, he would get up and leave me wherever we had been rolling, on the floor, on the bed. Last month he had banged my head on the cutting corner of the closet door after I kicked him close to his family jewels. If I was in the front room, he would turn on the TV while I yelled at him to leave. He loved it. He'd watch something that allowed him to make noise, a show he could laugh loudly at, a sporting event where he could shout instructions. He knew his voice echoed off the cement walls. If I lay on the bed, throbbing in spots on my legs or arms where he had pinched me or bent something backwards, I knew he had scratch marks and blood too, but he would flap his house shoes loudly into the kitchen, banging around pots, making something to eat, taking up all the space. "This is my place, I ain't gotta go nowhere," he crowed. "You don't like it, you go." Outside there was snow and cold, and he laughed.

Thundar called upon his magical powers. He was getting ready to fight some evil, so I got up from the shelf to leave, but Donnie's arm reached out to push me onto the bed. His skin was filmed with dried sweat, and I thought of the salty taste I had wanted that morning; now his skin only rubbed dull against me. "I don't feel like messing with you," I said.

"You used to kiss me all over my face after Cal State Merceno games, and I was more sweaty then," he said. "I was soaked."

"You were somebody special then," I said, sliding out of his hands and going into the kitchen.

"I'm somebody different now, and I don't gotta ask for what I want," he said, following me and raking me onto the floor. He held both of my hands against my chest with one of his, and pulled my sweats and underwear off like he was changing a baby. "I'm somebody mad now," he said. I waited, watching his small smile, and then he laughed and dropped my legs onto the floor. "I don't want none right now," he said, and slammed the front door.

My water glass fell off the couch onto the tile. I lay on the icy linoleum; it was gritted with sand from the streets. I tried to sweep it out every day, but it crept back on our boots. I knew Donnie's breath would be smoking out of his nose like a dragon when he walked to Three's in the cold, and when I closed my eyes and felt the floor touching my backbone, I thought, he hadn't even been hard when he pushed against me. It wasn't about wanting. The cold floor and my skin were getting friendly, and the tiny rocks pricked my bare thighs. At home, in Rio Seco, my skin and Donnie's had seemed to meld together, on those hundred-degree days. Was the linoleum warming to my body, or was my skin cooled and hard? They were growing together, fusing, so I stood up, and like a tongue stuck to a rough ice cube, I left skin behind when I pulled away.

The dust joined itself together like webs along the walls and between the spidery legs of the card table and two folding chairs. I swept the webs toward the door and mixed them with the glass shards, glinting like dew in the dust.

The air outside was very still and frozen; I pushed the dust and shards close to the wall and stood at the chainlink railing. When I sniffed, the dampness in my nostrils clicked, turning icy, and I started to feel the crying, the heat in my jaws when I held it back. I lifted up my face, and remembered Donnie's father teasing him about me, laughing with his uncles. "Is the boy in love?" "She got his nose wide open." "Don't let it come a storm and he look up, cause he drown in a minute." Donnie had taken it, wouldn't move his arm from around me even when his cousins joined in.

The broom lay on its side where it had fallen, and when I narrowed my eyes, it looked like a palm frond; at home, after the wind, curled stiff palm fronds would litter the streets and yards, the high school. We had searched for places to lie down, places where the cops wouldn't find us, and after one of his games, Donnie led me back to the field near the street. I had said, "This ain't no place," and he smiled, draping the fronds over the chainlink fence, hooked by the curved bark end, until he'd made a shack in the darkest corner, away from the streetlight. When we lay on the grass, I saw the papers and trash clinging to the fence where the wind had blown them, hiding us.

The pile of clothes was damp against my hands. I touched them where they hung on the railing, the shorts and practice jersey from Cal State Merceno, the tube socks long as my arm. I breathed in again, felt the air. I went back inside and turned on the weather channel; it was fourteen degrees. I brought the plastic pitcher outside and poured cupfuls of water over the clothes, my hands red in the cold, and watched the cloth cling to the metal. I poured again, waited, poured, standing there for a long time as the water shimmered down the bumpy surface and my ears ached with cold.

I waited inside, by the window, where the light from the yellowed, dirty window shade made everything golden. Donnie's face was beautiful in that dulled brightness. When we walked home, and I'd forgotten my gloves, he sat on the couch and put my fingers into his mouth, one by one, and sucked gently until they were warm again. His face was pale gold from the winter, glowing, when I leaned toward him. His eyes were closed, and the black fans of his lashes, his straight eyebrows, the thin-feathered wings of his faint moustache were like the markings on a tiger, soft and precise.

The light would shine over the three slanting scars on his cheekbone, arranged around a small black mole like Arabic writing that I couldn't read, and I would slide against his side like a palm against the tongue that's licking the sugar, or salt, from it.

I took paper to write him a note.

July will be seven years since I kissed you, after you lost the Dolorexx game. You lost again. I am going home to the Westside.

When I went back outside, the clothes were frozen to the railing, coated with ice in a dimpled opaque pattern thick as shower glass.

OFFSIDES

Marisa Labozzetta

"My father loved baseball, but he had no sons," Diana told Richard. "He did teach me how to pitch one time, but I never graduated to batting."

"Well, I'll show you how to play soccer!" He, Richard Grossman, coach of the Reddington Strikers, would give her a crash course so that on Sunday, when she came to watch her first game, his girls' game, she would not ask stupid questions of the crowd; rather, she would know exactly what was going on.

"I'm warning you," she said as they approached the vacant field at Bryant Park. "I used to sit out family softball games in my grandmother's bathroom where I conjured up the greatest excuses not to play, from tummy aches to acute diarrhea!"

"Soccer is nothing like baseball. It's a game where everybody gets involved, where you can be creative on the field and not be limited to second base. Diana, it's a game *that you play in the rain!*"

"Is that why you don't use your hands—so you can hold an umbrella?"

"Funny. By the way, the league doesn't allow jewelry."

"I think my age already disqualifies me."

He would never find a female of his own generation with a passion for soccer. Perhaps that's why he looked to teenage girls. Or was it the other way around? Had all the time he spent with them taken away his need for a woman? Some years, he coached two and three teams in one season. He knew people in town thought him odd for this reason. If he were still married and had a daughter of his own, would they? Absolutely not.

He removed a ball from the large fishnet sack he carried and began to juggle it from his toes to his thigh to the side of his foot back to his thigh.

"Jog slowly with the ball, touching the center of it at every step, like this," he said.

She did as she was told. Petite, well-coordinated, she could be mistaken from the back for one of the girls on his team. But it was clear she had no interest in what she was doing. "Girls didn't play soccer when I was growing up!" She wiped away beads of sweat from under her eyes, careful not to smudge her mascara.

"They play now!" He tossed the ball at her and she met it with her head, then said it gave her a headache. "How do those players keep doing it over and over? Doesn't it hurt?"

'Of course it hurts. Sports always hurt."

"Missy was lousy at practice today," he said as they got back into the car. "I know she's smoking pot. That senior she sees is trouble."

"What are you going to do about it?"

"Maybe have the girls sign an agreement not to do drugs and alcohol—but then some of them would just lie."

"You going to tell her parents?"

"There's only the mother. Anyway, I'd never betray the girls."

Diana leaned toward him. When she put her lips on his, he barely responded.

"Now who are you worried about? This is no good, Richard. I can't compete with a dozen fourteen-year-olds."

"Eighteen. A soccer team has eighteen players." He kissed her back quickly, then started the engine. It was Friday evening, the night before the play-offs, and it was getting late. He had to go home and make his calls.

They had met at Reddington Savings Bank. Triumphant after a 5–0 win, he had walked in, still wearing his blue and white team warmups and safari hat that resembled the one worn by the fortune-seeking movie hero, Indiana Jones. He believed it brought him luck, and was never without it at games or practices. Besides, it hid his receding hairline.

She had smiled at him as he made his way through the winding velvet ropes. Her long dark hair was pulled away from her face, emphasizing the wide grin and large straight teeth. When he stepped in front of her teller's grille, she glanced at the hat and said, "Welcome to *The Temple of Doom.*"

The following Saturday, he uttered what he had rehearsed all week.

"Can I take you to lunch when the bank closes?"

"Sorry, I have a management class at the college. How about dinner tonight?"

Her forwardness pleased him, yet made him anxious. Plus, she was ambitious. What would she say when he told her he'd been sorting zip codes in the Reddington Post Office for the last nine years? His ex-wife used to slip continuing education brochures in between the pages of his *Soccer America.*

Settled in his condo, a converted textile mill, Richard began to dial. Megan K., Megan O., Cara W., Cara M.—he flipped through his mental Rolodex. Did anyone name their daughters anything other than Megan, Cara, or Sara anymore? Whenever a coach yelled out one of those names at a game, at least five heads turned.

First he called Ari, his steady one, a solid defender and a great assister. The perfect teammate, she knew how to make the girls talk to each other on the field.

"I saw you downtown with your new girlfriend tonight," she told him. "You were skipping in front of City Hall."

"I skipped twice." It was one of what he liked to call his "rambunctious" moments—those urges he insisted acting upon, believing they'd keep him young.

"You were skipping all the same. Pretty lame, Grossman."

He'd been trying to keep his affair with Diana a secret. People were accustomed to seeing him alone. Grossman, the *girls'* soccer coach, tall and thin, with his khaki pants and red suspenders, sandy hair slicked back like his NBA coaching idol Pat Riley's. Lately, the sight of him with Diana was drawing extended stares from people who knew them. His compulsion to hide every time they encountered one of his girls aggravated his awkwardness in public. He just didn't know how to work Diana into his image. Perhaps that was what had gone wrong with his marriage; maybe he had never known how to fit a real woman into his life.

"And what did you think?" he asked.

"You were good, Grossman. You shot across the street before I could see your girlfriend's face."

"Go to sleep early. No babysitting this weekend. No sleepovers. No dates. Seven-thirty we meet in the bowling alley parking lot. Your parents coming?"

"Yup."

"Excellent. Most of you will need rides."

The girls had arrived at the Ludlow game half asleep last Saturday, stepping out of station wagons and vans with their warmup jackets hanging off their shoulders. After stretching out, they looked as if they wanted to lie down and curl up on the green. The Ludlow girls were already fiercely engaged in passing and shooting drills.

"Don't stand around!" he'd shouted. "Run! Get a ball! Get out there and juggle, but don't stand around!" It had irritated him to see them like that because it was exactly what the old boys at the Recreation Department were always screaming about: girls didn't take athletics seriously; girls were not worth the time or the effort, and especially not the money.

Missy had looked the worst of all of them that morning, her big green eyes reduced to slits. Sluggish throughout the game, she had obviously been up late with her boyfriend. The Strikers lost, but it hadn't been only Missy's fault.

"Second-half teams are losing teams," he had told them afterward. "Ludlow played a very clean, aggressive game. You've got to go in harder, girls. The harder you go in, the safer you are. You had your share of opportunities. You were outplayed. But we've got another chance at them in the play-offs. A little more commitment to be in there first, and we'll take it. Anybody got any thoughts, comments?"

"Yeah." Ari punched a soccer ball lying next to her. "How do we *really* beat Ludlow next week?"

"You beat them by taking shots. More shots at the top of the box. Next week I want everybody up. Push 'em out of there harder and faster. Wings can't trail behind the sweepers and fold."

Exhausted, Missy had asked him for a piggy-back ride to the parking lot, and he had given it to her, despite a disapproving look cast by Ari's mother. This "rambunctious" moment might have been wrong, but Richard liked to take care of Missy, maybe because she had no father. She was naive, different from some of the other girls. Shani, whose wild curly red mane was never secured in a ponytail, enjoyed lying on the ground propped up on her elbows during pep talks, knowing full well Richard could see down her V-neck jersey. Once she had fallen and pulled up her shorts to show him the strawberry on her rear end.

Belligerent, hostile, Liza was his real problem, though. When she was on, she was a great player; when she was off, a total disruption to the team who left a big gaping hole in the middle of the field, because if the center half isn't doing her job, the entire team falls apart. Once, when she was accidentally tripped by her own teammate, she went into such a rage they had to carry her off the field. That won her a yellow warning card from the referee. Another time, a teammate and she tried to win the ball; Liza whacked at the girl's ankles, threw elbows, just lost it.

One by one he phoned them all. He had no idea what their parents thought about the calls, although he once overheard Liza's mother say, as she handed the receiver to her daughter, "Tell him to get a life." What was the problem? Coaching was a serious endeavor. They wanted good teams, winning seasons? Well, this was part of it. Coaching four-teen- and fifteen-year-olds meant getting into their heads, reading their minds on and off the field, teaching them to trust him enough so that when he sent them out to perform, they had faith in his judgments, in themselves. Something happened to girls at their age. Just when they were beginning to believe they could do it, they turned self-conscious on him. Then, one by one, they dropped out, feeling more comfortable on the sidelines of some boys' competition.

Now it was the boys who had started cheering Grossman's teams, and lately that wasn't sitting so well with the recreational powers that be—the old boys' network of middle-aged men whose families had run the town's sports for generations. Richard wasn't sure whether they hated him more for having instituted the Reddington Soccer Club, which drew players away from "real" sports like baseball and football, or for not having the guts to coach boys. He had introduced fall soccer into the Recreation Department, but they had opposed his organizing spring teams. Fall was as far as they'd allow him to go. If kids didn't want to play baseball, then they should ride a bike, was their opinion. But Richard, who had gotten into soccer because he hadn't made his high-school baseball team, and because he was too short for basketball and too slight for football, had organized his own club in Reddington, one that hooked into a larger area league. On a Saturday morning in October, seven years ago, he turned up at the Rec Department soccer jamboree in his VW Rabbit, opened the sun roof, and held out a sign that said SPRING SOCCER SIGN UPS. Ninety-three boys and girls lined up to give him their names. The director of the Rec Department approached Richard's car and slapped his hand down on the hood. "Just what are you doing, Grossman?"

"Excuse me, but I'm a taxpayer. Please move aside because there are a lot of people trying to sign up."

Since then, each fall and spring he laid out the field: ten yards here, seventy there; ran the corners square; measured off the boxes around the goals; marked it all with string and pegs. Then he hauled two tons of lime in eighty-pound bags onto the green, filled the lining machine, and walked the perimeter. If the ball went beyond those lines, it was out of bounds—clear and simple. Some plays were trickier to call, however. One minute you could be onsides, ready to receive a pass, when the defender pulled up on you. Before you knew what had happened, the referee was calling, "Offsides," and awarding the other team a big fat indirect kick.

He hadn't always coached girls, but when spring soccer first began, the fifteen-and-under girls' team was stranded. If he hadn't taken them on, they wouldn't have played. Each season thereafter, the girls begged him to continue.

He wouldn't go back to boys now; they were too cocky. The girls let him care about them; he let himself care about them.

After he had made his last call, the ringing of the phone startled him.

"Good luck tomorrow," Diana whispered. "How about dinner tomorrow night?"

"I'll call you after the game. Diana—?" He wanted to tell her that he loved her; he had wanted to the last few times they'd been together, but he couldn't. He used to tell his ex-wife he loved her all the time, and what good had it done? She had gotten up one morning, told him they had nothing in common, and left. He thought he had learned something from his failed marriage: keep the dearest sentiments within. But this was difficult to do with Diana. She was the first person since his high-school soccer coach who made him feel he was good enough.

Tonight his passion was there, ready to be expressed through the telephone wires. "Like I just finished telling all my girls, get a good night's sleep," he said instead.

It poured on the first day of the play-offs, a cold hurricane-like Saturday in the middle of June. By the time the girls stepped onto the field, their cleats sank deep into the mud. They were hungry for a win, however. Enjoy the game, sure, but victory is what it's really about.

Within the first five minutes, Ludlow scored. His girls were faster, Richard had no doubts; they beat Ludlow to the ball each time, but Ludlow was bigger, and now with a wounded ego, the Strikers would give up the ball too easily, Richard feared. Toward the end of the first half, Sara B.'s father, who liked to coach from the sidelines, pacing to and fro, hands on his fat hips, confusing the hell out of the girls, shouted to his daughter as she lost the ball, "Sara, if you can't get tough, go home!" At that moment, Sara sent the ball in. And it would have been over by the end of the second half, the Reddington Strikers would have taken it neatly—had it not been for the weather conditions. Balls react differently to water than they do to dry ground. Cara W. dribbled the ball down the wing and crossed it high to Meghan K., who headed it to Missy. With the goalie out of the box, Missy booted it in; however, instead of rolling, the ball stopped short as it smacked into the puddle that had formed around the entire goal. And there it sat, waiting for the Ludlow goalie to lunge at it before Missy could come in for a second kick.

Double overtime went into penalty kicks; Meghan K.'s mother walked back to her car, unable to watch. After Ludlow had taken five shots and Reddington four, they were tied at three goals. Then Liza stepped up, kicked into the upper left-hand corner of the net, and the first game of the play-offs was over. Afterward, Richard had wanted to scoop Liza up and kiss her, but some calls were harder to make than others. In the past, when he had complimented her on her performance, she had become overconfident and screwed up in the next game.

"Nice job!" he congratulated her. She stared at him, full of expectancy; he just smiled, and chose to say nothing more.

.   .   .

They were sitting in Hunan Palace when Richard nonchalantly suggested to Diana that she not come to the Springfield game the next day.

"Why not?"

"You've never come to a game before. Why start now?"

"Because the season's almost over."

"It is over. These are play-offs," he reminded her.

"Whatever. It's a game, right? The last game."

"I still can't spend the night with you."

"Richard, I already know all that. No sex before games."

"Correct, an early night."

"How about early sex?" she grinned.

"Can't."

"Well, will you pick me up in the morning?"

He shook his head. He was getting that familiar feeling he always got with women—the fizzle that followed the sizzle and which usually came no later than after the second date. That his relationship with Diana had lasted so long astounded him, for at the moment she might as well have been some stranger sitting across from him. What had he seen in her anyway? Too much lipstick, too much jewelry. To think that he had almost told her he loved her.

"Fine. I'll come on my own. Give me directions." He scribbled them out on a napkin. "Are these directions to the field or a way out of a labyrinth? You don't want me to come, do you?"

"It's not *you*, it's just—I'm on a winning streak. I can't break it. You've never come to a game this season and we're seven and one."

"Now I'm bad luck? Is that what you're saying?"

"Sort of. But it's not only luck. It's the girls. They haven't seen you before. If you show up now, it might throw their concentration."

"It's not that you don't want them to see me, is it? It's that you don't want *me* to see *them!*"

"It's both."

"All your talk about my getting interested in soccer is a bag of bullshit, isn't it, Richard? You like to have your idolizing girls all to yourself. You don't want them to see that there's anybody else in your life, and you certainly don't want me to meet them because they *are* your life! You want them to think you're theirs alone! Well, they're almost women, Coach, and whether you like it or not, they're going to leave you. Soon, Richard. They always do."

She was crazy—way off base, he wanted to believe, but he knew better. He had to stop her from saying another word.

"Let's get out of this place," he said.

Later, he felt bad as he pulled in front of his apartment. Why did Diana frighten him? "The harder you go in, the safer you are. You win by taking shots," he always told his girls. *You win by taking shots. You are a coward, Richard Grossman. You are a loser.*

The Reddington Strikers managed to hold the Springfield Comets back the entire first half. Goaltender Shani took a dive for the ball at the same time the Springfield forward followed through with a kick that met Shani's trachea. She scared Richard the way she lay on the ground absolutely still. When the ref called him over, he didn't know what to expect; as he neared her, she lifted her head. Her jersey had become twisted around her torso, and one of her breasts was partially exposed through the shirt's neck opening.

"Want a sub?" Richard asked.

"Nope."

He was relieved. None of the others could punt like Shani; she was agile and fearless—had great hands. At halftime it was zero-zero.

"Always, always try to be first," he told them as they squirted water into their mouths. "If you can't, play the pressure and get that ball under control. If you can do that and have every player on the field marked, then we'll do fine."

They kept the field compact; they pressured. Their traps were the finest he'd seen all season. Then it happened. Sara B. and Liza went after the ball, but Sara B. won it and scored. Richard could see by the scowl on Liza's face that he had made a lousy call the day before; he should have commended her more on her winning penalty kick.

At the restart, Liza and a Springfield player engaged one another in a bout of name calling; the referee told them both to cool it. Volatile Liza wouldn't. "Put a lid on it, Liza!" Ari warned from midfield. That's when Liza held up her middle finger to Ari; the ref, in turn, gave Liza a red card and threw her out of the game.

Even with his team down one player, Springfield failed to score—until the last minute.

"Everybody up! Hustle!" Richard called as Springfield took off on a breakaway. They remained solid. Had they missed opportunities? Sure. Still, they had nothing to be ashamed of, and they felt good about that.

With the whistle blown and the hands slapped, the anxiety of a season was unleashed for all—players, parents, coach.

No one had noticed Diana standing on the other side of the field with the spectators. She wore tight jeans, a white tank top, and gold hoop earrings. Her face was made up and her hair perfectly styled. Now she stood out among the girls dripping with perspiration and the worn-out looking mothers in their baggy shorts and T-shirts. As Richard crossed the field, she approached him.

"I'm sorry," she clumsily offered.

"Yeah, tough one." He looked down at the ground, then back up at her, still surprised to see her there after the awkward way they had parted the night before. They were smiling at one another, not saying a word, when Shani crept up behind Richard and threw a large thermos-ful of cold water at his back.

"Got you, lover boy," she giggled.

He tore off after her, almost circling the entire field, his good-luck safari hat long fallen from his head. They were just about back in the center of the crowd when Richard caught her from behind by grabbing at a fold in her jersey and pulling her, face down, onto the ground. In a 'rambunctious" moment he straddled her, then picked up the cooler next to them, and poured melted ice water over her mass of red hair while she laughed and wiggled beneath him, her buttocks bobbing up and down, her breasts bouncing against the earth.

It wasn't the water that shocked the onlookers. They had grown silent just as he climbed over her. When he became aware of the stillness, he lifted himself off and met the confused gazes of parents. He had grossly misjudged his position; he had been offsides and out of bounds all at once. Word would reach the board members of the Rec Department, and they in turn would seize the opportunity to have him canned from the Soccer League. Even if his thoughts were running away from him, one thing he knew was certain. The story would spread around gossipy Reddington; word of mouth would keep the incident alive and make future soccer players' parents wonder if they should let their daughters be on Grossman's team.

Once again he had lost sight of Diana, until suddenly she was standing beside him. She held out a hand; with the other, she dragged his sack of soccer balls. She wore his warmup jacket draped over her shoulders, the arms tied around her neck, and his too-large hat floated on top of her head. Seeing her, he found the courage to speak. He thanked them all, parents and players alike, for a great season, and he told them he'd meet them again next fall.

"There'll be tryouts," he warned with a coach's decorum. Then he took the sack from Diana and hoisted it over his shoulder. "You smell good," he said, wrapping his free hand around hers and leading her away from the field toward the parking lot.

V

*Sudden
Death*

THE SECRET TO NOT GETTING STUCK

Jay Woodruff

That winter I was seventeen, and the *Post-Dispatch* was calling me the best high school wrestler in Missouri. I hadn't lost since the last match of my freshman year. I could bench-press more than twice my weight, go without eating for days at a time, start running as my father left the house to catch a flight at Lambert Field, and keep going until he'd landed in another state. When I looked at the soft bellies sagging over the belts of parents, teachers, and game-show hosts, I concluded that the world was a weakened, feeble, flabby thing waiting for me to whip it.

In February, near the end of my junior season, my father finally left for good. That night I sat on the edge of what had always been my parents' bed but was about to become my mother's alone. My father stuffed his black leather bag with hastily folded shirts, and wads of underwear and socks from the top drawer, where he'd always tossed his change at the end of the day and where I'd always found that extra nickel or dime or quarter I always seemed to need.

"Dad," I said, and he looked at me. He needed a shave. I felt the weight of important things to say but couldn't begin to find the words to shape them. "Your shaving stuff."

After tucking his razor and Old Spice into the toiletry kit he looked around the room with a frown, as if trying to remember what not to forget.

Outside, the night felt like spring. It was one of those winter warm spells in St. Louis, when the air seems to have come up from Louisiana instead of down from Iowa.

"I wish—" my father began, and I knew then that he too was searching for words, "I wish this could've waited till after state."

The state tournament was three weeks away. This was the first night in two years when no thought of it had crossed my mind. When he mentioned the word, I remembered again, suddenly, as if it were an urgent appointment I'd almost forgotten. I shifted beside him on the front walk, wearing the sweats I wore every night, my baggy gray uniform.

"I don't know . . ." He tried again. We were like a pair of wrestlers from the blind school my squad competed against every season: circling, tentative, groping for contact. "I don't know just what to say."

I watched him back out the driveway, and I followed the taillights of his Galaxie until they disappeared down the dark and quiet street. My mother was at a friend's. I didn't want to go inside. I had nothing to do, except what I did every night—run.

Back points cost me the state title my freshman year. I didn't get pinned, but my opponent, a towheaded senior named Hudson, with arms like Arnold Schwarzenegger, rode me the whole third period, cranking me over twice. I don't remember being on my back. All I remember is thinking *no!*, the lights of Hearnes Arena a blinding blur. On the films you could see I came within an inch or two of getting stuck. I only watched once: the idea of getting pinned, of giving in, made me sick. I got dizzy and almost puked when I watched myself struggling to avoid it. The moves I used to prevent it were called kicking, squirming, and twisting: no dignity in being forced to your back on the floor of a huge arena.

I took the five-mile route to the high school and walked down the alley between the cafeteria and the wrestling room. Coach Carson couldn't give us a key, but he never locked the window over the low brick entryway. If you were agile enough, you could scale the downspout and slide inside.

I liked working out alone late at night, when the building was dark and empty and the rest of the world was at home, eating Fritos, getting fatter. I did sit-outs till my sides ached, stand-ups till my legs wobbled, and push-ups till my pecs burned, my shoulders cramped, my arms buckled. The difference between you and the other guy at the end of six minutes might be one push-up, and before you ever step out there on the mat, you have to be able to look at him and say, "Adios, penci-neck."

I suited up in a set of plastics, grabbed a rope, and started skipping. My mother would get home soon. My father was probably already in his girlfriend's bedroom. They were weak, all of them. Dad couldn't last a period with me. He'd be sucking wind on his back in forty-eight seconds. The whole world was weak, just dozing out there, getting flabbier. If you worked hard enough, you could beat it.

The only sounds in the empty school were my feet shuffling on the mats, my breathing in rhythm with the *nick-nick-nick* of the rope, the rope's furious whir as it sliced through the gym's thick air. Sweat stung my eyes. For whatever reasons, I'd always felt about crying exactly as I felt about getting pinned.

"Your father, I'm afraid," my mother told me, "has become a very sad and sorry person."

She picked at her tuna salad with sharp, remorseful stabs. I was enjoying my usual dinner of celery and hard-boiled egg. We'd agreed last summer: I could lose twice as much as she could take off in the months leading up to the start of October practice. I had the slenderest mother in town.

"I don't see much hope," she continued. She looked worn out and older than I'd ever imagined she might. Her brown hair, flecked with gray, hung limp over one shoulder. "And it's not this . . . this *Kate* woman," she went on. "It's the goddamn booze. If he could just quit drinking."

She put down her fork and lit a cigarette, and I was struck, as I so often was, by the blind hopelessness of the adult species. Sure, Mom, I thought, slam one addiction while you get off on another. But I swallowed my celery without speaking. My mother rested her forehead on her left palm and began to cry.

I started wrestling because of Indian Guides, a YMCA father-son organization my mother got us to join. Each week our tribe met at a different tepee. We wore leather vests we had cut and sewn ourselves from patterns, and official Indian Guides headbands. We sat in a circle to pow-wow about Indian life, about the old bones and arrowheads we'd seen on weekend trips to Cahokia mounds or the Koster digs; ate roasted pumpkin seeds and wild blackberries; made tom-toms out of coffee cans and hide; clustered to see which boy could come closest to guessing when a minute was up or, after having been spun until dizzy, point north. And one night at Chief Crazy Horse's tepee we Indian-wrestled. I was the smallest in the tribe, but no boy lasted five seconds with me.

My father and I never talked a whole lot. At bedtime he'd read to me—Robin Hood, King Arthur, Tom Sawyer—and I would try to make him linger there by asking about the moon, the sea, distant dark forests and desert islands, but his progressively shorter answers always seemed to be edging toward the door. The night I discovered what I was good at, in Chief Crazy Horse's living room, my father's eyes glinted with a light I'd never seen in them before. He said nothing, but any child can sense even silent pride in a parent.

Each winter all the tribes in St. Louis gathered for the Snow Moon Council, a weekend in the cabins at Trout Lodge. We hiked across the frozen lake, the ice thick enough, my father reassured me, for a truck to drive on. We sledded down the sloping snow-covered roads of the Ozark hills, and on Saturday night everyone gathered at the lodge for a series of games. One of the events was Indian wrestling.

I tossed aside my first half-dozen opponents easily, to reach the finals, where I stood foot-to-foot with a tall skinny farm boy whose ears stuck out like handles. We clasped wrists, and, at "Go," I faked a tug and pushed as he faked a push and tugged. I tumbled to the floor.

I hid my face against my father's hip as he patted my shoulder.

"It's okay, Son," he said. "You did great."

I thought that I'd seen him blush when I fell and that I had embarrassed him in front of every Indian in the Missouri territory. Indians were strong and brave. They did not like to lose. They did not cry. If you won, you had no reason to cry. I was eight years old.

Near the middle of my sophomore season, just before the Mehlville holiday tournament, Coach Carson called me away from a king-of-the-mat drill and into his office.

"Your mother's on the phone," he said, and I immediately pictured my father's car, crumpled under an overpass on I–44, swept by firemen's hoses and the red lights of emergency beacons. My face must have looked as if I'd just been wracked on a front drop-cradle. "Nothing too serious," Coach said, handing me the phone.

Christmas was three days away, and our relatives were due in from Iowa. My mother had a bird about ready to come out of the oven, so she couldn't go pick up my father. He was drunk at a bar in Fenton. She sniffled over the kitchen noises.

I borrowed Mike Zumwalt's car. This wasn't the first time I'd had to drive my dad home. The previous summer, when he'd gotten me a maintenance job at the big Sears warehouse, I'd spent one Friday-afternoon happy hour playing pinball while he and his buddies got passout sloppy at Victor's. I'd driven him home that night, three months before I even had a license, creeping along at forty-five in the right-hand lane.

The bar, a seedy little hole near I–44, was dark, but I could see him at a table with Mr. Taylor and Willy Berner. A woman was sitting on his lap. He was rolling his head and laughing.

"Watch it, buddy," the woman said, one hand fending him off under the table, the other pushing his shoulder. I recognized her, a secretary from the warehouse.

"Hey, Del," Mr. Taylor said, standing to shake. The woman stood quickly, smoothed her skirt, and stepped toward the back of the bar.

"Kate was just taking dictation," my father said. He laughed alone. His cigarette bobbed, ashes falling onto his wrinkled shirt.

"Grandma and Grandpa are going to be here soon," I said.

My father ducked, glancing around. Then he laughed again.

"At the house."

"Oh, boy."

I steered him out to the car. I had to explain about a hundred times why we weren't using his Galaxie.

"I'll pick it up later," I said.

"Not going in anyone else's."

"Dad."

"Got my own car."

"Get in the car, Dad."

"My car."

"Get in the goddamn car."

His hand flew and my ear rang, and then began to burn and throb.

"Shit!"

"Don't you dare."

"My ear." I'd just gotten it drained for a cauliflower a month before.

"Don't ever let me hear . . ."

"My bad ear."

His feet were planted, and he swayed slightly, hands ready. He was just a medium-size man, though he had me by thirty-five pounds. My blood was rushing, my hands were shaking, and my throat went tight, squeezing the water into my eyes. Not because my ear ached, and not because of his anger, but because at that moment more than anything in the world I wanted to drop him on the asphalt and snap his damn neck, and I knew I could do it. He looked like a drunk from some sorry old movie.

"Del," he croaked, his hands dropping. He collapsed against Zummie's beat-up Pontiac. "I need help."

I got him into the car.

"I don't know what the hell," he moaned.

We called Mr. Furman "Scarlett" because he was a liar who wore a girdle and had a southern accent. Also, he turned bright red when he was angry, which was often in our class. He tried to disguise his nearly bald head with one eighteen-inch strand of hair wrapped from ear to ear and over his forehead. He taught English, and none of us doubted him for a second when he declared himself "somewhat of an authority on American fiction."

"He *is* American fiction," I whispered to Luke Jones, who blurted a laugh.

"Something to contribute, Mr. Jones?"

Luke froze. His nickname at school was Cool Hand, because he could work such magic with a basketball. On the courts he was graceful and fluent, but in the classroom he was awkward and tentative, and Scarlett was the kind of teacher who respected only one language—the one he taught.

"I was just telling him how much I love American fiction," I said.

"Oh, really." Scarlett smirked. "Any particular favorite, Del?"

Mr. Furman hated my guts. I didn't care about grades and did my assignments on the stationary bike in our basement, so my papers were always smudged with sweat. I made a point of carrying the latest edition of *Amateur Wrestling News* with my notebooks, and had even managed to cite that publication in my latest paper, a report on *The World According to Garp*.

"Halsey Taylor," I said. "I've been reading a lot of Halsey Taylor lately."

"Halsey Taylor?"

"Writes really weird stories about appliances and plumbing fixtures. Absurdist industrial fiction, they call it."

"Yes," Furman said. "I recall the name. Smart guy."

After class Luke followed me down the hall.

"I don't get it," he said. "How come he gave you an extra assignment?"

I waited as he drank at the fountain, his eyes only inches from the logo imprinted on the basin: HALSEY TAYLOR. Luke sprayed the wall.

"How was I supposed to know?" I said. "Didn't think he could bend down in that girdle."

Luke stopped me with his big hand, and we admired Linda Werner's wondrous profile as she passed.

"Eight steals and ten assists, but only six points. I foul out," Luke said.

"Step behind. Two takedowns and back points in the third period, but she escapes. No fall."

In Scarlett's class Luke and I normally spent the better part of the hour straining with every ounce of our energy to imagine beyond the fabric of Linda Werner's jeans. There she is, I'd think, no more than thirty inches from my face, nothing but a thin single skinny millimeter of cotton between me and her perfect beautiful nakedness. So close I'd spray her if I sneezed.

"I'd love to ask her out," Luke said.

"Do it."

"You crazy? She's married."

"To Hawkins?" I made a sour face. Brian Hawkins was a dweeb and a smart-ass, and Linda's eyes wandered as the two of them talked in the hallway.

"Another happy marriage."

"Yeah, yeah," I said.

That's how it starts, I thought. People come together for the wrong reasons, tell lies from the beginning, and pretty soon someone's wearing a hairpiece and filing for divorce.

·   ·   ·

My dad was staying at the Sunny Motor Court over on Route 66 while he looked for an apartment. It was a dingy little motel along a run-down strip of an old highway littered with other neon dives and fast-food joints. His room was cluttered with dirty T-shirts, and the bed was unmade. A half-full fifth of Cutty sat on the TV, an empty in the wastebasket.

"Nice place," my father said. "Bet you wish you had it so good."

His girlfriend had given him the hook, and his boss had warned him about missing work. My mother had told me this after a long, hushed phone conversation. "I'm sorry," I'd heard her say. "Not this time. No way." I'd found a lawyer's card on the table by her purse.

I wanted to ask him what was up. I wanted to ask him what he was doing. I wanted to ask him why he didn't quit drinking, what had happened to him, why he was acting this way.

"You like it here?" I asked.

"Think I'm nuts?"

I shrugged and stared at the wastebasket.

"Dad," I said. I wanted to tell him I was worried, worried about us, and even more worried about him, afraid he was going off the deep end. But how do you say those things to your father? "When are you moving?"

"Next week. This used to be a great place. Route 66. Remember?"

I didn't remember, although I recalled his stories about it. But as long as I'd known it, 66 had been a strip of crumbling blacktop and cheap cinder-block malls.

"St. Louis," he said, sitting on the edge of the rumpled bed and staring toward the window. "St. Louis, Misery. But this was some road, once upon a time."

My last dual match before the district tournament was against a guy named Wallor from St. Louis University High. He was pumped, but a fish, a sucker for ankle picks who always fagged out early. I'd already pinned him twice that year. Before every match Coach Carson used to tell me as he shook out my arms, "Just wrestle your match, hard as you can go, three full periods." What he really meant was, "Don't get cocky. Anything can happen out there."

True, for the most part. But Wallor was never a match; he was one of those guys who were so easy to beat that I got little pleasure in winning. He looked like a wrestler, and he was plenty strong and quick. I could never figure out what he lacked. But I tried not to think about it too much—why he lost, why he wasn't as good as he looked, how he felt about losing. The best way to deal with the idea of losing, I'd decided, was not to dwell on it.

I knew my dad was in the stands. This was the first dual meet he'd come to all year, the first my mother had skipped. I shook Wallor's hand, and at the whistle I circled, faked a shot, snapped him down, spun around for two points, sank my leg in for the cross-body, and started to crank.

But I was too high, way up on his shoulders. He shrugged, dropped and jerked back, and then was on me, digging his chin into my shoulder, burying a deep half-nelson, and pushing with his powerful chest.

I felt my shoulders tilting toward the mat. I kicked my legs the other way and rolled, but he caught me, my shoulders breaking ninety degrees. He was strong. The ref was kneeling, his hand waving the near fall points in front of my face. My shoulders were settling. The gym was a roar. I'd never been pinned.

"Get off your back, Del! Get off your back!"

I could see Coach Carson off his chair, waving, his mouth moving. "Get off your back, Del! Get off your back!" But the words weren't his.

I kicked and rolled again, arching my shoulders up as far as possible off the mat. Wallor's chin dug at my collarbone.

"Get off your back, Del! Please! Get off your back!"

It was my father. I could see him now at the edge of the mat, on his hands and knees, red-faced and barking at me.

"Off your back!"

He waved his trench coat at the edge of the circle, as if sweeping the seat off the edge of the mat.

"Get up, Del! Get off your back!"

His flushed face looked swollen, twisted, strained. The rest of the gym suddenly seemed silent, the only sound my father's hoarse shouts.

"Get off your back, Del! Get up, Son!"

He crawled closer to the edge of the circle.

Wallor tried to sink his hold deeper, and his arm shifted, loosening slightly. I bridged, spun, grambied, and shot back while he was still squatting, catching his ankle. The gym erupted again.

I sank my own half-nelson before he could roll, catching his other arm, weak from flexing to stick me, in a tight double-trouble. He left his legs sprawled open, so I cranked harder, spinning on top to lock them in an Oklahoma.

Forget about it: this hold was death. The ref slapped the mat.

I never looked into the eyes of the ones who went down easy, knowing what I'd see there and afraid of getting too close to it. But this time I looked Wallor in the face when we shook.

"Jesus," I said to Coach as I came off, the rest of the team slapping my backside.

"Way to go."

"Great job."

"Nice stick."

My dad was beside the bench, breathing as hard as I was, his forehead just as sweaty.

"Unbelievable," he said, squeezing my shoulder. He smelled like an ashtray sprinkled with Old Spice. "Scared the death outta me."

The gym had quieted, and I felt a lot of eyes on us. I wondered whether the place had really gone silent while my dad was on all fours. You can't trust your ears out there, where, normally, the crowd is just background noise, like TV static from another room. I wondered what my father had looked like to the crowd, crawling like that. He'd sweated clear through to his tie, his shirt half untucked.

"Took ten years off your old man's life," he said. "Don't expect me to come to another match."

I looked at his face and saw Wallor's eyes. It wasn't panic. It wasn't fear. It was a kind of weary resignation. The eyes of losing.

Twice a week at the end of practice—after jumping jacks, sit-ups, push-ups, bridges, takedowns, sit-outs, stand-ups, thirty-second drills, and running the stairs—we would hit the weight room. It was district-tournament time, the first step toward the state meet, an end to the clowning that began sometime in mid-season and continued into the lull after our last dual. Even Blake Simmons, a ninety-eight-pound senior who dedicated most of the season to finding freshmen he could figure-four and otherwise abuse, got serious.

In the weight room you wrestled yourself. The dumbbells were there to cooperate, to take you, each time you touched them, to the very edge. If you lifted right, you got stronger, so you could push further the next time, but the limit was always there, waiting for your muscles to quiver and gas out. Your limit is your own, not the iron's, and the guys who squirm against too many plates create only an illusion of strength. The only ones they fool are themselves. Those guys will let you beat them A guy like that will even help you.

"Okay, now," Coach Carson said, and we finished our sets and jogged back downstairs to the overheated wrestling room.

"Districts this weekend," Coach began. "I don't have to tell you what that means. This is it. Some of you are seniors. Enough said. But I want to tell you a story."

This was Coach's Dan Gable story. He told it this time every year. Once at the Midlands he'd wrestled the great Cyclone, had been turned on his back, and had spent half of the second period bridging and rocking to avoid the pin. He lost, but he lasted, against the greatest wrestler of all time, because he'd kept fighting.

"Do you know the secret to not getting stuck?" he asked. "It's no secret. It's pride and faith and stubbornness. That's all. You don't give in. No matter what, you keep going. You don't ever give up. That's it."

Coach worked out with us and was as fit as anyone on the team. His short Afro was gradually giving way to black forehead, but he didn't seem to care, so it looked good on him. He could take any one of us.

"There's no secret to it," he went on. "Never quit. Big secret."

I knew something was wrong as soon as I stepped into the house. You can smell bad news, feel it against your skin. Mr. Roe, an old friend of my parents' and the minister at the Congregational Church, was in the living room. He stood, and I could see it in his kind eyes.

"Del, I don't know how to tell you this." His hands sought a place to be. "There's been a terrible accident."

I stopped chewing my gum. I pictured my mother's Toyota upside down, on a median.

"They've found your father's body downtown."

I saw his car smashed deliberately into a pylon. I knew right off he'd done it to himself. What shocked me as much as anything was realizing suddenly that I'd expected this.

"He checked into the Marriott. Apparently he left a note. I'm so sorry. If I can do anything . . ."

"Where's my mom?"

"She had to go with the police. Marian went with her. They just left. This all happened very fast."

"Thank you," I said, and the words sounded stranger than any-thing I've ever heard come out of my mouth. "He was at the hotel?"

"Yes."

"Excuse me."

Three blocks from the house I dove behind a hedge and threw up. I cried like I'd never cried before and have never cried since, deep rushing waves that flowed without effort or thought. I hid my face in my arms, muffling the sounds against the cold ground. The street was dark and still. After a time I was empty, and I could hear the cars and trucks winding past, a few blocks away on the interstate.

Not far from our house was a pedestrian overpass where I often went to watch the cars. They had put I–44 through ten years before, slicing the town in two. After they'd paved it but before it was open, my father used to put our bikes in the car and take me there; we'd ride on the smooth new road all the way out past Kirkwood. He used to tell me about Route 66, the south border of our town, the great old highway, stretching from Chicago to L.A. It was like a river, and he'd felt like Huck Finn growing up beside it, watching trucks instead of barges, overloaded station wagons instead of rafts. He'd once hitchhiked it to California. And Highway 40, just north of our town, followed the trail of the explorers Lewis and Clark, he'd told me. And now a new one had been built, halfway between the old two. I'd go there often, after work-ing out, and stand on the overpass, following the taillights as far east as I could, closing my eyes to imagine the capital or New York, and then turning and watching the cars shoot out west, toward the Rockies and L.A. I'd close my eyes again, imagine myself alone in a car, pretend I was heading someplace.

That night I just stood there and thought of my dad, the eigh-teen-wheelers whooshing under the bridge. Each car was driven by someone who was alive, and my dad was dead. Maybe he'd still been alive when they'd gotten into the cars and started to drive, but he was dead now. The pavement was stained with oil and tread, and the cars never stopped, so I could barely imagine how clean it once was, that my father and I had ridden our bikes as far as we cared to go toward the Pacific.

My mother and I sat up almost all night at the dining-room table. We talked in low voices, and she cried every so often—just part of the conversation. But we also told stories that made us laugh, and each time that happened, the laughter echoed in my mind a moment after-ward and sounded very strange.

"God," she said. "Maybe I should have let him come back. He wanted to come back, you know. He asked me. If I'd let him come back . . ."

"Mom, you couldn't. It's not your fault."

On the table between us, beside her coffee cup and ashtray, his note lay upside down and wrinkled from when she'd wadded it up and thrown it away.

"I have decided," it read, "to quit smoking."

I didn't feel much when I looked at him in the casket. He didn't look like he was napping. He didn't look like himself. He looked dead, dressed up and made up, but dead. Looking at him was like staring at a wax replica.

After the funeral I shook hands and thanked people for coming to the reception at our house. Mr. Wilson, whose son and I had been in Indian Guides together, patted my arm.

"Bobby tells me you're really something," he said. "Says you're the strongest guy at school and that every time he sees you in the halls, you're surrounded with girls."

I smiled and denied the exaggerations and talked about Bobby, and the whole time, I watched the scene, thinking this was all very weird, to be joking about girls at my father's funeral.

I didn't face anyone new in the district tournament until the finals, when I was paired against an undefeated senior from De Smet who'd moved to the city from Ohio. I'd seen his name in the papers but didn't know much about him and didn't want to. I'd seen enough at the tournament to know he was quick on his feet and tough on top.

I'd worried that I wouldn't be able to concentrate on wrestling, but I was surprised to discover not only that I could but also that out on the mats there were moments when I forgot the constant dull ache I'd felt since that night. Then it would come back, the throbbing sense, like from a deep bruise.

I took down the senior from De Smet twice in the first period and again in the second, when I almost had him. I was ahead ten to three going into the final two minutes, and then we dropped to the mat in a whizzer and I felt something pop in my shoulder.

I froze a half second, and he pounced, driving me onto my back. I bridged. My shoulder burned. He was jerking at me to force me down. The gym was loud around us. He bounced on my chest. I kicked and rolled and bridged again, and then I heard it.

"Off your back, Del! Get off your back! Please! Get up, Del!"

I turned to look at the edge of the mat, but the only thing there was the scoreboard. I'd flattened out to look, and he wrenched my shoulder to tighten his hold. The pain knifed and burned, while this weird sort of dislocated sensation told me that part of my body was no longer properly connected.

"My shoulder," I said. It sounded like someone else's voice. *"My shoulder!"*

But the ref had already slapped the mat.

The Monday after the tournament I stayed home from school, propped up on the couch in front of the TV. I couldn't stand the commercials: my father was dead, I'd gotten pinned, and they were still merrily peddling Lemon Pledge, as if the world hadn't changed. I watched until the game shows and soap operas made me feel like I had the flu.

When I stood to turn off the set, the pain in my shoulder was sharp and hot. I'd have to rest the shoulder for four weeks, the doctor said. But nothing was broken and the joint was intact, so my biggest concern was how I was going to keep in shape during the few days I'd have to wait for the swelling to go down. Back on the couch I did leg lifts and flutters, using the ceiling to picture one-armed attacks.

My mother came home not long after three, and I listened to the clang of dishes from the kitchen.

"Mom," I called, trying to yell over the noise of the mixer. "Mom!"

"Yes?" she said, coming into the room, wiping her hands on her flour-sprinkled apron.

"What're you doing?"

"Making cookies. Chocolate chip."

My mother's cookies had come to signal the end of the season, when, during the break before AAUs, I could afford to put on a few pounds.

"Regionals are Friday," I said. "You want me to wrestle heavyweight?"

She gave me her motherly look, that mixture of tenderness, exasperation, and patience.

"Del," she said, in the quiet voice that hinted I didn't understand something. "Don't you think you can eat now? You know what the doctor said."

Although she was slender and fit, took long walks with friends, and sometimes rode her bike alongside me during runs, she'd reached that age when she needed three days to recover from an afternoon of raking leaves.

"Would you do me a really big favor?" I asked. She raised her eyebrows. "Downstairs by the bike. Could you bring me up a dumb-bell? Just one. One of the twenty-pound ones."

She frowned for a moment, as if she might say something, and then shook her head, sighed, and left. I raised my feet a few inches off the couch and held them as I listened to her trot down the stairs and then come back up more slowly. She lugged the black York iron with both hands.

"Criminy," she said. "I think I slipped a disc."

I took the weight and, with my right elbow at the edge of the sofa, began curling. I could feel the pull on my other shoulder. My mother slid out the coffee table for more room and then sat on the end of the couch, one hand on my ankle.

"Five, six, seven," she counted. The weight was a little heavy: I couldn't get a good angle and my elbow kept sinking into the cushion. I had to keep my bad side perfectly still.

"Nine, ten, eleven," my mother continued.

Should have asked for the fifteen-pounder and gone for more reps, I thought.

"Sixteen," she said. I wanted to crank out at least twenty. I took the weight back down.

"Del," she said, and I paused. "Take that weight all the way down. You're cheating."

I knew I'd have to take it a rep at a time, as many as it took. Just do what I could and hope for the best. No cheating.

DISAPPEARING

Monica Wood

When he starts in, I don't look anymore, I know what it looks like, what he looks like, tobacco on his teeth. I just lie in the deep sheets and shut my eyes. I make noises that make it go faster and when he's done he's as far from me as he gets. He could be dead he's so far away.

Lettie says leave then stupid but who would want me. Three hundred pounds anyway but I never check. Skin like tapioca pudding, I wouldn't show anyone. A man.

So we go to the pool at the junior high, swimming lessons. First it's blow bubbles and breathe, blow and breathe. Awful, hot nosefuls of chlorine. My eyes stinging red and patches on my skin. I look worse. We'll get caps and goggles and earplugs and body cream Lettie says. It's better.

There are girls there, what bodies. Looking at me and Lettie out the side of their eyes. Gold hair, skin like milk, chlorine or no.

They thought when I first lowered into the pool, that fat one parting the Red Sea. I didn't care. Something happened when I floated. Good said the little instructor. A little redhead in an emerald suit, no stomach, a depression almost, and white wet skin. Good she said you float just great. Now we're getting somewhere. The whistle around her neck blinded my eyes. And the water under the fluorescent lights. I got scared and couldn't float again. The bottom of the pool was scarred, drops of gray shadow rippling. Without the water I would crack open my head, my dry flesh would sound like a splash on the tiles.

At home I ate a cake and a bottle of milk. No wonder you look like that he said. How can you stand yourself. You're no Cary Grant I told him and he laughed and laughed until I threw up.

When this happens I want to throw up again and again until my heart flops out wet and writhing on the kitchen floor. Then he would know I have one and it moves.

So I went back. And floated again. My arms came around and the groan of the water made the tight blondes smirk but I heard Good that's the crawl that's it in fragments from the redhead when I lifted my face. Through the earplugs I heard her skinny voice. She was happy that I was floating and moving too.

Lettie stopped the lessons and read to me things out of magazines. You have to swim a lot to lose weight. You have to stop eating too. Forget cake and ice cream. Doritos are out. I'm not doing it for that I told her but she wouldn't believe me. She couldn't imagine.

Looking down that shaft of water I know I won't fall. The water shimmers and eases up and down, the heft of me doesn't matter I float anyway.

He says it makes no difference I look the same. But I'm not the same. I can hold myself up in deep water. I can move my arms and feet and the water goes behind me, the wall comes closer. I can look down twelve feet to a cold slab of tile and not be afraid. It makes a difference I tell him. Better believe it mister.

Then this other part happens. Other men interest me. I look at them, real ones, not the ones on TV that's something else entirely. These are real. The one with the white milkweed hair who delivers the mail. The meter man from the light company, heavy thick feet in boots. A smile. Teeth. I drop something out of the cart in the supermarket to see who will pick it up. Sometimes a man. One had yellow short hair and called me ma'am. Young. Thin legs and an accent. One was older.

Looked me in the eyes. Heavy, but not like me. My eyes are nice. I color the lids. In the pool it runs off in blue tears. When I come out my face is naked.

The lessons are over, I'm certified. A little certificate signed by the redhead. She says I can swim and I can. I'd do better with her body, thin calves hard as granite.

I get a lane to myself, no one shares. The blondes ignore me now that I don't splash the water, know how to lower myself silently. And when I swim I cut the water cleanly.

For one hour every day I am thin, thin as water, transparent, invisible, steam or smoke.

The redhead is gone, they put her at a different pool and I miss the glare of the whistle dangling between her emerald breasts. Lettie won't come over at all now that she is fatter than me. You're so uppity she says. All this talk about water and who do you think you are.

He says I'm looking all right, so at night it is worse but sometimes now when he starts in I say no. On Sundays the pool is closed I can't say no. I haven't been invisible. Even on days when I don't say no it's all right, he's better.

One night he says it won't last, what about the freezer full of low-cal dinners and that machine in the basement. I'm not doing it for that and he doesn't believe me either. But this time there is another part. There are other men in the water I tell him. Fish he says. Fish in the sea. Good luck.

Ma you've lost says my daughter-in-law, the one who didn't want me in the wedding pictures. One with the whole family, she couldn't help that. I learned how to swim I tell her. You should try it, it might help your ugly disposition.

They closed the pool for two weeks and I went crazy. I went there anyway, drove by in the car. I drank water all day.

Then they opened again and I went every day, sometimes four times until the green paint and new stripes looked familiar as a face. At first the water was heavy as blood but I kept on until it was thinner and thinner, just enough to hold me up. That was when I stopped with the goggles and cap and plugs, things that kept the water out of me.

There was a time I went the day before a holiday and no one was there. It was echoey silence just me and the soundless empty pool and a lifeguard behind the glass. I lowered myself so slow it hurt every muscle but not a blip of water not a ripple not one sound and I was under in that other quiet, so quiet some tears got out, I saw their blue trail swirling.

The redhead is back and nods, she has seen me somewhere. I tell her I took lessons and she still doesn't remember.

This has gone too far he says I'm putting you in the hospital. He calls them at the pool and they pay no attention. He doesn't touch me and I smile into my pillow, a secret smile in my own square of the dark.

Oh my God Lettie says what the hell are you doing what the hell do you think you're doing. I'm disappearing I tell her and what can you do about it not a blessed thing.

For a long time in the middle of it people looked at me. Men. And I thought about it. Believe it, I thought. And now they don't look at me again. And it's better.

I'm almost there. Almost water.

The redhead taught me how to dive, how to tuck my head and vanish like a needle into skin, and every time it happens, my feet leaving the board, I think, this will be the time.

PLAYING THE GARDEN

Chris Fisher

I can't understand the way some people's heads work. Mom has explained to me that if everyone thought the same, it would be a dull world. Dad disagrees. He thinks if everything was done his way, the world would run a lot more smoothly. I've been trying to figure things out by myself lately, watching people, deciding what makes them tick. Mom says I should stop staring.

Everything looked pretty rosy in the fall. I was heading into grade eleven and the twins, Kathryn and Kevin, were enrolled at the University of Saskatchewan in Saskatoon. Kevin, the southwest's best hockey prospect since Bryan Trottier hitchhiked out of Val Marie, was going to play with the university hockey team. There had been some heavy talks around the kitchen table about that decision. Dad was positive that the road to success lay with the Regina Pats, the junior club that held Kevin's rights. After countless examples, Kevin finally convinced him that National Hockey League scouts watched university hockey games, too.

The city is a four-hour drive north from the farm, so Dad rented the twins a three-bedroom house close to the university. They came home every weekend. The very first time Kathryn came home alone, even as she walked in the door and said Kevin had stayed in the city, I had a feeling something wasn't right. They aren't identical twins, they don't know what each other's thinking or weird stuff like that, but they usually travelled together.

Kevin is the oldest, three minutes ahead of Kathryn and eighteen months ahead of me. Being so close in age, Kevin and I did a lot together growing up. Dad claims that Kevin could have said he was hitchhiking to the North Pole and I'd have followed him out the door in my shorts. Sometimes during a game I would just lean back and watch him, pretending it was me scoring the goal or, for two months in the summer, pitching no-hitters and hitting the ball over the fence.

Kathryn and I spent our growing up time fighting. Mom says I pick on Kathryn because I'm jealous that she is Kevin's twin and I'm just a brother. That's too deep for me. I think anybody with a spaced-out sister like Kathryn would have to occasionally drag her back down to earth.

The second weekend in a row that Kathryn came home alone, everyone became suspicious. She said she was working on a psychology assignment, interpreting a dream of a member of the opposite sex. Since she wasn't dating anyone, proving to me that those university guys really were bright, she came home looking for a "male study." She asked Dad on Saturday morning, at breakfast, if he would participate. He said the only dreams he ever remembered were of tractors and grasshoppers, and even Hectare our cat could figure that out.

"Get Kevin to help," he said.

Kathryn and Mom exchanged looks. They knew something, that was for sure.

Mom said in her cheery, early morning voice that drives me nuts, "I imagine Kevin has enough to do. More bacon?"

Dad ignored the plate Mom was holding out and looked from Kathryn to her and back again.

"Why not him? Won't he have the same assignment?"

Kathryn shrugged. "Not sure. Different classes."

Dad pushed his plate away and leaned his forearms on the table. "You started in the same classes, didn't you?"

Kathryn nodded.

"Now you're in different classes."

She nodded, glancing again at Mom.

"Same university?"

"Yes."

"Still living in the same house?" Dad asked.

"Of course, Daddy. It's just that he's not around a lot. He hangs out with different people."

I could understand that. Kevin had met some people with good taste who only associated with quality women.

Dad nodded and pointed at me.

"Check out this dreamer," he growled, waving his half-eaten piece of toast at me. "See what button we have to push to get a little work out of him."

He had been upset with me ever since I told him I wasn't going to follow in his farmer footsteps, and I should spend next summer with Kevin in Saskatoon, looking for a part-time job. He said I would stay at home and earn my keep.

I didn't see any harm in helping Kathryn out. I remembered one dream I'd had pretty steady for the last few years, "recurring" is what Kathryn called it, and I thought it might be interesting to see what she came up with.

"Okay," I told her, "I'll do it on one condition. No smartass comments while I'm talking, and after it's done, you tell me what you wrote."

"That's two conditions."

"Your future's definitely in the math field," I said. "Is it a deal or not? I've got other things to do."

She agreed; the report was due the next week. We went into the living room and she told me to lie down on the couch. She dragged over the big recliner-rocker and sat down, holding a pen and paper. Then she leaned over the coffee table and flicked on her tape recorder.

"Now," she said, clearing her throat, "Case A, begin your dream dialogue."

"Okay, I started having this dream six years ago and—"

"Six? Are you positive? Why would you remember that?"

"I remember because our peewee team had just won provincials. Our deal was you wouldn't cut in."

"You mean after Kevin won."

I glared at her. One of Kathryn's most annoying habits is in stating the obvious. Everyone knew that Kevin was our whole team. He could have won with just himself and a goalie. We won the final 6–3 and he scored five of the goals. I got the other one. I fell in front of their net and the puck deflected in off my helmet. I consider myself a positional player.

"Sorry," I said. "I didn't realize you were telling this. Carry on, I'm curious about how it ends."

That shut her up. She zipped her mouth closed and motioned for me to continue. I leaned back and looked up at the ceiling so I could pretend she didn't exist.

"The New York Rangers are scouting for a center-man. They're Kevin's favorite team. Funny, though, it's my dream and I'm a Leaf fan. You'd think . . ." I could hear her pen scratching away by my ear. "Anyway, it's a Ranger scout watching us skate down at the Garden."

The Garden is our nickname for the rink Dad makes each year down behind the garage. He smooths out Mom's potato patch, puts up some plywood boards and floods until there's enough ice to skate on. It's our job to keep the ice clean of snow.

"This scout comes into the garage where Kevin and I are taking our skates off. He's got this million dollar contract and a big pen with a fancy feather plume on it. He waves it at Kevin and says, 'Sign here, my boy.' Kevin says, 'No way, José, not without my right-winger.' He points at me. The two of us are a unit, a package deal. Playing without me would be like playing with one skate. The scout winks at me and agrees. He pulls out another contract that I sign with a Bic."

Kathryn interrupted again.

"Do you recognize the scout?"

"Yeah, it's Fred Flintstone."

She started to scratch that down.

"No, I was joking, I was kidding. The scout isn't familiar."

She sighed and said, "Continue," real professional, like it was me who stopped in the first place.

"We immediately fly to New York for their next NHL game. There's cameras flashing and reporters scurrying around. We rush to Madison Square Garden, where a huge crowd's milling around out front. They sneak us in a side door. The players are in Ranger uniforms but they're all my favorites, Davey Keon and Paul Henderson and Bobby Orr and Anders Hedberg. They shake our hands and look relieved, like the U.S. cavalry just arrived. We get brand-new skates and as many sticks and rolls of tape as we want." I stopped, trying to find the right words. I had never explained the dream to anyone before, just lived and felt the scenes.

"There's got to be more," Kathryn said. "It has to be a ten-page report."

"Well, the opposition's never very clear, like it's not Montreal one night and Boston the next. And the players are kind of fuzzy, with no real shape to them. There's this mist clinging to everything, like fog. Our whole team, except me and Kevin, sits on the bench. The stands are a big blur but I can hear the crowd roaring, the rise and fall of the noise as the play develops. Whenever I look up, there's Kevin, either giving me a great pass or in perfect position to catch one. We weave through everybody."

I stopped, realizing something about the dream that I'd never noticed before. "It's weird, but we never finish the season, never play for the Stanley Cup. There's just miles to skate, goals to score, games to play forever. There's no end, just this feeling, this satisfaction, making the good play and knowing it's a good play and being . . . being . . ."

"Appreciated?"

"Yeah, that's the word, appreciated. You know what I mean?"

"I know the term, not the feeling." Kathryn stopped scratching on the paper and sighed. "Is that all?"

"Tha-tha-tha that's all, folks," I answered, sitting up.

Kathryn clicked off the tape recorder and gathered it up. She retreated into her room and shut the door, leaving her Garfield Do Not Disturb sign around the knob. At suppertime, Mom knocked on her door and went in. She stayed in there for almost an hour and came out alone. By then the potatoes were cold and Dad wouldn't eat because Hockey Night in Canada had already started. Mom seemed quieter than usual and went to bed early.

On Sunday morning, after a night of tapping away on the type-writer, the hermit emerged from her cave. She sat down at the breakfast table all smiles and didn't say a word.

"Well," I finally asked, "what's the verdict?"

"Hero worship," she announced, as proud as if she had just spouted off $E = mc^2$.

"Deep," I said, looking across the table at Dad.

"She'll go far," he said.

Mom broke in. "Very good work, dear. I'm sure Kevin will be pleased his brother admires him."

"Right, Mom," Kathryn said, and they exchanged another glance.

Dad noticed the look and thumped his cup down so hard that the coffee slopped onto the table. "What's going on here? Am I going to miss another meal before I find out anything? You and Kevin not talking?"

"We talk."

"What's up, then? You come home without him, someone's changing classes, you don't see him much. Is homework affecting his workouts? Should he cut his workload? Too many parties? Girls? Should I call his coach or what?"

When Dad hollers, we listen.

"Kevin should be telling you this," Kathryn said. "But since you insist, he's decided not to play hockey this year."

"Aha! I told him junior was better for him but would he listen? No. Now their season's started already. Has he talked to the Pats coach yet? Never mind, I'll call Jamieson right away. God knows he's called me enough over the years."

"Dad, he's—"

"That explains why he hasn't been home. His pride's been hurt, hates to admit I was right all along. Well, I'll call him, too, once I find out some news from the Pats."

Dad started to get up, to move toward the phone.

Mom reached over and put her hand on his shoulder. "Frank, he's not playing at all, anywhere, period."

Dad sat back down with a thump.

Someone had to have their wires crossed somewhere. Maybe I would end up playing right wing for the Dolguard Seniors but Kevin was different. He was going places, places for me, for all of us. Some day we'd watch him live in the Stanley Cup, or huddle around the TV on Saturday night and cheer when he was the first star.

Dad took a gulp of his coffee, swished it around in his mouth and swallowed. "If this is some practical joke, I'm telling you right now, I'm not laughing."

"It's the truth, Dad," Kathryn said. "They've started practicing and he hasn't gone. I shouldn't say anything. He would have told you when it was time."

"Maybe he'll change his mind," I suggested.

They all turned and stared at me.

"Well, what's his problem?" Dad asked.

"Dad, maybe he should tell you—"

"What's his prob-lem!" he hollered.

"It takes up too much time. His heart's not in it. He says he's had enough of hockey and now there's other things to do. He's got other interests, things he's never done before." Kathryn stood up. "He's switching classes, taking drama, going from education to arts."

Once, in grade eight, I was wrestling Ned Parker, my best friend, and he kicked me in the nuts. The pain didn't hurt as much as the surprise that he would even think of doing that to me. I felt that same emptiness now.

Mom stood up and started clearing off the dishes, even though no one had finished eating. "It'll straighten itself out. There's obviously been some mix-up. Frank, calm down. No use getting excited over something we can't change." She wiped up the coffee that Dad had spilled.

"I am calm, dammit. Kathryn, is there a girl?"

"Not that I know of. I told you, he hangs around with a group of guys."

"And they're not from the hockey team?" Dad asked.

Kathryn looked uncomfortable and Mom coughed.

"No," Kathryn said.

Mom moved to stand behind Dad's chair. She put her hand on his shoulder.

"Well, that's it," Dad said. "Years down the tube. Move to the city, get a little freedom, get into trouble."

"Oh no," Kathryn said. "Kevin isn't in any trouble."

"Wasn't, you mean. Tell him he can stay away if he wants to. He made his own bed, now he can sleep in it."

Dad rose from the table and stomped into the living room. He turned on the TV and slammed back into the recliner.

Mom was looking out the kitchen window. Kathryn moved over beside her.

"I had to tell him that at least, Mom," Kathryn said. "He'd have found out as soon as they played their first game."

"Maybe, dear. I still think it might all blow over."

"None of this is blowing over, Mom."

Mom turned and looked into Kathryn's eyes and they did that thing I always hate, when they stare at each other as if they are peering into each other's souls. It seems to calm them down so I never tease them about it. I just sat at the table, not really thinking anything.

Mom sat down at the table beside me while Kathryn poured them both some tea. She lifted the pot toward me but I shook my head. I thought I should get up and start chores before Dad yelled. Kathryn came around and sat down on my other side. She leaned in and looked across at Mom.

"It's not the time or place," Mom said.

"When is?" Kathryn asked. "When he hears it at school? Or when he goes up and visits?"

Mom shrugged. "Are we the ones to tell him?"

"Probably not," Kathryn said. "But I'd want to be told by someone here, and not on the street. We're all family."

Mom sighed. "It's not for sure."

"Mom, I live with him. You don't know how many times I've told myself the same thing."

I sat listening to the conversation bounce back and forth and felt like I was watching a tennis match. An annoying tennis match, because I hadn't asked to watch.

"What are you two talking about?" I asked. "If you're talking about telling me, Kathryn, then there's nothing you could tell me more surprising than what you already have."

So, with Mom sitting beside me there, just staring into her tea, Kathryn told me.

It's been six weeks now and there is still a tenseness in the air around home. Kevin has yet to make an appearance but Kathryn fills us in on his activities. She and I have had a couple of good talks, and I think she may turn out to be all right after all. Mom's been up to visit once but Dad wouldn't go. Mom asked if I wanted to go along, she said it was okay to miss school, but I had this biology project to work on. Mom sighed and gave me her sad look as I turned away. She knows how much I usually love an excuse to skip biology.

I've had everybody in the world ask me if the rumors about Kevin are true. I knot up inside and ask, What rumors? They look at me kind of funny and say they heard that Kevin wasn't playing hockey. I say, I don't know, I haven't talked to him lately. The day the question changes, I don't know what or how I'll answer.

Every year for as long as I can remember we've spent the end of

December flooding the Garden and building a respectable rink. Dad started early this year, clearing and raking the surface. He hasn't asked for my help or even mentioned that he's started. He put the boards up himself while I was at school. It hasn't been nearly cold enough, but he's been flooding every night after "The Journal," almost willing the water to freeze. I'm sure he's trying to have it ready by next weekend, when the twins come home for Christmas break.

I'm nervous about seeing Kevin but keep telling myself that he'll look and act the same and so should I. Mom says Dad will behave himself but Dad says a guy can do whatever he wants in his own house. I imagine that Dad plans on taking Kevin down to the rink for a chat, hoping that the magic of the Garden will transform Kevin into having the desire to play hockey again. Kevin will then tell Dad what the rest of us already know. Mom and Kathryn will busy themselves making another large meal and I'll go and do the chores early.

Of course I know Dad's dreaming, and I certainly don't believe in magic, but for the past two mornings I've been up at five. The ground is still wet and soft, and it's hardly cold enough for you to see your breath. I flood anyway, trying to step in Dad's tracks so he doesn't know I've been down there. The weatherman said temperatures could drop to ten below tonight. Maybe we'll get ice after all. If blood is truly thicker than water, even the frozen kind, then the healing will have to start down at the Garden.

REVENGE

Ellen Gilchrist

It was the summer of the Broad Jump Pit.

The Broad Jump Pit, how shall I describe it! It was a bright orange rectangle in the middle of a green pasture. It was three feet deep, filled with river sand and sawdust. A real cinder track led up to it, ending where tall poles for pole-vaulting rose forever in the still Delta air.

I am looking through the old binoculars. I am watching Bunky coming at a run down the cinder path, pausing expertly at the jump-off line, then rising into the air, heels stretched far out in front of him, landing in the sawdust. Before the dust has settled Saint John comes running with the tape, calling out measurements in his high, excitable voice.

Next comes my thirteen-year-old brother, Dudley, coming at a brisk jog down the track, the pole-vaulting pole held lightly in his delicate hands, then vaulting, high into the sky. His skinny tanned legs make a last, desperate surge, and he is clear and over.

Think how it looked from my lonely exile atop the chicken

house. I was ten years old, the only girl in a house full of cousins. There were six of us, shipped to the Delta for the summer, dumped on my grandmother right in the middle of a world war.

They built this wonder in answer to a V-Mail letter from my father in Europe. The war was going well, my father wrote, within a year the Allies would triumph over the forces of evil, the world would be at peace, and the Olympic torch would again be brought down from its mountain and carried to Zurich or Amsterdam or London or Mexico City, wherever free men lived and worshiped sports. My father had been a participant in an Olympic event when he was young.

Therefore, the letter continued, Dudley and Bunky and Philip and Saint John and Oliver were to begin training. The United States would need athletes now, not soldiers.

They were to train for broad jumping and pole-vaulting and discus throwing, for fifty-, one-hundred-, and four-hundred-yard dashes, for high and low hurdles. The letter included instructions for building the pit, for making pole-vaulting poles out of cane, and for converting ordinary sawhorses into hurdles. It ended with a page of tips for proper eating and admonished Dudley to take good care of me as I was my father's own dear sweet little girl.

The letter came one afternoon. Early the next morning they began construction. Around noon I wandered out to the pasture to see how they were coming along. I picked up a shovel.

"Put that down, Rhoda," Dudley said. "Don't bother us now. We're working."

"I know it," I said. "I'm going to help."

"No, you're not," Bunky said. "This is the Broad Jump Pit. We're starting our training."

"I'm going to do it too," I said. "I'm going to be in training."

"Get out of here now," Dudley said. "This is only for boys, Rhoda. This isn't a game."

"I'm going to dig it if I want to," I said, picking up a shovelful of dirt and throwing it on Philip. On second thought I picked up another shovelful and threw it on Bunky.

"Get out of here, Ratface," Philip yelled at me. "You German spy." He was referring to the initials on my Girl Scout uniform.

"You goddamn niggers," I yelled. "You niggers. I'm digging this if I want to and you can't stop me, you nasty niggers, you Japs, you Jews." I was throwing dirt on everyone now. Dudley grabbed the shovel and wrestled me to the ground. He held my arms down in the coarse grass and peered into my face.

"Rhoda, you're not having anything to do with this Broad Jump Pit. And if you set foot inside this pasture or come around here and touch anything we will break your legs and drown you in the bayou with a crowbar around your neck." He was twisting my leg until it creaked at the joints. "Do you get it, Rhoda? Do you understand me?"

"Let me up," I was screaming, my rage threatening to split open my skull. "Let me up, you goddamn nigger, you Jap, you spy. I'm telling Grannie and you're going to get the worst whipping of your life. And you better quit digging this hole for the horses to fall in. Let me up, let me up. Let me go."

"You've been ruining everything we've thought up all summer," Dudley said, "and you're not setting foot inside this pasture."

In the end they dragged me back to the house, and I ran screaming into the kitchen where Grannie and Calvin, the black man who did the cooking, tried to comfort me, feeding me pound cake and offering to let me help with the mayonnaise.

"You be a sweet girl, Rhoda," my grandmother said, "and this afternoon we'll go over to Eisenglas Plantation to play with Miss Ann Wentzel."

"I don't want to play with Miss Ann Wentzel," I screamed. "I hate Miss Ann Wentzel. She's fat and she calls me a Yankee. She said my socks were ugly."

"Why, Rhoda," my grandmother said. "I'm surprised at you. Miss Ann Wentzel is your own sweet friend. Her momma was your momma's roommate at All Saint's. How can you talk like that?"

"She's a nigger," I screamed. "She's a goddamned nigger German spy."

"Now it's coming. Here comes the temper," Calvin said, rolling his eyes back in their sockets to make me madder. I threw my second fit of the morning, beating my fists into a door frame. My grandmother seized me in soft arms. She led me to a bedroom where I sobbed myself to sleep in a sea of down pillows.

The construction went on for several weeks. As soon as they finished breakfast every morning they started out for the pasture. Wood had to be burned to make cinders, sawdust brought from the sawmill, sand hauled up from the riverbank by wheelbarrow.

When the pit was finished the savage training began. From my several vantage points I watched them. Up and down, up and down they ran, dove, flew, sprinted. Drenched with sweat they wrestled each other to the ground in bitter feuds over distances and times and fractions of inches.

Dudley was their self-appointed leader. He drove them like a demon. They began each morning by running around the edge of the pasture several times, then practicing their hurdles and dashes, then on to discus throwing and calisthenics. Then on to the Broad Jump Pit with its endless challenges.

They even pressed the old mare into service. Saint John was from New Orleans and knew the British ambassador and was thinking of being a polo player. Up and down the pasture he drove the poor old creature, leaning far out of the saddle, swatting a basketball with my grandaddy's cane.

I spied on them from the swing that went out over the bayou, and from the roof of the chicken house, and sometimes from the pasture fence itself, calling out insults or attempts to make them jealous.

"Guess what," I would yell, "I'm going to town to the China-man's store." "Guess what, I'm getting to go to the beauty parlor." "Dr. Biggs says you're adopted."

They ignored me. At meals they sat together at one end of the table, making jokes about my temper and my red hair, opening their mouths so I could see their half-chewed food, burping loudly in my direction.

At night they pulled their cots together on the sleeping porch, plotting against me while I slept beneath my grandmother's window, listening to the soft assurance of her snoring.

I began to pray the Japs would win the war, would come marching into Issaquena County and take them prisoners, starving and torturing them, sticking bamboo splinters under their fingernails. I saw myself in the Japanese colonel's office, turning them in, writing their names down, myself being treated like an honored guest, drinking tea from tiny blue cups like the ones the Chinaman had in his store.

They would be outside, tied up with wire. There would be Dudley, begging for mercy. What good to him now his loyal gang, his photographic memory, his trick magnet dogs, his perfect pitch, his camp shorts, his Baby Brownie camera.

I prayed they would get polio, would be consigned forever to iron lungs. I put myself to sleep at night imagining their labored breathing, their five little wheelchairs lined up by the store as I drive by in my

father's Packard, my arm around the jacket of his blue uniform, on my
way to Hollywood for my screen test.

Meanwhile, I practiced dancing. My grandmother had a black house-
keeper named Baby Doll who was a wonderful dancer. In the mornings
I followed her around while she dusted, begging for dancing lessons.
She was a big woman, as tall as a man, and gave off a dark rich smell, an
unforgettable incense, a combination of Evening in Paris and the sweet
perfume of the cabins.

Baby Doll wore bright skirts and on her blouses a pin that said
REMEMBER, then a real pearl, then HARBOR. She was engaged to a sailor
and was going to California to be rich as soon as the war was over.

I would put a stack of heavy, scratched records on the record
player, and Baby Doll and I would dance through the parlors to the
music of Glenn Miller or Guy Lombardo or Tommy Dorsey.

Sometimes I stood on a stool in front of the fireplace and made
up lyrics while Baby Doll acted them out, moving lightly across the old
dark rugs, turning and swooping and shaking and gliding.

Outside the summer sun beat down on the Delta, beating down a
million volts a minute, feeding the soybeans and cotton and clover,
sucking Steele's Bayou up into the clouds, beating down on the road and
the store, on the pecans and elms and magnolias, on the men at work in
the fields, on the athletes at work in the pasture.

Inside Baby Doll and I would be dancing. Or Guy Lombardo
would be playing "Begin the Beguine" and I would be belting out lyrics.

> Oh, let them begin . . . we don't care,
> America all . . . ways does its share,
> We'll be there with plenty of ammo,
> Allies . . . don't ever despair . . .

Baby Doll thought I was a genius. If I was having an especially
creative morning she would go running out to the kitchen and bring
anyone she could find to hear me.

"Oh, let them begin any warrr . . ." I would be singing, tapping
one foot against the fireplace tiles, waving my arms around like a
conductor.

> Uncle Sam will fight
> for the underrr . . . doggg.
> Never fear, Allies, never fear.

A new record would drop. Baby Doll would swoop me into her fragrant arms, and we would break into an improvisation on Tommy Dorsey's "Boogie-Woogie."

But the Broad Jump Pit would not go away. It loomed in my dreams. If I walked to the store I had to pass the pasture. If I stood on the porch or looked out my grandmother's window, there it was, shimmering in the sunlight, constantly guarded by one of the Olympians.

Things went from bad to worse between me and Dudley. If we so much as passed each other in the hall a fight began. He would hold up his fists and dance around, trying to look like a fighter. When I came flailing at him he would reach underneath my arms and punch me in the stomach.

I considered poisoning him. There was a box of white powder in the toolshed with a skull and crossbones above the label. Several times I took it down and held it in my hands, shuddering at the power it gave me. Only the thought of the electric chair kept me from using it.

Every day Dudley gathered his troops and headed out for the pasture. Every day my hatred grew and festered. Then, just about the time I could stand it no longer, a diversion occurred.

One afternoon about four o'clock an official-looking sedan clattered across the bridge and came roaring down the road to the house.

It was my cousin, Lauralee Manning, wearing her WAVE uniform and smoking Camels in an ivory holder. Lauralee had been widowed at the beginning of the war when her young husband crashed his Navy training plane into the Pacific.

Lauralee dried her tears, joined the WAVES, and went off to avenge his death. I had not seen this paragon since I was a small child, but I had memorized the photograph Miss Onnie Maud, who was Lauralee's mother, kept on her dresser. It was a photograph of Lauralee leaning against the rail of a destroyer.

Not that Lauralee ever went to sea on a destroyer. She was spending the war in Pensacola, Florida, being secretary to an admiral.

Now, out of a clear blue sky, here was Lauralee, home on leave with a two-carat diamond ring and the news that she was getting married.

"You might have called and given some warning," Miss Onnie Maud said, turning Lauralee into a mass of wrinkles with her embraces. "You could have softened the blow with a letter."

"Who's the groom," my grandmother said. "I only hope he's not a pilot."

"Is he an admiral?" I said, "or a colonel or a major or a commander?"

"My fiancé's not in uniform, Honey," Lauralee said. "He's in real estate. He runs the war-bond effort for the whole state of Florida. Last year he collected half a million dollars."

"In real estate!" Miss Onnie Maud said, gasping. "What religion is he?"

"He's Unitarian," she said. "His name is Donald Marcus. He's best friends with Admiral Semmes, that's how I met him. And he's coming a week from Saturday, and that's all the time we have to get ready for the wedding."

"Unitarian!" Miss Onnie Maud said. "I don't think I've ever met a Unitarian."

"Why isn't he in uniform?" I insisted.

"He has flat feet," Lauralee said gaily. "But you'll love him when you see him."

Later that afternoon Lauralee took me off by myself for a ride in the sedan.

"Your mother is my favorite cousin," she said, touching my face with gentle fingers. "You'll look just like her when you grow up and get your figure."

I moved closer, admiring the brass buttons on her starched uniform and the brisk way she shifted and braked and put in the clutch and accelerated.

We drove down the river road and out to the bootlegger's shack where Lauralee bought a pint of Jack Daniel's and two Cokes. She poured out half of her Coke, filled it with whiskey, and we roared off down the road with the radio playing.

We drove along in the lengthening day. Lauralee was chain-smoking, lighting one Camel after another, tossing the butts out the window, taking sips from her bourbon and Coke. I sat beside her, pretending to smoke a piece of rolled-up paper, making little noises into the mouth of my Coke bottle.

We drove up to a picnic spot on the levee and sat under a tree to look out at the river.

"I miss this old river," she said. "When I'm sad I dream about it licking the tops of the levees."

I didn't know what to say to that. To tell the truth I was afraid to say much of anything to Lauralee. She seemed so splendid. It was enough to be allowed to sit by her on the levee.

"Now, Rhoda," she said, "your mother was matron of honor in my wedding to Buddy, and I want you, her own little daughter, to be maid of honor in my second wedding."

I could hardly believe my ears! While I was trying to think of something to say to this wonderful news I saw that Lauralee was crying, great tears were forming in her blue eyes.

"Under this very tree is where Buddy and I got engaged," she said. Now the tears were really starting to roll, falling all over the front of her uniform. "He gave me my ring right where we're sitting."

"The maid of honor?" I said, patting her on the shoulder, trying to be of some comfort. "You really mean the maid of honor?"

"Now he's gone from the world," she continued, "and I'm marrying a wonderful man, but that doesn't make it any easier. Oh, Rhoda, they never even found his body, never even found his body."

I was patting her on the head now, afraid she would forget her offer in the midst of her sorrow.

"You mean I get to be the real maid of honor?"

"Oh, yes, Rhoda, Honey," she said. "The maid of honor, my only attendant." She blew her nose on a lace-trimmed handkerchief and sat up straighter, taking a drink from the Coke bottle.

"Not only that, but I have decided to let you pick out your own dress. We'll go to Greenville and you can try on every dress at Nell's and Blum's and you can have the one you like the most."

I threw my arms around her, burning with happiness, smelling her whiskey and Camels and the dark Tabu perfume that was her signature. Over her shoulder and through the low branches of the trees the afternoon sun was going down in an orgy of reds and blues and purples and violets, falling from sight, going all the way to China.

Let them keep their nasty Broad Jump Pit, I thought. Wait till they hear about this. Wait till they find out I'm maid of honor in a military wedding.

Finding the dress was another matter. Early the next morning Miss Onnie Maud and my grandmother and Lauralee and I set out for Greenville.

As we passed the pasture I hung out the back window making faces at the athletes. This time they only pretended to ignore me. They couldn't ignore this wedding. It was going to be in the parlor instead of the church so they wouldn't even get to be altar boys. They wouldn't get to light a candle.

"I don't know why you care what's going on in that pasture," my grandmother said. "Even if they let you play with them all it would do is make you a lot of ugly muscles."

"Then you'd have big old ugly arms like Weegie Toler," Miss Onnie Maud said. "Lauralee, you remember Weegie Toler, that was a swimmer. Her arms got so big no one would take her to a dance, much less marry her."

"Well, I don't want to get married anyway," I said. "I'm never getting married. I'm going to New York City and be a lawyer."

"Where does she get those ideas?" Miss Onnie Maud said.

"When you get older you'll want to get married," Lauralee said. "Look at how much fun you're having being in my wedding."

"Well, I'm never getting married," I said. "And I'm never having any children. I'm going to New York and be a lawyer and save people from the electric chair."

"It's the movies," Miss Onnie Maud said. "They let her watch anything she likes in Indiana."

We walked into Nell's and Blum's Department Store and took up the largest dressing room. My grandmother and Miss Onnie Mead were seated on brocade chairs and every saleslady in the store came crowding around trying to get in on the wedding.

I refused to even consider the dresses they brought from the "girls'" department.

"I told her she could wear whatever she wanted," Lauralee said, "and I'm keeping my promise."

"Well, she's not wearing green satin or I'm not coming," my grandmother said, indicating the dress I had found on a rack and was clutching against me.

"At least let her try it on," Lauralee said. "Let her see for herself." She zipped me into the green satin. It came down to my ankles and fit around my midsection like a girdle, making my waist seem smaller than my stomach. I admired myself in the mirror. It was almost perfect. I looked exactly like a nightclub singer.

"This one's fine," I said. "This is the one I want."

"It looks marvelous, Rhoda," Lauralee said, "but it's the wrong color for the wedding. Remember I'm wearing blue."

"I believe the child's color-blind," Miss Onnie Maud said. "It runs in her father's family."

"I am not color-blind," I said, reaching behind me and unzipping the dress. "I have twenty-twenty vision."

"Let her try on some more," Lauralee said. "Let her try on everything in the store."

I proceeded to do just that, with the salesladies getting grumpier and grumpier. I tried on a gold gabardine dress with a rhinestone-studded cummerbund. I tried on a pink ballerina-length formal and a lavender voile tea dress and several silk suits. Somehow nothing looked right.

"Maybe we'll have to make her something," my grandmother said.

"But there's no time," Miss Onnie Maud said. "Besides first we'd have to find out what she wants. Rhoda, please tell us what you're looking for."

Their faces all turned to mine, waiting for an answer. But I didn't know the answer.

The dress I wanted was a secret. The dress I wanted was dark and tall and thin as a reed. There was a word for what I wanted, a word I had seen in magazines. But what was that word? I could not remember.

"I want something dark," I said at last. "Something dark and silky."

"Wait right there," the saleslady said. "Wait just a minute." Then, from out of a prewar storage closet she brought a black-watch plaid recital dress with spaghetti straps and a white piqué jacket. It was made of taffeta and rustled when I touched it. There was a label sewn into the collar of the jacket. *Little Miss Sophisticate,* it said. *Sophisticate,* that was the word I was seeking.

I put on the dress and stood triumphant in a sea of ladies and dresses and hangers.

"This is the dress," I said. "This is the dress I'm wearing."

"It's perfect," Lauralee said. "Start hemming it up. She'll be the prettiest maid of honor in the whole world."

All the way home I held the box on my lap thinking about how I would look in the dress. Wait till they see me like this, I was thinking. Wait till they see what I really look like.

I fell in love with the groom. The moment I laid eyes on him I forgot he was flat-footed. He arrived bearing gifts of music and perfume and candy, a warm dark-skinned man with eyes the color of walnuts.

He laughed out loud when he saw me, standing on the porch with my hands on my hips.

"This must be Rhoda," he exclaimed, "the famous red-haired maid of honor." He came running up the steps, gave me a slow, exciting hug, and presented me with a whole album of Xavier Cugat records. I had never owned a record of my own, much less an album.

Before the evening was over I put on a red formal I found in a trunk and did a South American dance for him to Xavier Cugat's "Poinciana." He said he had never seen anything like it in his whole life.

The wedding itself was a disappointment. No one came but the immediate family and there was no aisle to march down and the only music was Onnie Maud playing "Liebestraum."

Dudley and Philip and Saint John and Oliver and Bunky were dressed in long pants and white shirts and ties. They had fresh military crew cuts and looked like a nest of new birds, huddled together on the blue velvet sofa, trying to keep their hands to themselves, trying to figure out how to act at a wedding.

The elderly Episcopal priest read out the ceremony in a gravelly smoker's voice, ruining all the good parts by coughing. He was in a bad mood because Lauralee and Mr. Marcus hadn't found time to come to him for marriage instruction.

Still, I got to hold the bride's flowers while he gave her the ring and stood so close to her during the ceremony I could hear her breathing.

The reception was better. People came from all over the Delta. There were tables with candles set up around the porches and sprays of greenery in every corner. There were gentlemen sweating in linen suits and the record player playing every minute. In the back hall Calvin had set up a real professional bar with tall, permanently frosted glasses and ice and mint and lemons and every kind of whiskey and liqueur in the world.

I stood in the receiving line getting compliments on my dress, then wandered around the rooms eating cake and letting people hug me. After a while I got bored with that and went out to the back hall and began to fix myself a drink at the bar.

I took one of the frosted glasses and began filling it from different bottles, tasting as I went along. I used plenty of créme de menthe and soon had something that tasted heavenly. I filled the glass with crushed ice, added three straws, and went out to sit on the back steps and cool off.

I was feeling wonderful. A full moon was caught like a kite in the pecan trees across the river. I sipped along on my drink. Then, without planning it, I did something I had never dreamed of doing. I left the porch alone at night. Usually I was in terror of the dark. My grandmother had told me that alligators come out of the bayou to eat children who wander alone at night.

I walked out across the yard, the huge moon giving so much light I almost cast a shadow. When I was nearly to the water's edge I turned and looked back toward the house. It shimmered in the moonlight like a jukebox alive in a meadow, seemed to pulsate with music and laughter and people, beautiful and foreign, not a part of me.

I looked out at the water, then down the road to the pasture. The Broad Jump Pit! There it was, perfect and unguarded. Why had I never thought of doing this before?

I began to run toward the road. I ran as fast as my Mary Jane pumps would allow me. I pulled my dress up around my waist and climbed the fence in one motion, dropping lightly down on the other side. I was sweating heavily, alone with the moon and my wonderful courage.

I knew exactly what to do first. I picked up the pole and hoisted it over my head. It felt solid and balanced and alive. I hoisted it up and down a few times as I had seen Dudley do, getting the feel of it.

Then I laid it ceremoniously down on the ground, reached behind me, and unhooked the plaid formal. I left it lying in a heap on the ground. There I stood, in my cotton underpants, ready to take up polevaulting.

I lifted the pole and carried it back to the end of the cinder path. I ran slowly down the path, stuck the pole in the wooden cup, and attempted throwing my body into the air, using it as a lever.

Something was wrong. It was more difficult than it appeared from a distance. I tried again. Nothing happened. I sat down with the pole across my legs to think things over.

Then I remembered something I had watched Dudley doing through the binoculars. He measured down from the end of the pole with his fingers spread wide. That was it, I had to hold it closer to the end.

I tried it again. This time the pole lifted me several feet off the ground. My body sailed across the grass in a neat arc and I landed on my toes. I was a natural!

I do not know how long I was out there, running up and down the cinder path, thrusting my body further and further through space, tossing myself into the pit like a mussel shell thrown across the bayou.

At last I decided I was ready for the real test. I had to vault over a cane barrier. I examined the pegs on the wooden poles and chose one that came up to my shoulder.

I put the barrier pole in place, spit over my left shoulder, and marched back to the end of the path. Suck up your guts, I told myself. It's only a pole. It won't get stuck in your stomach and tear out your insides. It won't kill you.

I stood at the end of the path eyeballing the barrier. Then, above the incessant racket of the crickets, I heard my name being called. Rhoda . . . the voices were calling. Rhoda . . . Rhoda . . . Rhoda . . . Rhoda.

I turned toward the house and saw them coming. Mr. Marcus and Dudley and Bunky and Calvin and Lauralee and what looked like half the wedding. They were climbing the fence, calling my name, and coming to get me. Rhoda . . . they called out. Where on earth have you been? What on earth are you doing?

I hoisted the pole up to my shoulders and began to run down the path, running into the light from the moon. I picked up speed, thrust the pole into the cup, and threw myself into the sky, into the still Delta night. I sailed up and was clear and over the barrier.

I let go of the pole and began my fall, which seemed to last a long, long time. It was like falling through clear water. I dropped into the sawdust and lay very still, waiting for them to reach me.

Sometimes I think whatever has happened since has been of no real interest to me.

VI

Dark
Victories

DOE SEASON

David Michael Kaplan

They were always the same woods, she thought sleepily as they drove through the early morning darkness—deep and immense, covered with yesterday's snowfall which had frozen overnight. They were the same woods that lay behind her house, *and they stretch all the way to here,* she thought, *for miles and miles, longer than I could walk in a day, or a week even, but they are still the same woods.* The thought made her feel good: it was like thinking of God; it was like thinking of the space between here and the moon; it was like thinking of all the foreign countries from her geography book where even now, Andy knew, people were going to bed, while they—she and her father and Charlie Spoon and Mac, Charlie's eleven-year-old son—were driving deeper into the Pennsylvania countryside, to go hunting.

They had risen long before dawn. Her mother, yawning and not trying to hide her sleepiness, cooked them eggs and French toast. Her father smoked a cigarette and flicked ashes into his saucer while Andy listened, wondering *Why doesn't he come?* and *Won't he ever come?,* until at last a car pulled into the graveled drive and honked. "That will be Charlie Spoon," her father said; he always said "Charlie Spoon," even though his real name was Spreun, because Charlie was, in a sense, shaped like a spoon, with a large head and a narrow waist and chest.

Andy's mother kissed her and her father and said, "Well, have a good time" and "Be careful." Soon they were outside in the bitter dark, loading gear by the back-porch light, their breath steaming. The woods behind the house were then only a black streak against the wash of night.

Andy dozed in the car and woke to find that it was half-light. Mac—also sleeping—had slid against her. She pushed him away and looked out the window. Her breath clouded the glass, and she was cold; the car's heater didn't work right. They were riding over gentle hills, the woods on both sides now—the same woods, she knew, because she had been watching the whole way, even while she slept. They had been in her dreams, and she had never lost sight of them.

Charlie Spoon was driving. "I don't understand why she's coming," he said to her father. "How old is she anyway—eight?"

"Nine," her father replied. "She's small for her age."

"So—nine. What's the difference? She'll just add to the noise and get tired besides."

"No, she won't," her father said. "She can walk me to death. And she'll bring good luck, you'll see. Animals—I don't know how she does it, but they come right up to her. We go walking in the woods, and we'll spot more raccoons and possums and such than I ever see when I'm alone."

Charlie grunted.

"Besides, she's not a bad little shot, even if she doesn't hunt yet. She shoots the .22 real good."

"Popgun," Charlie snorted. "And target shooting ain't deer hunting."

"Well, she's not gonna be shooting anyway, Charlie," her father said. "Don't worry. She'll be no bother."

"I still don't know why she's coming," Charlie said.

"Because she wants to, and I want her to. Just like you and Mac. No difference."

Charlie turned onto a side road and after a mile or so slowed down. "That's it!" he cried. He stopped, backed up, and entered a narrow dirt road almost hidden by trees. Five hundred yards down, the road ran parallel to a fenced-in field. Charlie parked in a cleared area deeply rutted by frozen tractor tracks. The gate was locked. *In the spring,* Andy thought, *there will be cows here, and a dog that chases them,* but now the field was unmarked and bare.

"This is it," Charlie Spoon declared. "Me and Mac was up here just two weeks ago, scouting it out, and there's deer. Mac saw the tracks."

"That's right," Mac said.

"Well, we'll just see about that," her father said, putting on his gloves. He turned to Andy. "How you doing, honeybun?"

"Just fine," she said.

Andy shivered and stamped as they unloaded: first the rifles, which they unsheathed and checked, sliding the bolts, sighting through scopes, adjusting the slings; then the gear, their food and tents and sleeping bags and stove stored in four backpacks—three big ones for Charlie Spoon and her father and Mac, and a day pack for her.

"That's about your size," Mac said, to tease her.

She reddened and said, "Mac, I can carry a pack big as yours any day." He laughed and pressed his knee against the back of hers, so that her leg buckled. "Cut it out," she said. She wanted to make an iceball and throw it at him, but she knew that her father and Charlie were anxious to get going, and she didn't want to displease them.

Mac slid under the gate, and they handed the packs over to him. Then they slid under and began walking across the field toward the same woods that ran all the way back to her home, where even now her mother was probably rising again to wash their breakfast dishes and make herself a fresh pot of coffee. *She is there, and we are here:* the thought satisfied Andy. There was no place else she would rather be.

Mac came up beside her. "Over there's Canada," he said, nodding toward the woods.

"Huh!" she said. "Not likely."

"I don't mean *right* over there. I mean further up north. You think I'm dumb?"

Dumb as your father, she thought.

"Look at that," Mac said, pointing to a piece of cow dung lying on a spot scraped bare of snow. "A frozen meadow muffin." He picked it up and sailed it at her. "Catch!"

"Mac!" she yelled. His laugh was as gawky as he was. She walked faster. He seemed different today somehow, bundled in his yellow-and-black-checkered coat, a rifle in hand, his silly floppy hat not quite covering his ears. They all seemed different as she watched them trudge through the snow—Mac and her father and Charlie Spoon—bigger, maybe, as if the cold landscape enlarged rather than diminished them, so that they, the only figures in that landscape, took on size and meaning just by being there. If they weren't there, everything would be quieter, and the woods would be the same as before. *But they are here,* Andy thought, looking behind her at the boot prints in the snow, *and I am too, and so it's all different.*

"We'll go down to the cut where we found those deer tracks," Charlie said as they entered the woods. "Maybe we'll get lucky and get a late one coming through."

The woods descended into a gully. The snow was softer and deeper here, so that often Andy sank to her knees. Charlie and Mac worked the top of the gully while she and her father walked along the base some thirty yards behind them. "If they miss the first shot, we'll get the second," her father said, and she nodded as if she had known this all the time. She listened to the crunch of their boots, their breathing, and the drumming of a distant woodpecker. And the crackling. In winter the woods crackled as if everything were straining, ready to snap like dried chicken bones.

We are hunting, Andy thought. The cold air burned her nostrils.

They stopped to make lunch by a rock outcropping that protected them from the wind. Her father heated the bean soup her mother had made for them, and they ate it with bread already stiff from the cold. He and Charlie took a few pulls from a flask of Jim Beam while she scoured the plates with snow and repacked them. Then they had coffee with sugar and powdered milk, and her father poured her a cup, too. "We won't tell your momma," he said, and Mac laughed. Andy held the cup the way her father did, not by the handle but around the rim. The coffee tasted smoky. She felt a little queasy, but she drank it all.

Charlie Spoon picked his teeth with a fingernail. "Now, you might've noticed one thing," he said.

"What's that?" her father asked.

"You might've noticed you don't hear no rifles. That's because there ain't no other hunters here. We've got the whole damn woods to ourselves. Now, I ask you—do I know how to find 'em?"

"We haven't seen deer yet, neither."

"Oh, we will," Charlie said, "but not for a while now." He leaned back against the rock. "Deer're sleeping, resting up for the evening feed."

"I seen a deer behind our house once, and it was afternoon," Andy said.

"Yeah, honey, but that was *before* deer season," Charlie said, grinning. "They know something now. They're smart that way."

"That's right," Mac said.

Andy looked at her father—had she said something stupid?

"Well, Charlie," he said, "if they know so much, how come so many get themselves shot?"

"Them's the ones that don't *believe* what they know," Charlie replied. The men laughed. Andy hesitated, and then laughed with them.

They moved on, as much to keep warm as to find a deer. The wind became even stronger. Blowing through the treetops, it sounded like the ocean, and once Andy thought she could smell salt air. But that was impossible; the ocean was *hundreds* of miles away, farther than Canada even. She and her parents had gone last summer to stay for a week at a motel on the New Jersey shore. That was the first time she'd seen the ocean, and it frightened her. It was huge and empty, yet always moving. Everything lay hidden. If you walked in it, you couldn't see how deep it was or what might be below; if you swam, something could pull you under and you'd never be seen again. Its musky, rank smell made her think of things dying. Her mother had floated beyond the breakers, calling to her to come in, but Andy wouldn't go farther than a few feet into the surf. Her mother swam and splashed with animal-like delight while her father, smiling shyly, held his white arms above the waist-deep water as if afraid to get them wet. Once a comber rolled over and sent them both tossing, and when her mother tried to stand up, the surf receding behind, Andy saw that her mother's swimsuit top had come off, so that her breasts swayed free, the nipples like two dark eyes. Embarrassed, Andy looked around: except for two women under a yellow umbrella farther up, the beach was empty. Her mother stood up unsteadily, regained her footing. Taking what seemed the longest time, she calmly refixed her top. Andy lay on the beach towel and closed her eyes. The sound of the surf made her head ache.

And now it was winter; the sky was already dimming, not just with the absence of light but with a mist that clung to the hunters' faces like cobwebs. They made camp early. Andy was chilled. When she stood still, she kept wiggling her toes to make sure they were there. Her father rubbed her arms and held her to him briefly, and that felt better. She unpacked the food while the others put up the tents.

"How about rounding us up some firewood, Mac?" Charlie asked.

"I'll do it," Andy said. Charlie looked at her thoughtfully and then handed her the canvas carrier.

There wasn't much wood on the ground, so it took her a while to get a good load. She was about a hundred yards from camp, near a cluster of high, lichen-covered boulders, when she saw through a crack in the rock a buck and two does walking gingerly, almost daintily, through the alder trees. She tried to hush her breathing as they passed not more than twenty yards away. There was nothing she could do. If she yelled, they'd be gone; by the time she got back to camp, they'd be gone. The buck stopped, nostrils quivering, tail up and alert. He looked directly at her. Still she didn't move, not one muscle. He was a beautiful buck, the color of late-turned maple leaves. Unafraid, he lowered his tail, and he and his does silently merged into the trees. Andy walked back to camp and dropped the firewood.

"I saw three deer," she said. "A buck and two does."

"Where?" Charlie Spoon cried, looking behind her as if they might have followed her into camp.

"In the woods yonder. They're gone now."

"Well, hell!" Charlie banged his coffee cup against his knee.

"Didn't I say she could find animals?" her father said, grinning.

"Too late to go after them," Charlie muttered. "It'll be dark in a quarter hour. Damn!"

"Damn," Mac echoed.

"They just walk right up to her," her father said.

"Well, leastwise this proves there's deer here." Charlie began snapping long branches into shorter ones. "You know, I think I'll stick with you," he told Andy, "since you're so good at finding deer and all. How'd that be?"

"Okay, I guess," Andy murmured. She hoped he was kidding: no way did she want to hunt with Charlie Spoon. Still, she was pleased he had said it.

Her father and Charlie took one tent, she and Mac the other. When they were in their sleeping bags, Mac said in the darkness, "I bet you really didn't see no deer, did you?"

She sighed. "I did, Mac. Why would I lie?"

"How big was the buck?"

"Four point. I counted."

Mac snorted.

"You just believe what you want, Mac," she said testily.

"Too bad it ain't buck season," he said. "Well, I got to go pee."

"So pee."

She heard him turn in his bag. "You ever see it?" he asked.

"It? What's 'it'?"

"It. A pecker."

"Sure," she lied.

"Whose? Your father's?"

She was uncomfortable. "No," she said.

"Well, whose, then?"

"Oh, I don't know! Leave me be, why don't you?"

"Didn't see a deer, didn't see a pecker," Mac said teasingly.

She didn't answer right away. Then she said, "My cousin Lewis. I saw his."

"Well, how old's he?"

"One and a half."

"Ha! A baby! A baby's is like a little worm. It ain't a real one at all."

If he says he'll show me his, she thought, *I'll kick him. I'll just get out of my bag and kick him.*

"I went hunting with my daddy and Versh and Danny Simmons last year in buck season," Mac said, "and we got ourselves one. And we hog-dressed the thing. You know what that is, don't you?"

"No," she said. She was confused. What was he talking about now?

"That's when you cut him open and take out all his guts, so the meat don't spoil. Makes him lighter to pack out, too."

She tried to imagine what the deer's guts might look like, pulled from the gaping hole. "What do you do with them?" she asked. "The guts?"

"Oh, just leave 'em for the bears."

She ran her finger like a knife blade along her belly.

"When we left them on the ground," Mac said, "they smoked. Like they were cooking."

"Huh," she said.

"They cut off the deer's pecker, too, you know."

Andy imagined Lewis's pecker and shuddered. "Mac, you're disgusting."

He laughed. "Well, I gotta go pee." She heard him rustle out of his bag. "Broo!" he cried, flapping his arms. "It's cold!"

He makes so much noise, she thought, *just noise and more noise.*

Her father woke them before first light. He warned them to talk softly and said that they were going to the place where Andy had seen the deer, to try to cut them off on their way back from their night feeding. Andy couldn't shake off her sleep. Stuffing her sleeping bag into its sack seemed to take an hour, and tying her boots was the strangest thing she'd ever done. Charlie Spoon made hot chocolate and oatmeal with raisins. Andy closed her eyes and, between beats of her heart, listened to the breathing of the forest. *When I open my eyes, it will be lighter,* she decided. But when she did, it was still just as dark, except for the swaths of their flashlights and the hissing blue flame of the stove. *There has to be just one moment when it all changes from dark to light,* Andy thought. She had missed it yesterday, in the car; today she would watch more closely.

But when she remembered again, it was already first light and they had moved to the rocks by the deer trail and had set up shooting positions—Mac and Charlie Spoon on the up-trail side, she and her father behind them, some six feet up on a ledge. The day became brighter, the sun piercing the tall pines, raking the hunters, yet providing little warmth. Andy now smelled alder and pine and the slightly rotten odor of rock lichen. She rubbed her hand over the stone and considered that it must be very old, had probably been here before the giant pines, *before anyone was in these woods at all.* A chipmunk sniffed on a nearby branch. She aimed an imaginary rifle and pressed the trigger. The chipmunk froze, then scurried away. Her legs were cramping on the narrow ledge. Her father seemed to doze, one hand in his parka, the other cupped lightly around the rifle. She could smell his scent of old wool and leather. His cheeks were speckled with gray-black whiskers, and he worked his jaws slightly, as if chewing a small piece of gum.

Please let us get a deer, she prayed.

A branch snapped on the other side of the rock face. Her father's hand stiffened on the rifle, startling her—*He hasn't been sleeping at all,* she marveled—and then his jaw relaxed, as did the lines around his eyes, and she heard Charlie Spoon call, "Yo, don't shoot, it's us." He and Mac appeared from around the rock. They stopped beneath the ledge. Charlie solemnly crossed his arms.

"I don't believe we're gonna get any deer here," he said drily.

Andy's father lowered his rifle to Charlie and jumped down from

the ledge. Then he reached up for Andy. She dropped into his arms and
he set her gently on the ground.

Mac sidled up to her. "I knew you didn't see no deer," he said.

"Just because they don't come when you want 'em to don't mean
she didn't see them," her father said.

Still, she felt bad. Her telling about the deer had caused them to
spend the morning there, cold and expectant, with nothing to show for
it.

They tramped through the woods for another two hours, not
caring much about noise. Mac found some deer tracks, and they argued
about how old they were. They split up for a while and then rejoined at
an old logging road that deer might use, and followed it. The road
crossed a stream, which had mostly frozen over but in a few spots still
caught leaves and twigs in an icy swirl. They forded it by jumping from
rock to rock. The road narrowed after that, and the woods thickened.

They stopped for lunch, heating up Charlie's wife's corn chow-
der. Andy's father cut squares of applesauce cake with his hunting knife
and handed them to her and Mac, who ate his almost daintily. Andy
could faintly taste knife oil on the cake. She was tired. She stretched her
leg; the muscle that had cramped on the rock still ached.

"Might as well relax," her father said, as if reading her thoughts.
"We won't find deer till suppertime."

Charlie Spoon leaned back against his pack and folded his hands
across his stomach. "Well, even if we don't get a deer," he said expan-
sively, "it's still great to be out here, breathe some fresh air, clomp
around a bit. Get away from the house and the old lady." He winked at
Mac, who looked away.

"That's what the woods are all about, anyway," Charlie said.
"It's where the women don't want to go." He bowed his head toward
Andy. "With your exception, of course, little lady." He helped himself
to another piece of applesauce cake.

"She ain't a woman," Mac said.

"Well, she damn well's gonna be," Charlie said. He grinned at
her. "Or will you? You're half a boy anyway. You go by a boy's name.
What's your real name? Andrea, ain't it?"

"That's right," she said. She hoped that if she didn't look at him,
Charlie would stop.

"Well, which do you like? Andy or Andrea?"

"Don't matter," she mumbled. "Either."

"She's always been Andy to me," her father said.

Charlie Spoon was still grinning. "So what are you gonna be, Andrea? A boy or a girl?"

"I'm a girl," she said.

"But you want to go hunting and fishing and everything, huh?"

"She can do whatever she likes," her father said.

"Hell, you might as well have just had a boy and be done with it!" Charlie exclaimed.

"That's funny," her father said, and chuckled. "That's just what her momma tells me."

They were looking at her, and she wanted to get away from them all, even from her father, who chose to joke with them.

"I'm going to walk a bit," she said.

She heard them laughing as she walked down the logging trail. She flapped her arms; she whistled. *I don't care how much noise I make,* she thought. Two grouse flew from the underbrush, startling her. A little farther down, the trail ended in a clearing that enlarged into a frozen meadow; beyond it the woods began again. A few moldering posts were all that was left of a fence that had once enclosed the field. The low afternoon sunlight reflected brightly off the snow, so that Andy's eyes hurt. She squinted hard. A gust of wind blew across the field, stinging her face. And then, as if it had been waiting for her, the doe emerged from the trees opposite and stepped cautiously into the field. Andy watched: it stopped and stood quietly for what seemed a long time and then ambled across. It stopped again about seventy yards away and began to browse in a patch of sugar grass uncovered by the wind. Carefully, slowly, never taking her eyes from the doe, Andy walked backward, trying to step into the boot prints she'd already made. When she was far enough back into the woods, she turned and walked faster, her heart racing. *Please let it stay,* she prayed.

"There's a doe in the field yonder," she told them.

They got their rifles and hurried down the trail.

"No use," her father said. "We're making too much noise any way you look at it."

"At least we got us the wind in our favor," Charlie Spoon said, breathing heavily.

But the doe was still there, grazing.

"Good Lord," Charlie whispered. He looked at her father. "Well, whose shot?"

"Andy spotted it," her father said in a low voice. "Let her shoot it."

"What!" Charlie's eyes widened.

Andy couldn't believe what her father had just said. She'd only shot tin cans and targets; she'd never even fired her father's .30–30, and she'd never killed anything.

"I can't," she whispered.

"That's right, she can't," Charlie Spoon insisted. "She's not old enough and she don't have a license even if she was!"

"Well, who's to tell?" her father said. "Nobody's going to know but us." He looked at her. "Do you want to shoot it, punkin?"

Why doesn't it hear us? she wondered. *Why doesn't it run away?* "I don't know," she said.

"Well, I'm sure as hell gonna shoot it," Charlie said. Her father grasped Charlie's rifle barrel and held it. His voice was steady.

"Andy's a good shot. It's her deer. She found it, not you. You'd still be sitting on your ass back in camp." He turned to her again. "Now—do you want to shoot it, Andy? Yes or no."

He was looking at her; they were all looking at her. Suddenly she was angry at the deer, who refused to hear them, who wouldn't run away even when it could. "I'll shoot it," she said. Charlie turned away in disgust.

She lay on the ground and pressed the rifle stock against her shoulder bone. The snow was cold through her parka; she smelled oil and wax and damp earth. She pulled off one glove with her teeth. "It sights just like the .22," her father said gently. "Cartridge's already chambered." As she had done so many times before, she sighted down the scope; now the doe was in the reticle. She moved the barrel until the cross hairs lined up. Her father was breathing beside her.

"Aim where the chest and legs meet, or a little above, punkin," he was saying calmly. "That's the killing shot."

But now, seeing it in the scope, Andy was hesitant. Her finger weakened on the trigger. Still, she nodded at what her father said and sighted again, the cross hairs lining up in exactly the same spot—the doe had hardly moved, its brownish gray body outlined starkly against the blue-backed snow. *It doesn't know,* Andy thought. *It just doesn't know.* And as she looked, deer and snow and faraway trees flattened within the circular frame to become like a picture on a calendar, not real, and she felt calm, as if she had been dreaming everything—the day, the deer, the hunt itself. And she, finger on trigger, was only a part of that dream.

"Shoot!" Charlie hissed.

Through the scope she saw the deer look up, ears high and straining.

Charlie groaned, and just as he did, and just at the moment when Andy knew—*knew*—the doe would bound away, as if she could feel its haunches tensing and gathering power, she pulled the trigger. Later she would think, *I felt the recoil, I smelled the smoke, but I don't remember pulling the trigger.* Through the scope the deer seemed to shrink into itself, and then slowly knelt, hind legs first, head raised as if to cry out. It trembled, still straining to keep its head high, as if that alone would save it; failing, it collapsed, shuddered, and lay still.

"Whoee!" Mac cried.

"One shot! One shot!" her father yelled, clapping her on the back. Charlie Spoon was shaking his head and smiling dumbly.

"I told you she was a great little shot!" her father said. "I told you!" Mac danced and clapped his hands. She was dazed, not quite understanding what had happened. And then they were crossing the field toward the fallen doe, she walking dreamlike, the men laughing and joking, released now from the tension of silence and anticipation. Suddenly Mac pointed and cried out, "Look at that!"

The doe was rising, legs unsteady. They stared at it, unable to comprehend, and in that moment the doe regained its feet and looked at them, as if it, too, were trying to understand. Her father whistled softly. Charlie Spoon unslung his rifle and raised it to his shoulder, but the doe was already bounding away. His hurried shot missed, and the deer disappeared into the woods.

"Damn, damn, damn," he moaned.

"I don't believe it," her father said. "That deer was dead."

"Dead, hell!" Charlie yelled. "It was gutshot, that's all. Stunned and gutshot. Clean shot, my ass!"

What have I done? Andy thought.

Her father slung his rifle over his shoulder. "Well, let's go. She can't get too far."

"Hell, I've seen deer run ten miles gutshot," Charlie said. He waved his arms. "We may never find her!"

As they crossed the field, Mac came up to her and said in a low voice, "Gutshoot a deer, you'll go to hell."

"Shut up, Mac," she said, her voice cracking. It was a terrible thing she had done, she knew. She couldn't bear to think of the doe in pain and frightened. *Please let it die,* she prayed.

But though they searched all the last hour of daylight, so that they had to recross the field and go up the logging trail in a twilight made even deeper by thick, smoky clouds, they didn't find the doe. They lost its trail almost immediately in the dense stands of alderberry and larch.

"I am cold, and I am tired," Charlie Spoon declared. "And if you ask me, that deer's in another county already."

"No one's asking you, Charlie," her father said.

They had a supper of hard salami and ham, bread, and the rest of the applesauce cake. It seemed a bother to heat the coffee, so they had cold chocolate instead. Everyone turned in early.

"We'll find it in the morning, honeybun," her father said, as she went to her tent.

"I don't like to think of it suffering." She was almost in tears.

"It's dead already, punkin. Don't even think about it." He kissed her, his breath sour and his beard rough against her cheek.

Andy was sure she wouldn't get to sleep; the image of the doe falling, falling, then rising again, repeated itself whenever she closed her eyes. Then she heard an owl hoot and realized that it had awakened her, so she must have been asleep after all. She hoped the owl would hush, but instead it hooted louder. She wished her father or Charlie Spoon would wake up and do something about it, but no one moved in the other tent, and suddenly she was afraid that they had all decamped, wanting nothing more to do with her. She whispered, "Mac, Mac," to the sleeping bag where he should be, but no one answered. She tried to find the flashlight she always kept by her side, but couldn't, and she cried in panic, "Mac, are you there?" He mumbled something, and immediately she felt foolish and hoped he wouldn't reply.

When she awoke again, everything had changed. The owl was gone, the woods were still, and she sensed light, blue and pale, light where before there had been none. *The moon must have come out,* she thought. And it was warm, too, warmer than it should have been. She got out of her sleeping bag and took off her parka—it was that warm. Mac was asleep, wheezing like an old man. She unzipped the tent and stepped outside.

The woods were more beautiful than she had ever seen them. The moon made everything ice-rimmed glimmer with a crystallized, immanent light, while underneath that ice the branches of trees were as stark as skeletons. She heard a crunching in the snow, the one sound in all that silence, and there, walking down the logging trail into their camp, was the doe. Its body, like everything around her, was silvered with frost and moonlight. It walked past the tent where her father and Charlie Spoon were sleeping and stopped no more than six feet from her. Andy saw that she had shot it, yes, had shot it cleanly, just where she thought she had, the wound a jagged, bloody hole in the doe's chest.

A heart shot, she thought.

The doe stepped closer, so that Andy, if she wished, could have reached out and touched it. It looked at her as if expecting her to do this, and so she did, running her hand, slowly at first, along the rough, matted fur, then down to the edge of the wound, where she stopped. The doe stood still. Hesitantly, Andy felt the edge of the wound. The torn flesh was sticky and warm. The wound parted under her touch. And then, almost without her knowing it, her fingers were within, probing, yet still the doe didn't move. Andy pressed deeper, through flesh and muscle and sinew, until her whole hand and more was inside the wound and she had found the doe's heart, warm and beating. She cupped it gently in her hand. *Alive,* she marveled. *Alive.*

The heart quickened under her touch, becoming warmer and warmer until it was hot enough to burn. In pain, Andy tried to remove her hand, but the wound closed about it and held her fast. Her hand was burning. She cried out in agony, sure they would all hear and come help, but they didn't. And then her hand pulled free, followed by a steaming rush of blood, more blood than she ever could have imagined—it covered her hand and arm, and she saw to her horror that her hand was steaming. She moaned and fell to her knees and plunged her hand into the snow. The doe looked at her gently and then turned and walked back up the trail.

In the morning, when she woke, Andy could still smell the blood, but she felt no pain. She looked at her hand. Even though it appeared unscathed, it felt weak and withered. She couldn't move it freely and was afraid the others would notice. *I will hide it in my jacket pocket,* she decided, *so nobody can see.* She ate the oatmeal that her father cooked and stayed apart from them all. No one spoke to her, and that suited her. A light snow began to fall. It was the last day of their hunting trip. She wanted to be home.

Her father dumped the dregs of his coffee. "Well, let's go look for her," he said.

Again they crossed the field. Andy lagged behind. She averted her eyes from the spot where the doe had fallen, already filling up with snow. Mac and Charlie entered the woods first, followed by her father. Andy remained in the field and considered the smear of gray sky, the nearby flock of crows pecking at unyielding stubble. *I will stay here,* she thought, *and not move for a long while.* But now someone—Mac—was yelling. Her father appeared at the woods' edge and waved for her to come. She ran and pushed through a brake of alderberry and larch. The thick underbrush scratched her face. For a moment she felt lost and looked wildly about. Then, where the brush thinned, she saw them standing quietly in the falling snow. They were staring down at the dead doe. A film covered its upturned eye, and its body was lightly dusted with snow.

"I told you she wouldn't get too far," Andy's father said triumphantly. "We must've just missed her yesterday. Too blind to see."

"We're just damn lucky no animal got to her last night," Charlie muttered.

Her father lifted the doe's foreleg. The wound was blood-clotted, brown, and caked like frozen mud. "Clean shot," he said to Charlie. He grinned. "My little girl."

Then he pulled out his knife, the blade gray as the morning. Mac whispered to Andy, "Now watch this," while Charlie Spoon lifted the doe from behind by its forelegs so that its head rested between his knees, its underside exposed. Her father's knife sliced thickly from chest to belly to crotch, and Andy was running from them, back to the field and across, scattering the crows who cawed and circled angrily. And now they were all calling to her—Charlie Spoon and Mac and her father—crying *Andy, Andy* (but that wasn't her name, she would no longer be called that); yet louder than any of them was the wind blowing through the treetops, like the ocean where her mother floated in green water, also calling *Come in, come in,* while all around her roared the mocking of the terrible, now inevitable, sea.

THE GIRL WHO LOVED HORSES

HORSES

Elizabeth Spencer

I

She had drawn back from throwing a pan of bird scraps out the door because she heard what was coming, the two-part pounding of a full gallop, not the graceful triple notes of a canter. They were mounting the drive now, turning into the stretch along the side of the house; once before, someone appearing at the screen door had made the horse shy, so that, barely held beneath the rider, barely restrained, he had plunged off into the flower beds. So she stepped back from the door and saw the two of them shoot past, rounding a final corner, heading for the straight run of drive into the cattle gate and the barn lot back of it.

She flung out the scraps, then walked to the other side of the kitchen and peered through the window, raised for spring, toward the barn lot. The horse had slowed, out of habit, knowing what came next. And the white shirt that had passed hugged so low as to seem some strange part of the animal's trappings, or as though he had run under a low line of drying laundry and caught something to an otherwise empty

210

saddle and bare withers, now rose up, angling to an upright posture. A gloved hand extended to pat the lathered neck.

"Lord have mercy," the woman said. The young woman riding the horse was her daughter, but she was speaking also for her son-in-law who went in for even more reckless behavior in the jumping ring the two of them had set up. What she meant by it was that they were going to kill themselves before they ever had any children, or if they did have children safely they'd bring up the children to be just as foolish about horses and careless of life and limb as they were themselves.

The young woman's booted heel struck the back steps. The screen door banged.

"You ought not to bring him in hot like that," the mother said. "I do know that much."

"Cottrell is out there," she said.

"It's still March, even if it has got warm."

"Cottrell knows what to do."

She ran water at the sink, and cupping her hand drank primitive fashion out of it, bending to the tap, then wet her hands in the running water and thrust her fingers into the dusty, sweat-damp roots of her sand-colored hair. It had been a good ride.

"I hope he doesn't take up too much time," the mother said. "My beds need working."

She spoke mildly but it was always part of the same quarrel they were in like a stream that was now a trickle, now a still pool, but sometimes after a freshet could turn into a torrent. Such as: "Y'all are just crazy. Y'all are wasting everything on those things. And what are they? I know they're pretty and all that, but they're not a thing in the world but animals. Cows are animals. You can make a lot more money in cattle, than carting those things around over two states and three counties."

She could work herself up too much to eat, leaving the two of them at the table, but would see them just the same in her mind's eye, just as if she'd stayed. There were the sandy-haired young woman, already thirty—married four years and still apparently with no intention of producing a family (she was an only child and the estate, though small, was a fine piece of land)—and across from her the dark spare still young man she had married.

She knew how they would sit there alone and not even look at one another or discuss what she'd said or talk against her; they would just sit there and maybe pass each other some food or one of them would get up for the coffeepot. The fanatics of a strange cult would do the same, she often thought, loosening her long hair upstairs, brushing the gray and brown together to a colorless patina, putting on one of her long cotton gowns with the ruched neck, crawling in between white cotton sheets. She was a widow and if she didn't want to sit up and try to talk to the family after a hard day, she didn't have to. Reading was a joy, lifelong. She found her place in *Middlemarch,* one of her favorites.

But during the day not even reading (if she'd had the time) could shut out the sounds from back of the privet hedge, plainly to be heard from the house. The trudging of the trot, the pause, the low directive, the thud of hooves, the heave and shout, and sometimes the ring of struck wood as a bar came down. And every jump a risk of life and limb. One dislocated shoulder—Clyde's, thank heaven, not Deedee's—a taping, a sling, a contraption of boards, and pain "like a hot knife," he had said. A hot knife. Wouldn't that hurt anybody enough to make him quit risking life and limb with those two blood horses, quit at least talking about getting still another one while swallowing down painkiller he said he hated to be sissy enough to take?

"Uh-huh," the mother said. "But it'll be Deborah next. You thought about that?"

"Aw, now, Miss Emma," he'd lean back to say, charming her through his warrior's haze of pain. "Deedee and me—that's what we're hooked on. Think of us without it, Mama. You really want to kill us. We couldn't live."

He was speaking to his mother-in-law but smiling at his wife. And she, Deborah, was smiling back.

Her name was Deborah Dale, but they'd always, of course, being from LaGrange, Tennessee, right over the Mississippi border, that is to say, real South, had had a hundred nicknames for her. Deedee, her father had named her, and "Deeds" her funny cousins said—"Hey, Deeds, how ya' doin'?" Being on this property in a town of pretty properties, though theirs was a little way out, a little bit larger than most, she was always out romping, swimming in forbidden creeks, climbing forbidden fences, going barefoot too soon in the spring, the last one in at recess, the first one to turn in an exam paper. ("Are you quite sure that you have finished, Deborah?" "Yes, ma'am.")

When she graduated from ponies to that sturdy calico her uncle gave her, bringing it in from his farm because he had an eye for a good match, there was almost no finding her. "I always know she's somewhere on the place," her mother said. "We just can't see it all at once," said her father. He was ailing even back then but he undertook walks. Once when the leaves had all but gone from the trees, on a warm November afternoon, from a slight rise, he saw her down in a little-used pasture with a straight open stretch among some oaks. The ground was spongy and clotted with damp and a child ought not to have tried to run there, on foot. But there went the calico with Deedee clinging low, going like the wind, and knowing furthermore out of what couldn't be anything but long practice, where to turn, where to veer, where to stop.

"One fine afternoon," he said to himself, suspecting even then (they hadn't told him yet) what his illness was, "and Emma's going to be left with nobody." He remarked on this privately, not without anguish and not without humor.

They stopped her riding, at least like that, by sending her off to a boarding school, where a watchful ringmaster took "those girls interested in equitation" out on leafy trails, "at the walk, at the trot, and at the canter." They also, with that depth of consideration which must flourish even among those Southerners unlucky enough to wind up in the lower reaches of hell, kept her young spirit out of the worst of the dying. She just got a call from the housemother one night. Her father had "passed away."

After college she forgot it, she gave it up. It was too expensive, it took a lot of time and devotion, she was interested in boys. Some boys were interested in her. She worked in Memphis, drove home to her mother every night. In winter she had to eat breakfast in the dark. On some evenings the phone rang; on some it was silent. Her mother treated both kinds of evenings just the same.

To Emma Tyler it always seemed that Clyde Mecklin materialized out of nowhere. She ran straight into him when opening the front door one evening to get the paper off the porch, he being just about to turn the bell or knock. There he stood, dark and straight in the late light that comes after first dark and is so clear. He was clear as anything in it, clear as the first stamp of a young man ever cast.

"Is Deb'rah here?" At least no Yankee. But not Miss Tyler or Miss Deborah Tyler, or Miss Deborah. No, he was city all right.

She did not answer at first.

"What's the matter, scare you? I was just about to knock."

She still said nothing.

"Maybe this is the wrong place," he said.

"No, it's the right place," Emma Tyler finally said. She stepped back and held the door wider. "Come on in."

"Scared the life out of me," she told Deborah when she finally came down to breakfast the next day, Clyde's car having been heard to depart by Emma Tyler in her upstairs bedroom at an hour she did not care to verify. "Why didn't you tell me you were expecting him? I just opened the door and there he was."

"I liked him so much," said Deborah with grave honesty. "I guess I was scared he wouldn't come. That would have hurt."

"Do you still like him?" her mother ventured, after this confidence.

"He's all for outdoors," said Deborah, as dreamy over coffee as any mother had ever beheld. "Everybody is so indoors. He likes hunting, going fishing, farms."

"Has he got one?"

"He'd like to have. All he's got's this job. He's coming back next weekend. You can talk to him. He's interested in horses."

"But does he know we don't keep horses anymore?"

"That was just my thumbnail sketch," said Deborah. "We don't have to run out and buy any."

"No, I don't imagine so," said her mother, but Deborah hardly remarked the peculiar turn of tone, the dryness. She was letting coast through her head the scene: her mother (whom she now loved better than she ever had in her life) opening the door just before Clyde knocked, so seeing unexpectedly for the first time, that face, that head, that being. . . . When he had kissed her her ears drummed, and it came back to her once more, not thought of in years, the drumming hooves of the calico, and the ghosting father, behind, invisible, observant, off on the bare distant November rise.

It was after she married that Deborah got beautiful. All LaGrange noticed it. "I declare," they said to her mother or sometimes right out to her face, "I always said she was nice looking but I never thought anything like that."

II

Emma first saw the boy in the parking lot. He was new.

In former days she'd parked in front of nearly any place she wanted to go—hardware, or drugstore, or courthouse: change for the meter was her biggest problem. But so many streets were one-way now and what with the increased numbers of cars, the growth of the town, those days were gone; she used a parking lot back of a cafe, near the newspaper office. The entrance to the lot was a bottleneck of a narrow drive between the two brick buildings; once in, it was hard sometimes to park.

That day the boy offered to help. He was an expert driver, she noted, whereas Emma was inclined to perspire, crane and fret, fearful of scraping a fender or grazing a door. He spun the wheel with one hand; a glance told him all he had to know; he as good as sat the car in place, as skillful (she reluctantly thought) as her children on their horses. When she returned an hour later, the cars were denser still; he helped her again. She wondered whether to tip him. This happened twice more.

"You've been so nice to me," she said, the last time. "They're lucky to have you."

"It's not much of a job," he said. "Just all I can get for the moment. Being new and all."

"I might need some help," she said. "You can call up at the Tyler place if you want work. It's in the book. Right now I'm in a hurry."

On the warm June day, Deborah sat the horse comfortably in the side yard and watched her mother and the young man (whose name was Willett? Williams?), who, having worked the beds and straightened a fence post, was now replacing warped fence boards with new ones.

"Who is he?" she asked her mother, not quite low enough, and meaning what a Southern woman invariably means by that question, not what is his name but where did he come from, is he anybody we know? What excuse, in other words, does he have for even being born?

"One thing, he's a good worker," her mother said, preening a little. Did they think she couldn't manage if she had to? "Now don't you make him feel bad."

"Feel bad!" But once again, if only to spite her mother, who was in a way criticizing her and Clyde by hiring anybody at all to do work that Clyde or the Negro help would have been able to do if only it weren't for those horses—once again Deborah had spoken too loudly.

If she ever had freely to admit things, even to herself, Deborah would have to say she knew she not only looked good that June day, she looked sexy as hell. Her light hair, tousled from a ride in the fields, had grown longer in the last year; it had slipped its pins on one side and lay in a sensuous lock along her cheek. A breeze stirred it, then passed by. Her soft poplin shirt was loose at the throat, the two top buttons open, the cuffs turned back to her elbows. The new horse, the third, was gentle, too much so (this worried them); she sat it easily, one leg up, crossed lazily over the flat English pommel, while the horse, head stretched down, cropped at the tender grass. In the silence between their voices, the tearing of the grass was the only sound except for a shrill jay's cry.

"Make him feel bad!" she repeated.

The boy looked up. The horse, seeking grass, had moved forward; she was closer than before, eyes looking down on him above the rise of her breasts and throat; she saw the closeness go through him, saw her presence register as strongly as if the earth's accidental shifting had slammed them physically together. For a minute there was nothing but the two of them. The jay was silent; even the horse, sensing something, had raised his head.

Stepping back, the boy stumbled over the pile of lumber, then fell in it. Deborah laughed. Nothing, that day, could have stopped her laughter. She was beautifully, languidly atop a fine horse on the year's choice day at the peak of her life.

"You know what?" Deborah said at supper, when they were discussing her mother's helper. "I thought who he looks like. He looks like Clyde."

"The poor guy," Clyde said. "Was that the best you could do?"

Emma sat still. Now that she thought of it, he did look like Clyde. She stopped eating, to think it over. What difference did it make if he did? She returned to her plate.

Deborah ate lustily, her table manners unrestrained. She swabbed bread into the empty salad bowl, drenched it with dressing, bit it in hunks.

"The poor woman's Clyde, that's what you hired," she said. She looked up.

The screen door had just softly closed in the kitchen behind them. Emma's hired man had come in for his money.

It was the next day that the boy, whose name was Willett or Williams, broke the riding mower by running it full speed into a rock pile overgrown with weeds but clearly visible, and left without asking for pay but evidently taking with him in his car a number of selected items from barn, garage, and tack room, along with a transistor radio that Clyde kept in the kitchen for getting news with his early coffee.

Emma Tyler, vexed for a number of reasons she did not care to sort out (prime among them was the very peaceful and good time she had been having with the boy the day before in the yard when Deborah had chosen to ride over and join them), telephoned the police and reported the whole matter. But boy, car, and stolen articles vanished into the nowhere. That was all, for what they took to be forever.

III

Three years later, aged thirty-three, Deborah Mecklin was carrying her fine head higher than ever uptown in LaGrange. She drove herself on errands back and forth in car or station wagon, not looking to left or right, not speaking so much as before. She was trying not to hear from the outside what they were now saying about Clyde, how well he'd done with the horses, that place was as good as a stud farm now that he kept ten or a dozen, advertised and traded, as well as showed. And the money was coming in hard and fast. But, they would add, he moved with a fast set, and there was also the occasional gossip item, too often, in Clyde's case, with someone ready to report first hand; look how quick, now you thought of it, he'd taken up with Deborah, and how she'd snapped him up too soon to hear what his reputation was, even back then. It would be a cold day in August before any one woman would be enough for him. And his father before him? And his father before him. So the voices said.

Deborah, too, was trying not to hear what was still sounding from inside her head after her fall in the last big horse show:

The doctor: You barely escaped concussion, young lady.

Clyde: I just never saw your timing go off like that. I can't get over it.

Emma: You'd better let it go for a while, honey. There're other things, so many other things.

Back home, she later said to Emma: "Oh, Mama, I know you're right sometimes, and sometimes I'm sick of it all, but Clyde depends on me, he always has, and now look—"

"Yes, and 'Now look' is right, he has to be out with it to keep it all running. You got your wish, is all I can say."

Emma was frequently over at her sister-in-law Marian's farm these days. The ladies were aging, Marian especially down in the back, and those twilights in the house alone were more and more all that

Deedee had to keep herself company with. Sometimes the phone rang and there'd be Clyde on it, to say he'd be late again. Or there'd be no call at all. And once she (of all people) pressed some curtains and hung them, and once hunted for old photographs, and once, standing in the middle of the little-used parlor among the walnut Victorian furniture upholstered in gold and blue and rose, she had said "Daddy?" right out loud, like he might have been there to answer, really been there. It had surprised her, the word falling out like that as though a thought took reality all by itself and made a word on its own.

And once there came a knock at the door.

All she thought, though she hadn't heard the car, was that it was Clyde and that he'd forgotten his key, or seeing her there, his arms loaded maybe, was asking her to let him in. It was past dark. Though times were a little more chancy now, LaGrange was a safe place. People nearer to town used to brag that if they went off for any length of time less than a weekend and locked the doors, the neighbors would get their feelings hurt; and if the Tylers lived further out and "locked up," the feeling for it was ritual mainly, a precaution.

She glanced through the sidelight, saw what she took for Clyde and opened the door. There were cedars in the front yard, not too near the house, but dense enough to block out whatever gathering of light there might have been from the long slope of property beyond the front gate. There was no moon.

The man she took for Clyde, instead of stepping through the door or up to the threshold to greet her, withdrew a step and leaned down and to one side, turning outward as though to pick up something. It was she who stepped forward, to greet, help, inquire; for deep within was the idea her mother had seen to it was firmly and forever planted: that one day one of them was going to get too badly hurt by "those things" ever to be patched up.

So it was in outer dark, three paces from the safe threshold and to the left of the area where the light was falling outward, a dim single sidelight near the mantlepiece having been all she had switched on, too faint to penetrate the sheer gathered curtains of the sidelight, that the man at the door rose up, that he tried to take her. The first she knew of it, his face was in hers, not Clyde's but something like it and at Clyde's exact height, so that for the moment she thought that some joke was on, and then the strange hand caught the parting of her blouse, a new mouth fell hard on her own, one knee thrust her legs apart, the free hand diving in to clutch and press against the thin nylon between her thighs.

She recoiled at the same time that she felt, touched in the quick, the painful glory of desire brought on too fast—looking back on that instant's two-edged meaning, she would never hear about rape without the lightning quiver of ambivalence within the word. However, at the time no meditation stopped her knee from coming up into the nameless groin and nothing stopped her from tearing back her mouth slathered with spit so suddenly smeared into it as to drag it into the shape of a scream she was unable yet to find a voice for. Her good right arm struck like a hard backhand against a line-smoking tennis serve. Then from the driveway came the stream of twin headlights thrusting through the cedars.

"Bitch!" The word, distorted and low, was like a groan; she had hurt him, freed herself for a moment, but the struggle would have just begun except for the lights, and the screams that were just trying to get out of her. "You fucking bitch." He saw the car lights, wavered, then turned. His leap into the shrubbery was bent, like a hunchback's. She stopped screaming suddenly. Hurt where he lived, she thought. The animal motion, wounded, drew her curiosity for a second. Saved, she saw the car sweep round the drive, but watched the bushes shake, put up her hand to touch but not to close the torn halves of the blouse, which was ripped open to her waist.

Inside, she stood looking down at herself in the dim light. There was a nail scratch near the left nipple, two teeth marks between elbow and wrist where she'd smashed into his mouth. She wiped her own mouth on the back of her hand, gagging at the taste of cigarette smoke, bitterly staled. Animals! She'd always had a special feeling for them, a helpless tenderness. In her memory the bushes, shaking to a crippled fight, shook forever.

She went upstairs, stood trembling in her mother's room (Emma was away), combed her hair with her mother's comb. Then, hearing Clyde's voice calling her below, she stripped off her ravaged blouse and hastened across to their own rooms to hide it in a drawer, change into a fresh one, come downstairs. She had made her decision already. Who was this man? A nothing . . . an unknown. She hated women who shouted Rape! Rape! It was an incident, but once she told it everyone would know, along with the police, and would add to it: they'd say she'd been violated. It was an incident, but Clyde, once he knew, would trace him down. Clyde would kill him.

"Did you know the door was wide open?" He was standing in the livingroom.

"I know. I must have opened it when I heard the car. I thought you were stopping in the front."

"Well, I hardly ever do."

"Sometimes you do."

"Deedee, have you been drinking?"

"Drinking . . . ? Me?" She squinted at him, joking in her own way; it was a standing quarrel now that alone she sometimes poured one or two.

He would check her breath but not her marked body. Lust with him was mole-dark now, not desire in the soft increase of morning light, or on slowly westering afternoons or by the nightlight's glow. He would kill for her because she was his wife. . . .

"Who was that man?"

Uptown one winter afternoon late, she had seen him again. He had been coming out of the hamburger place and looking back, seeing her through the streetlights, he had turned quickly into an alley. She had hurried to catch up, to see. But only a form was hastening there, deeper into the unlit slit between brick walls, down toward a street and a section nobody went into without good reason.

"That man," she repeated to the owner (also the proprietor and cook) in the hamburger place. "He was in here just now."

"I don't know him. He hangs around. Wondered myself. You know him?"

"I think he used to work for us once, two or three years ago. I just wondered."

"I thought I seen him somewhere myself."

"He looks a little bit like Clyde."

"Maybe so. Now you mention it." He wiped the counter with a wet rag. "Get you anything, Miss Deb'rah?"

"I've got to get home."

"Y'all got yourselves some prizes, huh?"

"Aw, just some good luck." She was gone.

Prizes, yes. Two trophies at the Shelby Country Fair, one in Brownsville where she'd almost lost control again, and Clyde not worrying about her so much as scolding her. His recent theory was that she was out to spite him. He would think it if he was guilty about the women, and she didn't doubt any more that he was. But worse than spite was what had got to her, hating as she did to admit it.

It was fear.

She'd never known it before. When it first started she hadn't even known what the name of it was.

Over two years ago, Clyde had started buying colts not broken yet from a stud farm south of Nashville, bringing them home for him and Deborah to get in shape together. It saved a pile of money to do it that way. She'd been thrown in consequence three times, trampled once, a terrifying moment as the double reins had caught up her outstretched arm so she couldn't fall free. Now when she closed her eyes at night, steel hooves sometimes hung through the dark above them, and she felt hard ground beneath her head, smelt smeared grass on cheek and elbow. To Clyde she murmured in the dark: "I'm not good at it any more." "Why, Deeds, you were always good. It's temporary, honey. That was a bad luck day."

A great couple. That's what Clyde thought of them. But more than half their name had been made by her, by the sight of her, Deborah Mecklin, out in full dress, black broadcloth and white satin stock with hair drawn trimly back beneath the smooth rise of the hat, entering the show ring. She looked damned good back of the glossy neck's steep arch, the pointed ears and lacquered hooves which hardly touched earth before springing upward, as though in the instant before actual flight. There was always the stillness, then the murmur, the rustle of the crowd. At top form she could even get applause. A fame for a time spread round them. The Mecklins. Great riders. "Ridgewood Stable. Blood horses trained. Saddle and Show." He'd had it put up in wrought iron, with a sign as well, Old English style, of a horseman spurring.

("Well, you got to make money," said Miss Emma to her son-in-law. "And don't I know it," she said. "But I just hate to think how many times I kept those historical people from putting up a marker on this place. And now all I do is worry one of y'all's going to break your neck. If it wasn't for Marian needing me and all . . . I just can't sleep a wink over here."

("You like to be over there anyway, Mama," Deborah said. "You know we want you here."

("Sure, we want you here," said Clyde. "As for the property, we talked it all out beforehand. I don't think I've damaged it any way."

("I just never saw it as a horse farm. But it's you all I worry about. It's the danger.")

Deborah drove home.

When the workingman her mother had hired three years before

had stolen things and left, he had left too on the garage wall inside, a long pair of crossing diagonal lines, brown, in mud, she thought, until she smelled what it was, and there were the blood-stained menstrual pads she later came across in the driveway, dug up out of the garbage, strewed out into the yard.

She told Clyde about the first but not the second discovery. "Some critters are mean," he'd shrugged it off. "Some critters are just mean."

They'd been dancing, out at the club. And so in love back then, he'd turned and turned her, far apart, then close, talking into her ear, making her laugh and answer, but finally he said: "Are you a mean critter, Deedee? Some critters are mean." And she'd remembered what she didn't tell.

But in those days Clyde was passionate and fun, both marvellously together, and the devil appearing at midnight in the bend of a country road would not have scared her. Nothing would have. It was the day of her life when they bought the first two horses.

"I thought I seen him somewhere myself."

"He looks a little bit like Clyde."

And dusk again, a third and final time.

The parking lot where she'd come after a movie was empty except for a few cars. The small office was unlighted, but a man she took for the attendant was bending to the door on the far side of a long cream-colored sedan near the back fence. "Want my ticket?" she called. The man straightened, head rising above the body frame, and she knew him. Had he been about to steal a car, or was he breaking in for whatever he could find, or was it her coming all alone that he was waiting for? However it was, he knew her as instantly as she knew him. Each other was what they had, by whatever design or absence of it, found. Deborah did not cry out or stir.

Who knew how many lines life had cut away from him down through the years till the moment when an arrogant woman on a horse had ridden him down with lust and laughter? He wasn't bad-looking; his eyes were beautiful; he was the kind to whom nothing good could happen. From that bright day to this chilly dusk, it had probably just been the same old story.

Deborah waited. Some way or other, what was coming, threading through the cars like an animal lost for years catching the scent of a former owner, was her own.

("You're losing nerve, Deedee," Clyde had told her recently. "That's what's really bothering me. You're scared, aren't you?")

The bitter-stale smell of cigarette breath, though not so near as before, not forced against her mouth, was still unmistakably familiar. But the prod of a gun's muzzle just under the rise of her breast was not. It had never happened to her before. She shuddered at the touch with a chill springlike start of something like life, which was also something like death.

"Get inside," he said.

"Are you the same one?" she asked. "Just tell me that. Three years ago, Mama hired somebody. Was that you?"

"Get in the car."

She opened the door, slid over to the driver's seat, found him beside her. The gun, thrust under his crossed arm, resumed its place against her.

"Drive."

"Was it you the other night at the door?" Her voice trembled as the motor started, the gear caught.

"He left me with the lot; ain't nobody coming."

The car eased into an empty street.

"Go out of town. The Memphis road."

She was driving past familiar, cared-for lawns and houses, trees and intersections. Someone waved from a car at a stoplight, taking them for her and Clyde. She was frightened and accepting fear which come to think of it was all she'd been doing for months, working with those horses. ("Don't let him bluff you, Deedee. It's you or him. He'll do it if he can.")

"What do you want with me? What is it you want?"

He spoke straight outward, only his mouth moving, watching the road, never turning his head to her. "You're going out on that Memphis road and you're going up a side road with me. There's some woods I know. When I'm through with you you ain't never going to have nothing to ask nobody about me because you're going to know it all and it ain't going to make you laugh none, I guarantee."

Deborah cleared the town and swinging into the highway wondered at herself. Did she want him? She had waited when she might have run. Did she want, trembling, pleading, degraded, finally to let him have every single thing his own way?

(Do you see steel hooves above you over and over because you want them one day to smash into your brain?

("Daddy, Daddy," she had murmured long ago when the old unshaven tramp had come up into the lawn, bleary-eyed, face blood-burst with years of drink and weather, frightening as the boogeyman, "raw head and bloody bones," like the Negro women scared her with. That day the sky streamed with end-of-the-world fire. But she hadn't called so loudly as she might have, she'd let him come closer, to look at him better, until the threatening voice of her father behind her, just on the door's slamming, had cried: "What do you want in this yard? What you think you want here? Deborah! You come in this house this minute!" But the mystery still lay dark within her, forgotten for years, then stirring to life again: When I said "Daddy, Daddy?" was I calling to the tramp or to the house? Did I think the tramp was him in some sort of joke or dream or trick? If not, why did I say it? Why?

("Why do you ride a horse so fast, Deedee? Why do you like to do that?" *I'm going where the sky breaks open.* "I just like to." "Why do you like to drive so fast?" "I don't know.")

Suppose he kills me, too, thought Deborah, striking the straight stretch on the Memphis road, the beginning of the long rolling run through farms and woods. She stole a glance to her right. He looked like Clyde, all right. What right did he have to look like Clyde?

("It's you or him, Deedee." All her life they'd said that to her from the time her first pony, scared at something, didn't want to cross a bridge. "Don't let him get away with it. It's you or him.")

Righting the big car into the road ahead, she understood what was demanded of her. She pressed the accelerator gradually downward toward the floor.

"And by the time he realized it," she said, sitting straight in her chair at supper between Clyde and Emma, who by chance were there that night together; "—by the time he knew, we were hitting above seventy-five, and he said, 'What you speeding for?' and I said, 'I want to get it over with.' And he said, 'Okay, but that's too fast.' By that time we were touching eighty and he said, 'What the fucking hell—' excuse me, Mama, '—you think you're doing? You slow this thing down.' So I said, 'I tell you what I'm doing. This is a rolling road with high banks and trees and lots of curves. If you try to take the wheel away from me, I'm going to wreck us both. If you try to sit there with that gun in my side I'm going to go faster and faster and sooner or later something will happen, like a curve too sharp to take or a car too many to pass with a big truck coming and we're both going to get smashed up at the very least.

It won't do any good to shoot me when it's more than likely both of us will die. You want that?'

"He grabbed at the wheel but I put on another burst of speed and when he pulled at the wheel we side-rolled, skidded back, and another car coming almost didn't get out of the way. I said, 'You see what you're doing, I guess.' And he said, 'Jesus God.' Then I knew I had him, had whipped him down.

"But it was another two or three miles like that before he said, 'Okay, okay, so I quit. Just slow down and let's forget it.' And I said, 'You give me that gun. The mood I'm in, I can drive with one hand or no hands at all, and don't think I won't do it.' But he wanted his gun at least, I could tell. He didn't give in till a truck was ahead and we passed but barely missed a car that was coming (it had to run off the concrete), and he put it down, in my lap."

(Like a dog, she could have said, but didn't. And I felt sorry for him, she could have added, because it was his glory's end.)

"So I said, 'Get over, way over,' and he did, and I coasted from fast to slow. I turned the gun around on him and let him out on an empty stretch of road, by a rise with a wood and a country side road rambling off, real pretty, and I thought, Maybe that's where he was talking about, where he meant to screw hell—excuse me, Mama—out of me. I held the gun till he closed the door and went down in the ditch a little way, then I put the safety catch on and threw it at him. It hit his shoulder, then fell in the weeds. I saw it fall, driving off."

"Oh, my poor baby," said Emma. "Oh, my precious child."

It was Clyde who rose, came round the table to her, drew her to her feet, held her close. "That's nerve," he said. "That's class." He let her go and she sat down again. "Why didn't you shoot him?"

"I don't know."

"He was the one we hired that time," Emma said. "I'd be willing to bet you anything."

"No, it wasn't," said Deborah quickly. "This one was blond and short, red-nosed from too much drinking, I guess. Awful like Mickey Rooney, gone and gotten old. Like the boogeyman, I guess."

"The poor woman's Mickey Rooney. You women find yourselves the damnedest men."

"She's not right about that," said Emma. "What do you want to tell that for? I know it was him. I feel like it was."

"Why'd you throw the gun away?" Clyde asked. "We could trace that."

"It's what I felt like doing," she said. She had seen it strike, how his shoulder, struck, went back a little.

Clyde Mecklin sat watching his wife. She had scarcely touched her food and now, pale, distracted, she had risen to wander toward the windows, look out at the empty lawn, the shrubs and flowers, the stretch of white-painted fence, ghostly by moonlight.

"It's the last horse I'll ever break," she said, more to herself than not, but Clyde heard and stood up and was coming to her.

"Now, Deedee—"

"When you know you know," she said, and turned, her face set against him: her anger, her victory, held up like a blade against his stubborn willfulness. "I want my children now," she said.

At the mention of children, Emma's presence with them became multiple and vague; it trembled with thanksgiving, it spiralled on wings of joy.

Deborah turned again, back to the window. Whenever she looked away, the eyes by the road were there below her: they were worthless, nothing, but infinite, never finishing—the surface there was no touching bottom for—taking to them, into themselves, the self that was hers no longer.

YELLOW

Don Lee

I

As a boy, Danny Kim had hated being little, always the shortest kid in his class. Oddly enough, growing seven inches when he was sixteen did not help matters much. The sudden spurt left him gangly, his face spotted with acne, and now he was truly skinny—an image of inconsequence he could not live with. That summer, with the single-mindedness he would apply to everything in his life, Danny vowed to become physically superb.

He went to the YMCA on the other side of town, near the barrio. He half believed that by lifting weights, his body would be transformed overnight. Immediately, standing among the older boys and men as they grunted and strained with their barbells, he felt foolish. He would do a few listless repetitions at the bench press, fake his way through some dips and curls, then leave the Y, his resolve disintegrating with each day.

Coming out of the weight room one night, Danny was thinking

that he should admit defeat and quit, when he saw a man at the drinking fountain in the hallway. He noticed him because he was wiry and not very tall, no more than five-five, but was somehow imposing, and neat. Extraordinarily neat. His undershirt and sweatpants appeared to have been ironed. He had a pencil mustache and a pompadour, both meticulously trimmed and looking tidy even now, despite the fact that he had clearly been exercising, a light sweat sheening his skin. His hands were bandaged, and he was washing out a plastic mouthpiece. He took a tiny sip from the fountain, inserted the mouthpiece, and jogged down a stairway near the end of the hall.

Danny hadn't known there were any exercise areas in the basement. He walked down the stairs and located the man in what he gathered was the boxing room. Danny sat down on a bench near the doorway. From its condition, he could tell the place was not a high priority at the Y. The dimensions of the room barely accommodated the boxing ring with its sagging ropes—hugged on three sides by padded walls, laid out flat on the floor, no platform—and the ceiling leaked onto the center of the ring. The man shadowboxed around a trash can that was positioned to collect the drops. There was a speed bag, two heavy bags patched with duct tape, and a wide, full-length mirror, concave in sections, distorting the reflection. All this was lit by low-hanging fluorescent tubes that made the room almost too bright; Danny had the impulse to squint as he watched the man.

Danny knew practically nothing about boxing—only what he had gleaned from Muhammad Ali's televised fights. He had thought it was a sport for big men, yet here was this little guy, flashing his bandaged fists, throwing combinations in a blur, bobbing and feinting with remarkable fluidity—a ballet—so light on his shifting feet his shoes did not squeak the vinyl canvas. It was beautiful to watch. It was—Danny knew the word was inappropriate, but he could think of no other— *pretty.*

A bell rang from somewhere. The man stepped out of the ring and toweled his face dry. Running a comb through his hair, he left the room, not glancing at Danny, who was confused that it had ended so abruptly. He finally concluded that the workout was finished, and, disappointed, walked to the base of the stairs. He heard the man coming back down. Danny quickly returned to his seat on the bench.

This time the man slipped his hands into a pair of boxing gloves. Eyes closed, he stood motionless for a moment, waiting. The bell rang again, and he started hitting the heavy bag, leaning into it with punches.

Danny read the label on the bell machine on the wall: "Ringmaster." He soon understood. The Ringmaster signaled three-minute durations—the length of a round in boxing—and the one-minute rest periods in between. The man did three rounds of each exercise, ritualistically toweling, combing, and going to the water fountain between rounds. He never missed a bell, always made it back with a few seconds to spare. After the heavy bag, whanging it with one-two-threes, he moved to the speed bag. The peanut-shaped sack thumped against the platform, rebounding back and forth faster than Danny could follow it, but the man stayed within its rhythm, hitting it precisely with different sides of his fists. Last was the jump rope: varying shuffle steps, heel-to-toe, double-time, arm crosses, the leather rope whistling the air, slapping the floor. When he was done, the man unraveled the bandages from his hands, rolled them up tight, unscrewed the speed bag from the platform, and packed everything into his gear bag. As he walked out, he hopped up to flick off the Ringmaster.

It was the most impressive thing Danny had ever seen.

Danny found the man in the locker room, a towel wrapped around his waist. Danny couldn't help staring at his stomach muscles, the rows of them. "Excuse me," he said. "Is there a boxing program here? Classes?"

The man sighed. He took a bottle of dandruff shampoo off the shelf of his locker. Hanging on a pair of wooden hangers was a dark silk suit, pressed and shiny. "It's ugly, you know. Boxing." He turned to Danny, looked him up and down. "Basketball's better for you."

"I don't plan to do it for a living," Danny said.

"No?"

"I'm only interested in training, what you were doing, to get into shape. I'm not interested in really fighting."

The man grabbed a woman's clear cosmetics bag—shaving cream, a tube of VO5, deodorant, baby powder inside—from his locker. "Monday, Wednesday, Friday, six o'clock," he said. "Bring a mouthpiece, hand wraps, and a cup."

"What do you mean? Are you going to train me?"

The man waved his hand up, resigned. "It's my job," he said as he headed for the showers.

Luis Porquilla was the new boxing instructor at the Y, an instructor who preferred not to have any students. This became clear on Monday when Porquilla rushed through the fundamentals with Danny—the three-quarters stance, the jab, and the straight right—and then threw him a headguard and a pair of gloves, and motioned to the ring. "Let's go," he said.

"You must be joking."

"Only way to learn."

As Porquilla tied Danny's gloves, he told him, "These here? Sixteen ounces. Pads like bath towels. But they make me tell you this: Every time you get hit—and you'll get hit, that's boxing—a blood vessel pops in the brain. You got a zillion, no sweat. But you walk into a punch, an accident, brain slams against the skull, you hemorrhage, you die." He turned on the Ringmaster and removed the trash can from the center of the canvas. "OK, ready?"

Porquilla didn't wear headgear. His gloves weren't even properly tied, the ends of the laces simply tucked inside with the hands. The bell sounded. Wide-eyed, alert, Danny went into a crouch, and jerked back when Porquilla extended his arm.

Porquilla smirked. "Touch gloves. Sportsmanship, OK?"

They circled clockwise. Danny tried a few jabs, none of them coming close, Porquilla just swatting them aside. Several times, Danny tried to tandem the jab with a right, lunging as Porquilla easily slipped away to his left. After thirty seconds, he was spent. It took all he had to hold his arms up. He'd never imagined three minutes could be so infinite. Porquilla began throwing jabs at him. Danny was incredulous. The man was *hitting* him. This must be against the law, he thought, or at least against the YMCA's principles of good conduct; he was being punched and bullied on his first day of instruction.

At the end of the round, he spat out his mouthpiece, Porquilla pulled off his gloves, and Danny walked out, not noticing the blood under his nose until he was in the locker room.

If Porquilla was surprised to see Danny come back on Wednesday and the succeeding nights, he didn't show it. He went through two more things with Danny—the left hook, the uppercut—then dropped the lessons altogether and just sparred with him. He no longer restricted himself to a single jab or hook at a time, and he even started taunting Danny, puffing out "boo" whenever he tagged him with a punch. Still, Danny kept returning. After two weeks, his stamina improved, and he could last the round without fading. After a month, he could slip Porquilla's jab and poke in a couple of his own. After six weeks, they were going two rounds—laying down a towel to catch the leak during the break—and Danny was able to sneak in his right once in a while, nearly hitting Porquilla flush, throwing him off balance.

"You Korean?" Porquilla asked.

"Yes."

"I thought so. Koreans got the killer instinct."

The next session, Porquilla began wearing a headguard, and since it was now apparent that Danny was there to stay, he commenced the training in earnest.

Boxing was so contradictory: the grace and economy of each motion, the connotation and promise of brutality. Danny thought it'd be the best of all worlds to have that sort of power—to know that if he had to, he could drop someone; that he was, despite appearances, lethal, dangerous. Danny had sensed from an early age that manhood was defined by physical strength.

His parents had immigrated to the States in 1953, a year before Danny was born. With the help of missionaries they'd met during the Korean War, they settled down in the small coastal town of Rosarita Bay, south of San Francisco. His father, Min Hong, who had been a history professor at Seoul National University, got a job at the local community college as a payroll clerk. His mother, Yong Soo, a small, elegant woman who, in her time, had been a member of the *jeunesse dorée*—privileged, wealthy, a radio announcer of brief renown—worked part time as a florist. They were an incongruous couple, Min Hong taciturn, seemingly passionless; Yong Soo compulsive about the maintenance of home and family, position. The resident debutante.

Sometimes, frustrated with this new, humbling life, she would become shrill, proclaiming she could have married any number of suitors, many of whom were now leaders in the ministry, industrial magnates. Danny's father reacted to these outbursts with utter silence. He was a hardworking man, dedicated to being a good provider, but he had no acumen for business, no ambition to follow the classic rites of other Far Eastern immigrants, beginning with a greengrocery or the like and rising to be an entrepreneur in real estate, own restaurant chains and factories. And in this country, where his degrees and intellect meant nil, where his English began as passable and never quite became fluent, he was severely limited in what he could do. Later, he would get a fairly well-paying job teaching Korean at the Defense Language Institute in Monterey, and throughout their children's teens they would be able to gather the accoutrements of the middle class, buying a house, three cars, and the necessary appliances; but Danny would always remember about his parents a forlorn resignation—the interruption of the war, the wrong choice made to emigrate, potential glory lost and now irretrievable.

Much attention and expectation, then, was given to Danny. They were, after all, a residually Asian family, and he was not only their sole son, but their first *American*-born child. Predictably, they wanted him to become a doctor or an engineer, and he excelled in the sciences in high school—his memory was nearly photographic. But he also pursued more amorphous interests. When he wasn't in school or at the local Safeway, where he worked as a stock boy, he was at the movies or in the public library. He listened to classical music through earphones, flipped through art books. He read novels. He cared nothing for aesthetics; his motives were purely utilitarian. He would memorize whole passages from novels and, in private, recite lines with careful enunciation, watching his mouth and tongue in the mirror. His tastes tended toward what he thought was sophisticated prose—Conrad, Lawrence, Flaubert, Henry James, Fitzgerald—and hence his diction became Anglicized, his expressions formal and stilted. Increasingly, and with unabashed condescension, he would correct his parents' and his two sisters' English. He refused to learn Korean, and when it was used in the house, he would sometimes burst out, "Speak English! Speak English!" His scorn extended to his mother's cooking: he would not eat traditional dishes like *pindaettok* or *kimch'i,* afraid the sharp smells of red pepper and garlic would linger on him. He rarely brought any of his few friends home with him.

He wanted to be exemplary, unquestionably an American, but where this need came from he did not know. There was quite an ethnic mix in the Rosarita Bay school system. The artichoke fields and cannery had brought workers from the cities and migrant families from the San Joaquin Valley to town, and the children of these Mexicans, blacks, Filipinos, and Asians were put together with the Anglos—a practical, rather than progressive, integration—so Danny never suffered prejudice to any great extent.

Certainly there were incidents, like the time his family had been vacationing in the Sierras and had stopped at a convenience store. A drunk, a big, florid man with his shirt open and his gut out, had staggered up to them. "I forgive you," he had said. "Pearl Harbor. I forgive you for Pearl Harbor." And then he had kissed Danny's father on the *mouth.* Danny had watched, horrified. It had been days before he could talk to his father, much less look him in the face.

But that incident alone, or even the accumulation of smaller ones (being called a chink or having people tease him by pulling their eyes slanty), could not wholly account for Danny's vague, perpetual sense of anger. He was, when it came down to it, a proud boy. Although he was an exceptional student and was generally well liked, he did not consider himself popular, and this irked him. He never dated. He felt he didn't have a chance with the fresh-faced, lissome blondes he most admired, and he would not compromise with lesser attractions. Surprisingly, he did not attribute his insecurities to racial difference. Rather, he blamed his acne and the lag in his physical development.

First pitifully short, now rail thin, he was routinely knocked to his ass in P.E. The irony was that he was naturally athletic. He just lacked the muscle mass for games like football and basketball, and he had gotten off to a late start in sports in general. (His parents had never encouraged him to do anything except learn how to swim. His mother had nearly drowned as a child, and she had enrolled Danny in Red Cross lessons, making sure he was certified as a lifesaver.) He had no aspirations to be a jock himself, but he could not tolerate the superiority of these bigger boys, dimwits like George Gilbertson, the center of the football team, who nicknamed Danny "Chopstick" and enjoyed lifting him over his head and depositing him on top of the hallway lockers. Danny wanted to be respected. He wanted to punish anyone who tried to humiliate him.

He went to the Y three nights a week for the next two years. He'd begin his routine with some stretching, check his technique in front of the mirror, then execute Porquilla's floor workout, mixed in with some hard sparring. Most of boxing, Porquilla stressed, was conditioning, and Danny did his on the intervening mornings before school. Push-ups, pull-ups, sit-ups, leg raises, neck bridges. Porquilla forbade weights— they hampered flexibility—and, rather than long-distance running, he had Danny perform intervals, first jogging a mile, then doing a torturous series of wind sprints, cooling down afterward with another mile job. On Sundays, Danny was allowed to rest.

In the initial months, he was sore all the time, groaning and wincing whenever he moved, walking bowlegged, his forearms so tight he couldn't make a fist. It *was* an ugly sport. He'd cramp, pull muscles, get bruised. Porquilla was careful—no black eyes, not a mark on the face—but periodically he would clip Danny with a hook and his jaw wouldn't close right for weeks. And the smells. Despite Porquilla's attempts to discourage initiates, eventually a handful of boys stayed on and joined Danny, so six people were sharing the same headgear and set of gloves. Danny learned why pros always bopped themselves on the head in the ring: it was a habit from constantly adjusting a sweaty, ill-fitting headguard while sparring. Even after showering, he could never quite get rid of the stink of glove leather from his hands.

The physical discipline was exhilarating. He enjoyed the feeling of exhaustion after a workout—a warm, cleansed sensation, the blood flowing, his mind absolutely lucid. And as he had hoped, his body changed. He gained pounds, his appetite ravenous now. He developed sinewy arms, biceps, the muscles on his back, legs, everywhere, hard and individually defined. He was proudest of his stomach. He liked to rub his hand over the knobbed tendon sheets. He frequently admired himself in his bedroom mirror.

There was a pleasure, too, in the camaraderie with the other young boxers, who couldn't have been more different from Danny. They ranged in age from fourteen to twenty-six, all Hispanic or black. Some were experienced amateurs, a couple semiprofessionals with a dozen smokers behind them. One of them, César, a Chicano the same age as Danny, made a living tarring roofs and was already, Danny was amazed to find out, the father of three. Danny got along with them all. They were a quiet, curiously gentle group. There were no displays of bravado, no loud machismo in evidence, and this was mostly Porquilla's doing. Porquilla, who claimed he only took the position as the Y instructor because he thought he'd be paid to work out—alone; who was a natural teacher, emphasizing safety and character as much as skill. He prohibited them from sparring with one another, serving as everyone's partner, sometimes going as many as sixteen consecutive rounds a night. He didn't let anyone off easy, yet he was inordinately polite, apologizing when he hit someone harder than he'd intended.

Danny never got to know very much about his trainer. He pieced together that Porquilla was from Guatemala, and until an opponent's thumb tore the retina in his right eye, he had had a bright future as a bantamweight, but everything else—even what his day job was—remained a mystery. Nonetheless, Porquilla had a profound influence on all of them, and for Danny, boxing was almost the least of it. There was his attention to hygiene (he told Danny to wash his face with Noxzema, not soap, for his pimples), his clothes, his entire manner. He appeared untouchable. Style was intrinsic to class, *dignidad*. Danny found himself imitating Porquilla. The key seemed to be a lack of excess, a measured slowness, in everything Porquilla did. He looked like he'd never been in a hurry in his life. He embodied absolute stoicism: giving in to emotion made you weak. What he ultimately said to you was this: I don't need you. And that in itself, that sort of self-possession, attracted people to him.

Just by adopting this attitude as his own, Danny felt more confident. He had reason to be. He was in terrific shape. At an even six feet, he still weighed no more than a hundred fifty pounds, but he was strong and quick. If he wanted to, he could probably lay out George Gilbertson with one punch, but George no longer bothered him. He hadn't told any of his classmates about the boxing, mostly because when he was still a neophyte, he worried he might be ridiculed or even challenged, but his classmates tacitly recognized the change in him, his ascension from boy to man. He was happy, perfectly satisfied with the way things were going, until one night Porquilla mentioned that all the boys should think about competing in the boxing tournament next summer, the Monterey County Amateur Championships.

The training intensified. In the ring, Porquilla would hold up punching mitts and call out numerical combinations, "one-two-one-three-bob-four-three," and they would hit the mitts with a jab, straight right, jab, and left hook, bob when Porquilla swiped at them, and counter with a right cross and another hook. While being commanded to "stick and move," they would weave under a clothesline stretched across the ring and throw uppercuts, slide to the other side, jab, weave again. With careful supervision, Porquilla now had them spar one another, matched deliberately—aggressive fighters with counterpunchers, Mutts with Jeffs—to give them a taste of what they might run into.

All the while, Danny tried to come up with an excuse to bow out of the tournament. What he had hidden from everyone was that from the very beginning, each time he climbed into the ring to spar, he was terrified. Thus far, he'd been able to ignore his fear, but now, faced with the prospect of going from the insignificant basement arena of the Y to the large civic auditorium in Salinas, he could think of nothing else. He knew he wasn't afraid of being hit or hurt. With the protective gear, the twenty-six joints in the hand were in more danger of injury than the head. He wasn't afraid of losing, either. No one would know, what did it matter?

It came time to submit the official entry forms to the competition. After distributing the applications, Porquilla took Danny aside. He leaned against the wall and scratched at the corner of his eye, almost bashful—this was plainly difficult for him. "For you, I know it's different," he told Danny. "You got college, maybe you'll be a lawyer someday. You got choices. That's why you could never be pro. You knew that coming in. If you'd said different, I'd've said walk. But you surprised me. You stuck with it. You've become a good boxer."

This was news to Danny. Besides a few words of encouragement here and there, like when he stepped into his jab instead of shooflying it, Porquilla had never hinted that Danny's skills were anything but pedestrian. "You mean that?"

Porquilla wagged his head grudgingly. "You're no Emile Griffith," he scowled, then he eased up and said, "Hey. You're going to do OK in this tournament," and he slapped Danny upside the head so hard it made his ear sing.

It was an unprecedented paternal gesture, and Danny felt trapped. In the end, he could not disappoint Porquilla, and he had no option other than to enter the tournament.

Danny would be competing in the novice division as a welterweight, one hundred forty-seven pounds. He was immediately reassured to see that most of the contestants in his weight class were smaller than he. Trying on the brand-new ten-ounce gloves and headguard provided by the tournament, Danny felt light, fast. He had a reach advantage; if he could stay cool through the three two-minute rounds, not get tempted into mixing it up, he had a competitive chance.

He forgot everything in the opening round of his first bout. His opponent, a black kid named Fedler, had no technique at all. He just came out and threw windmill hooks in a bunch. Danny got smacked with one, and, wild with anger and desperation, he stood toe-to-toe with Fedler, winging punches furiously.

Between rounds, Porquilla was *laughing*. "Danny, Danny," he said, shaking his head. "Just stick and move. You got this guy. He's gone. He's got nothing left. Lick him with your jab and move. He won't be able to touch you. Stick, stick, side to side, OK?"

It was OK. Doing what Porquilla told him, Danny outpointed

Fedler. A week later, he won the decision over his next opponent, and his next after that.

His family, noticing that his cheek was bruised, became worried. He had had to tell them about the training program when he started, yet they had acted indifferent about it, a reaction that had baffled him; perhaps they had not really understood what was entailed. As long as he continued to do well in school, it seemed, they were content. The bruise suddenly made them realize there was cause for alarm. Danny didn't care. He was exuberant. Porquilla told him not to get overconfident, he'd had an easy draw, but he, too, was obviously delighted with Danny's performance. Danny had made it to the quarterfinals of the championships.

Very early on, Danny had learned that boxing was about compactness—throwing punches within a tiny circle, the shortest distance to the target. In these three fights, though, he learned something else: you also boxed within concentric dimensions of time. He could anticipate a punch, and would slip and roll, counter. In the ring, he was in a circle of time—as well as space—*inside* of the other fighter's, calmly watching a slower pugilistic future. It was an immense feeling. He began to believe that, just possibly, he might win it all.

He fell apart in the quarterfinals. He knew he would lose in the first ten seconds. His opponent, Raymond Ríos, was taller than Danny by two inches and had a whip of a jab. Right away Ríos connected, two, three times in succession, and then lit into him with a combination. Danny was startled by the solid impact of the punches, considering how fast Ríos was throwing them; it was like having the end of a log shoved into his face. Occasionally he saw one coming, tried to block or weave, but it was always too late, his head knocked back and upward. He was clearly outmatched, and as the round progressed, he began to panic. He couldn't do anything. He was helpless. He was reduced to covering up, not fighting at all. The audience jeered. He'd get battered, grab Ríos's arms or waist, and hold him in a clinch. Several times the referee cautioned him to box, to stop holding, to keep his head up. Danny told himself to move, stick and move, but Ríos cut him off, quicker on his feet. Danny blindly reached for the boy's arms and accidentally knocked the top of his head against Ríos's chin.

"Stop!" the referee yelled. He pointed to Danny and issued a warning for a head butt, and then he pointed to each of the judges. A warning was as good as a foul in the amateurs; there would be a deduction from Danny's score. "Box," the referee said.

Eternal, the rest of the round. In the interval afterward, Porquilla pulled the elastic on Danny's trunks out to let him breathe, squirted water into his mouth, and held an ice bag against his left eye, which was swelling quickly. César, his Chicano mate from the Y, acting as the second, squeezed a sponge on the back of his neck and massaged him. Neither spoke to Danny. He could sense they were embarrassed by him. The timekeeper blew his whistle, signaling for the coaches and assistants to vacate the ring. Just before the bell, Porquilla, inserting Danny's mouthpiece, finally looked at him. "Be a man," he said.

It wasn't there. He wanted to fight, exhibit some *corazón,* some heart, but it just wasn't there. He understood now the root of his earlier fear. The truth had been too basic to comprehend. He had been afraid of being afraid.

Ríos started showboating—the Ali shuffle, bugging out his eyes, jutting out his jaw, talking to him. Most of it was unintelligible, garbled by his mouthpiece, but the mocking was intolerable. Danny wrestled him against the ropes.

The referee commanded, "Break! Stop!" He gave Danny another warning for a head butt; another point would be deducted. There were more jeers from the audience. "One more and you're disqualified, mister," the referee told Danny.

Resuming, Ríos popped him with a punch and said, " 'Ello." He did it again and again. " 'Ello, 'ello." Danny thought he was saying "hello," the way Porquilla used to rile him by breathing out "boo" when he hit him. Then he heard him distinctly. Ríos was saying *"yellow."* "Yellow," Ríos called him, disgusted.

Danny would never be able to figure out if what he did next was a conscious act or not. Certainly he was aware of the referee's last warning—another butt and he'd be disqualified—but it was, he believed, without premeditation, on impulse, that he leapt forward, head first, at Ríos. Perhaps it might have worked, he could have told himself the fight was stopped on a technicality, if Ríos, at that very moment, had not been jockeying backward, creating a gap between them, a short but conspicuous distance in which Danny's lunge, before his head cracked into Ríos's face, could only be construed as intentional, an overt attempt to end the fight.

The crowd was stupefied. The referee stepped between them and pushed Danny away, raising Ríos's arm as he led him to the corner, to a doctor for treatment of his nose, which was shattered and gushing blood.

The audience booed and tossed beer cups at Danny. He followed Porquilla out of the auditorium. *"Pendejo. Maricón,"* people shouted. Coward. Faggot.

II

At UCLA, Danny acquired a reputation as a cocky kid—a little smug. This struck him as strange at first, since he felt nervous and awkward all the time, but when he thought about it, he concluded it was only natural. That insolent pose of Porquilla's—he'd learned it well. He had also grown into a good-looking young man, his skin clear and smooth finally. He had a narrow nose with an adequately pronounced bridge, the epicanthic folds of his eyes were muted, his jaw was square, and he had retained the athletic grace and conditioning of a boxer, though he would never again put on a pair of gloves, never tell anyone that he had boxed at all. Moreover, Danny discovered he could be witty, sardonic. He'd get into philosophical and political discussions for the pure joy of it, relishing his newfound facility for argument. It was a heady time. Nineteen seventy-two. Vietnam. Nixon. The sexual revolution. In this new social milieu, where he had no history, he found his niche.

He endeared himself to the girls in particular because he could get them to talk about anything. One afternoon, as a freshman, he convinced six coeds in Sproul Hall to describe their masturbation habits (he had read Masters and Johnson and *Cosmo* in the public library). He lost his virginity to one of these girls a couple of nights later. Nancy, a cute blonde, just a little plump.

His college years weren't entirely genial, however, and Danny held the Vietnam War partly responsible. He was opposed to it for all the usual reasons, but something else rankled him. Whenever he watched the evening news and heard reports about the Viet Cong—the gooks, their devious guerrilla tactics, the tunnels and booby traps and snipers—Danny flinched internally. It was, to him, a blatantly racist war, as were the last two American wars. The yellow peril. The Japs, the Koreans, now the Vietnamese—all of them inhuman and atavistic.

So, despite his apparent solidarity with the students in Kerchoff Coffeehouse, the smokey, passionate talk about American imperialism and the bourgeois establishment, Danny privately thought, for a brief period, about enlisting. For him, for any Asian, there were deeper questions of patriotism that could not be easily ignored—a legacy of the days of internment. He knew, albeit secondhand, about the dangers of communism. When the North Koreans invaded Seoul, had his parents not escaped to the countryside, they might have been imprisoned or executed, along with many of the intellectuals and aristocrats, or taken away above the Thirty-eighth Parallel, never to be seen again.

In his heart, he did not believe in the antiwar movement. He kept his cynicism to himself, and endorsed it all because he recognized it as fashion, like long hair and fringed suede jackets, but the Vietnam War heightened his desire to repudiate his Asianness, and led to his decision as a sophomore to double-major. Studying mechanical engineering, he had become all too aware that the campus was separated by a demilitarized zone of its own, the North housing the arts and humanities, the South the sciences, which were dominated by Asians. The stereotypes that traditionally befell science majors were racially endemic at UCLA: thick glasses, a calculator on the belt, high floodwater trousers. They were regarded as geeks, goofballs, and Danny thought the Asians themselves were as much to blame as anyone. They were insular and provincial, and it was true: they were hopelessly square. He defected to the English Department. Since math was effortless for him, he continued his engineering courses on the sly. But as far as most people knew, he was exclusively steeped in, say, the Metaphysical poets, Donne's conceit of a compass as close as he got to vectors and wave diffractions.

As appropriate as Donne's love poems would have been for them, Danny met Jenny Fallows in a seminar called The Martyr in the Novel. For quite a while, he had been observing her—hanging around drama-student types who wore black and smoked Gauloises. She was exquisite. Heavy, lush hair hanging down her back, lambent skin, eyebrows thick and dark. She had a shape to her, too, which made him weak. Wonderful legs. The curve of her breast through a loose, sleeveless blouse. Once, they had eyed each other outside of Powell Library. He noticed that her mouth protruded because of a slightly crooked tooth. He liked it, that single flaw.

Not long into the seminar, they ran into each other at the Nuart, the retrospective theater, where To Catch a Thief was playing (about Grace Kelly, Danny was devout). In the theater, he turned and saw Jenny sitting at the end of the same row. She moved to the seat beside him. "This is a coincidence," she said.

Flustered, he looked down at the floor. She was wearing pointy, red suede boots. "I like your shoes," he told her.

"Thanks," she laughed, showing her crooked front tooth.

After the movie, they went to a coffee shop, Zucky's. She drank tea and watched him eat. "Do you know about François?" she asked.

"François?"

"I live with him. He's a director. Or he's studying to be one."

"I suspected there was someone. I didn't know his name."

"We can't see each other. Not the way you want. This is special. François just happens to be away."

He tilted his head, bemused—a practiced gesture. "Aren't you being a bit presumptuous? What makes you think I'm interested in you in . . . 'that way'?"

She rolled her eyes, irritated. "Don't be coy."

They went to class together, sometimes lingered afterward for coffee and analyses of *Lord Jim* and *The Great Gatsby*.

She got his address somehow and began sending him things in the mail, odd little clippings. There was a diagram of the constellation Orion, with Jenny's scrawled caption: "Orion has a zipper, a fly. There are subliminals in the sky, you know." A page from her childhood coloring book of a little girl crayoned black: "I've always believed in racial balance." And a photograph of Brando from *Last Tango in Paris*: "He accepts no substitutes. Only real butter will do."

Danny waited. It was only a matter of time. Finally, she told him François would be away again, on a film project in the Mojave Desert. Several days of clouds, then a gorgeous afternoon. After class, Danny invited Jenny to take a drive up Topanga Canyon, to a spot with a high view of the ocean. He had a cooler in the trunk of his car with cold fried chicken and beer, the lunch Grace Kelly and Cary Grant had shared in *To Catch a Thief*. Every other night that week, Danny had thrown out the old chicken, fried a fresh batch.

They made love that day. They cuddled on his bed, and she said that as a child, she had pronounced "bedraggled" as "bed-raggled," because that was what her parents looked like on Sunday mornings.

"I think I'm going to be bed-raggled with you a lot," she said.

He knew then that he would fall in love with her.

François proved difficult at first (tears, begging, then recriminations), but eventually, after about a month, he found his own place.

Jenny took on one roommate, then a second, to split the rent on the one-bedroom apartment—two lonely girls who stayed home all the time in a nihilistic funk. Jenny spent nearly every night at Danny's.

They were consumed. They saw no one, lost touch with all their friends. Frequently on weekends they did not leave his room. Sometimes they forgot to eat.

Danny had had a healthy string of affairs before meeting Jenny, and he had thought of himself as relatively experienced. Yet once he began sleeping with Jenny, he discovered just how much he didn't know—all the subtle ministrations which could only be learned through daily intimacy. She taught him everything. Their bodies fit together perfectly—a natural confluence. They had their routines, their preferences. At night, slow kisses, brushing of lips, Danny sliding down. Then he'd rise above her, be inside, hold himself up to watch her face, pressing against her while he moved in small circles. She would touch his nipples, run her nails lightly down the hollow of his back, between his buttocks. When one sensed the other getting close, it'd push them both over. Without miss, the first time, every time, they came simultaneously, a fact of which they were ridiculously proud.

In the morning he'd wake up with Jenny spooned against him. There was so much made of the male genitalia, he thought, but women . . . they had their differences, too. He'd curl into her, his morning erection spreading her distended labia—unusually exposed, a protrusion not unlike her mouth's—and he could not wish for anything sweeter, not entering yet, just rubbing along the furrow of this warm, plummy flesh.

During the summer, Danny worked at a firm that designed oil-drilling equipment, Jenny at a nursery. They took drives on Pacific Coast Highway, drank gin and tonics, read passages from *A Sport and a Pastime* to each other, cooked elaborate meals.

Danny was in love, wildly happy, and, as a consequence, he was sadder than he'd ever been in his life. He despaired that it had to end. Sometimes he'd accuse Jenny of having fallen in love with someone else. She was capable of it once, why not again. "Why are you doing this?" she'd cry.

In July, they thought she was pregnant. She wasn't, but before they were sure, he asked her to marry him.

"Oh, sweetheart, it'd be foolish," she said. "You'd always blame me for trapping you."

"No, I wouldn't."

"Yes, you would. In the back of your mind, you would."

"But I love you. I want to marry you."

"I know. But the timing's all wrong. We have to finish school first, decide what we're going to do with our lives." She told him she would get an abortion.

"Would you feel all right about doing that?" he asked her.

"Yes. Because I can't imagine that we won't have children together someday, that we won't get married."

They drove up into the Hollywood Hills that night. The Santa Ana winds were blowing, desert air buffeting the trees, and with the smog cleared out, they had a spectacular view of the city. "What will our kids look like?" she asked.

It took him a moment to understand; somehow he had never thought of it as an issue, a complication. "They'll have straight, brownish hair and brown eyes," he said. "They'll either be beautiful or homely. With mixed-blooded children, there are no in-betweens."

Jenny kissed him. "We'll have three. Two boys and a girl. They'll all be beautiful."

He was convinced, more than ever, that the romance was blighted.

Their senior year began. Danny was often moody, and whenever Jenny tried to nudge him out of it, he'd become more distant from her. Their studying sessions—before, filled with sighs, wistful looks—were now dry, businesslike. They no longer made love every day.

One afternoon, as they were walking on campus, they passed a group of male Asian students. One of them, under his breath, said, "Banana."

"What did he mean?" Jenny asked Danny when they were out of earshot.

He was tight-lipped.

"What?" she asked again.

"Yellow on the outside, white on the inside," he told her.

"That's hilarious! Banana! Now is 'Oreo' the same kind of thing? I thought it meant—how can we put this delicately—a double-entry transaction."

"I don't know."

"Food epithets . . . there must be something significant about that, don't you think?"

He would not respond.

For Thanksgiving vacation, he flew to Minneapolis with Jenny to meet her family. Mr. Fallows was an executive with Northwest Airlines; Mrs.

Fallows, a former flight attendant, ran her own travel agency. Their house in Edina, an affluent Minneapolis suburb, was filled for Thanksgiving with Jenny's many siblings and relatives. Danny felt overwhelmed, and his discomfort swelled when he was introduced to Jenny's aunt. She was clearly confused. "Are you from Vietnam?" she asked. She had been hearing about the recent wave of Vietnamese, Laotian, and Cambodian refugees, and was stuck on the idea. Even after his clarification, she continued to think Danny was an FOB—Fresh Off the Boat. "How do you like the United States?" she asked.

Jenny giggled. "Auntie, he's lived in California all his life."

After grace, everyone raised their wineglasses. "Happy Thanksgiving," they said to one another. The aunt warmly saluted Danny: "Welcome to America." Jenny nearly fell out of her chair. It perplexed him that she found this funny.

The following day she took him on a tour of Minneapolis and presented him to her friends. Later, Jenny told him, "You know what Amy said? She said, 'How come you've come back from L.A. with all these Oriental things? Your purse, your address book, your boyfriend . . .' "

"What did you tell her?"

"That I appreciate beauty. Even Dad says you're—his words—'exceedingly handsome.' He's never commented on any man's looks before."

"What do they think of me? Your family."

"They think you're charming."

"Nothing else?" Danny asked, not satisfied.

"Most people would take that as a favorable ruling, honey."

"They didn't mention anything about my being . . . an Oriental *thing?*"

"Auntie told me you don't *look* that malnourished after all those months at sea."

"No, really."

Jenny smiled impishly. "Kate wants to go to bed with you," she said, referring to her sixteen-year-old sister. "She can't believe anyone's skin can be so tight."

The trip, seeing the cozy, genteel world she came from, made him captious about Jenny. Her family and friends had been amiable enough, but they didn't seem to attend to him earnestly, as if he were only Jenny's latest distraction, not a prospective husband for her. To Danny, this had to reflect Jenny's own attitude about him.

They took their final exams, and then she left for Montserrat, another family gathering for Christmas. Danny had been invited, but he canceled at the last minute. He said he couldn't afford it, though the tickets and accommodations, arranged by Mrs. Fallows's travel agency, were at a cut rate. Jenny seemed relieved.

He visited Rosarita Bay for a week. His relationship with his own family was, at best, perfunctory these days. He had never cared for Jenny to meet them, but during this holiday, he thought it odd that she had not once suggested it herself.

They reunited in L.A. on New Year's Eve. She was tan, gorgeous. "God, I missed you," she said.

A movie producer was throwing a party in his Brentwood mansion, a *Feliz Año Nuevo* theme. Sombrero party hats, *tapas,* margaritas. It was a huge affair, at least seven hundred people. Jenny had been looking forward to it all month. She bought a short, red faille dress with a revealing décolletage for the occasion. Danny never fully understood the vague connections—a friend of friends of Jenny's—which put them on the guest list. They knew no one there, but Jenny mingled blithely.

As Danny was following Jenny through a throng in the main ballroom, he noticed two men ahead staring at her, at her breasts, then coolly at him. He and Jenny had to squeeze into them, turn face-to-face with one man to get by. "Did you know it's National Hate Chinese Week?" the man said to Danny. Jenny, who had heard, tugged him away.

"Ignore him," she said.

Jenny found some acquaintances to talk to. Danny was standing apart from the group when something hit him on the chest. He looked down at the floor. It was a wedge of lime.

"What's the matter?" Jenny asked, moving over to him.

Another wedge bounced off his temple. Across the room, the two men glared at Danny, sipping their margaritas.

"Come on, let's go out to the lawn," Jenny said.

Sweat trickled down his back. After a moment, he complied.

They didn't stay long. Danny was silent as they drove away from the mansion. He hated himself for having done nothing. He hated Jenny for dressing like a whore.

"Sweetheart, just try to forget it," she said.

"I can't forget it. It's what I have to live with every day."

"They were just a couple of drunk assholes."

"You have no idea. . . . It's a novelty to you. An interracial cou-

ple. So radical-chic. Even more rebellious than shacking up with François. What will it be next? A black man?"

"That's not fair," she said to him. "Your color's never been an
issue with me. I've never even thought about it."

He scoffed.

"It doesn't matter to me what other people think," Jenny said.
"I don't care."

"You are laughably naive."

"Danny, please . . ." She touched his arm.

He jerked away. "Don't," he said in revulsion.

He did not see her for several days. More than anything, he marveled at how deluded he had been, for he had believed—abstractly,
quixotically—that he *could* be white. Colorless. He realized he was
doomed. No matter what he did, no matter how much he tried to deny
it, he would never get past being Asian. It was untenable, and the
knowledge broke him.

He told Jenny it was over.

"You can't do this," she said.

They argued for many hours, at the end of which he told her, as a
coda, "You were never serious about me, anyway."

Sobbing, she slapped him. "I loved you. I wanted to marry you.
Don't ever lie to yourself that I didn't."

Danny was speeding as he entered the underground garage of his
apartment building. He had wanted to race toward the far wall, stomp
on the brakes, skid to a stop an inch away from impact. Someone had
hosed down the concrete to clean the garage. The tires locked and slid
over the sheet of water, the car's front end crumpled into the wall, and
the seat belt lassoed his waist as he folded over, snapping his face into
the steering wheel.

The surgeries on his nose and cheekbones were reconstructive. The op-
eration on his eyelids was elective, cosmetic. His appearance wasn't al-
tered that much—a little more exotic, more sculpted. He could have
returned to school in the spring, but he chose to wait until the summer,
until after Jenny had graduated.

He stayed in L.A. for another two years, working as an engineer
at Lockheed. For a while, she would call. They had lunch a few times.
She looked different, too. Her hair was shorter and she wore braces. She
was a production assistant for a film company. Eventually they lost
touch altogether.

III

At Harvard Business School, Danny—or Daniel, as he called himself now—kept to himself. He rented a studio apartment in the Back Bay instead of living in the B-school residence halls, and while he worked in small study groups, as was dictated by the program, he did not socialize with his sectionmates.

Romantically, too, he was passive. When he was the object of pursuit, he would sometimes try to go through the motions, but he never had his heart in it, and women found his disaffection frustrating and cruel. "There's something wrong with you," one of them said when they broke up. "You're so cold-blooded. You don't have any loyalties to anybody or anything. You have any feelings at all?"

Eight months later, he married a Korean American. His mother arranged it for him. For years, she'd prodded Danny, urged him to go out with Asian girls, showed him photographs, and he had refused unequivocally. She'd been shocked when he asked her to introduce him to someone.

Rachel Chung, born in Rochester, was the daughter of his mother's schoolmate from Seoul. A senior at Boston University when he met her, she was short but trim, cute with her thick, pageboy hair and rounded mouth. She was companionable, had her cultural finishes—a theater major who had wandered into costume design—and her values were patently Western, as far removed from the old country as he was.

The night he proposed, she took him back to her apartment. Heretofore, he'd only kissed her. "You don't have to be such a gentleman all the time," she said. They made love. She was the first Asian woman he'd ever touched.

For five years, he worked at Rayco Tech, a semiconductor company in Woburn, outside of Boston on Route 128. Despite the commute, Danny wanted to stay in the city, and he and Rachel bought a condo on Dartmouth Street. He was comfortable in the Back Bay. He felt relatively secure there, whereas elsewhere in Boston and its suburbs, he did not. The city was so plainly and historically stratified by class and color. At the better restaurants and hotels, at upscale functions and parties, at business meetings, it would dawn on him that everyone there, *everyone* except him, was white. He felt a kinship with prosperous blacks, a silent brotherhood of tokenism, and was ashamed of himself when he tolerated his colleagues' racist jokes and comments. It shouldn't have sur-

prised him, but it always did, to hear ostensibly liberal, educated North-
erners using the word *nigger*.

A more immediate concern for him, though, was the hostility toward Asians—specifically the Indochinese immigrants—that he saw in-
creasing with their presence in Boston; almost with regularity, he
thought he was becoming a victim of it. Sometimes it was subtle. His
flight was delayed at Logan once, and he went to the airport bar for a
cup of coffee. There was a group of salespeople at the next table, and one
of them, repacking her briefcase, pulled out a cellular telephone. A man
in the group said, "Hey, let me use that portable phone there. I want to
call Hong Kong. Order me some chop suey." They laughed. Danny
looked over to them, nervously wondering if the joke had been casual or
if he was being baited. Another time, he was waiting at a stoplight, and a
man in the passenger seat of the car next to Danny's said, "Fucking Orientals everywhere. Every last one of you should be crucified."

Occasionally, he would tell Rachel about these incidents, and she
would tell him about things that had happened to her (she'd given up
her dreams of an acting career when a famous director, whom she'd approached for advice, had said, "To be frank, honey, there aren't a whole
lot of plays with kimonos and rice paddies"). But Rachel had more
equanimity than Danny. "You have to rise above it," she'd shrug. She
didn't like dwelling on the subject, and she would discuss it with him
less and less. She was comfortable being Korean, was fluent in the language, and often spoke Korean to both their families in public, while
Danny anxiously glanced about them, not understanding what they
were saying.

As the years went by, he grew more alarmed. He followed reports on the resurgence of the KKK, racial assaults, boycotts of Korean
merchants, and the jingoistic fervor in Michigan, where people threw
rocks at Japanese cars, where two laid-off auto workers killed a Chinese
American with a baseball bat. Eventually, Danny could not help bris-
tling or feeling threatened whenever he was asked, "What are you?" He
was born here, he spoke perfect English, he was as mainstream as anyone could be. Yet, in this country of immigrants, Danny, as an Asian,
was regarded as a foreigner, a newcomer, someone who was not a *real*
American. Every day he expected, at any moment, at any place, to be
attacked.

Rachel gave birth to a son, Michael Jay Kim. He was a big baby, weigh-
ing in at nine pounds. He would be tall probably, but Danny was disap-

pointed with his looks. His head was squarish, his face broad and flat; his black hair poked out as stiff as porcupine quills, and his eyes were cut thin in slits. It was a dull physiognomy, characteristic of most Orientals.

"With the amount of time you're home," Rachel's older sister, who was visiting from New York, told him, "it must have been an immaculate conception."

"Beth, don't be *ongtoree*," Rachel said—Korean for "stupid."

"Haven't you ever heard of phone sex?"

"Daniel, Daniel, what do you get when you cross a rooster with a telephone pole?" Beth asked.

"A cock that wants to reach out and touch someone!" the sisters screamed at the same time. They howled, hit each other with sofa pillows.

Danny was unimpressed.

"You're such a poop," Beth said to him. "Don't you ever loosen up, do something besides work? You ever have any fun? Do you *know* how to have fun?"

Later, as they were readying for bed, Rachel asked Danny, "Tell me the truth, are you having any fun? You're so . . . serious all the time."

"I take what I do seriously. Is that a fault?" He arranged what he would wear to the office the next day on his wooden valet: Louis, Boston suit, Hathaway shirt, Charvet tie, cap-toed Brooks Brothers oxfords. Clothes were his one extravagance.

Rachel came up from behind and hugged him. "Sometimes I wish you hadn't taken this job."

Rayco Tech had ridden out the computer-industry recession in 1984, but it hadn't required too much insight to predict that the semiconductor market would remain in a downturn. Danny got out while he could. In 1985, he joined Delaney, Rhodes & Company, a prestigious management consulting firm in downtown Boston, known for its client base in manufacturing.

The hours were grueling, the demands for flexibility and dedication prodigious. The consultants were often called upon at a moment's notice to go to Chicago, Austin, Atlanta, for months at a time. DRC made sure they were comfortable: an apartment, rental car, generous per diem, and a round-trip plane ticket home every weekend. At the completion of one particularly big job, DRC rewarded the team and their spouses with four days in Mexico. For the annual Christmas party once, consultants from every branch nationwide were flown to New York and treated to an evening at the Rainbow Room. But despite all the perks, the strains on family life were inescapable. Even when Danny stayed in Boston, he worked most weekends. During the week, he came home long after Michael was asleep, too tired to do anything but share a late dinner with Rachel.

Yet he assumed Rachel was content. When she wanted to go back to work as a costume designer for the Huntington Theatre, he encouraged her. After all, Michael had turned five and was attending school now, and Danny could understand if she was restless. Then she told him that before a play began its run, she would have to be at the theater at night—weekends, too. Since day care ended at six o'clock, he would have to be home by that time during those months.

He didn't know what to say at first, the request was so unreasonable. "What happens if I get an assignment out of state?" he said.

"You'll have to give it to someone else."

He had to laugh. "Come on, that's inane."

"Why?"

"I'd be fired."

"No, you wouldn't," Rachel said. "You're too valuable to them. If you really wanted to work normal hours, demanded it, you could. They'd accommodate you."

"Is this a ploy to get me to spend more time with you and Michael? Because if it is, trying to undermine my career isn't going to accomplish anything."

"What about my career? It's just as important as yours."

"Your sister put you up to this, didn't she? Beth and her neofeminist ideas about the modern Asian woman."

"Beth has nothing to do with this. It's us. I don't even know why we're together anymore. Why did you marry me? You don't want to be with me much, that's for sure. Sometimes I think you hate me."

"I don't hate you."

"No, it's worse. You don't care enough to hate me."

They hired an au pair as a compromise, but they never reached a full level of rapprochement from that point on. He despised her theater friends. They were pretentious, loud, and went to ludicrous lengths trying to be hip. It wasn't until one Sunday, though, that he understood his aversion toward them had a secondary, subliminal basis. He went to the movies without Rachel or Michael, as was often the case these days, buying a ticket without knowing what the film was about—anything to get out of the house and the summer heat—and as he sat in the air-conditioned darkness, reading the opening title credits, he was startled to recognize a name: Associate Producer, Jennifer Fallows. He had never put the two together, Rachel and Jenny, the latter's clique of drama students at UCLA, François the director, Hollywood.

Over the next couple of weeks, memories visited him, eidetic glimpses of Jenny in the bathroom, wearing his shirt, the tails lifting to reveal her splendid behind as she dried her hair; of her in class, fondling him under the seminar table as she listened, primly, to the professor's lecture, which linked *Sons and Lovers* to the Freudian madonna/whore complex; of her dropping a rolled-up note in a bottle of wine they'd just finished, a note he tried to extract with a pencil, a wire hanger, finally smashing it with a hammer to read, the ink running over the wine-bled paper, "I cherish you, I adore you, I love you."

When they had stopped seeing each other, Danny had promised himself that he'd never risk being so vulnerable again. He had sworn never to fall in love with another white woman, and surrendered to the fact that being with an Asian was easier. If he wasn't in love with Rachel, he'd come to be fond of her, he had believed. But along the way, he had sacrificed more than he'd known. He had forfeited the part of himself that permitted the possibility of love.

In 1991, DRC's biggest client was Beal Microsystems, a minicomputer manufacturer in San Jose. It was a huge, intricate job, and Danny was heading DRC's team with another executive consultant, Kevin Sheridan, an interesting and not entirely coincidental arrangement, since it was no secret that they were competing for a partnership. Danny disliked Sheridan. They had been assigned together on several other jobs, and each time, Sheridan was industrious only in the variety of ways he invented to avoid or delegate his work. Quite simply—at least to Danny—he lacked the technical know-how to get down to business. Danny wondered how he had squeaked through MIT with an engineering degree, through Boston College with his MBA, and he was dumbstruck that Sheridan's deficiencies hadn't caught up to him yet, that he was allowed to stay—indeed, *thrive*—in the firm.

Taller than Danny, slim, with lank blond hair and an asymmetric grin, Sheridan was the personification of old-boy, blue-blood charm and assurance (his father had been an economic advisor to JFK). The clients loved him. In meetings and presentations, he was careful to give credit where credit was due, but he was always a bit too self-deprecating about his own contributions to the project, leaving the impression that he was being modest. The end result was that when a problem or question arose, the clients asked for *him,* not Danny. It wasn't difficult to imagine what got back to Dennis Rhodes, DRC's senior partner.

He was convinced that he would not be made partner. A traditional Boston firm like DRC might patronize him and exploit his talents, but it would never grant him full admission.

He and Sheridan wrapped the Beal job a week before Christmas, and, much to Danny's discomfort, they ended up on the red-eye to Boston together. They exchanged a few final notations, and then fell asleep. Everything was out of their hands now; most likely Dennis and the other partners had already made their decision. They'd attend DRC's Christmas party, Danny would go to St. John for a week's vacation, then he and Sheridan would learn who had been chosen in mid-January.

An hour and a half from Boston, Danny was awakened for the breakfast service. Groggily he peeled off the foil covering his omelet and tore open the cellophane packet of utensils. Sheridan, in the adjoining seat, was staring out the window. His face was averted, but, unmistakably, he was crying.

"Celie's leaving me," Sheridan said. "Did you know that?"

"No."

"Of course not. You don't know a single thing about me. You've never cared enough to ask. Tell me, how many kids do I have?"

Danny admitted he had no idea.

"Five. I've got five. They're what I live for. And now Celie wants me to move out. She can't even wait until after Christmas." He turned to Danny. "Do you love your family?"

Before Danny could answer, Sheridan said, his tone vacillating from maudlin to bitter, "What we do, it's pointless. We work like dogs, and we tell companies how to be more efficient, and a lot of times that means eliminating people's jobs so the profit margin goes up a few measly percentage points. What is it that we contribute? The only thing that makes it tolerable"—he began weeping—"the only thing that makes it worthwhile, is having a family to come home to. What will I do when I lose that?" He closed his eyes and whimpered, choked out loud sobs.

At first Danny thought this was some sort of bizarre trick—Sheridan, in an insipid reversal of tactics, attempting to elicit sympathy, pass himself off as a conscientious, God-fearing family man. But then, as Sheridan continued to cry, oblivious to the flight attendants and passengers glancing at him, Danny became embarrassed for Sheridan. He was repelled by this open display of weakness.

"Get ahold of yourself," he told Sheridan. "Be a man."

They landed, and Danny hurried off the plane. Sheridan caught up with him at the baggage carousel. He was composed now, and he stood by Danny silently for a minute or two before speaking. "I never liked you," he said. "I knew guys like you at MIT. You get into schools and get these great job offers and promotions because you're minorities, but you won't help anyone except yourselves, you'll only go out of your way for your own kind. I'm not gifted like you. I have to scramble just to be average, and you've never lifted a finger for me because you enjoy it, don't you? You enjoy seeing me fail. You're ruthless. You're vicious."

Danny accompanied Rachel to a benefit dinner for the Huntington Theatre at the Copley Plaza Hotel. The incident with Sheridan still stung him. Maybe Sheridan had been right: whatever their differences, he should have made an effort to work with him as a team, and he should have tried to console Sheridan on the plane. Yet the accusation that disturbed Danny the most had nothing to do with race or conduct or compassion. It was when Sheridan had asked if he loved his family. He had felt suddenly ashamed, because he had thought of Rachel and Michael, of his father and mother and sisters, and he had realized that he could not automatically declare, Yes, I love them.

At the benefit dinner, he was seated next to a skeletal old widow named Maggie Hartmann, a major patron of the Huntington. She seemed quite taken by Danny and was chatting jauntily to him. Preoccupied, Danny half listened to her ramble on about the bygone era of Boston theaters, the grand shows they'd had at the Colonial and Wilbur and Majestic; she couldn't understand why no one went to plays anymore; one of the primary reasons she split her time between Boston and New York was her love for the theater, though even the Upper East Side was becoming unlivable. "At least we have those wonderful Korean markets," Mrs. Hartmann said. "Those grocers work so hard, such long hours, and they keep their stores so well-stocked and clean. I don't know what I'd do without my Mr. Ahn. You Koreans are the hardest working people I know."

"Is that so?" Danny said. He was fully attentive to her now.

"Oh yes. I admire you so much, especially the sacrifices you make for your children. You know that Mr. Ahn's son is at Cal Tech and his daughter is at Cornell? Always studying."

"It's astonishing, the opportunities that are there if one is willing to make the effort," Danny told her. He noticed Rachel eavesdropping on the conversation.

"Yes. Absolutely."

"And the corollary to our success is obvious, isn't it?"

"Yes," Mrs. Hartmann smiled. Then she hesitated and said, "Well, I'm not sure I know what you mean."

"Laziness—the real bane of the black and Hispanic underclass. Do you believe that our talent in the sciences and in music is genetic, akin to rhythm or passion? Or maybe we're simply forced to sublimate because our dicks are so small."

"Oh my."

"Daniel!" Rachel said.

In the hotel lobby, Rachel seethed, "What's wrong with you? What's happened to you?"

"It's part of growing up—knowing that it no longer matters to be nice. I won't tolerate condescension. You shouldn't either."

"She was trying to give you a compliment."

"No stereotype is innocent. You can't excuse bigotry because it's well intended."

"God, listen to yourself," Rachel said. "That's all you talk about. This whole thing with Kevin. Everyone's a racist! You've become completely paranoid."

"Are you denying that racism exists?"

Rachel sighed. "Of course I'm not. But the thought of it has taken over your life, it's poisoned you, and that's sadder than anything anyone could ever say or do to you. Don't you see? Racism's not the problem. It's you." She gently pounded her fist against his chest. "You've got no heart, Daniel. You've got no soul."

DRC's Christmas party was held at the Charles Hotel in Harvard Square. All evening, Danny avoided Sheridan, who had come without his wife. He seemed strangely ebullient, however, greeting people jovially, which sank Danny's hopes: Sheridan knew something he didn't about the partnership. At the end of the party, Sheridan walked over to him, expansive and friendly. "No hard feelings?" he asked.

"Why would there be?" Danny said hatefully.

"Good." To Danny's amazement, Sheridan hugged him. "Take care of yourself," he said, and left.

Dennis Rhodes signaled to Danny. As he went to the corner to meet him, Danny composed some dignified words with which to tender his resignation. He would have to send out his vita tomorrow so he could arrange interviews immediately after his vacation.

"You know we're not going to announce this until January, but I thought you ought to hear this now." Dennis shook his hand. "You're the new partner. There was never any question about it. Even before the Beal job."

When he could speak, he thanked Dennis for his confidence in him. "When are you going to tell Kevin?" he asked.

"He knows already. Actually, he came to my *house* this morning and demanded an answer."

"I don't understand, then," Danny said. "He looked so . . . happy tonight."

He told Rachel the news as they pulled out of the hotel's parking garage. She beamed at him. "Does this mean you'll be able to relax in St. John now?"

"I think so," he said.

As they waited to turn left at an intersection, several colleagues and their spouses passed them, honking, wishing them a Merry Christmas. He and Rachel waved, and then Danny swung onto Memorial Drive, alongside the Charles. The river was partially frozen, a film of ice glowing a reflection of the moon. The sky was clear, and there were no other cars on the road, and soon there were glimpses of the downtown Boston skyline. "It's a beautiful night," Rachel said.

Danny was filled with relief and pride and—for the first time in years—genuine affection for Rachel. He moved one hand off the steering wheel to touch her, but then stopped and gripped the wheel again. Ahead of them was a car, going slowly, weaving, no lights. "Drunk driver," he said to Rachel.

They gained on him. "Stay away from the guy," Rachel said.

"I can't help it. He's barely moving."

The driver was bouncing crazily inside the car, lurching for the doors. "What's he doing?" Danny asked. It looked like he was rolling down his windows, every single one.

"Isn't that Kevin's car?" Rachel asked.

They got within thirty yards of him, and then, without warning, Sheridan floored it. Danny knew Sheridan hadn't recognized them. He wasn't running away, he was racing *toward* something. "Put on your seat belt," he told Rachel. He rapidly shifted up to fourth and chased after Sheridan. For a moment, he thought he might have lost him—nothing ahead—and then he saw a flash of red brake lights on a curve, a shadowed outline of his car. Sheridan was on a short straightaway now, and he was accelerating, not slowing down for the next bend.

"Jesus," Danny said.

Sheridan's car jumped the curb, flew across the grassy esplanade, and crashed through the railing into the river.

Danny skidded to a halt, jumped out of the car, and ran toward the tangled gap in the railing. He stripped off his overcoat and suit jacket, and dove into the water. For a second there was only blackness, no sensation, no sound, an abyss. Something touched his hands. Mud. It wasn't too deep, twelve feet or so. He surfaced, and the cold seized him, was electric. He dove again, and somehow, though he could see nothing, he found the car almost immediately this time. There was the hood, the windshield, the open driver's window. He reached inside, swept his arm back and forth. Sheridan wasn't there. He was searching from the wrong side—this was the back seat. He lunged into the other window and grabbed Sheridan, struggled to pull him out. He was unconscious and unbelievably heavy. Danny put his feet against the door, used his legs for leverage, and pushed Sheridan upward. They broke the surface. Danny saw Rachel standing at the railing, screaming at them. He flipped Sheridan over so he was supine and began hauling him to shore. Suddenly Sheridan regained consciousness. He coughed and retched out water, raspily hyperventilating for air, and clawed at Danny's arm.

"It's OK, I got you, you're safe," Danny said, but Sheridan panicked. He spun around and squeezed Danny in a bear hug, dunking them both underwater. Danny kicked his legs, and they bopped up, but he couldn't break Sheridan's embrace, his arms were pinned. Everything was noisy, the splashing and wrestling—vertiginous, as if he were upside down. It occurred to him that Sheridan might be trying to kill him. Danny was so tired, the idea of giving in, drowning, was dimly appealing; they would sink into the darkness, he and Sheridan, and it would be quiet, peaceful. Sheridan's eyes were wild; he was yelling unintelligibly. Danny swallowed water, strained to keep them afloat. He couldn't last much longer. He tried to recall the Red Cross lifesaving techniques he'd learned as a teenager, the escape from a front head hold. Another memory came to him—a perfect, inviolate rescue. He stretched back, and, as hard as he could, he butted his head into Sheridan's face.

Cinnamon Bay, St. John. He and Rachel lay on towels, side by side, on the beach. It was his first visit to the Caribbean. He had had the chance to come down with Jenny and her family long ago, and he wished that he and Rachel had made the trip earlier, because right now, looking out at the white sand and the warm, blue island water, holding Rachel's hand, he couldn't imagine anything more romantic than being here with her.

Rachel squirted suntan lotion onto his shoulders and massaged it into his skin, moving her fingers up his neck, his face, around the Band-Aid on his forehead. "We should change this," she said.

Danny had been cut, Sheridan unscathed. That night, Danny had admitted to Rachel that if he had had a chance to think about it, he might not have saved Sheridan. He had plunged into the river on instinct, without thinking. "There's something to be said for that, you know," Rachel had told him.

He saw Sheridan only once more, just before leaving for St. John. He visited him at McLean's, the psychiatric hospital, where Sheridan had asked to be admitted. They had nothing to say to each other, but Sheridan, who upon his release would move to New York, appreciated that Danny had come. He told Danny he actually didn't mind being there. For once, he could rest. Sheridan had not been trying to drown him, Danny knew, and he decided that Sheridan was not at heart a bigot; he had been, then and all along, just terrified.

Danny watched his son, Michael, run out of the ocean. He was naked. He had taken off his swimming trunks. He was laughing, and his body was slick and lithe, and as Michael bounded toward him, Danny marveled at the simple, pure joy of seeing his son's face, which was, he had to admit, becoming remarkably like his own.

BIOGRAPHICAL
NOTES

⸻

THOMAS FOX AVERILL is Writer-in-Residence and Professor of English at Washburn University of Topeka, Kansas. His story collections are *Seeing Mona Naked* and *Passes at the Moon.* In 1991 he won an O. Henry Award.

TONI CADE BAMBARA grew up in Harlem and Bedford-Stuyvestant, New York. She is the author of a novel, *The Salt Eaters,* and three collections of stories, *Tales and Stories for Black Folks, The Seabirds Are Still Alive,* and the highly acclaimed *Gorilla, My Love,* which includes "Raymond's Run."

The latest book of JONATHAN BAUMBACH—playwright, critic, and novelist—is a novel called *Seven Wives: A Romance.* He is also the author of *Separate Hours, Reruns, Chez Charlotte and Emily,* and *The Life and Times of Major Fiction,* and has served as chairman of the National Society of Film Critics.

T. CORAGHESSAN BOYLE is the author of five novels, including *Water Music, World's End,* and *The Road to Wellville.* He has also published four story collections, most recently *Without a Hero.* He lives outside Santa Barbara, California.

ETHAN CANIN's first book of stories, *Emperor of the Air*, won a Houghton Mifflin Literary Fellowship in 1988. Since then, he has published two other books, *Blue River*, a novel, and *The Palace Thief*, a collection of four novellas. He lives in California, where he is completing his medical residency.

CHRIS FISHER's first book is a collection of stories, called *Sun Angel*, which includes "Playing the Garden." His short fiction has also been published in Canadian literary magazines and aired on Canadian public radio.

ELLEN GILCHRIST, the winner of the 1984 National Book Award for fiction, is the author of many short story collections and novels. Two of her most recent works are *Starcarbon: A Meditation on Love* and *Anabasis: A Journey to the Interior*.

MARK HELPRIN, whose latest book is called *A Soldier of the Great War*, has served in the British Merchant Navy, the Israeli Infantry, and the Israeli Air Force. His other books include *Ellis Island and Other Stories*, *A Dove of the East and Other Stories*, and the novels *Refiner's Fire*, *A Winter's Tale*, and *Memoir from Antproof Case*.

DAVID MICHAEL KAPLAN is the author of the story collection *Comfort*, and *Skating in the Dark*, a novel.

GARRISON KEILLOR is a humorist who has worked in radio since 1963. The creator and host of the public radio program "A Prairie Home Companion," he has collected many of his radio stories in *Happy to Be Here*, *Lake Wobegon Days*, and *Leaving Home*. He has also published a novel, *WLT: A Radio Romance*.

MARISA LABOZZETTA's stories have appeared in *The American Voice*, *The Florida Review*, and the best-selling anthology, *When I Am an Old Woman I Shall Wear Purple*. She lives in Northampton, Massachusetts, and teaches foreign languages and Italian-American literature at area colleges.

DON LEE's work has appeared in *GQ*, *The Village Voice*, *Harvard Review*, *American Short Fiction*, and *Ploughshares*, where he is currently the editor.

ANN PACKER is the author of *Mendocino and Other Stories*. Her short fiction has appeared in *The New Yorker*, *Ploughshares*, *Threepenny Review*, and other magazines as well as in *Prize Stories 1992: The O. Henry Awards*. She lives in Oregon.

JOHN SAYLES is both a writer and a filmmaker. *Union Dues* and *Los Gusanos* are two of his novels, and some of his stories have been collected in *The Anarchists' Convention*. His films include *Matewan*, *Return of the Secaucus Seven*, *Lianna*, and *Baby It's You*. He lives in Hoboken, New Jersey.

JIM SHEPARD is the author of four novels, *Flights*, *Paper Doll*, *Lights Out in the Reptile House*, and *Kiss of the Wolf*. His short fiction has appeared in *The New Yorker*, *Harper's*, *The Atlantic Monthly*, and *The Best American Short Stories*. He teaches at Williams College in Williamstown, Massachusetts.

Born in rural Mississippi in 1921, ELIZABETH SPENCER has published eleven books, including the novels *The Voice at the Back Door, The Light in the Piazza, The Snare,* and *The Night Travelers,* and the story collections *Jack of Diamonds, Ship Island,* and *On the Gulf.* The recipient of the Award of Merit Medal for the Short Story, given by the American Academy of Arts & Letters, she lives in Chapel Hill, North Carolina.

SUSAN STRAIGHT has published three novels: *Aquaboogie: A Novel in Stories, I Been in Sorrow's Kitchen and Licked Out All the Pots,* and *Blacker Than a Thousand Midnights.* She was born and raised in Riverside, California, where she still lives, with her husband and two daughters.

JOHN EDGAR WIDEMAN has published six novels, including *Philadelphia Fire, Reuben,* and *Sent for You Yesterday,* which won the PEN/Faulkner Award in 1983. He is also the author of a memoir, *Brothers and Keepers.* His latest book is called *Fatheralong: A Meditation on Fathers and Sons, Race and Society.* He lives in Amherst and teaches at the University of Massachusetts.

NANCE VAN WINCKEL is a poet whose two collections of poetry are *Bad Girl, with Hawk* and *The Dirt,* and whose first collection of short fiction is called *Limited Lifetime Warranty.* She edits the literary magazine *Willow Springs* and teaches at Eastern Washington University.

MONICA WOOD's first novel is called *Secret Language.* Her short stories have appeared in numerous anthologies and magazines, including *Glimmer Train, Redbook,* and *The North American Review.* She lives in Portland, Maine, and is at work on a second novel.

JAY WOODRUFF's stories have appeared in *The Atlantic, Story,* and other publications. He lives in Durham, North Carolina, with his wife and three children.

ACKNOWLEDGMENTS

"Off-Season" by Susan Straight, from *Aquaboogie* by Susan Straight (Milkweed Editions, 1990), copyright © 1990 by Susan Straight. Reprinted by permission of Milkweed Editions.

"Coming To" by Nance Van Winckel, from *Limited Lifetime Warranty: Stories* by Nance Van Winckel, copyright © 1994 by Nance Van Winckel. Reprinted by permission of the University of Missouri Press.

"Doc's Story" by John Edgar Wideman, from *Fever: Twelve Stories* by John Edgar Wideman, copyright © 1989 by John Edgar Wideman. Reprinted by permission of Henry Holt and Company, Inc.

"Disappearing" by Monica Wood, copyright © 1988 by Monica Wood. First published in *Fiction Network*. Reprinted by permission of the author.

"The Secret to Not Getting Stuck" by Jay Woodruff, copyright © 1988 by Jay Woodruff. First published in *The Atlantic*. Reprinted by permission of the author.